A STORMY YEAR

The Sabblonti Series

Jantzi's Jokers

A Stormy Year

Love, the Tie that Binds

BOOKS BY SHEILA EISMANN

A STORMY YEAR

A WOMAN OF SUBSTANCE

HEART TO HEART FROM GOD'S WORD

LOVE, THE TIE THAT BINDS

JANTZI'S JOKERS

POETRY TIME – VOLUME ONE

RECOGNIZE YOUR CIRCLES

STIRRINGS OF THE SPIRIT

STRAIGHT FROM THE HORSE'S TROUGH

THE CHRISTMAS TIN

A STORMY YEAR

Book Two of The Sabblonti Series

S

Sheila Eismann

Desert Sage Press

WWW.DESERTSAGEPRESS.COM
WWW.SHEILAEISMANN.COM

This book is a work of fiction. Names, characters, places, cattle ranches or brands, and incidents are the product of the author's imagination or are used fictitiously. Any resemblance to actual events, locales, persons, living or dead, businesses, or companies is coincidental.

Published by Desert Sage Press. All rights reserved.
www.desertsagepress.com

Printed and bound in the United States of America.

Cover: Sharon Breshears Photography. All rights reserved.

Illustrated by Cathie Richardson. All rights reserved.
www.cathiericharsonillustration.com

Greeting card design ~~ Cathie Richardson Country Garden Cards. All rights reserved.

Stock photos:
www.dreamstime.com. Used by permission.
www.istockphoto.com. Used by permission.

ISBN: 978-0-9897133-3-7
Library of Congress Control Number: 2016917788

DEDICATION

Book Two of The Sabblonti Series is dedicated to women everywhere who have experienced life challenges, not only in cattle country, but all around the world. There's always an opportunity to look deeper into ourselves to see if we can make a difference, whether large or small.

It's impossible to go through life without experiencing some storms, but thankfully, they don't last forever. The sun is sure to shine, sooner or later.

ACKNOWLEDGEMENTS

My heartfelt thanks and sincere appreciation are extended to Cathie Richardson, JoEllen Claypool, and Lesta Chadez, each of whom brought a unique and challenging perspective, coupled with a large bouquet of encouragement, during the time in which I wrote ***A Stormy Year***.

It's been a special joy to share this experience with my oldest daughter, Cathie, whose artistic gifts and talents bless me beyond measure.

JoEllen, one of my fellow co-founders of ICAN (Idaho Creative Authors' Network), kept a sharp eye on the big picture as the many characters rode in and out of the vast western landscape.

Fifty-one years ago, Lesta and I lived in the same small rural area. Our paths reconnected at just the right time. Lesta's unique combination of mercy and exhortation are a bonus for any writer.

INTRODUCTION

As the author of this three-book series, I would like to extend a hearty welcome to you as you enter into a fictional world of a high desert mountain region comprised of six counties in the northwest.

The majority of the cattle ranches were homesteaded in the 1800's after the land was cleared of sagebrush and rocks. Some of the meadows containing native grasses have been in place since then, but new pastures and feeding areas were seeded in the decades after the turn of the century.

The cattle were driven into the high country during the summer months and brought back down to the lower elevations late in the fall. The ranchers sometimes sold and shipped cows to other parts of the country. Breeding bulls were a crucial aspect to the ongoing development of herds. There were bull pastures on some of the ranches. Beavers built their dams on the streams that flowed through these pastures which created ponds.

Bobcats, cougars, coyotes, and wolves were always lurking in the high country seeking to devour the cattle, horses, and cow dogs. There's an emergence of wolves in Book Three, *Love the Tie that Binds.*

More than ample snowfall in the mountains most years kept the rivers, streams and reservoirs full. Prior to the homesteaders arriving, there was a flood one spring which changed the course of the river as it cascaded down the mountain sides. When all this water came rushing down, it brought trees, brush, and debris with it. This made a new channel in the river in the northeastern portion of Chrebine County which flowed into the lower, southeastern part of Shadow Butte County.

With water being so vital, there's been only one major dispute in this regard when one of the characters forged a land deed to pirate the coveted Alder Creek and reservoir which is owned by the Merrill Ranch. This matter finally gets rectified in Book Three, *Love, the Tie that Binds.*

The Sabblonti Cattle Ranch is by far the largest spread. *Jantzi's Jokers*, Book One of the series, includes the details of the passing of the second generation of the family, Ace Sabblonti, and his wife, Jantzi Belle Siddonz Sabblonti. Pursuant to the specifications contained in Jantzi Belle's will, Stormy Castins, the oldest daughter, inherits everything. Sarita Sabblonti, her younger sister, is cut out of the will.

As the reader will discover in this second book titled *A Stormy Year,* it doesn't take long before Stormy lets the vast domain fall into shambles. As anyone in real life can attest, there's a drastic difference in working for an honest living versus inheriting a large fortune. She's created to be an enigmatic character. If you can figure her out, you'd be well on your way to becoming a psychologist or psychiatrist.

Just in case you might think that a somewhat sparsely populated region is void of any mystery, drama, intrigue or excitement, read on! The census of an area has no bearing upon whether or not there are characters who stay on the straight and narrow path or those who traverse the wide, dangerous, swaths of land. Mirroring real life, there are triumphs and tragedies along with victories and defeats.

Before starting to read this book, I would encourage you to take a few minutes to familiarize yourself with the family tree, map, and legend in the front of the book. Also, there's a cast of characters in the back.

After penning the first book, *Jantzi's Jokers,* I received emails, telephone calls, and written letters with reader's sentiments. They had definite opinions as to whether or not one character should marry another one; who should be punished for his or her actions; who they trusted and did not; and what made them happy or sad. I commented to someone, "Oh my goodness, some readers think these are real people!"

Obviously, none of the characters mentioned on any of the pages are real. Perhaps there are those with whom you can identify or relate.

Thanks for reading, and enjoy!

§ *Siddonz &*

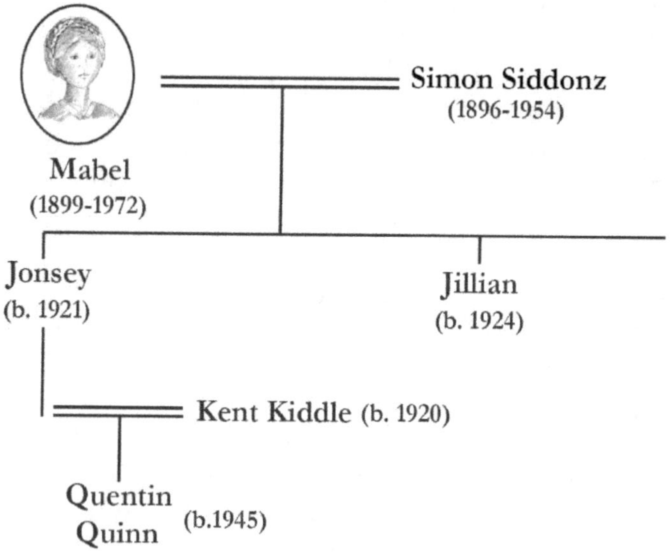
Simon Siddonz
(1896-1954)
Mabel
(1899-1972)
Jonsey
(b. 1921)
Jillian
(b. 1924)
Kent Kiddle (b. 1920)
Quentin
Quinn
(b.1945)

Sabblonti Family Trees

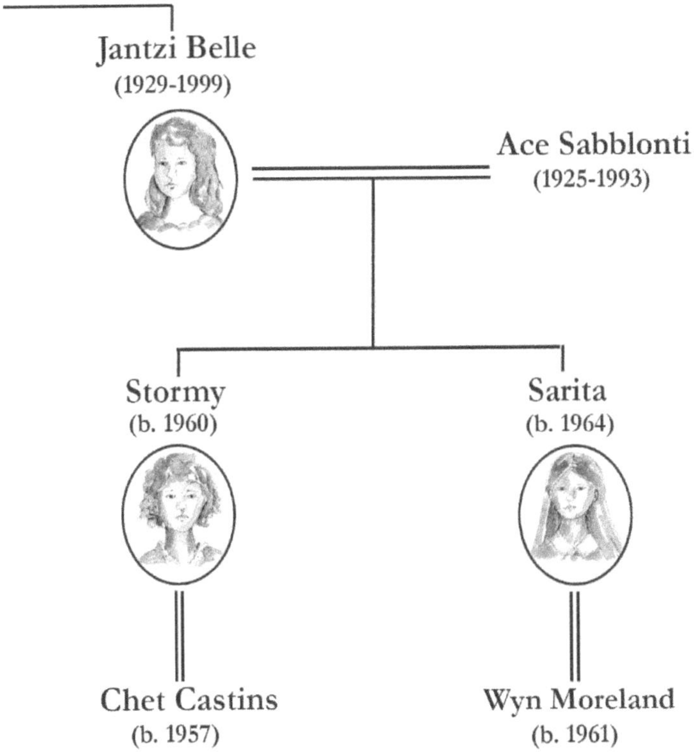

Legend

S Ace Sabblonti Ranch

Nelson Merrill Ranch

Tom Toppens Ranch

RB Rees Broomfield Ranch

W Wilbur Drebner Ranch

Main Highway

Ranch Road

Meadows/Pastures

Creek/River

Reservoir

County	* County Seat
Blunte County	Blademere
Chrebine County	Limnosa
Clarey County	Horsewood
Ignee County	Cinder Valley
Shadow Butte County	Ridgemonte
Tranquility Falls County	Fantone

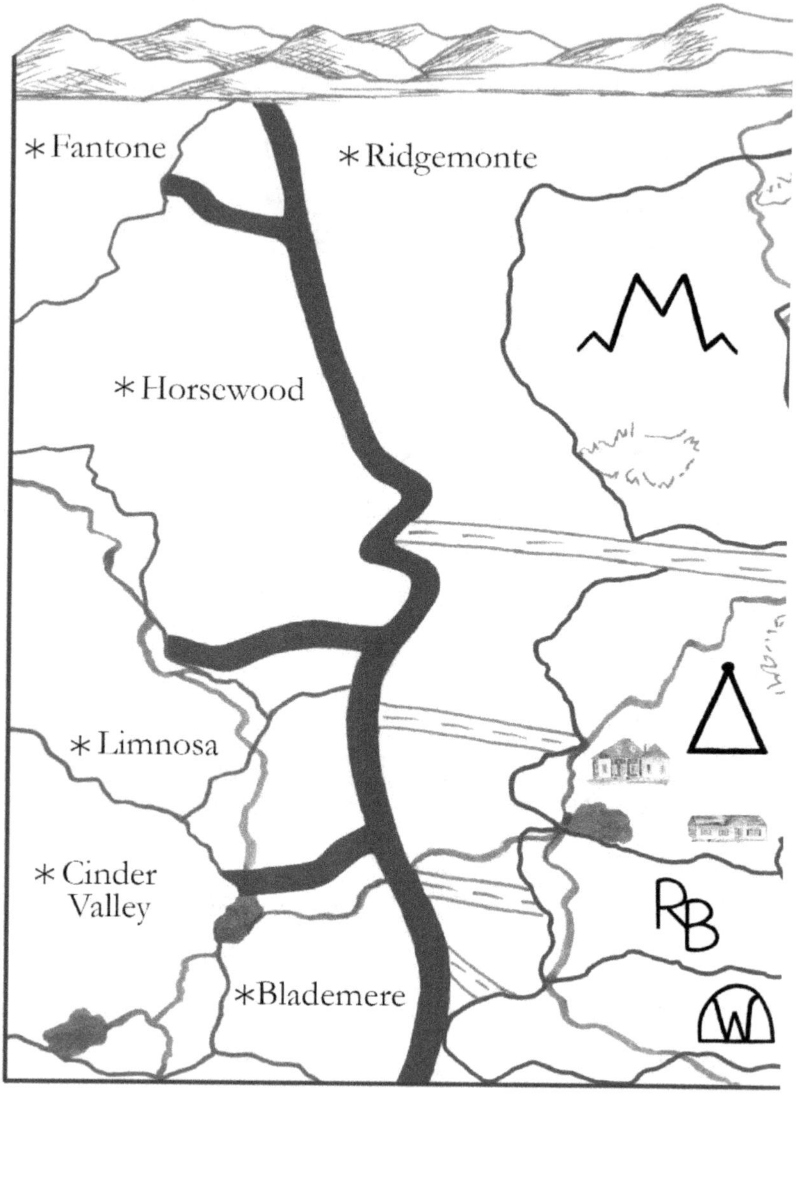
*Fantone
*Ridgemonte
*Horsewood
*Limnosa
*Cinder Valley
*Blademere
RB
W

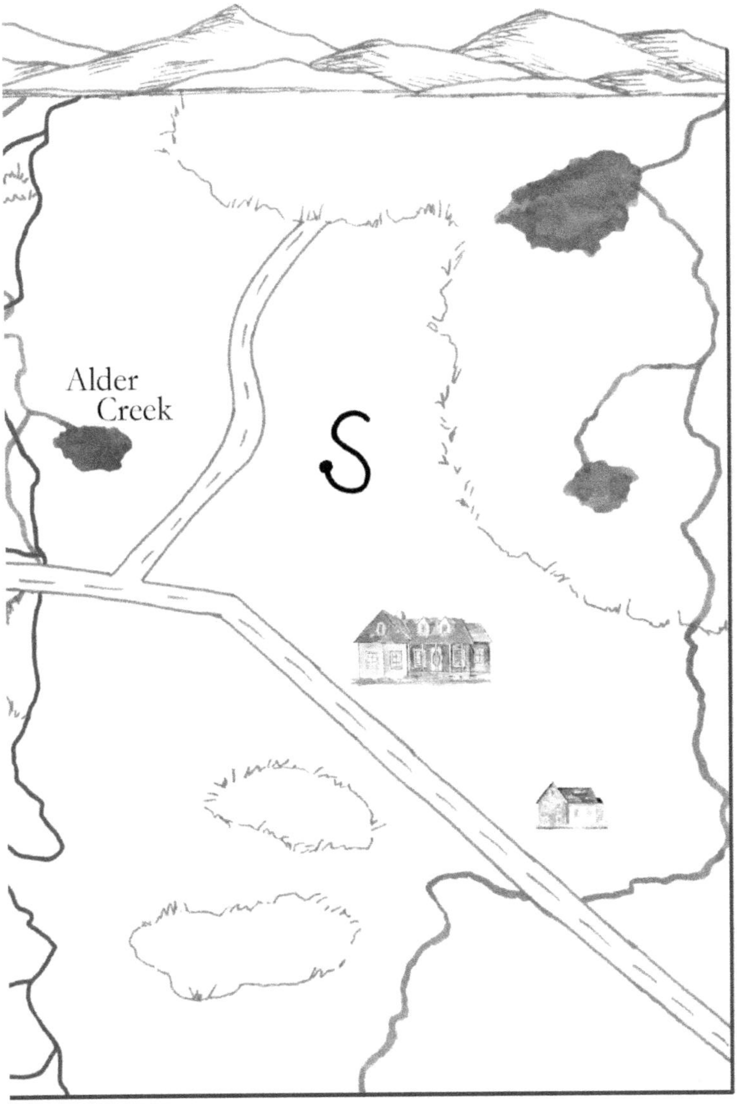
Alder
Creek
S

CHAPTER ONE

Sunday Evening, January 2, 2000
6:00 p.m.
Main Sabblonti Ranch House

A beleaguered Chet Castins rolled his dark moustache between his left thumb and forefinger as he watched the tops of the red cowboy boots glide down the steep staircase. He knew what he'd like to do with that footwear. Pitch from an oversized juniper log sizzled in the fireplace which reminded him that the flame in his heart died nine days ago.

Rising from the brown overstuffed leather chair and walking toward his wife, Chet flicked her curly black hair and gently placed his weathered hands around her waist. Towering almost a foot over her head and breathing in her Gardenia perfume he so often enjoyed, he waited momentarily to see if she would respond.

"Stormy, sweetheart, I've been doing a lot of thinking since Jantzi Belle's death. Let's plan a second honeymoon somewhere of your choice, so we can figure out how we're going to operate the Sabblonti Cattle Empire. I can hire some more short-term help at the ranch while we're gone."

Removing his hands from her slender hips while trying to push him backwards, Stormy guffawed, "Surely you jest! That's laughable. You want to take me on a second honeymoon? You didn't even take me on a first honeymoon. Do you love me more now that I've inherited the ranch and all the money that goes with it? That scene with you and Salina Bevvins at Mother's funeral plays over and over again in the theatre of my mind. I can't find the power switch to shut it off."

"I've never stopped loving you since the day I first met you. And I've repeatedly told you, I'm guilty of nothing as it pertains to Salina. I don't know what it's going to take to convince you."

Stormy walked to the bay window, picked up the pastel, multi-colored baby afghan and sat down in her chair. After lacing all her fingers through it, she rocked back and forth.

Chet approached the fireplace, selected the small shovel from the set of tools, and handed it to Stormy. "Can you go to the graveyard, find your old self, dig it up, and bring it back into our lives, so we can try again to start a family and live happily ever after?"

"I have an expansive cattle ranch to oversee at the moment. The only time I will be visiting the cemetery is to ask Mother some important questions and let her know how much I miss her."

"What could you possibly know about operating the Sabblonti spread? I think you know how to spell *cattle* and that's about the extent of it. All of that cold hard cash in those accounts at Cattlemen's Central won't make a dime's worth of difference if you don't let me help you call the shots."

Standing up and reaching into her right hip pocket, Stormy pulled out a small folded envelope. Opening it, she declared, "I've located Mother's decks of cards she kept in her office for decades and pulled out all of the jokers that will do my bidding. Look, here's one with your name on it."

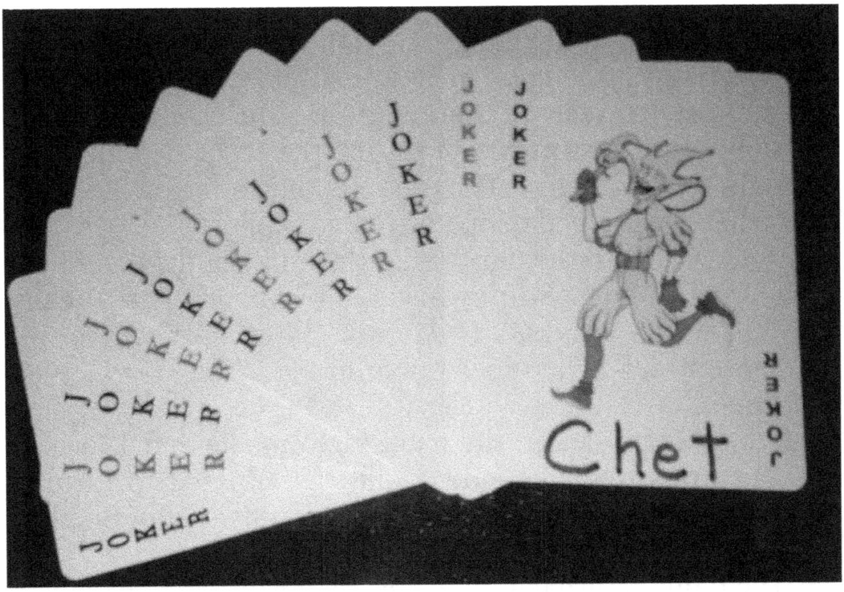

Chet grabbed for the card just as she jumped backward. "I'm nobody's joker, Stormy."

"Poobash, you preach!" Stormy threw the afghan on the floor, ran toward the fireplace and grabbed the steel, hand-forged thirty-two-inch fire poker. It looked like a black snake flying in mid-air as she hurled it directly toward Chet's head, narrowly missing him and shattering one of the windows on the southwest side of the house. Chards of glass splattered in the corner of the room and spilled onto the front porch.

Throwing his arms in the air and shaking both hands, Chet hurriedly walked down the long hallway into the mud room to collect his coat, hat, and gloves. The dark of the moon cloaked the desert landscape as he entered the front yard, got inside the cab of his pickup and headed toward the main highway.

The month of December 1999 seemed like ninety-nine long days during which time he lost his matriarchal mother-in-law, Jantzi Belle, and witnessed the changing of the guard of the Sabblonti Cattle Empire. As he drove, Chet's mind drifted in and out of various scenes, conversations, landscapes, and relationships. For the life of him, he couldn't discern the sudden personality change in his wife. During the prior years of their marriage, she had been such a joy and delight to him except during the times in which she had suffered three miscarriages. He longed for the good ol' days when life seemed to operate on auto pilot.

He spoke into the darkness, "Have I been living a lie all these years? Maybe Stormy never did love me. Was I really one of Jantzi's Jokers? Is Stormy taking over where her mother left off? What does my future look like? Do I even have one?"

When Chet reached the main highway, he opted to turn left and drive toward Cinder Valley as opposed to turning right and heading to Ridgemonte, the county seat of Shadow Butte County.

The temperature fell rapidly as the fog began to envelope the countryside. While Chet drove the next few miles, his mind was not in the Milky Way Galaxy. He accelerated as he rounded the "S" curve and felt his left-hand glide completely off the steering wheel. His attention was diverted when he glanced to his right and quickly grabbed the wheel to regain control of his pickup. When he looked straight ahead, all he saw was pure white. By that time, it was too late. Coming out of the curve after driving into the lane of oncoming traffic, he was definitely in the wrong place at the wrong time.

Chet's white face met the white face of the Black Baldy when the force of impact thrust the steer against the front windshield causing the pickup to veer off the left-hand side of the road, roll twice, and land in a ravine.

Smoke rose from the dashboard as the driver's air bag deployed. As Chet was losing consciousness, he screamed, "Help, help, get me out of here! I think my pickup's on fire!"

CHAPTER TWO

Southeast of the accident scene some fifteen plus miles, Sarita Sabblonti and her fiancé, Wyn Moreland, stopped by to visit Tom and Merna Toppens at their ranch house. They told them what had happened during the reading of The Last Will and Testament of Jantzi Belle Siddonz Sabblonti just a few hours earlier that afternoon.

Warm, motherly, and comforting, the yellow hue in Merna's hazel eyes seemed to twinkle like small holiday lights as she served warm apple pie with melted cheddar cheese slices on top to her guests. Despite her small five-foot frame, she was blessed with boundless energy, and was the consummate hostess sporting a vast array of colorful aprons, all hand-crafted. There was not a gray hair mixed in with her natural honey brown color after seventy-three years.

"Your dessert really hits the spot, Merna," said Wyn. "Now that you and Tom have become like parents to me since I started working for you, I just had to see you before taking Sarita back to Ridgemonte for the night."

"We're so thankful that you did. You and Sarita are like our own grown children. Please feel free to visit us anytime you like. We love to have company."

The pain from Tom's wrenched back held back much of his speech from the evening, but that did not mean his mind was not working overtime. His black XXL back brace was draped over an empty kitchen chair along with his blue striped suspenders. He realized that he was not going to be able to cover as much range land in the ensuing year as he'd done in prior decades.

"Now that we've enjoyed something sweet, how about we

sit by the fire?" asked Merna. An atmosphere of peace and tranquility settled over the wood paneled living room. The only sound that could be heard was the crackling of the large mahogany log burning in the middle of the stove. No one seemed to be in a hurry to do much of anything.

Sarita studied Tom and Merna's 50th wedding anniversary picture that hung between the two large living room windows draped with fabric showcasing a herd of cattle grazing in a golden, grass covered meadow. *Since she was getting such a late start at marriage, would she achieve that major milestone?*

Next to the anniversary photo was a dark brown frame with a small heart etched across the top. The picture was taken on Toby's second birthday. He sat on a little wooden rocking horse and held his straw cowboy hat with his right hand as he gripped the wooden peg with his left one. The photographer managed to capture a full grin. Merna had transferred the Toppens cattle brand onto the little beige vest she'd made for Toby to compliment his western shirt. He'd been so excited to wear his new little cowboy boots to have his picture taken that day.

Tom broke the silence, "Wyn, I've been doing a lot of thinking the past month or so. These golden years aren't all they're cracked up to be. About all that happens is the gold is draining from our ranching reserves. My aging body can't keep up with my young cowboy mind, so I need to make some major changes. I want to offer you the job of Toppens' Ranch foreman starting immediately. Part of your salary will include a new manufactured home that we'll place on the property somewhere. We'll get that figured out right away."

Wyn had been sitting with his elbows on his knees with his hands cupping his face as he stared into the fire. At the sound of Tom's offer, he quickly sat up straight. "Did I hear you correctly, Tom? The job of ranch foreman is a tall order. I'd be willing to take it if you'd agree to be available in the wings for counsel and advice."

"Oh, I'm not going anywhere anytime soon. I wouldn't offer you the job if I didn't think you could do it. Merna and

I have talked at great length about this, and she is in full agreement with me. During our entire married life, we've always made the major decisions together. None of this *One Man Show* stuff for me!"

Merna chimed in, "Yes, Wyn, I fully support Tom's decision. Since you've become like a son to both of us, it will be a complete joy to hand over the reins to you. Actually, it will be to you and Sarita, assuming you still plan on getting married this year."

"Well, we've not had a lot of time to talk about a specific wedding date," said Wyn. "Life has been like a runaway stagecoach since our Christmas Day engagement."

Sensing Sarita's reticence, Merna looked at her and inquired, "Are you doing okay tonight? You seem quieter than usual. I'm sure it came as quite a blow to you that you received no inheritance when your mother died."

"Yes, Merna, I'm doing just fine. Since I'm not a material girl, the Sabblonti fortune is not where I've staked my future claim." Extending her left hand to allow Wyn to hold it in his right, she continued, "I've chosen to walk with Wyn and follow his dreams which will become our dreams."

An enthusiastic grin revealing the large gap between his front teeth graced Tom's face as he boomed, "Now that's the kind of talk I like to hear! Those are just about the same words I heard from my beautiful bride way back in 1947. Gee, that seems like an eternity ago. Merna and I have worked very hard to get the Toppens' Ranch in tip-top shape, so we need to be very wise concerning our choices for the future."

"How will all of this foreman business settle with my fellow cowhands, Shane and Spence?" asked Wyn.

"You can plan to leave all of the delegating to me. I've been keeping my eyes peeled the past year and making some notes about all of my ranch hands to determine where I want to place each one of them. Thankfully, I still have another month to put the finishing touches on my master plan before we start the busy spring calving and branding seasons. We'll need to round up a few more hired hands before we get into haying and shipping the steers to the feed lot in the Midwest this fall. I'm also working on possibly selling a few of our heifers to one of my ranching buddies in Ignee County."

Merna, holding the blue and white flowered coffee pot in her right hand, re-entered the living room after placing the dessert plates in the kitchen sink. "Do you think you two cattle barons can take a little break from talking ranch business, so we can discuss a very important date?" Turning to address Wyn and Sarita, who were seated on the love seat, she continued, "Tom and I've also talked about offering our ranch for your upcoming wedding if you'd be interested."

Without missing a beat, Sarita replied, "Oh, that would be wonderful! Wyn, what do you think of that idea?"

"It's totally fine with me. Since I have no family, it would mean the world to me to be married on the Toppens' spread."

"Well, then that settles the matter," said Merna. "After our little Toby drowned in the stock tank when he was two and a half years old and we never had any more children of our own, I spent many therapeutic hours designing and developing our back yard. I did some research as to what types of trees, shrubs, flowers, and flowering plants would thrive in the high desert region. It's as if I knew all those years ago that someday there would be a beautiful bride and a handsome groom standing under the archway that I placed back there. If your wedding date was in July, I just know those bright yellow, wild roses would be poking their glorious blooms through the white lattice. Yellow roses are symbolic of friendship and caring, and I care deeply for you two lovebirds."

"Merna, do you happen to have a calendar for 2000?" inquired Sarita.

"I most certainly do! The Shadowy Merc was giving them to their customers during the month of December. I will get it from the kitchen wall so you can decide on a wedding date."

Observing Tom's profile, Wyn wondered how he'd trained his ultra-thick gray hair to form four distinct waves on the top of his head. During one of their prior range riding weekends, Tom had informed Wyn that he'd not entered a barber shop since the day he and Merna were married. She cut his hair and trimmed his lamb chop side burns. Looking down at Tom's feet, Wyn had never seen anyone with such wide, flat ones. They were probably at least a size 15EE.

Turning the calendar pages to July, Sarita traced her right index finger to the final weekend of the month. "July 29th is the last Saturday. Wyn, what do you think of that date?"

"Suits me just fine, my sweet. It sounds sort of silly, but I've never even been to a wedding. Growing up in the boy's home after my mother abandoned me, I didn't have much of an opportunity for social occasions."

Sarita beamed as she decreed, "July 29th it is. Just the thought of it almost takes my breath away! Oh dear, with my daddy having died in 1993, who will give me away at our wedding? I'll worry about that tomorrow instead of today. Merna, I would be honored if you'd be willing to make my white wedding gown and veil."

"I'd be happy to help you any way I can, Sarita. I'd consider it an honor and a privilege."

Sarita, gazing intently at Wyn, proclaimed, "My handsome cowboy, I want to walk through life with you and lean against you so neither one of us falls."

"On that note," continued Wyn, "I think we better let these fine folks get some much-needed rest and take you back to Ridgemonte. The normal drive might take twice as long as usual since the fog decided to fence us in tonight."

CHAPTER THREE

Blake Benson, Southwest District Brand Inspector, was traveling from Cinder Valley to his ranchette on the outskirts of Ridgemonte. Truth be known, he was concentrating more on the words to the song "Dance with Me in My Home Town" than the infamous "S" curve on the main highway dead ahead. He caught a glimpse of what looked like headlights of a pickup. Blake continued to drive and braked suddenly when he noticed fresh blood on the road. "Good night, what do we have here?"

Parking his pickup where it could be safely viewed as much as possible through the fog by oncoming traffic, Blake switched the hazard lights on. He grabbed his flashlight, jumped from the driver's seat, and made his way through the waist-high brush to the bottom of the ravine.

With the passenger side of the pickup dented in, the hood folded up like an accordion, and someone slumped over the steering wheel, Blake felt like he was going to black out. Walking around to the driver's side, he opened the door, and started shaking the driver. After recognizing that it was Chet, he yelled, "Can you hear me?" Blake removed Chet's driving glove and jerked his shirt sleeve up so he could check his pulse which still registered.

Chet began to groan as he regained consciousness. "I can't feel my right leg or my right arm. I hurt all over. Everything looks dark. Where am I? What happened?"

"Appears to me like you hit something head on, Chet. You're one lucky cowboy right now. Looking at your rig, it's a miracle you lived through this. I'm going to run back to my pickup and call the emergency services. I knew I shouldn't have removed my first aid kit from my pickup. I'll be right back."

Using the phone in his pickup, Blake called the Shadow Butte County authorities since the accident had occurred just inside their county line. He located an additional flash light in the jockey box of his pickup along with a horse blanket in the back seat and headed back down to check on Chet. Halfway down the hill, Blake noticed a flash of white. As he walked closer to it, he came upon the steer. "Sheesh, I'm going to have to call the dead animal wagon tomorrow morning."

Amidst the dense fog, smells of the coolant of the cracked radiator, chemicals from the deployed air bag, and burned rubber from the tires hung in the air like an iron curtain. Blake secretly hoped he wouldn't lose his prime rib dinner onto his new black leather jacket, the one the waitresses admired when he wore it to The Sage Hen Café. He'd spent about an hour posing in front of the mirror earlier in the day trying to decide upon which hat to wear with his new coat. His salt and pepper hair was affecting his ego. Surely The Shadowy Merc or The Ridgemonte Rx sold hair coloring products in bottles.

Snapping back to reality, Blake asked, "Are you cold?" He draped the horse blanket over Chet's shoulders. "I don't dare move you before the EMT's get here, especially since you said you can't feel your leg or your arm." There was no immediate answer from Chet. Blake continued, "It's colder than a well digger standing out here in this dreaded fog." Straining his right ear, Blake thought he heard the shrill sound of the ambulance siren piercing the present darkness. "Hold on, Chet, help is on the way!"

Arriving at the accident scene, the ambulance driver and two attendants parked behind Blake's pickup. They removed their equipment from the back and hurried down to the wreckage site. Upon completing a preliminary check of Chet's vitals and stabilizing his back along with the right side of his body, he was loaded onto the gurney. They carried him up the hillside and loaded him into the ambulance to be transported to Mintner Medical Center in Ridgemonte.

Just as the ambulance driver turned around on the main highway to drive to town, Jeff Jensen, Shadow Butte County Sheriff, arrived on the scene. He spoke with the ambulance crew briefly before they departed.

Sheriff Jensen was not completely familiar with Blake since he was fairly new on the job, having replaced Sheriff Koslen during the summer of 1999. Jeff had heard what he deemed were a few tall tales regarding Blake's possible involvement in some shady cattle rustling deals a few years back, but he didn't put a whole lot of stock into cowboy campfire folklore. The sheer size of the geographic area of Shadow Butte County could easily employ several sheriffs along with their trusted deputies, but the county commissioners didn't place a high priority on such matters. There seemed to be a lot more ready revenue in Ignee County. Small wonder those law enforcement jobs rarely became available.

"The Sabblonti outfit has sure had a run of bad luck lately," Sheriff Jensen opined. "Deputy Whillson is still trying to add up everything that happened at the main ranch house on Christmas Eve. I guess I'd better tend to the duties at hand. Blake, were there any other witnesses to the accident or vehicles that drove by?"

"None that I know of unless I missed hearing one while I was standing down here next to Chet's pickup. The highway seems pretty quiet tonight. Most of the time I'm not out and about on a Sunday evening, but I was just returning from visiting one of the ranchers on the other side of Cinder Valley who'd invited me for a New Year's weekend dinner. I saw the flash of Chet's headlights before he veered off the side of the road. Most people have enough horse sense not to be driving on nights like this one. Since I'm smarter than the average cowboy, I knew I could handle it."

"I'm surprised my deputy hasn't arrived yet," Sheriff Jensen said with a bit of concern in his voice. "Blake, until he gets here, can you walk to the highway and keep an eye out for oncoming traffic to help warn them? I placed some flares on the road, but with this super thick fog, I need to take some extra precautions. Also, trying to take pictures is going to be a real challenge, not to mention determining the coefficient of friction, measuring the radius of that sharp "S" curve, and calculating Chet's combined speed using the Pythagorean Triangle method."

"Sure, I'd be happy to help. With all that fancy *Sheriff Speak*, one would think you could certainly land a better job than that of a local yokel county sheriff."

"Mr. Brand Inspector, why don't you concern yourself with keeping the brands straight and the cattle safe while I tend to my duties? The combined counties in these parts would highly benefit from those honest practices."

Blake turned sharply on the heel of his right alligator-skin cowboy boot and walked up the hill to the main highway. Looking to his left, he saw a pair of headlights in the distance.

Deputy Leo Jeelon parked the county vehicle behind Sheriff Jensen's pickup. After introducing himself to Blake, he remained on the main highway as Blake headed down the hill to join the sheriff.

"Blake, can I get you to write out your witness statement? Here's the form and the clipboard. Maybe you can sit in the cab of your pickup and use the dome light so you can see what you're writing. It's best to do this while it's still fresh in your mind. Plus, the insurance company is going to want a copy. Just a note of caution, write down exactly what you observed and not what you think you saw."

"Yes, I can do that for you. When I'm finished writing my statement, do you want me to call Zib's Towing or are you going to take care of that?"

"We'll take care of that, Blake. Since it's the dark of the moon married up with lousy weather conditions, I don't want what's left of Chet's pickup moved tonight. I'll take what pictures I can, and then plan to take some more in the morning. Hopefully we'll be able to see our hand in front of our face by then."

Blake continued, "I was going to call the dead animal

wagon, but I'll wait until Tuesday to do that so those characters don't interfere with your ongoing investigation."

Upon completion of his witness statement, Blake walked down the hill and handed it and the clipboard to Sheriff Jensen. "I've had enough excitement for one night, so I'm headed home."

"Thanks for your help, Blake. If we need anything further regarding your appearance out here this evening, we'll contact you."

After Blake left, Deputy Jeelon walked down to join Sheriff Jensen, and commented, "I don't know what it is about that guy, but he sure makes me uneasy. Do you know any history or background on him?"

"No, Leo, I don't, but I do agree with you. I sense something very different when I'm around him. I can't quite put my finger on what it is. Time will tell. I can remember my mother saying, 'If you wash something often enough, something usually gets washed out. If there's anything hidden, it will get washed into the open areas where everyone can see it.' It could be that since he's only 5' 2" tall, his height bothers him. I've overheard a couple of the local ranchers talking about how he struts around like a Banty Rooster most of the time."

CHAPTER FOUR

"Oh, Wyn, even though I can't see the moon tonight, I'm just over the moon with this whole wedding business! To tell you the truth, I wondered if this season of my life would ever appear. I want the ride to Ridgemonte to last for hours."

"Sarita, come on and admit it. You just needed to wait until I rode in, swept you off your feet, and helped you onto my horse to ride behind me. Have you given any thought as to how much longer you're going to work for Dr. Diller? We have a lot of ground to cover if we're going to get hitched the end of July."

"Dr. Diller has been such a fantastic boss and his dental clinic is the best bar none. When I go to work tomorrow, I'll ask to speak to him during our lunch hour, so I can let him know our plans. I want to give him as much time as possible to select a replacement for me."

The bride and groom to be were immersed in their private thoughts as they traveled down the road. There was so much to think about as their lives were changing dramatically.

Wyn tried to imagine what Sarita would look like on their wedding day. He hoped she wouldn't wear heels since he was only one-half inch taller than she was. Would she wear her super-straight, ash brown hair on her shoulders or piled on top of her head underneath her veil?

"Wyn, if you're in agreement, I would rather not have to drive into Ridgemonte every day to work unless you really want me to. I'd love to settle down and learn how to be a good cattle rancher's wife like Merna has been for Tom.

There are a lot of things she could teach me, especially if we lived close by their house."

"Agreed. I really want you to learn the ropes from Merna. Wow, just think how nice it will be for me to move from the bunkhouse and you from your small apartment in Ridgemonte into a home of our very own! I only have until July 28th to get it ready."

Wyn started silently calculating the number of days until their BIG day.

"Do you think Shane will be more upset than Spence when he hears the news of your new job offer?"

"Probably. Shane keeps a lot of things bottled up inside, so it's hard to tell what he's thinking at any given time. Uh, did you feel the backend of the pickup fishtailing a little bit? I'd better switch it into 4-wheel drive. It seems like we're on a little stretch of black ice here. What would I have done if Merna had not entered my name in that year-end *Rigs For Ridgemonte* drawing?"

Sarita entertained the idea of asking Wyn about other ways in which Merna had helped him, but she didn't want to remind him of what few belongings he actually owned.

"I'm in dreamy wedding land right now, so no, I didn't feel the pickup doing anything strange. You're a careful driver which I appreciate a lot. Where did you learn how to drive anyway?"

"The boy's home was for children ages newborn through high school, so they had a full curriculum which included driver's ed. I took advantage of it before I graduated. The only problem was the vehicle was an automatic transmission instead of a standard one. It was a good thing I had a lot of open range on the Toppens' spread when I first signed on there to get used to the older models with clutches and stick shifts. That one old red truck Tom has is really the bomba chumba!"

"The what?" Sarita asked as she repeated Wyn's lingo.

"The bomba chumba. Shane, Spence, and I've pretty much assigned a name to most everything at the Toppens Ranch. Keeping it all straight is the key. It helps to pass the time of day, especially when we work long hours. I'm the one that dreams up most of the names."

"So, does that mean you'll be naming our children as well?"

"Not totally. With something as important as our kids, we'll both be working on that project. But, we have a lot of time to think on that one. I want to get good and settled before we start our family."

Sarita could feel her heart rate increase. She would be thirty-six years old this year and had no clue how to take care of a newborn. Alas, that's where *Momma Merna* would come in handy. She resumed the conversation, "So do I. In one of the magazines in Dr. Diller's office, I read an article recently advising newlyweds to wait five years before they had any kids. While we're on the subject of kids, I wonder if any of them will have your high cheekbones, boyish face and grin or your dark chocolate brown widow's peak. I don't want to put the cart before the horse, so shall we talk a little bit about who's going to be in our wedding party?"

"Since Shane and Spence are my two closest friends right now, I'm going to ask them to be in our wedding. No one else really comes to mind. I could ask a couple of the other ranch hands, but I don't really feel inclined to do that. As far as I'm concerned, the size of the wedding party doesn't mean *Jack Diddly* when compared to the overall wedding."

"Who's *Jack Diddly*?"

"*Jack Diddly* isn't an actual person. It's another way of saying, 'it doesn't really matter a hoot or a holler.'"

"I'm going to let bygones be bygones with this whole reading of Mother's will business. Stormy is my one and only sibling and sister, so I'm going to ask her if she wants to be in my wedding. If she agrees, Chet could be one of your groomsmen. Even though she's considerably older, I also want to ask Aunt Jonsey to be part of my bridal party along with a couple of my co-workers. I deem it's really important who we have standing with us in front of the gazebo when we recite our wedding vows."

Wyn and Sarita rode in total silence for a couple of miles

while Sarita continued to squirm back and forth in her seat. Wyn thought momentarily about kidding her but then reconsidered. “Let’s just see how things come together over the next few weeks. We still have some time to make our final plans. Okay, my sweet, it looks like it’s *Apartment Small Apartment* time. I’ll walk you up the stairs to your humble abode. Just think, only 208 days until we get married up. And this is a leap year to boot! What’s the deal with getting married during a leap year anyway?”

“It’s supposed to bring bad luck according to those tall wives’ tales. There are some people who think that no major decisions should be made during a leap year concerning marriage, having a child, entering into business relationships, changing jobs, and so forth.”

Stopping half way up the flight of metal stairs, Wyn stated, “That’s just a bunch of hog wash as far as I’m concerned. Granted, we raise cattle and not hogs, but those are just stories blowing in the wind. You hide and watch. We’ll be doing most everything you reeled off except starting our family during a leap year. We’ll be just fine.”

Standing in front of Sarita’s apartment door, Wyn kissed and hugged her tightly, bid her goodnight, and drove back toward the Toppens Ranch. He turned from the main highway onto the side road leading to the ranch house. An uneasy feeling came over him which he attributed to making so many major changes in such a short period of time.

CHAPTER FIVE

"Is Meadows on shift tonight?" inquired Dr. Linke as he approached the nurse's station on the west wing of Mintner Medical Center.

"Just a minute, Doctor, while I check who's covering the 3:00 to 11:00 shift," replied Nurse Joyce Stone. "Yes, it looks like Macey Meadows has been here since 2:45 p.m., so she should be somewhere in the building."

"Just when I thought we were going to have a relatively calm night, the weather must have decided otherwise," commented Dr. Linke. "The ambulance crew just brought in somebody who rolled his pickup and landed in a ravine south of Ridgemonte. Some people don't have enough sense to come in out of the rain or refrain from driving excessive speeds in dense fog. It's a good thing I'm not the one issuing driver's licenses in these parts."

Leaning to her right, Joyce said in a hushed tone to her co-worker, Dawn Rowann, "I think the doctor would benefit from a few of your cookies made with those dark chocolate chunks and pecans. We need to do something to sweeten him up a bit."

Dawn nodded her head up and down as she giggled out loud and replied, "Oh, Joyce, just how long have you worked at MMC anyway?"

"A little over three decades now, with probably that many more to go."

After completing his initial exam of Chet and exiting the emergency room, Dr. Linke ordered, "Meadows, arrange for x-rays of his ribs, right arm, and right leg. I rather suspect the tibia and fibula are both broken. He might have several cracked ribs along with a fractured ulna and radius. Picking that glass out of his hands was quite the project. He must have shielded his face with both hands as his pickup was rolling down the side of the hill. Miraculously enough, he has no internal injuries. I thought for sure his spleen would have ruptured. You could not pay me to live anywhere near that nasty stretch of road on that highway. Residing a few blocks from the hospital in Ridgemonte does have its distinct advantages."

"Yes, Dr. Linke, I'll get those x-rays ordered and get Chet moved to his room as soon as I can," assured Nurse Meadows. "It might be a while before he can get back on his horse."

"Ride his horse? I didn't think this patient was a cowboy. I had him confused with someone else. Even though I've worked at Mintner for over ten years, I still maintain there's an inherent risk to horses and motorcycles. We don't see many hogs in this area, but lots of horses." Realizing how that sounded, Dr. Linke chuckled before he said, "Actually, there are some four-legged hogs in the county, but not many two-wheeled ones! I think I'd better find a cup of coffee or a protein shake somewhere."

"The patient is Chet Castins of the big Sabblonti Cattle Ranch. That's what's engraved on the inside of the large silver belt buckle he was wearing."

"Is that supposed to mean something?"

"Well, I guess it does to some people."

"You guessed wrong on my account. Maybe Chet should plan to drive horses in the future and leave his pickup parked at his ranch. Owners of big cattle spreads never did impress me even if they help to pay for my extravagant annual hunting safaris."

Macey knew better than to ask Dr. Linke what kind of people he deemed noteworthy or important. She reminded herself, "In my type of work, I need to be more concerned with a doctor's professional skills than his social skills."

Despite being fairly young, Dr. Linke's seventy-eight-inch bean pole frame was hard to miss as he maneuvered throughout the hospital. He had trouble finding suitable hospital clothing to fit him. His extra oily skin and hair presented quite a challenge to him as he would periodically wipe his face with a paper towel. For some reason, the flesh on his boney hands was very thin revealing his large textbook veins and protruding knuckles which he cracked often. His steely gray eyes could not have been more than an inch apart if that much.

Returning to the nurse's station and leaning over the counter, Macey grinned from ear to ear before posing the obvious question, "Which one of you fabulous co-workers wants to accompany me to the ER and then to Room #131 to get our patient settled for the night?"

"Oh, you know I will," agreed Dawn. "Since I'm current on my charting, I can help you. Joyce, if we don't return for about three days, it means we've slipped out the back door and headed for parts unknown! Don't bother to send out a search party." The three nurses laughed in unison.

Macey and Dawn wheeled Chet's hospital cart into the assigned room and proceeded to get him as comfortably situated as possible in the bed. Macey commented, "At least this is not one of those fakealoo inflatable mattresses on this bed. Last month I had a patient who became so frustrated with his lack of sleep due to the mattress rising and falling that he unplugged it, threw it on the floor, and proceeded to sleep there for awhile. When I saw him lying there, I let him know in no uncertain terms that I did not approve of what he he'd done. Suffice it to say, we brought in another kind of bed for him. I can't remember his first name, but he had a German last name. That patient is proof positive that one should never try to out-stubborn a German."

Dawn lifted the bed sheet and pinched the side of the mattress. "Thanks for the unsolicited marital advice, Macey. I'll make a mental note to find out the last name of my prince charming when he shows up on the scene. It will be your job to determine his origin and ethnicity from that point forward."

After checking Chet's vitals, Dawn expressed her concern, "Macey, we need to keep a sharp eye on this one.

His temperature has spiked three degrees since he was brought in. There might be some infection brewing in his body."

Chet moaned as he turned his head from side to side on his pillow. He lifted his chin and opened his mouth but no words came out.

Dawn continued, "Well, there's one saving grace. At least Chet didn't suffer any facial injuries. I wonder if his wife realizes what a prize she won the day she married him. Wow, I could sit and stare at him for days on end! He's got that total movie star look about him. You know, the full black eyebrows, extra-long black eyelashes, robin egg-colored blue eyes, square jaw and full lips that form that perfect small "v" in the middle. Oh, just so dreamy!"

Macey cautioned, "Earth to Nurse Rowann, come in, Dawn. You'd better keep your eyes on the instruments behind Chet's bed and monitor those for the time being. I'll locate King Linke and let him know about the rising temp."

"What did you call our good doctor?"

"I referred to him as *King Linke* which was in very poor taste. That was probably unwise. If his neck was any stiffer, he couldn't bend over and tie his shoes. On second thought, I need to change my attitude toward him so that the wrong words don't spill out at the wrong time. I wouldn't want to have to move to Ignee County to work there after Linke ordered me out of here. I'm starting to settle into Shadow Butte County."

"Oh, surely there are other hospital personnel who share the same opinion of Dr. Linke, but for the most part, I think we should consider ourselves most fortunate to have someone of his caliber who's willing to work here. He might not have settled in this area if it were not for his fond childhood memories of visiting his maternal grandparents. It's one of those *returning to your roots* sort of things. I'm surprised he's still unmarried."

"Well, I'm not in the least bit surprised! Would you marry him? After all, money's not the most important thing in life."

Reflecting upon the last half hour of her shift, Macey opted to first check the doctor's lounge to see if Dr. Linke was in there rather than have him paged to apprise him of Chet's increased fever. Opening the door, Macey was trying to detect the source of the foul odor. The doctor's back was turned to her, so she walked to the front of the table.

Macey glanced down at the paper plate sitting on the table in front of her boss. Narrowing her focus, she guessed his sandwich was comprised of sardines and thinly sliced hot white onions overlaid with sardine oil. She thought she was going to regurgitate onto her uniform. *Is this why his skin looked like it did most of the time? What kind of shampoo did he use anyway?*

"Dr. Linke, after getting Chet checked into his room and taking his vitals, Dawn informed me that his temperature is rising. I thought it best to let you know in case you wanted to write the order for some additional antibiotics."

"Listen, Meadows, I'll be down when I get good and ready. Those cowboys are supposed to be full of grit, so he can just hang tough for a while longer. Since I've never been to the area where he rolled his pickup, I don't know what it looks like, but there might be something out there that would contribute to a bacterial infection. The outsides of his hands were pretty sliced up when he got here. I'll order some additional blood work from the lab, too. It would be nice if we had some medical history on him. Has his immediate family been notified that he's here?"

"I will double check on that to make sure. I've never met his wife or any of his family. His mother-in-law, Jantzi Sabblonti, passed away shortly before Christmas. I read her obituary in *The Ridgemonte Rider*."

"You actually take the time to read that fish wrap?"

"Yes, Dr. Linke, I enjoy reading the local newspaper. In fact, a copy is delivered to the hospital every week in case you are interested."

"If I could not find anything better to do with my time, I would quit before I wasted one minute reading that *Ridgemonte* whatever you called it. I'm still on my much-needed break if you don't mind, Meadows."

Macey exited the lounge.

Forty minutes later, Dr. Linke stood up, tore the magazine he'd been reading, left the scraps of paper on the table, and walked into the hallway. The last time he checked, other people were paid to clean up after him.

Returning to Chet's room, Macey opined to Dawn, "make that two items on the premarital list – never marry a German or some guy with a choleric personality."

"What's a choleric personality?"

"You know, someone who drinks rattlesnake venom for breakfast every morning, so he can breathe fire and speak with a forked tongue the remainder of the day! How's our patient doing? Oh, do you happen to know if anyone has contacted Chet's family to let them know he's in here?"

"I'll check with Joyce at the nurse's station to find out for sure before we both wind down our shifts for the night. Hopefully we can get on the day shift starting next month. Wouldn't that be nice?"

"Dream on, Nurse Rowann! Dream on!"

"Joyce, do you happen to know if Chet's family has been notified of his admittance to Mintner Medical Center? I've been so busy during my shift that I forgot to find out."

"Come to think of it, Dawn, I don't think they have. I'll look up the number for the Sabblonti Ranch and place a call right now. The Sheriff's office might have already notified someone, but sometimes those investigations can take a while to complete, especially on foggy bottom nights."

Dialing the phone number listed in the book, Joyce let it ring twenty-eight times. "Either no one is home, they're still at the accident scene, or everyone has gone to bed, and they can't hear the phone ringing." Checking the clock on her desk, Joyce said, "I'll be sure to leave a note for Caroline to remind her to keep trying to call during her shift."

CHAPTER SIX

"Mundane Monday, I guess I'd better get you on track by calling that hired hand husband of mine to get him on task," sang Stormy as she puttered in the kitchen. Carrying her cup of green tea into the living room, she plopped down in her recliner. Just as she was about to dial the number for the Lower Sabblonti Ranch house, the phone rang. Picking up the receiver she stated, "It's high time you called me. Where have you been, anyway? Get home. You have work to do."

Sarita extended the phone from her left ear. "Stormy, is that you? Who are you talking to?"

"Sarita, what do you want? Make it snappy as I'm very busy today."

"Wyn and I've been planning our special day which is set for Saturday, July 29th, at 7:00 in the evening. We're blissfully in love and can't wait to get married. I was calling to ask you to be in my wedding. Let's just let the past be the past. Mother and Daddy would want it that way. Both of us need to put our best foot forward. We are family."

Stormy held her cup at eye level. Her mother, Jantzi Belle, had a penchant for peacocks, not only for pictures of them adorning her kitchen walls, but some of her accessories as well. As Stormy looked at the feathers, she said, "Sarita, my life is so busy, and I'm not really all that interested in being in your wedding. Since you seem to have so many city friends, why don't you just fill up the spaces you need with them? They could probably find some used jeans at the *Second Time Around* shop in Ridgemonte. You were never one for uniformity anyway, so the fact that they'd all look different ought to suit you just fine. Mother's no longer with us. No need to worry about her being horrified over your ten-cent wedding. I really need to drink my antioxidants and get going. Goodbye."

Stormy dialed the number for the Lower Sabblonti Ranch house. The phone rang innumerable times, but no one answered it. She voiced her irritation, "I would imagine that Chet is ignoring me by not taking my call. I suppose I should've called him last night after he left to go home, but I really wasn't in the mood to talk to anyone. It took me two hours to clean up that glass and board up the broken window. I needed to spend some quality time in my office calculating my new-found wealth. I'll be able to keep far more of it than I'd originally planned since hubby will be doing twice as much work as he did before. He doesn't know that yet, but I'm in charge of the Sabblonti Empire now.

I think I'll just rest for a day or so while I draw up my master plan for the next few months. Loungewear and lots of caffeine will be the order of the day. I need to call the insurance company about that shattered window. I'll have to spin some kind of twisted yarn as to how it was broken. Those people don't need to know every intimate detail."

As Stormy sauntered down the hallway, she heard the phone ringing at 8 o'clock. *Since that horse head husband of mine was in no hurry to answer my call, I'm in no hurry to answer his call. Two can play this game. Water runs both ways through the pipe on this one.*

Eventually lifting the phone receiver to her left ear, Stormy chided, "Chet, you dunce, why didn't you answer the phone when I called you earlier?"

The voice on the other end of the phone replied, "Hello, could I please speak to Mrs. Castins?"

"This is Mrs. Castins. Who did you think it was?"

"This is the Mintner Medical Center. Chet Castins was admitted to the hospital last evening following his car accident. We've been trying to reach you, but no one answered the phone."

"I've been here the entire time. Knowing you people, you

probably dialed the wrong number."

"We've been calling the number listed in the current phone book."

"You have no way of proving that."

"Mrs. Castins, your husband is in Room #131 at the hospital."

Stormy slammed the receiver down as she muttered, "Now what has that half-baked husband of mine gotten himself into? It looks like I'll have to hire that babysitting agency after all to keep tabs on him the rest of the year. That was definitely money I was not planning on spending. Serves him right for not paying attention while driving. He can just doze in that hospital bed for a day or two until I find time to go check on him. He said he'd not been sleeping very well lately anyway. Chet Carleton Castins is not high on my priority list at the moment."

S

Trying to catch her breath after her brisk walk from The Shadowy Merc to Daisy's Floral Shop in downtown Ridgemonte, Salina Bevvins opened the front door and took in a quick view of the few floral arrangements on display. "Hello, is anyone in the shop right now?" she yelled.

Proprietor Daisy Freemille answered from the back room, "Yes, I'll be there in just a minute. Hold your horses."

Emerging through the arched doorway of the south wall, Daisy dried her hands on a *Happy New Year* themed hand towel. "Good morning, how can I help you?"

Salina removed her black leather gloves and stuffed them inside her purse. "I need a male floral arrangement."

Daisy tried to keep from laughing out loud, but she could not. "Did you intend to say that you need an arrangement put together for a male rather than a female?"

Feeling her face blushing, Salina responded, "Well, yes, that's what I meant to say. It's been such a hectic morning as I just found out that Chet's in the hospital. I asked my boss if I could take an hour or so off work so I could drop by your shop and then head over to see Chet. Time is of the essence."

Daisy had her back turned to Salina when she opened the refrigerated display case and looked through the arrangements she had for sale. The word *hospital* registered with Daisy. Whirling around, she gasped, "Oh dear, did you say your husband was in the hospital? What on earth is the matter with him? I hope it's nothing serious!"

"Oh, Chet's not my husband. He's just a good friend of mine. Shortly after I arrived at work at The Shadowy Merc around 7:15 this morning, Deputy Jeelon came in to buy some doughnuts, so that's when I heard about it. Thankfully, Chet did not perish when he rolled his pickup on that nasty "S" curve."

Standing at the counter Daisy commented, "My fresh flowers have not yet arrived this week since it's only Monday. My local supplier, Catherine Harrison, keeps me well stocked in the summer and fall with her wildflower collections, but the dead of winter can present some challenges. What about a flowering plant? Do you think that would work for Chet?"

Salina walked through Daisy's shop touching the tops of various plants with her fingertips. "Great idea! The main thing is I want Chet to know that he's always on my mind. Do you happen to have any *Get-Well* cards that I could include with the plant?"

"I have a nice selection of a variety of types of cards in that revolving rack next to the wall over there. I try to keep them away from the moisture, so that's why they're in that corner by the ceramic planters, vases, and related items. I mentioned my childhood friend Catherine a moment ago. She's been such a gift to me and is a big help and encouragement in my business venture. Being a free-lance artist and graphic designer, she has created some lovely cards. I'm sure you can find one to suit your needs."

Salina continued to verbally plan, "Let's see, I should probably get more of a masculine looking *Get Well* card to go along with that green flowering plant. Chet would be horrified if I showed up with some fancy feminine looking bouquet of flowers and a frilly looking card." Bending down, Salina plucked a blue card from the rack as she expressed her approval, "This one is just perfect, and I like the fact that it's blank on the inside so I can pen my own thoughts. Most of the time when I try to purchase a greeting card, I like the outside of the card, but don't necessarily like the wording inside. Those kinds of cards are probably designed by people who have zero love life."

After paying for her merchandise with a personal check, Salina left the shop, walked to the grocery store parking lot, got inside her Aunt June Slader's dark brown pickup, and drove to the hospital.

As soon as the shop was empty, Daisy went to the *Employee Only* section and called her friend who answered on the first ring. "Catherine, do you know some people in these parts named Salina and Chet?" Somewhat puzzled, Catherine replied, "Not that I recall right off hand. We didn't grow up with any kids in our class who had those names. I don't go into town that often, so I'm not that familiar with folks who are moving in and out."

"Salina mentioned something about Chet being involved in an auto accident or some such. She seemed to be overly concerned and could not get out of my shop fast enough to get to Mintner Medical Center."

"No clue, but if you happen to find out what's going on, dial me up again. I'll be in my alpine art studio working on my greeting card line today. I hope it was not a serious accident. The roads can get treacherous in a hurry around here in the winter."

"Stay warm, dear friend, as you continue with your creative designs."

S

Salina drove as quickly as she could to Mintner Medical Center and parked close to the front door. She dug around in her black-fringed, leather purse to find a pen as she contemplated expressing her inmost thoughts. *I must find the exact balance of words to write so Chet will know what I'm feeling in my heart this very morning. There cannot be any doubt once he reads the card.* Romantic phrases flitted in and out of her mind, but she was having trouble concentrating. She remembered a conversation from years ago with one of her life-long friends. During that time, Salina mentioned to her, "I have something to tell you, but don't know how to say it."

Her friend replied, "Try words."

That's it! Try words. Just write some words.

Opening the card and laying it across the overdue library book titled *A Crash Course in Finding A Rich Western Husband* which rested on the passenger seat of the pickup,

Salina began to write,

To my dear friend, Chet,

I hope you are up and around soon. I was so sorry to hear that you were in a bad accident, but am very thankful you did not die! Please let me know if there is anything, large or small, that I can do for you. Now I know the reason I moved to Ridgemonte. I needed to be here for you when you were going through a rough time. You know where to find me. I miss your warm smile.

You are in my thoughts every waking and sleeping moment,

Salina

Salina walked around to the passenger side, opened the door, retrieved the plant, and nestled it inside the bent elbow of her left arm. *It's below freezing this morning, so I hope this thing is not as fragile as those poinsettias. Surely a few seconds in cold weather will not damage it.*

Approaching the information desk, Salina inquired as to Chet's room number. The clerk responded, "Are you family? Visiting hours end in half an hour."

Salina answered, "Family? Well, sort of, extended, you know how that goes. I just need to drop off this plant and card for Chet to let him know I'm thinking of him."

"Let me double check our records here. Okay, it looks like Chet Castins is in Room #131. That's down the hall, turn to your right, and it's almost to the end. If the door is closed, be sure to knock first in case the nurses are performing their timely tasks."

"Thank you," Salina replied. She walked hurriedly to locate Chet's room. When she arrived at Room #131 the door was closed. She knocked quietly, but there was no answer. She waited for a couple of minutes and everything seemed quiet. Opening the door, she peeked inside and saw that Chet was sleeping soundly. His right leg was in traction which caused her to rear back as she was not expecting anything like that. Tip-toeing to the window closest to his bed, Salina set the plant on the window shelf, opened the *Get-Well* card, and propped it against the plant. She looked longingly into his face. Gentle tears welled up inside her eyes and fell onto her black cape. Before exiting the room, she held her right forefinger to her mouth, kissed it, and gently placed it in the middle of Chet's closed lips. She waited to see if he would move or awaken. When he did not, she left the hospital and wondered how long it would be before Chet could return to the Sabblonti Ranch or stop in and do some grocery shopping at The Shadowy Merc.

S

Sarita had made prior arrangements with Dr. Diller to meet him fifteen minutes before his first dental patient was to arrive that morning. Even though she'd worked for him for a number of years, she was surprised at how emotional she was just thinking about talking to him.

Dr. Diller was already in his office when Sarita arrived at the clinic. His door was wide open. "Good morning, and thank you kindly for making extra time for me."

"Of course, Sarita. What's on your mind?"

"This will come as no surprise to you in light of my recent engagement. Wyn and I plan to be married on July 29th, so after discussing it with him, we deem it's best if my last day here is June 30th. That should give you ample time to hire someone else. I've so enjoyed working here, and you've been a fabulous boss. I couldn't have asked for anyone more considerate and gracious, but it's time to write a whole new chapter in my life. I'm so excited to be getting married!"

"Congratulations, Sarita." Dr. Diller leaned forward, crossed both arms, and rested them on his desk. The corners of his lips turned downward.

"I apologize, Dr. Diller. I should have told you earlier that I was leaving, but Wyn and I've not really had a lot of time to talk about things, so we just made this major decision. I wanted to let you know right away in fairness to you and the rest of your staff."

"Sarita, I'm not upset that you didn't tell me earlier that you would be working until the end of June and then leaving. That will give me ample time to find a replacement, and you've been a stellar employee. If permissible, my concern is more along a personal line. In a fatherly sort of way, I'm concerned that you don't know Wyn very well at all. I would like to see you take some more time to get to know him on a much deeper psychological level."

"But I do know him, Dr. Diller, and he's just been promoted to Ranch Foreman for the Toppens Ranch. Tom Toppens would not have given him that assignment if he didn't think he could trust him."

Dr. Diller leaned back in his chair. "It's not that I disrespect Tom's judgment or am trying to interfere where I don't belong, but completing ranching duties is far different on an emotional level than being married to someone. It's easy to go work every day and just go through the motions without investing any emotion."

"You and Anne-Marie have a very good marriage, or so it would seem."

"Yes, we do, but a lot of factors have gone into that. We grew up as kids together in a small coastal town. We got married during my undergraduate years and then Anne-Marie worked to help put me through medical school. We also had a lot of financial and emotional support from both of our rock-solid families. Even with all that, it was still a major project. Marriage is wonderful, but you have to go into it with both eyes wide open and a real heartfelt commitment. Also, you have to construct real strong boundaries around it."

Sarita continued to fidget with the bracelet on her left wrist. "Do you think Wyn is not committed to me in the long run or is not in it for the long haul? Do you want to talk to him before we get married? Would that make you feel better? I think you're prejudging someone you don't even remotely know."

Dr. Diller lifted his eyeglasses toward the ceiling lights and carefully peered through them. "Sarita, I'm not trying to rain on your special day. No, I don't need to talk to Wyn before you get married. He's an adult and can make his own decisions. There's an old saying that comes to mind which is, 'Look before you leap, still water runs deep.'"

"Dr. Diller, I have looked. The water is still, and it's not that deep."

CHAPTER SEVEN

As Stormy walked down the hall toward Chet's hospital room, Blake Benson rounded the corner and almost ran into her.

"Blake, what are you doing here? Have you been in Chet's room?"

"Yes, I have. Is there a law against it?"

"I could care less what laws are in force and effect right now. The last time I checked, you were merely a brand inspector and not deputized via Shadow Butte County. You probably don't have what it takes to be a sheriff or deputy anyway."

"Who's going to be running your Bigshot Sabblonti Show now that your better half will be laid up for so long?"

"First of all, Chet is **NOT** my better half. I'll have him scurrying around and carrying out my orders in a couple of days."

Blake grabbed both sides of his leather jacket and pulled it towards the middle of his stomach. He pushed the brim of his cowboy hat up a couple of inches. "A couple of days? That's hilarious unless you also believe in miracles! Have you forgotten that Chet's right leg is still in traction? Not to mention that he's not even had the surgery yet to fix the compound fracture. He'll be laid up for months."

"You have no idea what you're even talking about. Chet is only faking having something wrong with him to get a little extra attention."

"Well, if broken bones and lacerations are your idea of faking it, then God help you, woman. Surely you saw what kind of condition Chet was in when you visited him. Hold on a minute – you've not even been inside Chet's room yet, have you? What's with you, anyway?"

Stormy raised her right hand to slap Blake, but held it in check. "You have no right to question me or my whereabouts. I've been very busy the past few days. On second thought, and assuming that Chet will be unable to ride herd for me for a while, do you know of anyone I could hire right away? I know it's the dead of winter and most of the itinerant cowboys don't blow in until early spring."

Sneering and then laughing out loud, Blake replied, "Come to think of it, I do. The Alottos just happen to be in the area paying me a long overdue visit. Less was the foreman for a big cattle spread in South Dakota, but it just sold after a century of ownership. That sorta left him high and dry, but he's got tons of experience. So does his wife. Meg's her name. She was the bookkeeper for the ranch where they both used to work. Less and Meg are as honest as the day is long. I would highly recommend them, and I know they would sure appreciate finding a job right away."

"Where are they living now?"

"They're staying with me until they can find something a little more permanent."

"Do they have any kids?"

"No, their two sons are grown and own a ranch in Montana."

"Why didn't their parents go to work for them once they lost their jobs on the big ranch in South Dakota?"

"I don't know exactly. I didn't want to pry into their personal business, so I didn't ask them."

Checking the time on her wristwatch, Stormy ordered, "Meet me in the waiting room in ten minutes, so we can talk some more about this."

Shoving the door open with her right forearm, Stormy marched into Chet's room and walked to the side of his bed. "Your charade is over, Chet. I know you've conned these inept nurses and buffoon doctor into tying your leg up to look like you have some major injuries, but you can't fool me. I'll give you another day and then you'd better be ready to walk out of here. No one has even checked on your prized animals of late, so that might be some incentive to get up off your blessed assurance and get to work!"

Stormy had not noticed Nurse Meadows standing behind the bathroom door during her tirade.

Nearing Chet's bed, she said, "You must be Mrs. Castins."

"What gave you the first clue, Mrs. Sherlock?"

"Your husband has suffered a broken leg and will be in traction for a few more days before surgery. I just finished checking on him, so I can give you a few private moments if you wish."

"Maybe you're not as dense as you look. Yes, I need only a couple of minutes to speak to *Bonehead*."

"Chet, was the nurse speaking the truth?"

"Yes, she was, unfortunately," he muttered. Extending his right bandaged hand to touch her, Stormy stepped back. "Stormy, I love . . . "

Stomping her right foot on the floor and raising her voice, Stormy said, "It's a little hard to feel one bit sorry for you. Maybe next time you'll pay closer attention when you're driving instead of daydreaming or nightdreaming or whatever you were doing."

Just as she turned to exit the room, Stormy noticed the flowering plant in the windowsill. "Let me see, I'll bet I can guess who this is from." Picking up the card, reading it, and then laying it face down, she calmly declared, "Chet Carleton Castins, there's no way you can try to convince me that you're not guilty of setting your sights on that grocery store clerk."

"I've never taken my sights off you, Stormy."

"It's going to take more than a feeble explanation to convince me of that!"

Stormy joined Blake in the first floor waiting room. She found a pen and small tablet in her purse so she could take some notes. "Okay, Mr. Benson, time to talk business."

"I prefer to be called Blake."

"Fine, Blake. Give me your schpeel on this Less Alotto. What can he do, and why do I need him instead of someone else? How old is he anyway? If he's got one foot on the banana peel and the other one in the grave, I'm not interested. Keep in mind that I don't intend to turn my newly acquired inheritance over to some unlearned cowpoke who thinks he's a big-time operator. My empire is running on auto ranch now, so I don't want to endanger it in any way, shape or form. Do you understand?"

Blake removed his cowboy hat and set it on the end table. He reached into his pocket, took out his pocket-knife and opened it. He started cleaning his fingernails with the smaller of the two blades. Small bits of a black substance flipped into the air and landed on the hospital floor.

Stormy glanced down at her feet. *Maybe Chet wasn't such a bad catch for a husband after all.*

"Yes, I understand completely. You act as if I'm a total stranger to cattle country and how it operates. I have a lot of experience under my belt as a brand inspector and am very well connected in this state along with our two neighboring ones. You can fully trust me. As for Less and Meg, they're in their mid to late fifties and both as healthy as a horse."

"Some horses are not that healthy. Chet just dumped a lot of cash into that horse flesh of his called *Braezee.* She sure in the world was not very healthy."

"Seems to me like she was before she picked up that nail in her foot."

"How'd you know about Braezee's nail injury?"

"I told you that I was very well connected."

"You might just have too much time on your hands rather than being well connected. What kind of experience does Meg have as I'm looking to hire someone to help me with some bill paying and light office work?"

"Meg took care of the books and all related office work in her prior job. I can make arrangements with the Alottos for you to meet and interview them. Just name the date, time, and place. I will make it happen. I'm an expert at making things happen, especially important things."

Stormy continued to write some notes to herself on the tablet. "Job interviews bore me, and I have so much to do these days. I'm hiring them this very minute based upon your advice. Let's see, today is Wednesday, January 5th, so have them meet me at 8:00 sharp Friday morning at the Main Sabblonti Ranch house. Since Dunce Chet has not fed his animals for a few days, some of them might be getting pretty famished by now. Oh, and tell them to come alone. You don't need to accompany them."

"Not a problem. Anything else?"

"No. This kind of horsing around just about sends me over the edge. Today is the first day of the rest of my ranching life, so I need to get on with it." Retrieving her pickup keys from inside her coat pocket, Stormy walked out the front doors of the Mintner Medical Center.

Blake stood up and spotted a mirror on the far wall. He walked toward it and continued to place his hat in different positions on his head as he made various facial expressions. He reminded himself that he needed to keep practicing in case his picture ended up in a popular western magazine somewhere. Lost in his thoughts, he reflected, *Now that's one thorny woman. I've never met someone who was so uncaring and unkind. What would have happened if I'd not been on the main highway the night Chet drove off the road? He might well have lain in the bottom of that ravine for hours or even a couple of days before someone found him. Well, now is not the time for what ifs. It's high time for the past to step on the heels of the present.*

CHAPTER EIGHT

"Dawson's Dealership, how may I direct your call?"

"Yes, hello, Tom Toppens of Toppens Ranch here. I need to talk to Delbert. Can you get him on the horn for me?"

"Yes, please hold while I find him. He's in the building somewhere."

Lifting the telephone receiver while pressing the blinking red light on line four, Delbert Dawson said, "Well, howdy old timer, how are you doing today? What can I peddle you to start the new year?"

"I need one of your F350's with the marker and running lights. Do you have one hidden in plain sight on your regular or extended lot?"

"There's one that I've kept tucked away for you on the very end of the regular lot. It's dark blue and the only one I've got right now, but I can order one in a different color if you would prefer."

"How'd you know that I'd be ordering one so soon?"

"I keep pretty close tabs on all of you ranchers."

"It's a good thing somebody does. If I pay cash on the barrel head like I usually do, how much will you knock off the price?"

"Oh, I can discount it by about 10%, give or take. Will that work for you?"

"Sounds like a great deal to me. Are you going to be there around noon so I can drop in, cut you the check, and drive my new rig off the lot so that it immediately loses 10 Grand in value?"

"Gee, you drive a hard bargain, and yes, I'll make sure to be here at noon."

Donning his outdoor clothing, Tom walked down to the bunkhouse. The aroma of fried bacon permeated the air as he knocked on the front door.

Spence, one of the hired hands, greeted him, "Well, good morning, Tom! What brings you down so early? Do you need help at your house?"

"Howdy, Spence. No, everything's just fine up yonder. Must be your turn to do the cooking today. Smells like you've had a mighty fine breakfast. Did you fry some grits to go with your bacon and eggs?"

"Sure did! There's nothing quite like some good hearty vittles on these cold mornings. Would you like to try some of my cooking?"

"Not right now. I need you to ride into Ridgemonte with me. I'll be leaving here in about half an hour."

"Can do, Tom. Let me put the one easy, quick clean job on these pots and pans, and then I'll walk up to meet you. I dare not leave the kitchen messy since Wyn's sort of a *Neat-Nick*, and it's his turn to cook tomorrow. On second thought, I better just let this one pan soak while we're gone. I went to sleep at the switch when frying the grits, so there's some gradue in the bottom."

As Tom headed back to his house, he heard some yelling coming from the barn. Opening the door, he saw the dust filled air and looked on the ground where two men were wrestling.

"You're not pulling your weight around here, Luger," Shane shouted.

"Liar! I'm not only doing my share but part of yours as well. I'm not the one crawling out the bedroom window at night and returning right before the sun comes up."

"Knock it off you two," ordered Tom. "Grow up, and get your chores done."

Oblivious to what was happening inside the barn, Spence's mind began working overtime in search of a reason as to why he would need to accompany Tom into town. He hoped neither Tom nor Merna were experiencing any urgent medical issues. Both of them were extremely private people and did not telegraph much of what was transpiring on a day-to-day basis. *Never really thought about it until now. With Toppens not having any children or grandchildren of their own, who will help take care of them as they continue to age? My co-cowpoke, Wyn, would most likely help out, but Shane, on the other hand, seems pretty self-centered to me. Maybe he's not along for the full ride.*

Merna looked out the kitchen window and saw Spence walking onto the front porch. Opening the door, she greeted him warmly. "Oh, good morning, Spence. Please come inside from the cold. How's everything at the bunkhouse? Are you keeping nice and toasty down there? Thankfully, the snow has not started to fly just quite yet today. Let's hope we don't get any of those hair-raising storms where the snow looks like vertical white-out. We had enough of those last year! According to the *Farmer's Almanac* our winter is supposed to be fairly dry with deep freeze temperatures."

Removing his gloves, Spence extended his right hand to pat Merna on the shoulder. "Yes, all of us are doing fine. One nice thing about the winter months is there are fewer of us inside the bunkhouse, so we have more elbow room. It gets very crowded during branding and calving seasons. Speaking of the *Farmer's Almanac*, is there any truth to that business of the correct time to dehorn cattle and so forth?"

The stove timer sounded as Merna removed a pan of freshly baked cinnamon rolls and set them on some hot pads. "Some folks don't put any stock into the *Almanac's* recommendations at all, but Tom swears by them, so we've implemented those practices for years. There seems to be some truth to the connection of performing ranching chores according to the phases of the moon since the moon itself is directly tied to moisture. That's especially true in the high desert mountain regions."

Spence's mouth started watering as he looked at the rolls. Since he'd just eaten, he didn't ask for one. "Always something to learn, isn't there Merna? Oh, you asked if everything was okay at the bunkhouse. There's one thing I might mention. That old washing machine seems to be making some strange noises. Maybe I'm just over-loading it too much with my heavy winter clothing. When I washed the last batch of heavy-duty overalls, it sounded like a grain grinder. It was really lugging down. About the only difference seemed to be there wasn't any dust flying out the top of it!"

"It's probably past time to install a new washer and dryer set. Come to think of it, I can't even remember when we moved those down there. After I purchased my new washer and dryer for this house, we had the hired hands take my old ones and put them in the bunkhouse. I'll call Jed's Appliance Center and see what they might have on hand. Thanks for mentioning it. All of you need clean and dry clothing, especially this time of year. On another note, I meant to ask you about the New Year's Eve gathering at Merrills. Thanks for delivering the jars of preserves to us. They're so delicious on warm toast. If there was enough time right now, I'd fix you some so you could sample it."

"The barbeque was great and we met some nice folks. The evening was just starting to look like it had some promise when Shane got a severe gut ache, so I had to call it a night and drive him home. I made a complete fool of myself in front of Priscilla Fletcher. I doubt I'll ever see her again. She probably thinks I'm the biggest *chucklehead* in seven states. I'm trying not to dwell on it too much, but as you can probably tell, I'm still replaying the night in my mind."

"What on earth happened anyway? You and Shane were not gone too awfully long that evening."

Before Spence could continue to pour his heart out to motherly Merna, Tom emerged from the back of the house and entered the kitchen. He patted his front shirt pockets along with his jean pockets. "Can't seem to find my checkbook anywhere. Merna, have you seen it? Got to find it in a hurry so we can skedaddle out of here."

Merna walked into their bedroom, pulled Tom's top dresser drawer open, and located his well-worn, leather-covered checkbook secured by a thick rubber band. Walking into the kitchen, she waved it in the air. “Here you go, Tom. Safe travels into town and back. I’ll have your dinner waiting for you when you get back. Would you rather have beef stew or beef pot pie?”

Tom opened his checkbook to see how many blank checks were inside. “Yep, looks like there’s plenty for today. Oh darlin’, whatever you want to whip up is fine with me. How about we have the stew for dinner and the pot pie for supper? But you can leave the dried hay leaves out of my pot pie if you please.”

“Hay leaves, Tom? What on earth are you talking about? You know I don’t go to the hay barn, break a bale apart, scoop up some dry leaves, bring them to the kitchen and put them in your food.”

“I saw something that looked like dried hay leaves in that pot pie you made last time.”

“For heaven’s sake, Tom! That’s dried tarragon from my herb garden that I grow each year. I harvest it which helps to add a wonderful flavor when married up with beef dishes.”

“Well, never mind what *gone* you called it, since it needs to be gone!”

Just the mention of that fine homemade cooking made Spence start to salivate. While he could not remember the last time he had beef pot pie with gravy, he appreciated getting inside the warm cab of Tom’s pickup.

“On these cold mornings it’s important to get the engine of your rig warmed up before driving it,” instructed Tom. “Those dudes in town walk to their garages, turn on the ignition, and back their pickups into the street. That really takes a toll on the engine after a while.”

“Thanks for the maintenance tips, Tom. Operating in this region is a whole new learning curve for me.”

Spence’s stomach was in knots. Perhaps he should not have gorged himself on seven slices of bacon, three over-easy eggs, and a mound of grits sprinkled with hot sauce. It was as if his mouth was sealed with duct tape and he couldn’t think of anything to say.

The ride into Ridgemonte was on the quiet side except

for a few lines of small talk. Spence wondered if Tom was just going to take him into town and dump him off at the bus depot. Did the old buses even make trips back and forth from Ridgemonte anymore? Tom hadn't mentioned anything about Spence's job being terminated, and more importantly, had not instructed him to pack his belongings into a duffle bag before leaving for town.

Tom turned onto a street located on the outskirts of town, drove several blocks, and entered Dawson's parking lot. "Spence, have you met Delbert before?"

"No, can't say as I have. Who's he?"

"None other than the owner of the dealership. He's a real straight shooter, and I've horse traded with him for decades. Well, not actually horse traded. I should say ranch rig traded. He's probably getting ready to retire and hand the reins to his oldest son, Brent. You should probably get to know him, too."

Spence accompanied Tom as he walked into the dealership, through a set of swinging doors, and straight into Delbert's office. Tom acted like he owned the joint.

"Howdy, Delbert! Nice of you to give up your dinner hour for me. I would like to introduce you to one of my hired hands, Spence."

Shaking hands with Delbert, Spence said, "Good to meet you, Delbert." All of this happened so quickly and methodically that Spence hoped Delbert hadn't noticed his trembling right hand.

"Pull up a chair while we tend to the matters at hand," directed Delbert. "Now Tom, I want you to know that I came within an Ace of selling that dark blue F350 on Monday. Just at the last minute, the buyer backed out. He was willing to pay cash as well. Must be your lucky day or mine or both!"

"I'm a firm believer that everything in life happens for a reason," said Tom. "The helping hand usually comes back around just when we need it the most. You got the paperwork all drawn up?"

"Sure do, but don't you want to give it a test drive first so you can be certain it's exactly what you want? That's a lot of cash to part with all at once."

"Nah, you've never sold me a bum steer in the past. I've learned over the decades that your word is your bond, so if there are any problems, I know you'll plan to deal with them straight out of the shoot."

"Why don't you take a look-see at these documents and if they meet with your approval, sign on the bottom line, and I'll get some keys rounded up? You didn't mention anything about a trade-in, so I didn't include anything on the sales order to reflect that."

Tom reached inside his shirt pocket to locate his reading glasses. He spent the next several minutes looking over the sales slip. Standing up, he bent over Delbert's desk to find a black pen, and signed the paperwork. Then he wrote a check for the full amount of his new pickup. Spence noticed that after Tom signed his check, he drew his cattle brand.

Delbert returned to his office about twenty minutes later and handed two sets of keys to Tom along with his copy of the sales slip, warranty information, and related documents. "Spence, I assume you're the relief driver for today?"

"Must be."

After shaking hands once again with Delbert, Tom and Spence exited Dawson's Dealership.

"Spence, I'll hoof it down to the end of the lot and fire up my new rig. When you see me drive by, follow me. Here's the keys to my old pickup."

Walking to Tom's pickup, Spence reached around to pat his left rear hip pocket. "Whew, I was so shook up I couldn't remember if I even picked up my wallet this morning."

Not having previously driven that much in Ridgemonte

or spent much time in town, Spence wondered if Tom was leading him on a wild goose chase as he zigzagged through several streets. Tom stopped in front of a large red brick building complex and motioned for Spence to get out of his pickup.

Spence opened the main door of the building for Tom and walked through after him. "I can't recollect if that licensing outfit is on the first or second floor. Spence, do you see one of those boards on the wall listing the different offices?"

"Right over yonder. Looks like we need to head to #204. On second thought, Tom, let's take the elevator."

Tom and Spence walked to the front counter where Tom laid his paperwork down. The head clerk, Lorena, inquired as to how she could help them.

"I assume you know how to do all this fancy transfer stuff," said Tom. "Let's see here. I just bought a new pickup from Dawson's outfit, so I need to get the title, vehicle registered in my name, and I want to use the same plates that I had on my old pickup."

"What's the license plate number on your old rig?" asked Lorena.

"It's Toppens. That's T O P P E N S. Most people want to put an *i* where the *e* goes in my last name. Don't know why."

"Thank you for spelling that for me."

Tom unzipped the inside pocket of his coat and pulled out another creased piece of light orange paper. It looked like it had only been folded once in the past. "I need to sign this title so it can be transferred."

"I can help you with all of that."

"That's one of the things I like the most about Shadow Butte County. Most folks pretty much seem to know what they're doing. The last thing I need is some paperwork foul up. I'm planning on riding prosperously on the high hills from this point forward."

Spence cocked his head to his right after he heard that last comment. What did he know? After all, he was just along for the ride.

"Mr. Toppens, please complete the reverse side of this old title."

"You can call me Tom. None of this *Mister* stuff for me."

Glancing at Spence, Tom asked, "What's your last name again?"

"Woodson."

As Tom leaned his head back to fill in the information inside the small space provided on the paper title, he inquired, "Is that *sen* or *son*?"

"It's *son.* W O O D S O N."

"Okey, dokey, Lorena. I think that does it for me. All I need to do now is cut a check to this government outfit."

Lorena started to add the different figures on her adding machine when she stopped suddenly and said, "Wait a second, Tom. You'll need new plates for that older model pickup since you're transferring those to your new one. That's a separate form so give me a minute while I locate one. Okay, here you go. Just fill this out and give it back to me. I'm in no hurry. You hit it just right as the noon hour has come and gone when we seem to be busiest most days."

Tom slid the paper to his right which landed in front of Spence who was leaning into the counter while resting his chin on his right hand.

"Here you go, Spence. Go ahead and fill this out. Do you want just standard plates with any old number on them or do you want something else like personalized plates?"

"Me, fill out the paperwork?"

"Yes, you fill out the paperwork since you're the new owner. Don't just stand there like a cow lookin' at a new gate."

"I'm the new owner!" exclaimed Spence. "Boy, howdy. I didn't see that coming. Okay, I can certainly do that."

"Just don't plan on making a cattle career out of trying to get that paper completed. Figure out what you want on your plates and let's hightail it out of here. Merna's got dinner waiting for me at home."

Spence filled in the necessary blank spaces on the piece

of paper and handed it back to Lorena.

"It looks like you want your license plates to read S P E N C E. Is that correct?"

"Correct."

"Tom, the personalized plates are more expensive as you well know from having them on your vehicle for years."

"Not a problem, Lorena. Just add that amount on your fancy machine and give me the grand total."

"Your new title will be mailed to you in about three weeks so be on the lookout for it. Thanks for stopping in and have a nice day. Oh, just a second, Spence. Here's the temporary pink sticker to place inside your window until your new license plates arrive."

The word *pink* struck a nerve in Spence's recent memory. He had flashbacks of Priscilla Fletcher who he'd met a mere five days ago at Merrill's New Year's Eve Barbeque wearing her pink leather jacket and matching pink cowgirl boots.

As they left the building and walked toward their rigs, Spence looked at Tom and said, "I never dreamed in a million years that I'd have a pickup to start a new millennium. How can I ever thank you enough? What will Shane say about this?"

"I suppose you could give him a lift every now and then if you wanted to, but I would be more concerned about your new job responsibilities than Shane's reaction to anything. We still have that old tan job at the ranch that's up for grabs. I've been hearing some reports of Shane's bellyaching. Cattle ranches are not built or maintained by complainers. We need good, solid, and honest workers."

"Just what are my new job responsibilities?" asked Spence.

"You are my new Assistant Ranch Foreman as of right now."

Spence was speechless. "Thank you, Mr. Toppens, ur, I mean, Tom. Wow, a new-to-me pickup and a new ranch job title all in the same day. Is this for real?"

"Yes, it's for real and you better get your tail feathers

back to the ranch. The temperature is dropping like dead flies out here, and I aim to head home."

Spence left Dawson's Dealership parking lot ahead of Tom since he was parked closer to the exit. En route to the Toppens Ranch, he was having trouble concentrating following the events of the past two and three-fourths hours. He recalled one of his mother's favorite sayings, "Suddenly, life can change on a dime." Spence envisioned a dime in his mind which is about three-quarters of an inch in diameter. *Is this what a "suddenly" is all about?*

When Spence entered the driveway of the Toppens Ranch, he wondered where he should park his new-to-him pickup. If he was the assistant ranch foreman, Tom must still be the ranch foreman, and it was of the utmost importance to remember one's rung on the ladder. Not wanting to ruffle anyone's feathers at this point, he started to drive toward the barn, but braked suddenly when he saw Merna scampering about in the front yard. He turned the ignition off, got out of his pickup, and ran toward her.

"Merna, what are you doing out here in the cold wearing just a sweater? Is something wrong?"

"Spence, help me catch this sweet thing. It's freezing out here, and I don't want her to get cold."

"Never mind about whatever sweet thing you're trying to find! What about you getting cold? Where's that big, fur-lined coat with the hood that you normally wear along with your winter gloves? You know, your go-to-town coat?"

"I didn't have time to put on any coat before she darted out the front door. We need to find your belated Christmas gift."

"My belated Christmas gift? Out here in the cold? The only belated gift I got was being left out in the cold by a pretty, petite, strawberry blondie."

"Spence, we're searching for something that's black, brown, and white."

"Black, brown, white, and a moving object?"

"She's not an object. She's a living, moving being, and just adorable!"

"Women drive me nuts! Merna, cut to the chase, and tell me exactly what I'm supposed to be chasing and finding."

When Spence walked past a frosted boxwood bush, he thought he heard a strange noise. Retracing his steps, he caught a glimpse of something that looked like pink satin. Separating the branches as he bent down, Spence picked up a furry thing that was black, brown, and white alright. "My, my, my, look at you! How'd you find your way clear out here complete with a pink satin bow tied around your neck?"

Merna dashed toward Spence and his new-found gift. "Thank heavens you found her. Let's get inside by the stove so all of us can warm up a few degrees. There's Tom coming into the driveway right now."

CHAPTER NINE

Taking a little more time than usual with her plastic princess routine on Thursday morning, Stormy frowned as she stood in front of the full-length mirror. *Something doesn't look quite right. This dark purple just isn't going to cut the mustard today. I need something more empowering.*

Hurriedly flipping through the blouses and sweaters in the closet, Stormy selected a redhaven colored turtleneck to match her boots. "Oh, I feel better already! Why on earth did I apply that cotton candy, pink colored lipstick anyway? What was I thinking? Where's mother's cold cream so I can get that stuff removed and go with a shade of red to complete my ensemble?"

Stormy entered her office down the hallway on the third floor of the Main Sabblonti Ranch house. Living alone had its distinct advantages. Looking through the various checkbooks in the top drawer of the desk, she located the one for the operating account. It suddenly dawned on her that she would need to get new checks ordered for each of the accounts, but that would have to wait until later. On second thought, she decided to count out $70,000 in cash for her outing for the day. She remembered seeing her mother's briefcase somewhere upstairs which she would need to find post haste and secure the cash in the bottom of it.

"With nothing to worry about, I'm as free as can be today. No husband, no animals, no nothing, but just little ol' me. Time to invest in myself as it's sure to pay great dividends in the not-too-distant future."

As Stormy drove into Ridgemonte, she decided to swing by the local day care. She parked in front and contemplated going inside to inquire about volunteering to help so she could hold newborn babies. Sorrow overcame her as she sobbed into her monogrammed handkerchief. Regaining her composure, she drove to Mintner Medical Center. She looked into the mirror and determined that enough redness had disappeared from her eyes and cheeks, so she could go inside and see Chet. Just as she got out of the pickup and started to walk toward the entryway, Salina emerged from the front door. Stormy's tears returned. She couldn't shut them off. "Why can't that woman leave my husband alone? What could she possibly have that I don't?"

En route to Cinder Valley, Stormy gave considerable thought to the last twenty-one days of her life. *What did other people do when their world dissolved right before their very eyes, but had no money, land, servants, or cattle empires? Heaven help those poor sapheads!*

Thankfully, Stormy had accompanied her mother to the hair styling salon in Cinder Valley a few times before, so she knew exactly where to go. She parked near Eighth & Belmont Streets which meant she would need to walk only a short distance.

Entering *The Mane Place*, Stormy spotted Vonnetta, her mother's hairdresser, who walked toward her and gave her a big hug.

"Stormy, it's so good to see you! Please forgive me for not attending your mother's funeral. I had four cut and colors that day and couldn't get anyone else to take my customers for me. Did you have a nice service? I sure hope so."

"It was a lovely funeral. Mother looked just radiant, of course. There weren't a lot of people there, however. As I thought about it afterwards, most people were so jealous of her because she was such a loving and kind person. They must have had their noses on crooked and chose to do other things that day. Whatever happened to common decency anyway?"

Using the broom to sweep cut hair from the floor, Vonnetta answered, "Seems to me like there are a lot of people who are just into themselves and no one else these days. Stormy, in honor of your mother, Jantzi Belle, I would love to treat you to a facial massage, haircut, shampoo, and blow dry style."

Stormy reared back on her heels. "Not on your life! What do you think I am – some charity case? Sabblonti's lack for nothing. There's nothing Sabblonti money cannot buy."

Vonnetta leaned on the old yellow broom. "I wasn't inferring that you were a charity case. I just wanted to do it as a gesture of kindness. I need to rinse out the wash bowl where I was working on my last customer. It should only take about five minutes. Would you like to wait or make an appointment for some other time?"

Looking around the shop for a clock and not finding one, Stormy said, "My time is extremely valuable. I could probably wait five minutes, but not much longer than that. You have to realize that I drove all the way over here from Ridgemonte today."

"Please have a seat across from the counter. There are some hairstyling magazines in case you're interested along with other reading material."

As she sat down, Stormy spotted the recent issue of the local newspaper, *The Cinder Valley Scoop.* She quickly leafed through the pages. An article featuring an upcoming retirement party piqued her interest.

Vonnetta called from the back of the salon, "Stormy, all ready for you now."

"Do you happen to have space in one of your supply drawers where I could put my briefcase while you cut and style my hair?"

"You can just set it next to my blow dryer there if you like. No one will bother it."

Stormy held the briefcase close to her stomach. "I would feel safer if it was out of sight."

"Suit yourself. Here, you can set it inside this bottom drawer if you like."

"Say, Vonnetta, who's that lady that's retiring from the Ignee County Rodeo Board?"

"Oh, you must mean Gwen Hybrenth. She's been on that board forever or so it seems."

"Do you happen to know her?"

"Yes, I know of her, but I can't say as I know her very well. She frequents the shop regularly, but is not one of my customers."

"The announcement said that the event was open to the public. Are you planning on attending?"

Vonnetta secured the purple plastic cape around Stormy's shoulders. "I have no idea. I live my life very sporadically and make most of my decisions on the fly. When is it?"

"I would have to double check the date. It seems like it's Friday night, February 4th, at the Grange Hall."

"Well, at least it's not a Friday the 13th! Those dates along with black cats always spook me."

"Seriously? One day's the same as the next to me. As far as black cats go, I wouldn't think they have the power to control or influence anything. I mean, after all, Vonnetta, it's just a cat that we're talking about here." Stormy was starting to think she'd made a mistake asking Vonnetta to cut her hair.

"Stormy, do you have any superstitions or what kinds of things rattle you?"

"Nothing moves me. No one moves me. I have nerves of steel."

Selecting a brush from the sanitized ones, Vonnetta commented, "Must be nice. I sure don't."

"Back to this retirement party. What's the whole purpose of something like that anyway?"

"I can't say as I've ever been to one for a rodeo board, but I think it would be just what it says. Gwen is getting ready to hang up her cowgirl hat and silver spurs. I think someone said she was the first rodeo queen in Ignee County. You know, back in the days when a young woman could wear a white blouse along with a pair of blue jeans, tie a wild rag around her neck, and be crowned. Some people in these parts really get into this whole rodeo business. It's not for me. I will say, however, that I make a lot of extra money during rodeo week since so many people are in town. That's the nice aspect of it. Has your hair always had a lot of natural curl in it?"

Stormy smiled as she looked in the mirror framed into the aged, barn wood door placed in front of the styling station. "Yes, unfortunately, for as long as I can remember. My sister ended up with the straight hair, and I got the curls."

"Your sister's name is Sarita, right?"

"Yes, it's Sarita. Let's move on to a more pleasant topic, shall we?"

All Vonnetta wanted to do was sit down, prop her feet up, and have a cup of strong coffee with several teaspoons of real cream.

"I can follow this conversation anywhere you want to go. How much do you want me to trim from your hair?"

Reaching up and pulling down a few strands by her left shoulder, Stormy said, "Why don't you whack about three inches off? Will that get rid of these split ends of mine?"

"Let me comb the back some more and see what taking that much off would look like."

Handing Stormy a small hand mirror as she turned the chair around to where a rear view could be seen, Vonnetta gestured to Stormy what her hair would look like. "Keep in mind when curly hair dries, it will look much shorter. Have you ever thought of wearing western hats? I think you'd look cute in one. That's merely a suggestion."

After shampooing, cutting, and styling Stormy's hair, Vonnetta directed her back to the counter. "Did you want to make an appointment for some time in the future? I'm leaving for two weeks starting the 17th to travel to North Dakota for a family wedding."

"North Dakota? Isn't that one of the coldest places this time of the year? Who gets married in North Dakota in the dead of winter?"

"It's my niece who's getting married. Stormy, people are born, die, get married, and all sorts of other life events happen every day of the week. Life goes on whether it's convenient or not."

"Do you have any openings on Friday the 4th of February?"

"I would doubt it, but let me check my calendar. I almost forgot! I had one of my Friday *regulars* call this morning and cancel. It's for 4:00 in the afternoon on that very day. Will that give you enough time to get all dolled up for the retirement party?"

"That'll be fine. I'll just need my hair shampooed and styled that day, so it shouldn't take too much of your time."

"Okay, then, the 4th it is. Oh, don't forget your briefcase back there in the drawer."

"Thank you, Vonnetta, I almost walked out of here without it."

When Stormy was out of earshot, Vonnetta commented, "She might as well have been Jantzi Belle herself sitting there."

Stormy drove to the end of the business district in Cinder Valley, but couldn't find what she was looking for. Since she could only scope out the businesses on one side of the street as she drove, she decided to turn around and make one more loop through the main shopping area. "Oh, there it is!"

Parking in the adjacent lot next to the store, Stormy grabbed her briefcase and walked to Jodell's. She looked in the window to see if there was something that appealed to her, but didn't find anything. There was a male clerk standing behind the counter as she entered the store.

"Good afternoon, what can I show you today?"

"I need to look at your displays first. Are all of your new styles in the glass cases or do you have others that are not on the main floor?"

"Christmas sales were the real boon. We have some nice things left, but they're more on the expensive end. The boss usually rolls in one or two of the high dollar items just for grins. What exactly are you in the market for right now?"

"I don't want anything in a marquise, oval, or pear. I prefer the princess cut. What do you have available in that in white gold?"

"Do you know what size of a ring you normally wear?"

"I believe it's a six. Might be a six and a half."

"If you would like to walk over to this next display case, there's one princess cut in there. The clarity on it is very good. As I said, be prepared for sticker shock, however."

"Get it out of there so I can try it on. I don't have all day."

The clerk reached inside his pocket to locate the key to unlock the display case. He bent down to select the ring to show it to Stormy. "Here you go, Ma'am."

"Don't 'Ma'am' me! Don't they teach you low-life clerks anything in these towns? Anyone from a grocery store clerk to any kind of a sales clerk seems to be void of most anything." The clerk clenched his teeth.

Stormy removed the red leather glove on her left hand along with her horseshoe shaped diamond wedding set and laid them on the counter. The clerk looked down at the ring and contemplated making a comment, but decided that he would rather not stir up the hornet's nest any further.

Slipping her new ring on her finger, Stormy proclaimed, "It fits just perfectly! My, my, my, I love the way that looks on my left hand. I really wanted the *boing* effect, and it seems like this will do the trick. You can dump that old ring of mine into the red, velvet case that my new ring came in. You don't need to write up a receipt or anything as I plan on wearing this ring from this day forward."

"I have to write up a receipt for our business records."

"I'm not the least bit interested in what your business practices are. Just give me that old cast-off ring and let me know what the total will be for my new one."

As the clerk finished his calculations and paper work, Stormy was lost in the moment as she admired her new jewel on her left hand. *There's no way that Salina Bevvins will ever own a diamond as expensive and beautiful as this one. Who can stand before envy?*

"The total for your ring, including sales tax, is $15,900."

Stormy sat down in the black and gold, brocade fabric-covered chair on the far side of the counter, unzipped her briefcase, counted out $16,000 in cash, and laid it on the counter. "Here, keep the change. Maybe you can buy yourself a new, white, western shirt or black vest to wear to work here. It might help your appearance. Or maybe you could buy some of that teeth whitening goop they sell to help your smile along a little. Make that several teeth whitening kits while you're at it."

The clerk counted the money, looked at Stormy, and said, "Thank you very much, have a nice day, and enjoy your new wedding ring."

Collecting her brief case and gloves, Stormy exited the store. With time slipping away quickly before sunset, she needed to kick it into high gear to make her next two stops.

The sign hanging above the store window read, *Country Cate's Western Wear Red Tag Sale*. Upon entering, Stormy was drawn like a magnet to a display in the far corner featuring a mannequin draped with a black, semi-sheer, hand-beaded designed blouse complete with tucked front. She was beyond confident that the fake-looking diamonds sprinkled throughout the black overlay fabric would really accentuate her new found authentic diamond ring. Hopefully the red and black, ankle-length tartan, 100% pure virgin wool skirt was available in her size. She would need some new, black, dress boots and perhaps a hat, too.

Shasta, one of the store's employees and the head merchandise buyer, walked up behind Stormy who was completely lost in her own thoughts.

"Hi there! Could I help you find something?"

Somewhat startled, Stormy whirled around and said, "Good grief, you scared me! I was just envisioning what I would look like in this outfit. I really like the color combination. I have an important event coming up and need to find some appropriate clothing."

"What size do you wear?"

"Either a four or a six. It really depends upon the clothing."

"Let me see what we have in stock. With our big after

Christmas red tag sale in full swing, I'm not quite sure what we still have on hand. If the display items are the last ones we have, I'll let you purchase those for your special occasion."

"Well, it's about time someone started doing something nice for me. After all, don't people know who I am?"

Shasta, quite taken aback at what she'd just heard, pretended that she heard nothing and walked to the center aisle to check on sizes of clothing for sale. "It looks like I don't have either one in your size. I can order them for you if you'd like. It should take about three weeks. Even though the ones we have in stock are too large for you, it might be a good idea to try them on together so you could determine if you like the overall look. Our dressing rooms are over there on the left toward the back of the store."

"I'm in a real hurry this afternoon, so I need you to get the lead out and help me get this outfit completed right away. Also, I need a pair of knee-highs, black, dress boots with a one-inch heel in a size six. And do you have any hats that would match? I have no idea what hat size I wear. You seem to be able to figure out this whole complete country look, so I need you to do it in short order. I could even leave you a little tip if you work hard and fast enough."

"Thank you. Tips are always appreciated. I'm pretty sure we have those boots in your size."

Stormy emerged from the dressing room radiant as ever. "Wow, this looks far better on me than I thought it would! Hand me those boots and that hat you're holding in your left hand. Don't just stand there gawking at me. I'm sure that I'm not the first raving beauty you've ever seen."

Donning the red, felt hat with a black, grosgrain ribbon accent tied in a bow in the back and slipping on the black boots, Stormy rushed to look at herself in the full-length, oval mirror. "I look absolutely stunning to say the least!"

After changing into her business attire, Stormy walked to the front counter where Shasta was waiting for her. Looking at her name tag pinned to her blue sweater, Stormy asked, "Is your name really Shasta? I thought that was a brand of pop."

"Yes, my name is Shasta, and I happen to think it's a lovely name. And yes, there's a soda pop brand by the same name as well. I like to think that the pop was named after me, not the other way around."

"Think what you like."

"Would you like me to place your hat box and the box containing your boots inside a large bag with a handle?"

"Of course, what do you think I want?"

Shasta took meticulous care with the packaging of Stormy's purchases. "Your total, including our red tag discount sale, is $532.50. Unzipping her brief case, Stormy counted out $535 in cash and laid it on the counter. Keep the change. You deserve it since you worked so quickly to help me get this done. Nice store you have here. Do you own it?"

"No, Cate owns it. My name is Shasta, remember?"

"How could I possibly forget?"

Carrying the oversized bag in her left hand, Stormy walked out of the store and toward her pickup. After getting everything carefully situated inside the cab, she pushed the cuff of her faux fur jacket back to check the time and look at the next store on her list. *I have no idea where this place is. Whoever designed the layout of this town was definitely one bale short of a full stack.* She drove up and down the streets of Cinder Valley and finally stopped at a gas station. Going inside, she obtained the necessary directions that she needed.

Driving west of town for approximately twelve minutes, Stormy pulled into the parking lot. A salesman in a black wool jacket emerged from the show room with a jovial greeting, "Happy New Year from Carl's Car Corral!"

"Who's in charge here? Is it you?

"Well, I'm Clark, and I'm one of the salesmen. I'd be happy to help you try to find what you're looking for. Are you shopping for yourself or someone else?"

"For myself, otherwise I would not be wasting my precious time. Why did you build this new dealership so far out of town? It's highly inconvenient for me."

"Truth be known, I had no say as to where it was built. I just peddle the pickups and trucks. What'd you have in mind, and do you have a trade in?"

"No trade in, and that red job right there is exactly what I'm in the market for."

"Let me get the keys so you can test drive it to make sure it meets with your approval."

"I don't need to test drive anything. Let's get inside, so I can pay you and get on down the road."

Clark removed the 8.5 x 11-inch piece of light-yellow paper inside the cab of the pickup with the specifications, price, etc. and walked inside where Stormy was waiting for him.

"Please come into my cubicle so we can get the paperwork drawn up. We have a special financing promotion going right now. It's zero percent interest for thirty-six months."

"Forget all that nonsense. I'm paying cash. There's nothing that Sabblonti money cannot buy. Oh, there's one specific thing I need done on the pickup before I drive back here to get it. I want my cattle brand painted on both doors using black paint."

"That's not a problem. Carl does that sort of thing for his customers all the time. We even have a special form already printed for that detail work." Clark reached inside his desk drawer and handed the paper to Stormy. "Can you please provide the information on this form?"

Stormy commenced filling in the blanks on the preprinted form and inserted the Sabblonti Cattle Brand in the blank square provided.

S

She handed the completed form back to Clark who commented, “Interesting brand. What cattle ranch is that one?”

“It’s the Sabblonti Ranch. We’re the largest cattle operation in this area, bar none. It doesn’t bother me that you’ve never heard of us before. At least all of the important people in the state know who we are.”

“I don’t think I’ve heard of it before, and I’m familiar with most of the ranches in these parts.” Clark continued to study the information on the form Stormy had completed in order to finish his set of paper work. “The pickup comes with a standard three-year or 36,000-mile warranty. Did you want to purchase an extended warranty?”

“Why would I want an extended warranty? Could you please just stop asking your foolish questions? It’s beyond me as to why it should be so difficult to sell a vehicle.”

Clark read out loud, “Let’s see here. You must be Stormy Castins. I take it Sabblonti was your maiden name.”

“Yes, Sabblonti is my maiden name. I’m surprised your mother didn’t name you Super-Sleuth.”

“I was named after my Uncle Clark, and I quite like my name, thank you very much. Do you normally have an issue with people’s names?”

It was obvious to Clark that Stormy was not in a chatty mood, so he laid the sales slip down in front of her. “If you could please sign on the bottom there where the red “x” is that would be great. Your total, including sales tax and dealer doc fee, is $53,465. You can make the check to Carl’s Car Corral, please.”

“I already told you I’m paying cash.” Stormy proceeded to count out the full amount and laid it on Clark’s desk. “You have my phone number in case you have any questions, Clark. Is there any way my new red rig could be ready by next Thursday, the 13th?"

"I should be able to dial that up by then. If there's a delay, I'll let you know."

Stormy gathered her things and left Clark's office.

Clark slapped his right knee, raised his left hand, ran his fingers through his red hair, and exclaimed, "That's by far the easiest sale I've ever made. Now, if I had one of those every day of the week, I'd be cuttin' a fat hog!"

CHAPTER TEN

The savory aroma of homemade stew greeted Tom, Merna, and Spence as they entered the kitchen of the Toppens Ranch house. "What's that sticking out of that old red coffee can, Merna?" asked Spence.

"Oh, that's Tom's favorite homemade bread. We'll have some with our dinner."

"Since when does bread come out of a can like that? Wouldn't it taste a bit like coffee?"

Merna suppressed a laugh as she covered her mouth with her left hand, "Not in the least. I've made countless loaves of bread in that old container and it just never seems to wear out."

"When I first walked into the kitchen, I thought I smelled lamb stew," commented Spence.

"Oh, don't let Tom hear you say that! This is cattle country through and through. Not that cattle and sheep can't graze in the same areas, but these old-time ranchers are the die-hard cattle type."

Handing him a clean orange hand towel, Merna asked, "Spence, are you going to spend the day holding that girl or are you going to get washed up for dinner?"

"She's just so adorable that I don't want to put her down. How'd she get clear out here in these frigid temperatures?"

Merna ladled the stew into large soup bowls, filled pint mason jars with milk, sliced the fresh bread, and set butter and the jar of Currant Conserve on the kitchen table.

Spence sat down and immediately picked up the jar of conserve. "Just another friendly reminder from New Year's

Eve. It seems like I can run, but I can't hide from that night."

Tom tucked the large, faded-yellow dishtowel under his chin and began to eat his stew. "This tastes mighty fine. Glad you left those hay leaves out of it this time. No wonder it's so good. Thanks for making my favorite bread."

Their new guest started to whimper, so Merna rose from the table, picked her up, and walked over by the stove where she had lined the wood box with a flannel blanket. She patted the box and said, "Oh, sweetie, come over here and get warm. I'll hold you after I eat some dinner."

"What's with that goofy, pink ribbon?" asked Tom. Spence wondered the same thing.

"That's just the way she was delivered," answered Merna.

"She's a mighty fine-looking specimen, that's for sure," said Tom. "But let's get that thing off her neck. It's driving me nuts looking at her sportin' that bow."

Spence set his spoon on the table. "Curiosity has gotten the best of me, so I can hardly eat, Merna." She sliced a few more pieces of the freshly baked bread, then explained, "Shortly after high noon, I looked out the kitchen window and saw an unfamiliar vehicle enter our driveway. I could tell there were two girls inside the car. I could also see something jumping up and down in the back seat. For a minute there I thought it was some people out for a scenic drive on the weekend, despite the cold, but then I remembered that it was a weekday.

"The girl in the passenger seat got out first and opened the back door of the car. I did not recognize her at all. I could tell she was trying to get something from the back seat. I wondered at first if they were lost or were getting low on gas for their car and needed a few gallons to get back to town. The girl wasn't wearing a heavy coat, hat, or gloves. I could tell in short order she was getting pretty chilly just standing out there. The driver got out and I recognized her.

"I turned from watching out the window to check on my bread that was baking. When I answered the front door, I was pleasantly surprised to find Priscilla Fletcher and one of her co-workers standing there. I invited them in, and when

Priscilla set this little darling on the floor, it started scampering all over the place.

"According to Priscilla, someone dumped a litter in front of the Shadow Butte County Courthouse before it opened for the day. I'm surprised the pups stayed there and didn't run off. Whoever it was must have deposited them there at 7:55 a.m. Priscilla said she was really drawn to this one, but knew there was no way that she and her mother could keep her in town. That's when she got the bright idea to bring her out here and gift her to you, Spence, as a belated Christmas gift. And you know that since everything with Priscilla seems to have a pink theme, she found that ribbon in a box of odds and ends in the recorder's office and put it to good use."

Spence ate his bowl of stew and consumed four slices of bread. "That's amazing! I sure never expected this to happen. Did Priscilla say anything else when she was here? I'm surprised our paths didn't cross at the courthouse when Tom and I went there to take care of the paperwork for the pickups."

"No, she was in quite a hurry as they were on their lunch break and were having to take more than an hour as it was to drive out here and get back to work. Oh, before I completely forget about it, Priscilla did leave something else for you. I laid it on the buffet. I'll be back in a minute."

Merna handed the loosely wrapped package to Spence who ripped the paper off, wadded it up, and stuck it under his right hip. Unfolding the brown and burgundy hand knitted winter scarf, he said, "What a thoughtful gift. It's like I will have Priscilla wrapped around my neck every time I wear this thing."

Tom could not resist, "At least it's not pink!"

Spence ate a second bowl of stew and scooped the puppy into his lap. "Looks like a Bermese Mountain Dog to me. Is that right, Tom?"

"Did you say Bermese?"

"Yes, Bermese."

"Spence, you're still pretty green around the ears. If we marry that up with that red neck of yours, you'll be quite the sight come next Christmas. It's a Bernese Mountain Dog. Looks like you've still got some of that *city slicker* blood running through your veins. You and your bunk house buddies will have fun training her. She's a beauty for sure!"

Rubbing his face against that of his newfound friend, Spence declared, "I think I'll call you Miggy."

"Miggy?" Tom asked as he choked on a big chunk of bread. "Well, to each his own, I say. That's quite the name for a dog that will be herding cattle, serving as a watchdog, and most importantly, a lifelong loyal companion. They were developed in Switzerland to herd cattle and pull carts. Now I don't want you fellers getting any bright ideas down there at the bunk house. No building tinky little carts from that scrap lumber pile and expecting her to pull it, even if she does have a name like *Miggy*."

Spence pushed his chair back from the table. "Merna, could I possibly borrow that old flannel blanket and take it down to the bunk house with me?" When she did not answer right away, Spence thought he saw a tear tumble down her right cheek.

"Actually, Spence, I have another blanket that you could use. Just a minute while I get it for you." Merna disappeared down the hallway, pulled out a large drawer, and plucked an old, dark grey, thermal blanket from the stack. When she came back into the kitchen, she handed it to Spence. "Here, this is a bigger blanket that will work better. I want Miggy to be nice and warm." Merna carefully folded the yellow flannel blanket and drew it close to her chest as she bowed her head. Spence's eyes fell on the design on the quilt which was that of a little boy wearing a red cowboy hat sitting on a little pony. Surely, that little quilt was full of heartache and had its own story to tell.

Wrapping Miggy inside the thermal blanket and heading toward the front door, Spence said, "Tom and Merna, how can I ever thank you for all that you do for me?"

"Just work hard and help us out, Spence," replied Tom.

Walking toward his pickup, Spence opened the front door and gently placed Miggy on the front seat. Tom had his right arm around Merna's waist as they stood at the front window and watched. Tom leaned into his bride as he said, "Spence will make a great daddy some day for a flock of little kids."

"Yes, he shall."

Tom kissed Merna gently on the side of her face and drew her close to him. Toby had been gone for almost fifty years, but the memory of their young son remained forever in their hearts. "Whoever would've thought all those years ago that we would end up being like a mother and father to grown men?" whispered Tom as he gently dried Merna's tears with the edge of the dishtowel.

Spence drove down to the bunkhouse and took Miggy inside to introduce her to Wyn and Shane. He unrolled the blanket as Miggy started sniffing around the inside and crawling in and out of the bunk beds.

Wyn was in the tack shed repairing one of the saddles. Shane emerged from the side of the haystack where he had been collecting the bales for the night feeding when he caught sight of Tom's pickup. He beat feet to the bunkhouse as he presumed Tom was waiting to talk to him. When he got inside, Tom was nowhere to be seen.

"Hey, Spence, is Tom down here? I saw his pickup over there by the haystack." Miggy approached Shane and started sniffing his boots. Shane lifted his right foot and pushed Miggy backward. "Well, whose mutt are you?"

"She's no mutt, Shane! She's my belated Christmas gift. Isn't she beautiful, just like Priscilla?"

"I don't see a whole lot of connection between a drab strawberry blonde and a dog. This has sure been an upside-down day. Where have you been anyway? I looked high and low for you, and you were nowhere to be found. Wyn said he had no idea either."

"Oh, brother, where art thou? Are you your brother's keeper?"

"I'm not in the mood for your humor, Spence."

"Lighten up, Shane. Have you been chewing on crab grass again or duking it out with Luger? You two are like oil and water. I had to ride into town with Tom to take care of some business, and he needed someone to drive his pickup back home."

Shane removed a glass from the cupboard and slammed it shut. "That still doesn't explain where this thing came from."

"Don't you like dogs, Shane? Every rancher has one."

"Agreed, every rancher has one, but you're no rancher. You're a ranch hand. There's a big difference."

Spence scooped Miggy into his arms and sat in one of the brown, corduroy-covered kitchen chairs.

"Shane, it occurs to me you've got the same clothes to get glad in, and get rid of that cross-patch attitude you've got. There's no time like the present to tell you which cow ate the cabbage, so here goes. Since I just got promoted to assistant ranch foreman this morning, Tom's old pickup has now become my new pickup. Priscilla Fletcher delivered this stray pup to the ranch while Tom and I were in town getting his new pickup. Her name is *Miggy*. I think it's a great name and suits her looks and personality."

"You haven't had her long enough to know what her personality is going to be like. *Miggy* sounds like the name of a dog that someone would have if they worked on an air force base or some such, not a ranch. And if you're the assistant foreman, who's the ranch foreman?"

"Didn't Wyn tell you?"

Shane plucked one of the knives from the wooden block sitting on the counter. He started shaving a few hairs on his forearm. "Wyn has said very little to me since he got engaged to that Sabblonti outfit. His head is in the clouds and his eyes are full of dollar signs. It's like he's been trying to avoid me."

"Wyn's the new ranch foreman. I don't think he's trying to avoid you. I deem he has a lot on his mind these days. I can't imagine what all it would take to get ready to get married, especially after just getting a promotion. He has to come up with a place to live after he gets married, not to mention ride herd on the whole outfit here."

“He has you as his assistant, doesn’t he?”

“Now that you mention it, I guess he does. I better get on down to the tack shed. On second thought, come on Miggy, no time like the present for you to get acquainted with our new boss.”

When the bunkhouse was quiet, Shane shoved the knife inside the wooden block, walked down the hallway, stood in the doorway of Spence’s bedroom, and carefully surveyed his belongings.

CHAPTER ELEVEN

Stormy chided herself, "What could I have possibly been thinking when I instructed Blake to have those dolts here at eight this morning? I need to get some serious sleep this weekend as I'm fast losing my edge."

Wading through most of her ready cash the day before in a wild spending frenzy in Cinder Valley, Stormy realized she needed to collect what was left prior to her appointment with the Alottos. She had wanted to get all gussied up before they arrived, but due to her late start, that idea flew straight out the window.

Donning her blue jeans and sweatshirt, Stormy shuffled down the hallway and entered her office. Retrieving the remaining cash from the top drawer, her eyes darted around the room looking for someplace to stash it. She spotted a wooden container on top of one of the filing cabinets. Had that been there before? She could have sworn that she hadn't seen it. Walking to the cabinet and grabbing the box, she brought it down to eye level. A picture of Jantzi's beloved mare, Diamante, was showcased on the top of the beautiful cherry wood music box. Directly beneath this was the Sabblonti cattle brand. She opened it carefully to the tune of "Home on The Range." This had to have been a gift to her beloved mother from her father, Ace. Lifting the top ivory colored velvet portion that was divided into three compartments, she quickly determined this would be the perfect place to stash the remaining cash. It struck her odd that the music box had never been used since the metal knob inside to turn the music on was still sealed with cellophane. How did it get on top of that filing cabinet? The last time Stormy was in the office it was not there. Hearing the front door knocker down stairs in unison with the mantle clock bonging eight times, she quickly set the velvet liner in place and closed the lid. She ran into her mother's bedroom, lifted the burgundy dust ruffle, and shoved the box under the bed. Her slippered feet glided down the three flights of stairs.

Opening the front door, she greeted her new guests. "Come in. It looks like it might be cold out there this morning. When I looked outside the window at the thermometer, it registered seventeen. We can sit around the kitchen table. I would offer you some coffee, but I've not even had time to make myself a cup as of yet, so that means there's none for you either."

"Good morning, allow me to introduce myself. I'm Lesster Alotto. Just call me Less. That's with two s's. Where would you like for us to hang our coats and hats, Stormy?"

"No place, Less. You're not going to be here long enough to concern yourself with such trivial things. You can just hold them in your lap or wear them. You choose. Okay, let's get started here. I hired you based upon Blake Benson's recommendations. He said you both had a lot of experience working a big cattle ranch. Is that correct?"

"Yes, that's correct," said Less. "We would still be with the *Sliding S* if it wouldn't have sold."

Stormy continued, "Tell me about the *Sliding S*."

"That stands for the Selmer Seward Sampler's Cattle Ranch in South Dakota. Huge spread with lotsa cattle. Big bulls with extra-long horns and the whole bonanza. The *Sliding S* is sorta my own lingo. Instead of saying all those *'S's,* I decided to shorten it a bit."

Smiling her best fake smile, Stormy asked, "Why was it that the new owner didn't keep you on to run the ranch?"

"Didn't ask. He was some *BHOR* sportin' a ten-gallon hat. He didn't know straight up about ranching, but thought he did. He brought in his own dog and pony show when he blew into town."

"Oh, how sad that he was boring, but he did have dogs and ponies, too?"

Less pinched the skin of his face between his left thumb and fingers to keep from laughing. Releasing his hand, he answered, "You could say that, yes. By the way, I have no idea if he was boring or not. *BHOR* stands for *Big Horse on the Ranch.* So, Mrs. Castins, just what were you wanting us to do here at the Sabblonti spread?"

Stormy glared at Less. "Don't ever call me Mrs. Castins or you'll be fired as soon as you're hired. My name is Stormy Sabblonti. As far as your job goes, I need you to run this whole shootin' match. I don't want any foul ups whatsoever or you'll be sorry you even entertained the thought. My paternal grandfather and father worked tirelessly to get this showcase ranch in the shape it is today, and I fully expect it to stay that way."

Less hesitated somewhat, then inquired, "What about your husband? I thought he worked on the ranch, too."

"What about my husband? Just because he might have worked on the ranch doesn't mean that he contributed to the prosperity of the ranch. I mean any flunkee can run a ranch. There's no place here for you to live so you'll either have to continue to live with Blake Benson or find someplace else. Can you start to work this morning? I have no idea when the last time any of the animals were fed. There were a couple of part time cowhands who worked during the winter months, but I haven't seen hide nor hair of them lately."

"When's your husband due to get out of the hospital?"

"Oh, that horse head, who knows? He has those doctors and nurses totally buffaloed as to what might be wrong with him. His bones have turned lazy, and I don't think he wants to work that much anymore. I've got way too much at stake here to not have someone slaving from sunup to sundown and beyond every day to keep me in the manner to which I've become accustomed. I assume you have your own vehicle. I don't have one you can borrow after Chet wrecked his. That's his problem as to when he gets all that ironed out with his insurance company."

Less pressed, "What does the job pay?"

"I plan to pay you $1,000 per month, a small bonus in December, and one steer that you can have butchered if you like. If you're the tightfisted type, you can slaughter it yourself. The beef is a little incentive if I deem that you've done a good job for me all twelve months. Now, don't get any wild ideas because that amount does not include any type of benefits. You're on your own for all that stuff. Have you always had those big, saggy bags under your eyes? I guess you and Blake do have one thing in common. You're both skinny cowboys."

Less stood and spread his feet apart as he crossed his arms. "I'm not that skinny, and your offer is not that dandy of a monthly salary. I mean, after all, Meg and I have to pay rent to Blake and help with the utilities and some of the grub. Would you consider at least $1,500 a month for me?"

"Not on your life! Ranch foreman are a dime a dozen in this country. Your personal financial arrangements with Blake are not my concern."

"As you wish. Both of us prefer to be paid in cash."

"Well, that won't be a problem since your wife will be the bookkeeper. You can take care of that any way you want."

Turning to face Meg Alotto, Stormy said, "My, my, my, aren't you a quiet one. Don't you ever talk or does your big man do all of the talking for you? I hope you realize that a big mouth does not make a big man. Come to think of it, if you don't say much, you and I'll get along just great. Are you a CPA?"

Meg looked straight at Stormy, and without flinching or hesitating, replied, "Yes."

Glancing down at the ring finger of Meg's left hand and waving her left hand so Meg would be sure to see her new flashy, princess-cut, five-carat, diamond ring, Stormy continued, "My mother, a fantastic business woman, had her favorite CPA, and I'm confident she would want me to continue in like manner. As far as your wages go, I'll pay you $500 a month since you are a CPA and all. After all, those are just letters after a name. It can't be that difficult to add and subtract, now can it, especially when it comes to counting money? Any questions, Meg?"

"None."

Stormy folded her hands. "Okay, all settled then. Less, get outside and get to work. Meg, follow me up the stairs, and I'll show you what I need done. If you finish with your office work before Less finishes outside, then you can plan to sit on the bench on the front porch or inside your husband's pickup with the heater running while he finishes up. Your coat doesn't look any too warm. I can't believe you didn't own a warmer coat than that living in South Dakota. Oh well, I've got far more important things to concern myself with than your wellbeing. One more thing before I dismiss you for the day. Less, I need you to clean up outside. Following mother's death, there are some blood stains on a few things. Figure out how to get rid of them."

Following Stormy up the stairs, Meg felt like she was walking on eggshells. Stormy sat down in her office chair. "Guess there's not another chair around, so you can just stand there for as long as it takes while I explain some things to you. We'll drive into Ridgemonte after dinner so I can add your name to some of the accounts. You did bring something to eat during the day, didn't you? I don't feed the hired help. You're on your own in that regard. Did you bring some rubber bands so you can keep that long, frayed, dirt-brown hair out of your face? I don't want it interfering with your calculations of my money."

For the next ten minutes, Stormy showed Meg the stack of bills and told her to get them paid. Meg said very little and asked virtually no questions. "Since you are a CPA, you can plan to talk to Mother's CPA at the end of the year. Her business is in Blunte County."

As she pulled her hair away from her face and started twisting it into a bun on the back of her head, Meg replied, "I can take care of that once you provide me with a name and telephone number."

After Stormy left her office, Meg sat down only to discover her feet did not reach the floor. She spotted a cardboard box in the corner. "This will have to do until I can find something else. And, my hair does not look like dirt!"

Meg proceeded to write out checks to pay various bills for the household and Jantzi Belle's funeral as well as the ranch. She went ahead and signed them since they would be mailed in town later that day after going to Cattlemen's Central.

At one o'clock sharp, Stormy stood in the threshold to her office. "Meg, let's hit the road. We need to get to the bank, stop at a couple of other places, and get home before dark. I really don't like to drive after the sun sets."

Meg rode to Ridgemonte with Stormy in total silence. Truth be known, she didn't care if she made small talk with her or not.

After parking her pickup near the bank, Stormy marched toward Cattlemen's Central with Meg in tow, walked in, and demanded to see a manager.

Just then Lonnie Browne, one of the assistant managers, happened to be walking through the lobby. He spotted Stormy and greeted her enthusiastically, "Happy New Year, Stormy! I was very sorry to hear of Chet's recent accident. I hope he's recuperating well. How can we help you today?"

"Inside your office, Lonnie," demanded Stormy. "I don't want these dimwitted folks to know anything about my life."

"Please follow me. I would be happy to help you." Opening the door and gesturing to two comfortable, ivory-colored, Italian leather chairs, Lonnie extended his right hand to Meg. "Hello, I'm Lonnie Browne. It's nice to meet you."

Meg remained silent.

Lonnie positioned himself behind his desk as he asked Stormy, "So what can we do for you?"

"I've hired Meg as my bookkeeper and need to get her name on the bank accounts."

Lonnie inquired, "Meg, do you already have an account with us?"

"No, we just moved from another state and are getting settled here."

"No problem. I need to see two forms of identification such as a driver's license and a major credit card. That should suffice."

Meg unzipped her small purse, reached inside her wallet and produced her driver's license. "Actually, I have only one piece of identification, so I hope that's sufficient. We don't use credit cards. We're cash only folks and pay-as-we-go types." Standing on her tip-toes, she leaned across the desk and handed her license to Lonnie.

"Oh, looks like you're from sunny California. Too many folks in those parts for me. I like these high desert mountain areas that are more sparsely populated. What part of California?"

Stormy interrupted, "California, Meg? I thought Blake said you worked on a big cattle spread in South Dakota?"

Before Meg could reply, Lonnie said, "This California license is fine. Zigzagging back and forth between *The Golden State* and *The Mount Rushmore State* is not a big deal. The picture on this license looks like you, and I'll double check the signatures as soon as you sign this paper which will authorize the bank to accept your signature on the checks. Stormy, which accounts do you want Meg to be able to sign on as far as the Sabblonti Ranch goes?"

"All accounts, Lonnie."

With a raised eyebrow, Lonnie wanted to confirm Stormy's directive, "ALL ACCOUNTS?"

"Yes, I did not stutter, Lonnie. What is it about the two words, ALL ACCOUNTS, that you don't understand? Are you're sure you're even qualified to be a banker?"

Lonnie continued to type information on the keypad of his computer as he updated each account and printed off the corresponding paper work. He handed the documents to Meg who signed each one of them. "I'll make a set of copies for you, Stormy."

"Don't bother, Lonnie. It would just be a waste of paper for both of us. Meg is a CPA, so she sure in the world doesn't need any more paper than what she already has to deal with."

"So, Meg, you're a CPA, is that right?"

"That's right."

"Well, definitely then if you're a CPA, it really doesn't matter from which state you've gotten your driver's license." After collecting the signed documents, Lonnie stood to his feet, walked around his desk, and shook hands with both women. "Has Cattlemen's Central provided for all of your needs today?"

"You've already wasted enough of our time, Lonn-Job. We need to get going."

CHAPTER TWELVE

Pulling the light blue, flowered drapes apart in Chet's room to let in some of the sun's rays, Nurse Macey Meadows tried to spread some sunshine of her own. "How are you doing this morning? Are you about ready to head home? I would imagine that you're chomping at the bit to get out of here! I saw where Dr. Linke signed your discharge orders for tomorrow."

"What day is tomorrow anyway? I've lost track of time being cooped up in this joint."

"It will be January 13th. You've been with us now for eleven days. It seems as though you're progressing well enough with your physical therapy to be released. Of course, you'll still have to continue that at home. Do you have a lot of help with your ranching chores since you won't be able to return to those right away?"

Sitting on the side of the bed, Chet arched his back to stretch his muscles. "Yes, I plan to hire a couple more part-time winter ranch hands, so I can tell them what needs to be done."

Macey removed the additional blanket from Chet's bed and placed it in the linen bin to be cleaned. "That's great news! I'm sure it will help you to heal faster if you know that everything is being taken care of properly. Since I grew up in town, I don't have the first clue what it would take to run a ranch, especially one as big as yours. I'm okay around most animals, but horses scare me to death."

"There's more to it than meets the eye, that's for sure. What is it about horses that frighten you so much?"

Shrugging her shoulders, Macey replied, "They seem like they're so big and strong. There was a girl in my high school graduating class that had a horrible accident on her horse during our senior year. She was riding across a set of railroad tracks in town when her horse caught its foot in one of the rails, fell on its side, and pinned my friend, Denise, on the asphalt. She suffered a broken jaw which had to be wired up for about three months. Fortunately, we had just taken our senior pictures right before that happened."

"I'm sorry to hear about your friend, Denise. Is she doing okay these days? How'd her jaw turn out?"

Macey collected Chet's clothing and personal belongings. "I think she is, but I have no way of knowing. I've not seen her since we graduated. Her father was a contractor who built homes and she helped him in the business. I knew that I wanted to become a nurse someday, so I started college three months after graduating."

Chet's laugh startled Macey. "None of that high falootin' higher learning for me. I'm a *learn as you go* type of guy."

"Oh, I forgot to mention that there are a few prescriptions that Dr. Linke wrote for you as well. One is an additional round of a different antibiotic. Your vitals look good this morning, so that's encouraging. When you talk with your wife today, please let her know that you'll be discharged tomorrow after 1:30 p.m. That will give Dr. Linke sufficient time to make his rounds. You'll need to have a wheelchair at home for a short while along with some crutches. Do you already have anything like that or shall I get some from the hospital pharmacy for you?"

"Wheelchair? I imagined that all I would need is crutches for a couple of days."

Macey lowered her head, pursed her lips, then spoke, "Chet, it's not going to be quite that easy and fast once you return home. You'll need extensive physical therapy for that right leg of yours. It's important to allow it to heal properly, so Dr. Linke doesn't have to re-break it and re-set it."

"We don't have a wheelchair or crutches or anything of the sort. We're tough as nails out there on the range."

As soon as Nurse Meadows left the room, Chet dialed the number for the Main Sabblonti Ranch house.

On the fifteenth ring, Stormy finally answered, "This is Stormy Sabblonti."

A smile graced Chet's face. "Harmonica music to my ears this morning, sweetheart! It's great to hear your voice. I just received some fantastic news! I get to head home tomorrow afternoon. Dr. Linke is going to release me, so can you please be here at about 1:15? That will allow you a few minutes to take my things to the pickup in the parking lot. Then you can drive around to the front entrance where the hospital attendant will assist me from my room to the pickup and load my wheelchair into the back. If there's something already in the back of the pickup, can you please take it out of there so there will be plenty of room?"

Sitting in her recliner, Stormy rested the left side of her face between two of her fingers and thumb. "How long are you going to have to be in a wheelchair?"

"I don't know for sure. I suppose it depends upon how fast I can get through my physical therapy workouts. I need you to bring a checkbook, too. The doc is giving me some more prescriptions. You can get those at the pharmacy before you pick me up."

"I don't plan to be in town tomorrow or at the ranch for that matter. I have other pressing business to take care of, so I guess you'd better find somebody else to do your bidding. Since all of the bedrooms in the main ranch house are upstairs, you can plan to recuperate down at the lower ranch house. All of your stuff is there anyway. If your physical therapist cannot drive to your house every day, you're really going to be in a world of hurt, aren't you?" Stormy slammed the receiver down, walked throughout the main floor, and lighted the dozen, oversized, strawberry-scented candles she'd purchased recently.

Chet lowered his head and massaged the top of it for a couple of minutes. As soon as Macey returned to the room, Chet asked, "Nurse Meadows, could I ask a favor of you, please?"

"Sure, Chet, what do you need?"

"Can you locate the phone number for the Shaw Vet Clinic?"

"I would be happy to, but you know that a vet cannot help you with physical therapy. Is the clinic here in Ridgemonte?"

"I realize that, and yes, Dr. Shaw's practice is in Ridgemonte. Speaking of physical therapy, are there ones that do in-home therapy, especially since I live so far out of town?"

"Yes, there are. I'll talk to Dr. Linke about that. I've not seen him yet this morning, but he's scheduled to be here sometime today. I know there are a couple of the PT's at Shadow Butte Physical Therapy who do in-home care."

Obtaining Dr. Shaw's phone number a few minutes later, Chet sincerely hoped that he could score a friendly voice on this call.

"Shaw Vet Clinic, Jacobe Davone speaking, how may I help you?"

"Hello there, Jacobe, this is Chet Castins. Is your boss floating around there somewhere close by I hope?"

Jacobe closed the vet supply catalog he'd been ordering from. "You just happened to call in the nick of time. He was headed out the door on a call. Seems one of the local ranchers has some cows with mastitis this morning. Hold on to your hat!"

Jacobe ran out the back door of the clinic and motioned for Dr. Shaw to turn his truck's ignition off.

"Doc, it's Chet Castins. He needs to talk to you."

Walking inside the front door of his clinic and lifting the phone receiver, Dr. Shaw said, "Howdy, Chet! Sure didn't expect to hear from you so soon into the New Year. Everything okay at your ranch?"

"I have no idea."

"What do you mean you have no idea. Where are you anyway?"

"I've been laid up in the hospital the past few days after I wrecked my rig."

"You what? When?"

"The "S" curve won the battle on the night of January 2nd. I rolled my pickup and landed in the bottom of that ravine. I'm surprised you haven't heard about it."

Dr. Shaw leaned against the wall. "We've been on a dead run here at the clinic. Some of the cattle in these parts are suffering from a viral infection. It seems like it broke out all at once. Sorry to hear about your wreck. Are you doing okay? I would've been down to see you had I known."

"I'm doing well enough to be discharged from the hospital tomorrow which is the reason I'm calling you right now. I need a lift home. Could I get you or Jacobe to lend me a helping hand?"

"Yes, you can count on one of us for sure. What time do we need to be there?"

"If you could be here at one-thirty that would be great. I need to take a wheelchair back home with me, so if you could make sure there's room in your rig for that I would appreciate it."

"You bet, Chet. See you soon."

Dr. Shaw gently placed the telephone receiver back in its cradle. After explaining to Jacobe what little he knew of Chet's recent misfortune, he opined, "I don't even want to know why Stormy can't be bothered to pick her husband up at Mintner Medical Center and drive him to their ranch. Chet Castins is the most longsuffering individual I know."

CHAPTER THIRTEEN

Dr. Shaw arrived at Mintner Medical Center at twenty-nine minutes past one and parked in the closest *Patient Parking* space. *It seems like my life is a constant theme of close shaves.* Walking to the Information Desk, he said, "Hello, I'm Dr. Ben Shaw, and I'm here to pick up Chet Castins. He said he was due to be discharged today. I thought he might be out here in the waiting area, but I don't see him."

"Well, Dr. Shaw, let me check with the nurse's station to see what's going on down there," said the clerk. "You can take a seat if you like."

"No, thanks, I've been driving quite a bit this morning, so I think I'll just walk around the waiting area and drink in some of this fabulous western, framed, art hanging on the walls. Boy, someone has to be one talented photographer to capture a shot of the bull rider coming out of the shoot like that! I wonder if it was taken at the National Finals Rodeo. I didn't make it to *Sin City* for that one."

The call was returned quickly. "Information Desk, how may I help you? Oh, got it. I will let Dr. Shaw know. Can he just go to the room? Thanks."

Peering over the desk, Dr. Shaw asked, "I take it the patient has not been released from his room yet?"

"Correct, Doctor. You can either wait here or go to Room #131, whichever you choose."

Dr. Shaw found his way to Chet's room, walked in, and greeted him like a long-lost brother. "If you aren't a sight for sore eyes! We'll just have to get you back in the saddle el pronto. What's the hold up on getting out of here anyway?"

"Thanks a million for coming to my rescue, Doc. It's been a while since the nurse has been in here. I have no idea where Dr. Linke is this morning. He's the one who'll bust me out of here."

Dr. Shaw did not hear someone walking up behind him. "If you'll excuse me, sir, I need to check on my patient, get him packed up, and ready to go."

"Pardon me. Sorry, I didn't hear or see you. Let me step aside here. I know what it's like to have someone in your way when you're trying to get medical things done."

Nurse Macey Meadows continued, "You're not in the way at all. I'm thankful that Chet has finally had a visitor. It's been quite lonely in here for him since he arrived. You can sit in that gray chair over there if you like."

As Dr. Shaw walked toward the window, the *Get-Well* card caught his attention. He didn't want to ask Chet who it was from because he suspected he knew the answer to the question before he even asked. *Was Chet withholding information from him? Was there more to this picture than met the casual country eye?*

Turning to address Chet, Macey said, "Dr. Linke had an emergency C-section to take care of, but since he already signed your discharge papers, he indicated you can go. I'm sure that's welcome news to you. Remember, you'll need help when you get home, and you have quite a rigorous physical therapy schedule along with follow up doctor appointments. Don't forget your prescriptions in the pharmacy."

Chet's countenance fell as he looked down at his folded hands resting on his lap.

Macey glanced at Dr. Shaw sitting in the chair and then back at Chet again. She could discern nothing from the two poker-faced country gents. "Is there anything I should know or is something wrong?"

Following a brief silence, Chet spoke, "Nothing's wrong. I'm trying not to get discouraged thinking about what it's going to take before I can walk without crutches and get back on Blitz again."

"Is Blitz your horse?" inquired Macey.

"Yes, Blitz and Braezee are my two favorite horses. Blitz is my black gelding with a star, stripe, and snip for face markings along with four white stockings. Doc here helped me save my beloved mare, Braezee, a short while ago."

"Chet, that will be some incentive for you to work very hard and do exactly what your physical therapist tells you to do. I'm happy for you that you like horses so much. I already told you that they frighten me."

"You're right about ramping up the physical therapy, Macey. Just think, if you wouldn't have traded shifts this morning, I would've been gone by the time you got to work today. And horses aren't so scary once you get used to being around them. Thankfully, I've been able to spend most of my adult life working with horses. They're really smart animals and interesting too. Just ask Dr. Shaw. I'm sure he'll agree with me."

Dr. Shaw was distracted thinking about the greeting card. The only word he heard was *horses*.

Macey continued, "It seems like things happen for a reason, Chet. Stay encouraged, and you'll do just fine. I'm sure of it."

"I would not say everything happens for a reason. It's hard for me to think of my accident in those terms, at least right now."

Macey patted Chet's left shoulder. "Someday you might be able to make sense of it all."

"Someday I just might. I forgot to introduce you to my trusted friend, Dr. Shaw."

"I gathered that since he showed up to take you home."

Nurse Meadows glanced at Dr. Shaw as she smiled and said, "Hi, I'm Macey Meadows. It's nice to meet you."

Instinctively reaching up to tip the brim of his white Beaver Stetson, but realizing he was not wearing it, Dr. Shaw replied, "Nice to meet you, too."

Dr. Shaw was struck with Macey's milky white teeth showcased inside her lovely pomegranate-tinted lips, her ivory complexion, high cheekbones, and intense, emerald green eyes. He glanced down at her left hand which revealed no jewelry. Then again, some nurses don't wear their wedding rings while on shift. Oh, could he possibly start to get his hopes up once again only to be dashed? Hope deferred makes the heart sick. He'd made a fool of himself with Sarita Sabblonti as it turned out in the end and didn't even want to entertain the thought of women folk at the moment.

"Shaw, let's see. Is that a German name?" Macey asked.

"No, it's of English and Scottish origin, and a topographic name for someone who lived by a copse or a thicket. Why do you ask?"

Flashing her pearly, milky whites once again, Macey answered as she chuckled, "No particular reason. People's ancestry intrigues me somewhat. It's kind of a little inside baseball I guess you could say."

"Or maybe inside hospital? I should probably spend my evenings studying my ancestry a little more in depth."

"Oh, no need to do that. Your life is probably quite full as it is. Interesting hat you're wearing. I'm sure it helps to keep you warm on these cold winter days."

"My hat, ah, yes. It's a Double Mackinaw Cap. Have you ever heard of those?"

"No, can't say that I have. The description sounds like something you'd get at a fast-food drive in. You know, *Double Mackinaw with lettuce, onions, . . . "Macey's* own words made her burst out laughing. "Excuse me, I'm not laughing at you. Sleep deprivation makes me a bit daffy at times. This is not my normal work shift. Please don't take anything I say personally."

"Not a problem. As a matter of fact, I quite like my hat. It shows that I have good taste."

Macey wondered what Dr. Shaw would look like if he wasn't wearing his hat. His blue-green eyes seemed to smile when he smiled. Considering smiles, she'd never seen a more inviting one. There were two faint creases on both cheeks and a slight dimple in his chin. His face radiated kindness and intrigue. Nurse Dawn Rowann may have raved about how handsome Chet Castins was, but Macey would prefer Dr. Shaw's looks to his any old day of the week. Where had this guy been hiding?

"Chet," Macey continued, "I've arranged for one of the hospital personnel to take you down to the entry way in your wheelchair. I think I've bagged up everything that was with you the night you came in. Just a second. I forgot your card in the windowsill. Let me get that for you."

"You can throw that away along with that green plant if you would please, Macey. I definitely don't need either of them."

Macey grabbed the card which slipped from her fingers and landed on the floor. She saw the name Salina and the red heart banner. "Who's Salina anyway? Is she one of your relatives? I don't recall her visiting your room."

No one answered.

Macey slipped the card inside the large plastic sack along with Chet's other belongings.

Dr. Shaw paid for Chet's prescriptions at the hospital pharmacy. When helping him get inside the pickup, Chet noticed the white sack in the back seat. "Those must be my happy pain pills and antibiotics. Just add that to my tab, Doc. How much do I owe you for those?"

"I would have to double check, but I think the total was $112.49 or some such."

"If I add the prescriptions and the groceries you bought me from the Shadowy Merc last month that brings my total to $139.63."

"Who's counting?"

Chet held up his left hand. "I'm counting. Maybe my brain is not as blown out as I thought it was following my accident. Perhaps there's hope after all."

"There's always hope, Chet. The day we no longer have hope is the day we call it quits. A quitter never wins and a winner never quits."

Driving out of the parking lot of Mintner Medical Center, all Dr. Shaw could see in his mind's eye were those milky white teeth and those dark emerald green eyes. *Was Macey wearing colored contacts to accentuate her eyes?* He surely couldn't ask Chet such a frivolous question. *Chet had probably not even noticed her eyes during his eleven day stay, or had he?*

"What's with that Nurse Meadows anyway?" asked Dr. Shaw as he left Ridgemonte and headed for the main highway leading to the Sabblonti Ranch.

"What do you mean 'what's with that Nurse Meadows?'"

"Just what I said. I mean, what's her story?"

Remembering Dr. Shaw's failed attempt to date Sarita, Chet's sister-in-law, he opined, "I have no idea. She normally works the 3 to 11 shifts and was there every day at that time except for today. She's terribly nice, merciful, and oh, so kind. She seemed to treat all patients the same way. She just happened to be in the room the day Stormy came in to see me. I was embarrassed to have her in there. Stormy was her usual sweet self. Her few words nearly peeled the paint off the wall."

"Was that after she saw the *Get-Well* card?"

Chet unbuckled his seat belt momentarily so he could get more comfortable. Buckling it again, he resumed, "Not exactly. Stormy was in a sour frame of mind when she first came into my room. As far as that bloomin' card goes, I have no idea when Salina came into my room and left it in there. I should've asked one of the nurses to deep six it as soon as I discovered it. I don't know how many days it was in there before I saw it. As far as Nurse Meadows goes, the only thing for certain I know about her is that she's very fearful of horses. One of her friends suffered a bad accident on a horse during their senior year of high school, and that incident has haunted Macey ever since."

"Perhaps she just needs to discover that horses aren't nearly as big and bad as she's made them out to be in her mind," said Dr. Shaw.

"Perhaps. If you're thinking of making a play for that nurse, I wouldn't wear that hat. What's with you, your hats, and country ladies? At least you removed that rattlesnake hat band from your white Beaver Stetson upon my advice following Jantzi's funeral. I guess I could hire myself out as your personal hat coach or some such to help offset all of the favors you're doing for me. What do you think?"

Both men laughed.

"It might not be a half bad idea after all. Are you in any pain now, Chet? Let me know if I'm driving too fast and making it uncomfortable for you to ride."

"I have some pain in my leg right, but it's not as intense as it was before the surgery. Your driving is fine."

"Am I taking you to the main ranch house or your lower ranch house?"

"To the lower ranch house, please. The bedrooms are on the main floor of that house which will make it easier all the way around for me."

"Does Stormy plan to stay down there and help take care of you once you're home?"

Chet shifted in his seat and looked out the passenger window. "I have no idea what her plans are. There's not been a whole lot of difference between her and the outside temperatures lately."

"Well, you'll need someone down there to help you. I don't know if there's one of those home health outfits in Ridgemonte that you could contact to see if they have employees who do home nursing kinds of things. Do you want me to check into it and let you know?"

"Sure, that would be a huge help to me. Dr. Linke was supposed to let me know, but I never heard back. Looks like Linke dropped the ball."

"I don't suppose you have much in the way of food down there either, do you?"

"Not much at all. Going into The Shadowy Merc would mean another encounter with Salina Bevvins which is the dead dog last thing I need right now."

"That makes two of us."

Arriving at the Lower Sabblonti Ranch house, which was where Chet and Stormy lived prior to her mother, Jantzi Belle Sabblonti, passing away, Dr. Shaw helped Chet inside the house. He carried in Chet's belongings and placed them in the living room.

"Chet, I can heat up a can of chow for you before I drive back to town if you want me to."

"That would be so helpful. Now that I'm home, I'm hungrier than I thought I would be."

Dr. Shaw looked inside Chet's pantry and selected a can of beef soup along with cans of carrots and sweet corn. "I'll just mix these three together which ought to taste pretty good. I've done that before and it's not too bad. I'm going to lay your prescriptions here on your counter so you'll know when to take them. If you want, I can check inside your fridge and make sure you've got some milk. Actually, we should probably get a supply list written out for you. I'll have my assistant, Jacobe, go to The Merc and get the grub, and then I'll drive back here and deliver it. On second thought, I could ask Jacobe to drive back here later this afternoon with your groceries and he could plan to stay with you until we get things settled a bit. That's just a suggestion."

Chet stood up, leaned on his crutches, and tried to walk. "Doc, help me into the wheelchair. Not ready for the crutches quite yet. Your plan sounds good. This is a horrible time to be without family members to help me out. I really appreciate all that you and Jacobe are doing for me."

"What about Wyn and Sarita? Could you ask them to help you? I'm sure they would. Neither one of them seem that cold hearted to me."

"They never came to the hospital to see me, so maybe they don't even know that I had the bad accident. When Stormy conducted the reading of her mother's will on Sunday, January 2nd at the main ranch house, you could say there was not a very friendly parting of the ways."

Dr. Shaw heated Chet's food and placed it on the kitchen table along with a glass of milk and some bread and butter.

"Thanks a ton, Doc. Aren't you going to have dinner with me?"

"I'll take a rain check on that one. I want to get back to

town and get Jacobe farmed out on the grocery store run, so he can get back here and help you with your animals as well as whatever else you need."

"How can I ever repay you, Doc?"

"I'm not looking for repayment, now or ever, for that matter. That's not the reason I help people. I treat people the way I want to be treated. That's my golden rule."

Dr. Shaw's mind was all over the desert as he drove from the Lower Sabblonti Ranch house toward the main highway. He slowed down as he approached the main ranch house on the right-hand side of the road. He contemplated stopping by to see if Stormy was home, but thought he better not chance it. She might order him off the place. Glancing down at his watch, he realized that Jacobe was going to have to throw it into overdrive to get the supplies purchased and get back to Chet's place. He pulled into a turnout on the main highway and turned the engine of his pickup off as he placed a call to his clinic on his pickup mobile phone.

As they spoke together, he and Jacobe compiled a list of supplies to be delivered to Chet's house. Dr. Shaw coached Jacobe to give out zero details to Salina Bevvins if she happened to be working inside The Merc when he went in there. The less said the better. Dr. Shaw instructed Jacobe to take some money from the petty cash drawer to cover the groceries and they would sort out the financial transaction later. Maybe it could just be a pay out from the Shaw Clinic benevolence fund.

A flash of inspiration came to Dr. Shaw just as he was on the outskirts of Ridgemonte. He pulled into the parking lot of Mintner Medical Center, got out, walked inside and headed for the nurse's station on the first floor.

After he arrived at the desk, he inquired, "Is Nurse Meadows still on shift? I'm Dr. Ben Shaw and was in here earlier today. I talked with her when I picked Chet Castins up to take him home."

Charge Nurse Joyce Stone grinned broadly as she looked squarely at Dr. Shaw, "You look like a man on a mission. Nurse Meadows is unavailable. Is there something I could help you with?"

"Yes. I was wondering if you could supply me with the name and number of one of those home health outfits as Chet's going to need their services."

"There's one in Ridgemonte. They're pretty new and I can't vouch for them obviously. Doesn't Chet have any help at home? He surely shouldn't have been released if he doesn't."

"Oh, yes, he has help forthcoming, but he was looking for additional help."

"What do you mean by *forthcoming?* Isn't Mrs. Castins available to help him?"

"Well, it's a little more complicated than that. Mrs. Castins was unavailable to pick her husband up this afternoon, so I drove him to the lower ranch house which is more suited for what he needs right now as the bedrooms are on the main floor. There will be a medical assistant available to help Chet for a couple of days, but he cannot commit to long term since he's also working another job."

Joyce closed the local phone book and said, "Okay, Dr. Shaw, here's the information for the company. It's *Hearts & Hands 2 Help Home Care* and the number is listed below that."

"Thanks so much. Hopefully the quality of their care lives up to their business name."

"I'm sure it does, Dr. Shaw. All company personnel are certified. Was there a message you wanted me to deliver to Nurse Meadows or is this the information you were needing?"

Dr. Shaw blinked twice and smiled. "No message for Macey. You gave me the contact info I needed. You might mention to her that I stopped by if you feel so inclined. Thank you."

"You're most welcome. Your ears look red. You should try wearing a hat in this cold weather. It doesn't take much to damage the skin."

"I cannot win for losing on this hat business!"

"Say, are you a milliner?"

"A what? I'm a vet. Time is getting on. Thanks, again."

CHAPTER FOURTEEN

It bothered Dr. Shaw considerably that Chet had so few visitors during his stay at Mintner Medical Center. Come to think of it, some of his extended family members had probably not even been notified. What was happening to this ranching community anyway?

Pulling into the local *Gib's Gas*, Dr. Shaw filled the two tanks in his pickup and lifted its hood to check the oil which registered one quart low on the measuring stick. He parked in the far corner of the parking lot and walked into the front entrance.

The baldheaded cashier with dark brown, horn rimmed glasses looked up from the counter, "You new in these parts, stranger?"

"No, I've been here for some time now. I own the vet clinic in town. I need to cut a check for the gas I just purchased and get a quart of that 10W-40 you've got on the shelf behind you."

"Well, you must've been running on the fumes because you just rung up 39 ½ gallons of fuel so that'll be $58.85 and the quart of oil added to it brings your total damage to $61.54. We've been getting some rubber checks lately, so I'll need to take a gander and see if your name's on our official list."

"I don't make a habit of bouncing checks unless of course my trusty assistant hasn't made a deposit in a few days."

"Where'd you get that off-beat hat, anyway? About the only thing I can say about it is your ears would stay warm. Your wife like the way you look in it?"

"I quite like my hat, thank you."

Dr. Shaw secured the receipt in his left hand, picked up the quart of oil in his right, and walked to his pickup. "Small towns require thick skins to absorb insults."

The main highway was busier than usual as Dr. Shaw headed out of town toward the Toppens Ranch. He reasoned with himself that he would be able to sleep better tonight if some more of the ranching neighbors were apprised of Chet's plight. After parking in the driveway, he removed his Mackinaw before getting out of the pickup. He was not about to subject himself to more ridicule. The day had been long enough already.

Wiping her floured hands on her green and blue plaid apron, Merna answered the front door. "Why, Dr. Shaw, what a pleasant surprise! Please come in. What brings you our way tonight, and where's your hat? You're going to catch pneumonia without keeping your head covered."

"Thanks, Merna, and about the hat, well, never mind. I left it in the cab of my truck. Is your boss around?"

"He sure is. His back has been bothering him quite a bit, so he laid down on the heating pad for a few minutes before supper. Please come in and have a seat by the fire while I round him up."

Tom emerged from the hallway fastening his right, front, navy blue striped suspender. "Well, howdy, Doc! Did one of the hired help call you from the bunkhouse or something? None of them mentioned anything to me about one of the critters being down."

Dr. Shaw extended his right hand. "Hello, Tom. It's nice to see you, and no, I didn't get a cattle call. I've come to see you about another matter."

Merna walked into the living room. "Dr. Shaw, we'd be honored if you'd join us for supper. You can wash in the mud room if you'd like. I just placed a clean towel on the wall hanger."

"It's been about three weeks since I've had a good old-fashioned ranch-cooked meal. I really didn't plan to drop in during supper time. My day has been all over the place. In fact, I made a second trip out this way in just the past few hours."

Seated at the kitchen table with Tom and Merna, Dr. Shaw talked non-stop as he savored every bite of the beef goulash, home canned green beans with bacon and tomato chunks, freshly baked sourdough bread and butter, and garlic dill pickles Merna had soaked in her ceramic crock before canning them. He informed them of everything he knew to date regarding Chet's accident and hospital stay. Suddenly, Dr. Shaw noticed that Merna had set her eating utensils on her plate, folded her hands, and sat staring at him. Her food was untouched. The color drained from her face. "Land sakes, I had no idea all of that happened. I feel so terrible. It's like we've not been good neighbors. Even though it's the dead of winter, every day seems beyond full, and I can barely keep up."

After finishing with the main course, Merna suggested they sit in the living room around the fire while she served chokecherry pie and freshly brewed coffee with real cream she'd obtained from Rees Bromfield's Jersey milk cow. Just then she heard five knocks at the front door. As she opened it, a gust of wind caught the door and blew it wide open. "Spence, get in here out of the cold."

"I came to ask you for a couple of extra blankets for Miggy if you have any."

"Yes, I have some old ones in a trunk in the guest bedroom. Let me get them for you. You know Dr. Shaw, don't you?"

"Sure do! Howdy, Doc. What brings you out on a windy night like this one? I didn't think we had any issues with the Toppens herd. At least Wyn didn't mention anything to me or give me any orders."

"Good to see you, Spence. I didn't receive a call regarding any of the cattle or horses. I guess you could say this is a neighborly concern call of sorts."

Merna returned with two old handcrafted quilts draped over her left arm. "Here you go, Spence. This should keep little Miggy nice and warm, especially this denim and flannel one. Would you like a big piece of warm pie and a cup of coffee?"

"That would be fantastic, Merna. It looks like Miggy started shivering at the right time which sent me up here in search of blankets. The pie and coffee are the bonus."

Curiosity got the best of Dr. Shaw. "Who's Miggy? Your son or daughter?"

Spence had just taken the first bite of pie which he promptly spit onto his black and grey plaid flannel shirt. "A kid! Get a grip; I'm not even married. How would I get a kid? I couldn't wrangle one by my lonesome."

"My job is to keep up with the critters in the county. I am clueless as to peoples' kids and their stories."

"Miggy is a Bernese pup. She's a belated Christmas gift from a lady I met at the Merrill's New Year's Eve party."

Tom added his two cents worth. "Spence has this cat and mouse game going with one of the clerks in the Shadow Butte County recorder's office. He's real sweet on her. She's as cute as a bug's ear and sorta fond of the color pink too. Wouldn't surprise me none if she got hitched wearing a frilly, pink dress or some such."

"Maybe I should've gone to that New Year's Eve party instead of sitting home and pining away for someone that was already spoken for," lamented Dr. Shaw.

Spence and Dr. Shaw continued to banter back and forth for the next several minutes.

"Well, I better get on down to the bunk house. Wyn was camped on the phone with Sarita when I left. Hopefully he will be done by now, so we can have some peace and quiet. Shane's been stove up ever since the double pickup exchange deal. He stays holed up in his bedroom after dark and isn't very friendly these days. Plus, he's been picking more fights with Luger who can't seem to ignore him. I'm in the middle of reading a good western. I think the stagecoach is about to get robbed."

Not flinching when Sarita's name was mentioned as he'd done so many times in the past, Dr. Shaw asked, "Have you heard what happened to Chet Castins of the Sabblonti

Ranch?"

"No, I've not. In addition to our daily chores of feeding and minding the cattle and horses, we're repairing all of the saddles, bridles, and tack in preparation for riding the range when it warms up. We've got miles and miles of barbed wire fence to check this spring. The upshot of it all is that Miggy will be my new constant companion. It'll be great training ground for her. Because I've been so busy, I've not had time to run into anybody to hear any news about anything. What's up?"

"Chet was in a bad accident on January 2nd and is all bunged up. He's recuperating down at the Lower Sabblonti Ranch house. He's in a wheelchair and will have to be on crutches for a while. It's a miracle he survived that wreck. My assistant, Jacobe, is taking some supplies out there tonight and staying with him for a couple of days until Chet can hire some medical help."

Spence carefully pushed his plate forward a few inches. "I'm so sorry to hear Chet's in bad shape, and it's odd because Wyn's engaged to Sarita Sabblonti, and he didn't mention a thing. He's pretty tight lipped, but I would imagine he would've said something about all that misfortune. I wonder if he even knows about it."

"If he doesn't, you need to tell him immediately. If that would have happened to me, I would want some people checking in to see how they could help. There's a whole lot of country in this area, and the ranches are miles apart. We've got to stay connected the best we can."

Standing to his feet, Spence looked around the room and flashed a big grin. "Miggy thanks you for the blankies so she can go *beddy bye basket*, and I thank you for the dessert. Good night, all."

Merna collected the remainder of the pie, a pint jar of pickles, a fresh loaf of uncut sourdough bread, two cubes of real butter, and a jar of red rosehip jelly. She handed the cardboard box to Dr. Shaw.

"What's this?"

"Let's just call it a belated Christmas gift. That seems to

be one of the themes of the month. Stop in anytime. We enjoy having company."

CHAPTER FIFTEEN

Wyn's right hand grabbed the alarm clock as it fell onto the bunkhouse floor. *That was one short night!* The aroma of fresh side pork wafted underneath his bedroom door. Forgetting to comb his tousled hair after dressing, he made his way into the kitchen where Spence was dusting the cast iron skillet and everything in it with lots of freshly ground black pepper.

As he fastened his left front shirt pocket, Wyn commented, "Sure glad it's your turn to cook breakfast this week, pardner. Say, can I ask a huge favor of you? Now that you've told me about Chet's misfortune, I want to drive over and check on him this morning after we do the first round of chores. If you can take care of my mid-morning to noon shift, I'll trade you sometime when you need a favor. How does that grab you?"

"Yep, works for me. I never have a reason to leave this place anyway, so don't rightly know when I can collect on the favor. Shane must be fasting this morning. When I knocked on his door there was no answer. I don't see any lights in the barn, but maybe he's already down loading the feed truck," Spence speculated. "Luger fixed oatmeal and beat feet a few minutes ago."

Wyn continued, "There's no telling what's going on with Shane. I tried to explain to him that neither you nor I had anything to do with the assignment of duties on the ranch or the vehicles that went with them. He just started to rant every time I tried to speak to him, so I just quit talking until he gets an attitude adjustment. He told me I could just 'blow it out my barracks bag.' That's the last I heard from him. He's been making himself pretty scarce. I've heard his bedroom window opening late at night a couple of times."

Wyn was so preoccupied with the Sabblonti news that he ate his breakfast standing up. Not being a big fan of pepper, he left three of the four strips of fresh side pork on the red, chipped plate. "Here, Miggy, you can finish this off. Hope you like yours on the hot side. One more thing before I take off. You're not chapped that Tom made me the foreman, are you?"

"No, I think it's great!" exclaimed Spence. "I'm just living my dream here at the ranch and trying to gobble up as much first-hand experience as I can."

Spence finished his breakfast and replaced Miggy's blanket in her makeshift bed with the denim one Merna had loaned him. Looking into Miggy's eyes, he said, "Now don't you get into mischief while I'm gone. It's a titch chilly out there first thing this morning. I'll be back to get you pretty soon. I've doggy-proofed everything in this bunkhouse that I can think of, but I don't want to come back to any surprises. Be a good girl. Maybe we can take a ride into town later and pay Priscilla a visit to thank her. She'll be amazed how well you're doing."

Donning his outerwear, Spence traced his hand across the metal hooks on the wall by the front door. *Gee, that's odd. I could've sworn I hung my new Christmas scarf here last night.* He spent the next half hour looking through his bedroom, the laundry area, kitchen, and remainder of the bunkhouse minus the bedrooms, but couldn't find the hand knit muffler. "I'll ask Wyn when I see him later today. Normally he's not a jokester, but since he's getting married soon, he might be changing."

Blue, Chet's blue heeler that he inherited from his deceased mother-in-law, Jantzi Belle, announced Wyn's arrival at the Lower Sabblonti Ranch house. He applied heavy pressure to the horseshoe door knocker, but no one answered. After a few minutes, he walked around the house and down by the barn. "Anybody out and about this morning?" The horses' whinnies were the only answer. He would try one more time.

Jacobe Davone opened the front door just as Wyn grabbed the black horseshoe. "Come on in. I'm Jacobe, and I'm here to help Chet for a spell. Are you one of the local ranchers?"

"Thank you. I'm Wyn Moreland. I work up at the Toppens spread. I'm engaged to Chet's sister-in-law, Sarita."

"Oh, so you're Wyn. I've heard a lot about you. It's nice to finally meet. Please have a seat in the next room by the fire. I'll let Chet know we have a visitor. I'm sure he'll be glad to see some family."

A quick survey of the room pressed heavily upon Wyn's spirit. The singed lower corner of the blue, polar fleece blanket was draped over the wheelchair. He moved the stacks of unfolded laundry so he could sit on the couch. Unwashed soup bowls and dinner plates littered the hearth around the fireplace. A ten-inch stack of unopened mail sat in the far corner.

Wyn felt like an intruder. Should he get up and leave? Since he'd been abandoned by his mother at a young age and grew up in the boy's home, he didn't't' feel overly confident in awkward situations. He'd never been to a dance, wedding, or funeral. Was Chet going to be civil to him?

Time seemed to stand still. Wyn glanced around the room for a clock, but didn't see one. Suddenly, he heard Chet groan as he walked on the crutches down the hallway. When he entered the living room, Wyn stood to his feet. He bit the inside of his right cheek to avoid letting out a loud gasp.

It was comforting to watch Jacobe get Chet situated in

his chair and drape the blanket over his lap. With the gentleness he exhibited, Wyn wondered if he had a lot of medical training. A scene from an old movie Wyn had watched in the bunkhouse flashed through his mind where a trail-riding hand had gone into the local watering hole and requested a close shave. The barber wrapped his scraggly beard in a hot towel and went about his business. He realized afterward there was no blade in the razor. Some viewers may have been fooled by this, but Wyn wasn't. Too bad he couldn't arrange for Chet to have an actual shave and some *TLC*.

Jacobe excused himself to go into the kitchen to brew some coffee.

"Chet, first of all, let me say that I'm sorry to hear of your accident. I sincerely apologize that I didn't stop by to check on you sooner. Dr. Shaw paid a visit to the Toppens last night is the only reason I knew you were laid up. Do you have help with your cattle and horses?"

"No need to offer an apology, Wyn. I'm sure Stormy has everything under control with the ranch. She's been gone a lot, so I would imagine she's rounding up all sorts of cowhands. She's been through a lot with the sudden death of her mother. I'm just giving her a wide berth while I get healed up. I've got to have a physical therapist come down here and help me out."

Laying his hat and coat in the chair next to him, Wyn asked, "What about Jacobe? He seems like he's got everything in hand."

"Nah, he's just Dr. Shaw's office assistant. I'm not sure he'd even know how to give a shot to a critter. Guess I could ask him, but it's not shots that I need. Don't get me wrong. He's a really nice kid, and I appreciate him a lot. I really did a number on the right side of my body. Lucky to be alive I guess you could say."

Wyn leaned forward in the recliner. "Sarita and I are thankful you're still with us. We harbor no hard feelings for anything. What happened up there at the main ranch house with the reading of the will and all that malarkey is past us now. We're not dwelling on it. We've set our special date for this summer and want you to be all healed up so you and Stormy can dance at our wedding."

Chet adjusted the blanket to cover his shoulders. "I'm not much for dancing, but we'll sure be at your wedding. Where are you getting hitched anyway?"

"In the Toppens' back yard. Merna says she'll have it all fixed up right nice and pretty for the last Saturday in July. I've got a lot of ground to cover between now and then to get a place ready for my beautiful bride."

"Yes, your bride-to-be is beautiful, and she's as nice as she's pretty. She got the sweet side of the family. Stormy flipped an internal power switch after Jantzi died."

Wyn repeated that last sentence to himself three times.

Jacobe served the coffee in small two-tone, brown ceramic soup bowls with three-inch handles.

"Here you go, gents. I looked for some cream, but couldn't find any. Does anybody want sugar? Not sure how strong I made it. Could be more like sheepherder's coffee."

"Looks like an earthquake hit this place," lamented Chet. "It needs a woman's touch, that's for sure. Stormy should be down any day now to get it all spruced up. Sorry, Wyn, I'm just not very talkative this morning. Some of the pain pills I have to take make me feel *rum-dum*. Nothing personal. I've been sleeping a lot. I'm hoping that's going to help me heal up quicker."

Wyn asked for a piece of paper and a pencil. "Here's the numbers for the Toppens Ranch and the bunkhouse. If you need anything, give us a call. We're not so busy we can't come over and lend a helping hand. Spence is covering for me this morning, so I better head out. Thanks for the coffee. It wasn't half bad."

Maybe Chet hadn't heard a word Wyn said. He waited for him to speak or say *goodbye*, but nothing came forth. Jacobe was busy in the back of the house, so Wyn closed the door behind himself.

Driving from the Lower Sabblonti Ranch house to the main ranch house, Wyn pondered the interaction with Chet. He must be careful not to read too much into what was going on. As he approached the main house, he slowed down, and parked in the driveway. There was a part of him that wanted to put his pickup in reverse, back up, shift into 2nd gear and head on down the road. Instead, he got out of the cab and walked to the front porch. No one answered after repeated knocks. He thought he heard country western music coming from the window of the top floor of the house. Just as he turned to leave, he noticed the large piece of wood taped over the broken window. *What happened here?* Chet hadn't mentioned he needed any help with repairs at the house, but then again, maybe he was unaware. What else was broken besides this window? There was a part of Wyn that didn't want to know.

With more questions than answers, Wyn drove slowly from the ranch house onto the main highway. Several miles passed. Not realizing he was driving below the speed limit, a cattle truck suddenly appeared behind him. The driver laid on the horn which helped to bring Wyn back to sudden reality. He slowed down so the driver could pass him. A mile from the turn off to the Toppens Ranch, Wyn noticed something flapping in the breeze. He couldn't tell exactly what was entangled in the rabbit brush, but he thought he'd seen it somewhere before.

CHAPTER SIXTEEN

Spence gathered up his overalls, jeans, and one of Miggy's blankets to start a load of laundry. "I guess Merna did get a newer washer and dryer down here. This washer has a larger tub which is going to be a real boon now that I'm washing for two." Talking to himself and Miggy, Spence did not hear Wyn enter the bunkhouse and walk down the hall.

"Who are you talking to, Spence? Did Shane ever surface this morning?"

"Nope, so we have extra chores to do. We need to pay Tom a visit and let him know. Hope he decides to hire on another hand now that you have the fiancé and things are looking up for me."

"Have you checked Shane's bedroom since I left?"

"Sure did, and it's as clean as a whistle. He even made off with the alarm clock and the few odds and ends that Merna insists stay in each of the bunkhouse bedrooms for the ranch hands. No note, no nothing."

Wyn opened the drawer and grabbed a package of jerky. "That's just plain weird. He must have hoofed it to the main road and started hitchhiking. I guess he didn't care one lick about collecting his wages for the last two weeks. He was sort of a strange duck all along."

"No use crying over spilled milk. I completed the first round of feeding and all is quiet on the western front, so let's head up to the main ranch house. Tom should be up and around. Sure do hope his back isn't out of commission today."

Tom answered the front door. “Both of you up here at once? Is there a problem down yonder? Come in out of the cold, and warm your hands by the stove.”

Wyn and Spence started talking simultaneously.

“One at a time,” instructed Tom. “Wyn, you go first.”

“Spence did some of my chores this morning so I could pay Chet a visit. Cattle and horses are fine. We are minus one cowhand, however.”

“Shane decide to call it quits?”

“Guess so. Spence can fill in that part of the story.”

“Yeah, Shane didn’t show up for breakfast. I thought he might be sleeping in, so I didn’t rap on his bedroom door. I went about my business and got Miggy all comfy before heading down to the barn. When I got back to the bunkhouse, I checked his room and he’d cleaned it out. Even stole the alarm clock and other things Merna has in the rooms for the hired help. Must have walked to the main road and hitched a ride with a long-haul trucker or cattle truck driver. Doubt he would try to bum a ride with one of the local ranchers.”

Tom had a coughing spell. Wyn handed him a pint jar of water. “I had an uneasy feeling about him after I decided to hand the reins to Wyn and named you two the ranch foreman and assistant ranch foreman. I’ve been a good judge of character most of my born days, and this one proved to be true as well. Gotta go with your gut feeling most of the time. I’ve had my eye on another hired hand. I’ll see if I can round him up and bring him on board.”

“My hand-knit muffler has disappeared, too,” explained Spence. “I’ll bet you dollars to doughnuts that weasel stole it before he headed outta Dodge.”

“Wait a minute!” exclaimed Wyn. “When I was driving back from paying Chet a visit and right before I turned off the main road onto the side road leading to the ranch, I spotted something hanging from a big rabbit brush. It sorta looked like a winter scarf. What color was it again?”

“Burgundy and brown.”

“Well, there’s only one way to find out for sure. Tom, do

you mind if we make a quick trip to the main highway to see if we can find Priscilla's handiwork?"

"As long as you don't make a career of it. Fine by me. I wouldn't have given you that pickup or named you the foreman if you couldn't be trusted."

Wyn reached into his jean pocket for his pickup keys. "Who's driving, you or me?"

"How about you drive, so I can be on the lookout for my prized possession? I sure hope it's still there."

"Well, with no desert wind this morning, you just might be in luck."

"Who does those sorts of things anyway? Shane knew how much that gift meant to me."

"Which is precisely why he took it to the main highway. He probably hoped someone else would steal it, so he could wash his hands of any guilt."

Wyn came to a complete stop at the end of the side road leading to the Toppens Ranch. Spence looked ahead. "Let's ease onto the main road."

"Let me roll down the window on my side so I can hear if any vehicles are on the main road. Can't hear a thing."

Wyn drove slowly onto the main highway. "Keep your eyes peeled. I think it's only about a mile or so down here. It's early enough in the day that the rubberneckers aren't usually out and about."

"I thought you called them turkeyneckers."

"Same difference. They're a hazard on the road either way."

Spotting something frayed hanging in the distance, Spence shouted, "Hit the skids! There it is."

Looking in his rear-view mirror and seeing no traffic, Wyn came to an abrupt stop. Spence bailed out, ran into the barrow pit, and unwound his muffler from the brush. "Ugh, the threads on the ends are ruined, and there's a big chunk taken from the middle of it. Quite the worse for wear."

"At least you found it, Spence. Now you have a second good excuse to pay your lady friend a visit. You can give her the sob story about *our good riddance to bad rubbish* and let her love on Miggy for a while."

"You better not let Merna hear you say that *rubbish* line. She's pretty strict with manners and how folks are supposed to act in all situations. How about I collect on that favor right before dinner at the bunkhouse? If I time it just right, I can hit the recorder's office at high noon. I better get Miggy and her blankie loaded into my rig. First, I've got to shower and shave so I'll look more irresistible."

"Just thought of something."

"What's that?"

"Now that Shane's gone, so is that skunk bait cologne he always put on. Could never figure out why he sprayed himself just to feed critters. They could care less what we smell like. I can cover the afternoon shift for you. Just don't get lost on me now. I don't know of a search party. Guess they do have the Shadow Butte Sheriff's Posse though."

Spence dressed in his best western wear, collected his hat and winter coat, and loaded Miggy into the warm cab of his pickup. "Uh oh, almost forgot the second important thing. Gotta get that ruined scarf. Be right back, Miggy. Sit tight."

As Spence drove into Ridgemonte, he rehearsed various lines of imaginary conversation to Miggy as he viewed the firs clinging to the crevices and shallow shelves on the precipitous face of the glacier-honed peak. "Too bad you can't give me some girly advice, girl. You're too young anyway for all of this romance stuff. Better keep a close eye on you though because you're a beauty!"

Arriving at the Shadow Butte County office building complex a mere five minutes before high noon, Spence checked the reader board, walked hurriedly down the hallway, and opened the door. Walking to the front counter, he frowned when he did not see Priscilla Fletcher.

"Hello, how may I help you?" asked one of the deputy clerks.

"Is Priscilla working today by any chance?"

"Yes, she's in the employee break room. We're closed from noon until 1:00 for lunch. She's probably already started eating. Can I tell her your name, please?"

"I'm her recent friend. She'll know who I am."

"I'll give her the message. Be right back."

The deputy clerk poked her head into the break room. "Priscilla, your recent friend is standing at the counter."

"What? Describe him to me. Recent friend sounds pretty vague to me."

"Well, he's about medium height with a full round face. His eyebrows are really different."

"How can somebody have different eyebrows?"

"This guy's are sorta like upside down "V" ones, so it looks like he's got little Alpine shaped roofs over his eyes."

Gluing one of the rhinestones to the frames of her pink glasses, Priscilla asked, "He's not some drifter, is he?"

"I would not call him a drifter. Just go out there and find out. I'll be with you, so there will be two of us."

Priscilla emerged from the room down the hallway wiping her mouth with a pink napkin. Spence pursed his lips together to keep from laughing. *Does this lady's entire life consist of pink?*

"What a nice surprise, Spence! I can't believe you're here during the middle of the day. Are you doing business for the ranch or something?"

Spence was tongue tied. Taking a deep breath and exhaling, he replied, "Two things brought me to town actually. I need to show you both of them if you have time."

"I just started my lunch hour. I could visit with you for a few minutes though. I would invite you to our employee's break room, but that's totally against the rules, so no can do. Would you like to visit in the hallway?"

"I have a little show and tell in the cab of my pickup. Let me help you into your coat so you can follow me out there."

"I guess I could be persuaded to do that. No arm twisting required."

Priscilla's faux pink fur coat with a white trimmed hood and fur-lined, pink, leather gloves might not be the best thing for an overactive puppy. Spence opened the door and gestured for her to walk through first. "After you."

"Such a country gentleman."

"Well, I would hope so. I'm certainly no country hick."

Priscilla giggled all of the way to the pickup, letting out a squeal of delight when she saw Miggy through the passenger window. "Oh, look at you! My, how you've grown since I last saw you. Spence, what are you feeding her, raw beef steak every day?"

Spence opened the pickup door for Priscilla and closed it gently behind her. He walked around to the side, opened the driver's door, and crawled inside. *Oh, what a feeling*!

Priscilla petted Miggy as she placed the pup on top of her lap. "Look here. You even have your own blanket!"

"I named her Miggy. Hope that meets with your approval."

Priscilla rubbed her nose against Miggy's and giggled. "Miggy's a delightful name! I doubt there's another range dog with that name. I could not think of anywhere else to take her since she was deposited on the steps of the building so early in the morning. Mother and I couldn't possibly keep a dog like her in town. We have crabby neighbors who are not fond of dogs. They have these birds in cages inside their house that squawk and talk, so we have to suffer through that during the summertime when our windows are open. You said there were two things. Where's the other one or are you hiding it from me?"

"No, I'm not hiding it. Can you please open the jockey box in front of you?"

"Jockey box. What's that? Do you mean the glove compartment?"

"They are one and the same. Cowboys call it the jockey box. Don't ask me why."

Turning to Spence as she tilted her head to the right, Priscilla asked, "Is there something alive in there that's going to jump out and scare me? I don't know you very well yet, so can't judge if you're going to play a trick on me."

"No tricks, Priscilla. I can guarantee that."

"That's a relief." Opening the jockey box and reaching into it, Priscilla felt the yarn. Pulling out the scarf she had knit for Spence, she looked at him quizzically. "What did you do to this? You've not had it that long for it to look like this!"

"I didn't do anything to it. As near as I can determine, Shane, one of the hired hands, stole it from me, cut a hunk from it, and hung it on some rabbit brush on the main highway near the turn off to the Toppens Ranch. I think he did it just to be spiteful. He was super chapped because he didn't get a promotion or a vehicle when Tom Toppens announced the new ranching arrangements. I was wondering if you could mend the muffler for me. I've been wearing it every day. It was such a thoughtful gift. You're very kind."

Rubbing the frayed edges with her fingers, Priscilla said, "Think nothing of it. I don't have much to do during the winter evenings when I get off work. I help Mother around the house some, but it doesn't take long to do what she needs done. If I knit and crochet, it helps to keep my mind occupied."

Just then Priscilla heard a tap on the passenger windshield. A cowboy grabbed the right-side brim of his black cowboy hat and smiled broadly at her. He stepped back a few feet, placed his hands on his hips, and laughed out loud. Lifting his left hand, he opened his palm and motioned for her to get out of Spence's pickup. Priscilla stiffened as Spence sat upright in the driver's seat. The cowboy bent over at the waist, stood up straight, shook his head, and started laughing once again as he continued to walk down the sidewalk.

"Who was that and what was he trying to prove?" Spence asked.

"That was Lane. I don't even know his last name. He has been bugging the workers in the recorder's office. None of us will give him the time of day. Actually, I think it's a good thing he saw me with you today. Maybe he'll leave me alone. There's safety in numbers, so we've been sticking together in the office. Thankfully, I don't live far from work."

Spence continued to watch Lane make his way down the street. "You don't walk home from work every day, do you?"

"No, I drive home most days, and sometimes I have to stop at The Shadowy Merc for groceries or other supplies."

"How long has that shady character been hanging around here?"

Priscilla gently rubbed Miggy's back. "I have no idea. He's been showing up at the office since last Thanksgiving. Most western men are not strolling up and down the sidewalks in town during the noon hour unless they're here conducting ranch business. I've never seen one act like he does. One of my co-workers said he smelled strongly of alcohol one day when he was standing at the counter. He probably spends a lot of time at the local bar."

"Can't your boss have him arrested for drunken and disorderly conduct? She should talk to Sheriff Jensen about that. It would help to cure the problem."

"I'll have to mention that to Betty Lou Bradford since she's the elected clerk now. So, back to your scarf. Yes, I'll be happy to mend this for you. I would imagine you'd need it sooner than later since it's been so cold. I could have it ready for you in a few days."

"Would you mind calling the bunkhouse and letting me know when you have it finished?" I know it's not proper for a woman to call a man on the phone, but maybe we could make an exception this one time."

"Yes, I could call, but I don't have the number."

"Oh, right. I'm still thinking about that Lane guy. Can you reach inside the jockey box one more time and hand me that little tablet in there?"

Spence dug around in the front pockets of the pickup seat covers and located a pen. Picking it up, he noticed *Dawson's Dealership* on the side. Rolling it around between his thumb and right forefinger, he commented, "Well, that's the least Dawsons could provide for all of the dough Tom has given them over the decades." Spence wrote the number for the bunkhouse on the piece of paper and handed it to Priscilla. "Now don't lose that. It's the most important number you'll need from now on."

The corners of Priscilla's mouth turned upward as she

tucked the piece of paper into her right pink pant pocket.

"Priscilla, you look beautiful in pink. Do you mind me asking if you own any other color of clothing? I hope that does not sound too fresh. Pardon me if it does."

"Why, yes, I own other colors of clothing. I have some pale blues, soft lavenders, sage greens, light apricots, and so forth. It must be that every time you see me, I'm decked out in pink. You don't mind, do you?"

"Not at all." Spence winked with his left eye at the same time he flashed a big grin. His face looked like a smiling full moon.

"Spence, I just had an idea. When I get your scarf mended, would you like to come to the house for supper? That way you could meet Mother. Be sure to bring Miggy with you. Mother was in a real dither as to what would happen to that poor little pup. Can you imagine someone so cold hearted they would leave a newborn on a doorstep in the dead of winter?"

"You've heard Wyn Moreland's life story, haven't you? Same thing happened to him."

Priscilla frowned. "No, I've not. That's very sad."

"Just let me know when everything is a go, and Miggy and I'll be there in our country finest. Miggy, you stay here while I get Priscilla safely situated in the office."

CHAPTER SEVENTEEN

Seated comfortably in the black chair inside Stormy's upstairs office, Meg propped up her 8.5 x 11-inch hardback book titled *Flow Charts for Ranching Businesses* as she placed her feet in just the right position on top of the small stool underneath the desk. She carefully positioned the romance novel she was reading in front of the larger book. To the casual eye, it would appear as though Meg was deeply engrossed in improving the subject matter for which she had been initially hired. Hearing a door open down the hallway, she suddenly closed the novel, opened the top desk drawer, and placed the book behind the row of checkbooks.

"Knock, knock, Mrs. Alotto. We need to leave for Cinder Valley right now. Grab your purse and make sure you have your current driver's license, not that flashy California one. I thought you just moved from South Dakota. Didn't you drive in that state when you lived there for so many years? How do you square that circle?"

Meg collected her belongings, turned the light switch off, and closed the office door. As she followed Stormy outside to her pickup, she wanted to ask about the repair for the front window of the house, but let it slide for now. "Will we be gone long, Stormy?"

"I have no idea. Certainly, you have nothing better to do than what I need you to do at any given time, do you?"

"Definitely not."

"I want peace and quiet inside the cab during the drive to Cinder Valley. I have a lot on my mind and need to be able to concentrate. Small talk is a sheer waste of time."

Stormy drove to Carl's Car Corral and parked smack dab in front of the main door. For a mere moment, Meg thought Stormy just might keep driving straight into the showroom.

"Meg, you stay put until I come to get you. Twiddle your thumbs or find something to do."

Clark, one of the salesmen, was holding the door open for a customer who was exiting as Stormy prepared to enter. "That bright red rig is ready for you Mrs. Castins, er, I mean, Stormy. I think you're going to be plum pleased with it. Now all you need is a pile of whipping cream and a red cherry on top. Cream sure wouldn't melt in this weather."

"Where's my new pickup? I'm dying to see what my family cattle brand looks like painted on both doors."

"It's parked around back. Please follow me or I could drive it around here for you. Your choice."

"Wait a couple of minutes. I need to dispatch my relief driver."

Stormy returned to Jantzi Belle's pickup and motioned for Meg to open the door. She handed her a standalone key. "Here. Drive this back to the ranch and plan to get it there in one piece. You're supposed to be highly educated, so I'm sure you can figure out how everything operates."

Meg got situated in the driver's seat, turned on the ignition, and pushed the heater switch to the maximum level. She couldn't find the correct switch to adjust the side mirrors. She turned the key to the far left, got out of the pickup, and tried to manually move the side mirrors to no avail. She planned to wait until Stormy exited the parking lot, and then she would go inside and ask for help. How humiliating. Where was Less when she needed him most?

Walking back into the dealership, Stormy did not spot Clark right away, so she approached the front counter to speak to the one of the employees.

"Where is he?"

"Where's who? Does he have a name?"

"Clark something or other. I need him front and center right now."

The young woman spoke into the intercom, "Clark, can you please come to the showroom counter?" Turning her back to Stormy, she proceeded to file invoices inside slots of the pine wood organizer resting against the back wall.

Stormy drummed her long fingernails on top of the counter for the next few minutes, sighing periodically.

"Sorry, Stormy, the detail crew forgot to shine your doors after your brand was applied on there. Here's two sets of keys, one for your husband and one for you. Carl thanks you for your business, and come back soon!"

Stormy jerked the keys from Clark's right hand. "Don't bother following me. I can find my own way out of this zoo."

Meg watched for Stormy to exit the parking lot and went inside to locate some assistance. Walking to the front counter, she explained her dilemma. After mentioning to her that she could have consulted the driver's manual inside the glove compartment, Clark followed Meg outside to give her the one easy lesson on how to adjust all of the mirrors. Meg replied, "I don't know why I didn't think to check the owner's manual instead of taking up your valuable time."

Clarke flashed a big grin, "I've got nothing but time."

S

"Country Cates. You're next on my list. My reinventing project needs some additional upgrades." Just then Stormy drove the right rear wheel of her new pickup over the curb as she turned the street corner. "I forgot this pickup bed is longer than the one I'm used to driving. I hope I didn't damage that new tire on the back. Oh, forget about it. I can park here and walk for a few blocks. It's not that cold."

As Stormy approached the intersection, she walked a few steps to the right to avoid running into what looked like a young mother and her two little children huddled under a sleeping bag. There was an empty bean can sitting next to them.

"You should be arrested for child abuse. Don't you know better than to have your kids out on a day like this?" Looking down at the young mother's left hand, Stormy saw no wedding ring. Removing her red leather glove and flashing her new, five-carat white gold wedding ring, she asked, "Where's your wedding ring? They say that a diamond is a girl's best friend. Obviously, you don't have a best friend. Probably don't even have a husband, either. Why don't you get up off your dead rear, get a job, and get a life? I won't ask where that jagged *J*-shaped scar on your hand came from. Probably a knife fight in the back alley behind the bar. What's your name anyway?"

Warm salted tears stung her cold face and mucous freely flowed from both nostrils as the young mother softly replied, "Aprilily."

"Well, Aprilily, wipe your nose with your shirttail. The world is never interested in losers, whiners, and criers. If you're going to beg for money, the least you could do is wash out that bean can so it doesn't look so gross."

Stormy squared her shoulders, looked to her left and right to check for oncoming traffic and walked another thirty steps. She could hear the sobbing of one of Aprilily's young daughters, so she turned around and walked back to where they were seated cross legged under the sleeping bag. Feeling around in the bottom of her purse, Stormy located the red velvet jewelry box. She removed her three-carat, horseshoe-shaped wedding ring that Chet had given her nine years ago when they got married in the large meadow of the Sabblonti Cattle Ranch. "Here Aprilily, you can just have this old ring of mine. Take it to the pawn shop and see what that old geezer will give you for it."

Through tear-filled puffy eyes, Aprilily looked at Stormy.

"Thanks, but no thanks. I'm waiting for an honest cowboy to ride into town who will love me just as I am."

"How will you know he's honest and that he will truly love you?"

"I will know that I will know that I will know. He'll give me the perfect wedding ring . . . someday . . . one that's all my own. He'll place me first in his heart above family, friends, and the rest of the world."

"Maybe reality will set in for you when the sun goes down and the temperatures drop."

Stormy thought about taking the two young children home with her and caring for them, but remembered that probably wouldn't interface too well with her present reinventing project.

A gust of wind blew in front of Stormy as she walked toward the western wear store. She fastened the top button of her fur coat. "I have no idea how people function without money, power, and prestige. Poor fools."

S

Meg had no time to lose. She studied the map she'd found last week when snooping through Ace's upstairs room. Lifting the keys to Jantzi Belle's pickup from the wooden key board mounted in the kitchen, she drove to Blademere, the county seat of Blunte County. Her heart skipped a couple of beats when driving up and down the city streets until her eyes spotted exactly what she was looking for. Parking several blocks away, she walked inside the building and approached the counter. "Good afternoon, I need to open a checking account, please."

"Perfect timing! Our assistant manager just left for a late

lunch, but I see that Mr. Tilmore is in, so I'll check to see if he has a few minutes to meet with you. It's pretty straight forward, but he does like to become acquainted with our new customers."

"Please come in, Meg. It's a pleasure to meet you, and welcome to the Bank of Blunte. As we like to say, 'Business is always better in Blunte!' Are you new to our region?"

"Relatively, I guess you could say. My husband and I actually live in the next county over. I have my own business, so I need to open a checking account."

"We can certainly help you with that. What kind of business?"

"Marketing, mostly. I also have a part-time bookkeeping job, but it's my self-employment that really keeps me hopping."

"What kinds of things do you market?"

"Just about anything I can dream up or get my hands on."

Ed leaned down to the right-hand side of his desk, opened the second drawer, and removed a set of papers that were clipped together. "If I can get you to fill these out for me, that would be great. We still implement the friendly country practice of the original owner of the bank all those decades ago."

"And just what might that be?"

Ed explained, "A new customer only has to come into the bank once to open an account. After that, you can mail in your deposits. This seems to work best for folks spread out over these big cattle counties. It's not such a chore for those in the city, but we like to accommodate people everywhere. We can mail your monthly statements to you as well. Sounds like that might be a good fit for you since you don't live in Blunte County."

"I've never really heard of such a thing, but that will work really well for my new set up. I can just plan to pick up my mail where I work and balance my monthly statements while performing my regular bookkeeping job." Meg felt inside her coat pocket. "Do you have a monthly service charge?"

"If you keep a minimum monthly balance of $500, there's no service charge, and the printing of your checks is free. Do you write very many checks each month for your marketing business?"

"Come to think of it, I do, so that feature will be especially nice. Maintaining the minimum $500 balance will never be a problem. I need a triple order of the deposit slips."

"Business must be booming!"

"Yes, it's starting to which is such a relief."

During the time Meg was completing and signing the paperwork to open her new account, Ed quickly reviewed two other cattle ranchers' operating loan applications.

Meg handed the paperwork back to Ed. "You don't have anyone else listed on your account. Don't you want to put your husband's name on here in case something happens to you, so he can have access to it?"

"No. I'm the only one on the account. My husband thinks I spend way too much money on my marketing business, so to avoid any hassles, I just go the solo route. That's the way I've handled it in the past. There's never been any problems."

"Okay, looks like the only other thing I need is your driver's license, so we can make a copy of it."

Meg located her wallet and nearly produced her South Dakota one, but decided at the last minute to hand over her California license. Ed asked one of the tellers to make a copy for their records. Meg selected the style of checks that she wanted and placed a large order.

"California? You can declare your residency in our state once you've lived here for one year. How much will you be depositing today in your new account?"

Reaching inside the old briefcase she'd taken from Stormy's office closet, Meg pulled out a large envelope containing $10,000. "This should do it for today. I don't usually like to carry a lot of cash with me, but since I was looking for a bank, I didn't deem it a problem."

As Ed secured the cash to the new deposit slip using a large rubber band, he commented, "These bills smell sort of like wood burned in a fireplace. That's odd. In all my years of banking, I don't think I've ever experienced that before." He drew the stack of bills close to both nostrils, inhaled deeply, and set them on his desk.

Pretending to be trying to locate something else in the bottom of the briefcase, Meg said, "I didn't even notice. Some of my customers pay me in cash. I've been collecting it for a bit until I could carve out the opportune time to open an account."

"You didn't want to open an account closer to where you live?"

Meg flicked her hair to her right side. "I just got this wild hair to drive over here to check out more of the neighboring counties and discovered you had a bank, so I thought I would pop in and take a look."

Ed stood as he creased Meg's paperwork and placed it inside the blue and white folder. "Since we're a privately-owned bank, we appreciate each and every one of our customers. Your newly printed checks and deposit slips should arrive in about a week to ten days. Here's wishing your business, *Double A Enterprises*, much success in the days ahead. It seems as though you're quite a proficient business woman. Perhaps you can treat yourself to a new briefcase since your business is so brisk."

"Yes, getting more so by the day. Thank you so much for all of your help, Mr. Tilmore."

"You're welcome. Just call me Ed."

CHAPTER EIGHTEEN

Salina Bevvins heard the sound of the male robin from the twelve-bird-themed clock hanging on the south wall of The Shadowy Merc, so she knew it was 4:00 in the afternoon. She had offered to open the store for the manager so she could get off work earlier than normal. During her morning and afternoon breaks in the back portion of the grocery store, she'd prepared and cooked a bacon topped meatloaf, baked potatoes, and cream style corn in glass oven wear dishes. Salina purchased the ingredients along with a package of frosted brownies from the bakery. She didn't know if every other country mercantile was as accommodating to their employees as this one was, but there was no time for comparisons right now.

At the stroke of five, Salina cleaned out her cash register and placed all of the bills, coins, checks, and coupons from the weekly circular inside the black, zippered pouch. She turned it into the office manager and hung her store vest on a hanger in the break room. She selected a large, metal, milk container located outside the walk-in cooler to place the oven dishes inside and walked outside to wrap it in the blanket inside her Aunt June Slader's pickup. Placing it on the floorboard of the passenger side of the front seat, Salina started the engine to warm up the cab and defrost the windows. She made one more trip inside the store, returned with brownies in hand, and placed them in the pickup bed behind the driver's seat. Her carefully penned get well sentiments were taped to the package. Secretly hoping she had sufficiently studied the county maps well enough, Salina left Ridgemonte just as the darkness was settling in.

Keeping a sharp eye on each mile marker and staying below the speed limit, Salina's blood pressure was rising as the country drivers were becoming quite impatient with her driving. They honked their horns and turned on their bright lights as they passed her while it seemed as if she was standing still. She turned onto a side road off the main one and hoped all the while she was on the correct one. Suddenly, she heard a loud *ding* coming from the dashboard of the pickup. She looked down and saw the yellow neon light warning her that she only had 1/4th of a tank of fuel remaining. Oh, my! Her uncle, Denny Slader, had told her that driving below the speed limit helped to conserve fuel. She sure hoped he knew what he was talking about.

Not having traveled this stretch of road before, Salina approached the main ranch house, but had the distinct feeling she should still keep driving. Was she taking too much of a chance with such limited fuel? She could have kicked herself for not taking a test run over the weekend so she would have a better feel for the lay of the land.

Salina drove for what seemed another half hour. There was nothing and no one around. Didn't people get lonely out here? Just as she was about to press her personal panic button, she spotted a dim light in the distance. Cautiously entering the driveway, she parked next to the brown van, got out of the driver's side and carried the metal container to the front porch and set it down. Salina made a second trip to get the brownies.

After striking the horseshoe door knocker on the front door several times without anyone answering, Salina tried the door handle which freely turned to the right and the door opened. She could see a light shining in the hallway, but the remainder of the house was dark. She called into the house, "Hello, anyone home? Is this Chet Castin's place?" Salina heard footsteps approaching her.

"Smells good! How neighborly of you to bring us some supper. Frosted brownies are my favorites. Let me see. I'll just set the container in the entry way. Oh sorry, I'm Evan Briarley, Chet's physical therapist. This is my second week of staying down here. And who might you be?"

"I'm a very close friend of Chet's. My name's Salina. I heard through the high desert grapevine that Chet's out of the hospital. How's he doing? Any chance I could visit with him for a few minutes? I'm just dying to see him."

Evan bent down to move the brownies so he would not step in the middle of them. "He's, uh, not really. Now's not the best time for visitors. He's getting around slowly on crutches and his right leg is still very sore. I'm hoping he's not gotten some kind of internal infection going on. His temperature has been up and down the past couple of days. I have a call into his doctor, so I'm waiting to hear from him. He might need some prescriptions picked up from the local drug store. I've not quite figured out how we're going to arrange all of that."

"I'd be more than happy to drive back out here and deliver whatever you and Chet need now that I know my way around a little better." Salina unzipped her purse. "I've got an old grocery list. I'll write the number of The Shadowy Merc on there. That's where I work. Here you go. Just let me know what Chet needs and when he needs it, day or night."

"Forgive me for not inviting you inside as I know it's getting pretty frosty out there right now. We've not had many visitors show up since I started helping Chet down here. Maybe I'd better get the place straightened up a bit so the next time you bless us with your domestic endeavors I'll be more prepared."

"I fully understand. It's not a problem at all. Please tell Chet hello for me and that I miss him terribly."

"I'll deliver the message. Be safe driving home."

"I will, but can you please empty that metal milk container and give it back to me? There are more meals where that came from."

Evan opened the metal box and set the serving dishes in the entryway. "Thanks again. Goodnight." Salina turned to walk to the pickup, made a fist with her right hand, and slammed it into the palm of her left hand. "Why, the nerve of him not to invite me in from the cold!"

One of Chet's crutches fell to the bathroom floor as he was trying to stand to his feet. "Evan, I really need your help. Seems like you were gone an awfully long time."

"Sorry about that, Chet. You had company. Let's get you settled in the living room."

"Did my lovely wife finally decide to pay me a long overdue visit? I could sure use a big kiss and hug."

"If her name is Salina, then yes, she did. We have a mighty fine supper waiting for us in the kitchen. It was all I could do to resist snitching one of the pieces of crisp bacon off the top of that country meatloaf."

Chet was taking longer than normal to walk on his crutches. He grimaced with pain as he eased into his recliner. "I have a big enough headache tonight without concerning myself with Salina."

"You still want to eat, don't you? I mean, I could heat up a can of chili from the pantry if you'd rather I do that. Getting something to eat might help with your headache. You've not had much of an appetite the past couple of days."

"Meatloaf does sound better than canned chili. Sure, fix me a helping of that."

Evan emerged from the kitchen carrying a flat cardboard box with two-inch sides all the way around. He laid it on the end table next to Chet's chair. "I couldn't find any kind of a serving tray, so I rounded up this box off the pantry floor. Hope that's not going to be a problem."

"She brought all this for supper? I thought there were just the beef and the bacon."

"Salina's quite the detailed person or so it would appear. She even included four gallons of milk, a pound of butter, a two-pound package of shredded cheddar cheese, and bacon bits for your fully loaded baked potato. That's cream style corn in that glass dish. You're losing so much weight, I cut three big brownies from the pan so you could indulge. Oh, and there was a little card or note taped to the top of the brownies. Just a minute. I'll get it for you."

Chet ate every morsel of what Evan had served him in the various dishes inside the cardboard box. "I don't know when I've had a better home-cooked meal. Seems like it's been years. I wonder what Salina put in that meatloaf?"

"Since Sabblontis own a huge cattle herd, doesn't your wife cook with a lot of beef?"

"She never did much cooking with much of anything during the time I've been married to her. My deceased mother-in-law, Jantzi Belle, convinced Stormy to stay razor thin for some stupid reason. Maybe that's why she had three miscarriages. She didn't eat enough to keep a bird alive most days. I ate out of a can a lot of the time. You can get most anything down with half a loaf of bread lathered with lotsa butter."

When cleaning up the kitchen, Evan remembered what he'd forgotten to tell Chet. "When I returned from the barn the other day, there were three large cardboard boxes of canned and packaged goods sitting on the front porch. The receipt was still in the box. It was from the grocery store in Cinder Valley."

"Cinder Valley?" asked Chet. "I don't know anybody down there that would be bringing groceries to me clear up here. What all was in the boxes?"

Glancing at the pantry shelves, Evan replied, "Soups, stews, one-man dinners, boxed scalloped spuds, and so on. Oh, and four packages of those chocolate chip cookies with the coconut in them."

"Those are my favorite store-bought cookies. Seems to me only Stormy knows that, but she doesn't shop in Cinder Valley. And if it was her that brought the supplies all the way down here, why didn't she come in and see me? I miss her so much!"

Evan opened his mouth to ask about Stormy as well as Salina, but promptly shut it. He decided to file those questions away until a later time. "It's a good thing you did your exercises before you ate that huge meal. Maybe you'll sleep better tonight. Is there anything else you need before I finish cleaning the kitchen, feed the dogs, and fold the laundry?"

"Not that I can think of right now. Thanks."

Thinking about the packaged cookies, remorse filled Chet's stomach following consumption of Salina's special delivery supper.

S

Salina was as nervous as a cat on a hot tin roof driving back to Ridgemonte. She kept glancing down at the gas gauge on the dashboard and nearly ran off the road in a couple of places. *Oh, how I would love to have been there to watch Chet eat his supper. You know what they say, 'The way to a man's heart is through his stomach.' That's it! The more I prepare for his stomach, the more he will prepare his heart for me. I knew that sooner or later the strategy would come to me.*

Gib's Gas was four blocks away when Salina entered town. The pickup stopped suddenly in the middle of the street. She tried to restart the engine, but knew that it must be out of gas. Getting out of the cab, she surveyed the landscape to see if there was anyone to help her. She turned on the hazard lights and walked to the gas station.

Travis Fisen was standing next to Lambent's Funeral Home hearse. He removed the gas nozzle from the tank and hung it on the pump. His hands were cold and he was having trouble screwing the gas cap onto the tank, so he didn't notice Salina walking toward him. There was no one else in the vicinity.

"Hello, would you mind lending me a helping hand? My pickup ran out of gas a couple of blocks up the street. I need someone to get behind it and push while I steer it down here."

"Wait a minute. Don't I know you? You look very familiar. Now I remember. You were one of the handful of people who attended Jantzi Belle Sabblonti's funeral. Weren't you the woman dressed in jet black?"

Salina batted her long black, fake eyelashes and smiled. "That was me. Can we forget about that funeral business and get me some gas? I don't have any extra money to pay you, but I could fix you a nice meal, dessert, or something personal as a thank you."

"It would reflect poorly on Lambents if I didn't help you. I need to park this hearse around the side of the building and pay for the gas, so give me a minute. No thanks on the meal or personal offer."

Salina followed Travis inside the station. Looking at the clerk he said, "That hefty gas bill on pump number one would be mine. Hearse's get two miles per gallon if that much. While you're at it, could I please borrow a one gallon can? It seems the person standing behind me wasn't watching her gas gauge closely enough and managed to run out a couple of blocks from here. You can just add that amount to my total. It's under Lambent's account, so I'll just sign for it. Thanks."

Travis filled the gallon can with gas and carried it to Salina's pickup. "Do you have a locking gas cap or just the screw top cover?"

"Just the screw top cover, and why didn't I think of borrowing a gas can from the station?"

"It's probably because your mind is in la-la land otherwise you wouldn't have run out of gas in the first place. Don't worry. Explanations aren't necessary."

After pouring the gas from the can into the pickup tank, Travis secured the lid and started to walk back toward the station.

"Wait a minute! Aren't you going to stay here with me to make sure the engine starts? I'd really like to do something nice for you since you were kind to me."

"Plan to do something kind for someone else besides me."

"Don't worry. I already have."

CHAPTER NINETEEN

Friday morning, February 4th, arrived much too quickly on Stormy's calendar. She'd received a telephone call earlier in the week notifying her that the special clothing she'd ordered from Country Cate's Western Wear had not yet arrived. In her mind, she was not going to be able to *put on the dog* to the extent to which she had originally planned. Flexibility was not often exercised in Stormy's world.

After dismissing Meg from her office at high noon, a flash of inspiration brightened Stormy's day. Chet was supposed to clean out Jantzi's clothing closet following her death along with some other mundane chores, but since he was involved in his bad auto accident, that had not been done. Stormy deemed this a blessing in disguise as she tried on different combinations of Jantzi's wardrobe while standing in front of the full-length mirror. She would need to select something right away as her hair appointment with Vonnetta was fast approaching. The emerald green sweater with accents was striking, but was there an ankle-length skirt to match it? Stormy was not in the mood to wear the regular clothing she'd recently purchased from Cate's store. Somehow it did not seem fancy enough to wear for the special occasion. After all is said and done, there's never a second chance to make a first impression. At the last minute, Stormy located an orange-red suede skirt hanging at the back of the closet. "This might work. Let me take a look in that mirror one more time. I guess I could wear that off-white cashmere sweater with the opal accents and Mother's matching opal earrings that Daddy gifted her."

Stormy hurriedly collected a few other things that she would need for the Ignee County Rodeo Board Retirement Party and placed them inside her leather suitcase. She collected her makeup along with her other accessories, briefcase, and purse. Locking the front door securely behind her, she drove to Cinder Valley.

Vonnetta paced the floor of *The Mane Place*. Clearly unhappy that she'd not yet received a telephone call from Stormy or heard from her, she stood looking out the front window and declared, "It's 4:35 now, and if Stormy isn't here in the next ten minutes, I'm closing up shop. At least Jantzi Belle was always on time for her appointments."

Tugging at the front door of the beauty shop, Stormy could not open it. Finally figuring out that she needed to push it forward, she offered no apology. "I'm running late, Vonnetta. I'm sure you won't mind staying open an extra half hour or so for me. I could tip you a $5.00 bill maybe. Just do your magic."

Exercising restraint as she shampooed and styled Stormy's hair, Vonnetta was perplexed as she studied Stormy's clothing combination, but wasn't about to make any sort of comment. It was Friday afternoon, and it had been a very long week. Vonnetta wanted to go home and soak her tired feet.

Staying true to her self-absorbed self, Stormy exclaimed, "I'm just so excited for this party tonight. Why, there's no telling who I'll meet. Just think of all of the important people who are going to be there. It's going to be my big chance! Vonnetta, you're sure quiet today. Are you having a bad day? I didn't think hairdressers ever had anything go wrong. How tough can it be to simply cut and curl hair all day long? I guess if you really wanted to make some money you sure could've learned to do something else besides use a comb, brush, and pair of scissors."

"Here's the hand mirror, Stormy. Take a look at the back of your hair and let me know if it meets with your approval."

Holding the mirror in her right hand, Stormy stood up, and walked backwards a few steps so she could be closer to the wall mirror. "Looks fabulous. I must say you have the perfect touch with hair stuff. The overall effect you have created is probably at least worth a $4.25 tip."

"Last of the big spenders."

"Pardon me, Vonnetta. I didn't quite hear you. Did you say something about suspenders?"

"Would you like to make another appointment?"

"Not right now. Let me see how tonight goes, and then I can call and schedule one if that's the way I want to proceed. Off to the big party!"

Vonnetta locked the beauty shop door behind Stormy. *It takes all kinds to make the world go around, and Stormy is going around on her own merry-go-round. I wonder when it will stop.*

Highly irritated that she needed to park four blocks from the Silver Jack Motel, Stormy chided herself for not changing shoes before she left the ranch house. There was no one standing behind the counter so she could check in for her overnight stay. Rory, a heavily-bearded young man with broad shoulders, finally sauntered down the stairs, pushed the right side of the swinging door open, and plopped down on the stool. "How can I help you, Miss?"

"I need a room for the night and make it your best one. You act like you've got all night, but I'm in quite a hurry. You're about as slow as trying to pour molasses in January."

Rory sharpened the pencil in the hand-held sharpener. The lead broke a couple of times, so he persisted until he'd achieved the length of lead at the top he desired. "January's gone. This is February." Turning around to reach for the small wooden box behind him, he continued, "What's your last name, so I can pull your registration card? You did make a reservation, didn't you?"

"Sabblonti is my last name, and no, I did not make a reservation. Since when do I need one in this jerk-water town for this second-rate joint?"

"Normally you wouldn't, but we've got big doin's here tonight. People came from far and wide for the Ignee County Rodeo Board shindig. We have people staying with us from

Blunte, Chrebine, Clarey, Shadow Butte, and Tranquility Falls counties. Hotel's never been this full in years. We even slapped an extra paint job on some of the rooms to spiff them up a bit. There's some hoity-toity elderly lady that's retiring or some story like that." Pulling out a drawer underneath the counter, Rory surveyed what looked like a small white board with names and numbers written with a black marker. "According to this chart, we have zero rooms available."

Reaching inside her hand-tooled leather wallet, Stormy plucked a $100 bill and laid it on the counter. "Here, this might give you some incentive to find one."

"You could try to bribe me with all of the money you might have, but it's not going to do you an ounce of good. I guess you could sleep in the hallway for free."

Just then, one of the hotel maids rounded the corner and slipped behind the front desk. "Apparently the spare room above the kitchen just got freed up. One of the cowboys scheduled to play in the band for tonight's dance couldn't make it for some reason. If someone else is in dire straits, I guess you could rent it out."

"I'll take it! I don't care what it rents for. There's nothing Sabblonti money cannot buy."

"Fine. It goes for $45.00 a night. How many nights do you want?"

"Just one. I need $55.00 back in change. Don't forget that."

Counting out the money and laying it on the counter in front of Stormy, Rory spotted her wedding ring. "That's some fancy rock you got there. Is it real or one of those fake jobs?"

"It's every bit as real as I'm standing here. What's the matter, haven't you ever seen expensive diamonds before in your whole life?"

Rory handed Stormy the tarnished key attached to a wooden key ring. "Checkout time is 11:00 o'clock tomorrow. Of course, you might well be out of here before then. Sleep tight, and don't let the bed bugs bite."

Stormy glanced down at her wristwatch which read straight up 6:00. That would give her only one hour to carry everything to her room, refresh herself, and get to the Ignee Grange Hall by 7:00. Oh well, she'd been in tight places before and managed just fine. She was confident this would be no exception.

Carrying as much as she could in both arms on the first trip, Stormy set her suitcase and accessories down in the hallway. She stuck the key inside the slot, turned it to the right, and nothing happened. Turning it to the left proved to be no different. *Maybe that clown didn't give me the correct key.*

Hurrying back down the hallway and the flight of stairs, Stormy found no one behind the counter on the first floor of the motel. Rory returned a few minutes later. "Can I help you with something else?"

"Here's that blasted key you gave me. It must be the wrong one because I can't get the door open."

"Look on the back of it. Does it have *AK* scratched on it? If so, that's the one for the room above the kitchen. You know, *Above Kitchen.*"

Turning the key over, Stormy saw that it matched the description provided by the clerk. "Yes, I see the *AK*, but there's no way this key works in that lock."

"Hand it over, and follow me up to that room. I'll prove to you that it does work."

Rory lumbered up the flight of stairs, turned to his right, walked down the hallway, inserted the key into the lock, and the door opened immediately.

"When I tried it, I couldn't get it open. I did exactly the same thing you did, but it wouldn't open for me. What will I do if I can't get the door open when I return later tonight?"

"If you're here by 10:00 o'clock it's no problem as I'm still on shift. After that, you're on your own."

Stormy carried her suitcase and accessories inside the room and set them on the bay window overlooking the alley. She pulled the dusty drapes closed. "I can't believe they rent this place for $45.00 a night. When's the last time someone cleaned in here? It gives me the creeps." She walked over to the twin bed and sat in the middle of it which caused the mattress to sag in the middle. A picture of Chet lying in his hospital bed flashed through Stormy's mind. *I would have driven home later tonight instead of staying in this rat hole, but I just don't want to risk it until I learn the nighttime road a little bit better.*

With about twenty minutes to pull herself together, Stormy opened her suitcase and dug through her belongings to find the off-white colored, cashmere sweater. Not finding it, she looked through her large bag of accessories. "You've got to be kidding me! I can't believe I left that at home." When she looked for her western dress boots, she couldn't locate those either.

There was no full-length mirror to be had, and the only resemblance of any kind of a mirror to apply her makeup was a rusted, splintered one mounted above the orangish-brown stained wash basin in the bathroom. Stormy pulled the end of the chain to turn the light bulb on so she could see herself in the mirror. Either the light switch didn't work or the bulb was burned out. Just as she was ready to depart for the big event, she realized she'd left her full-length fur coat at home as well.

Approaching the hotel counter one more time, Stormy asked, "Say, can you give me directions to the local Grange Hall?"

Rory directed, "It's nine blocks from here. On the southwest side of town. Can't miss it."

Stormy drove around for the next forty minutes trying to locate the building. "This is ridiculous. This town is not so big that I can't find some two-bit Grange Hall." The longer she drove, the more disoriented she became. She ended up on the main highway back to Ridgemonte. Turning around, she followed a pickup back into Cinder Valley. She determined if she couldn't find the hall this time around, she would have to stop and ask someone for help. "Well, maybe the driver of this pickup knows where he's going. I'll just see if he ends up where I need to be."

The white Chevy Silverado made several trips around the Grange Hall as there was no space close by to park. This was obviously the place to be this Friday night. Stormy had to park about ¼ mile away and walk to the Grange Hall. She could not move very fast in the uncomfortable shoes she was wearing. The event started almost an hour ago. She certainly never expected a crowd this size to be in attendance.

Stormy struggled to open the overly large, heavy, wooden front door. She stepped five feet inside and instantly froze. Everyone was seated at eight-foot circular tables draped with horse-themed, western tablecloths. The tables were placed so close together there was barely enough room to walk between them. Scanning the room, she didn't recognize one person. The master of ceremonies presented Gwen Hybrenth with a large engraved plaque and posed for pictures for the local paper, *The Cinder Valley Scoop*. The man hurriedly entering the hall right before Stormy was the newspaper reporter. Since there were no empty chairs available, she walked a few steps to her left and stood against the wall.

Gwen gave her retirement speech which droned on for the next twenty minutes followed by a standing ovation. She motioned for the master of ceremonies to come to the podium and whispered something in his ear after which she took her seat.

The emcee asked, "Would someone kindly locate a folding chair for the young lady standing against the back wall? Thank you."

An older gentleman looked in the anteroom next to the kitchen, but couldn't locate an extra chair, so he offered his to Stormy who politely declined.

The dinner portion and program of the evening were obviously finished as people got up from their chairs and started milling around. Stormy started to walk to the door when someone called out, "Young lady, you just got here. What's your hurry to leave?"

Blushing bright red, Stormy explained, "I had all sorts of

interruptions before I could get here tonight, and didn't realize that the dinner and program would be over so quickly."

"That's not a problem. We plow right through the groceries when they're served. No horsing around on this rodeo board. Let me introduce you to some people here along with our honored guest, Gwen. She was the first Ignee County Rodeo Queen way back when. Oh, by the way, I'm Trent Davies. I'm on the rodeo board along with several other guys. Follow me to the front of the room. What's your name? Are you from around here?"

"I'm Stormy Sabblonti Castins. We own the largest cattle spread in all of this part of the state. I'm sure you've already heard of my family."

"So, is it the Sabblontis or the Castins that own the large spread? Can't say as I've ever heard of the Castins outfit. Sabblonti sounds very familiar though. Was your dad's name Ace by any chance?"

"Yes, Ace Sabblonti was my father. He passed away a few years ago, and my mother just recently died."

"Sorry to hear that. Please accept my sincerest sympathies or however you're supposed to say that."

Was it Stormy's imagination or was everyone staring at her? She wanted to shout, "Take a picture! It will last longer."

"Gwen, this is Stormy Sabblonti Castins. Being as how it's your last night with us on the board, I'm trying to round everybody up, so they can shake your hand and sign their name in your fancy lavender and gold foiled guest book."

"Thanks, Trent." Gwen made no effort to shake hands with Stormy as she scrutinized every square inch of her. She covered her mouth as she tried to keep from laughing uproariously. "Quite the outfit you're modeling tonight. You look like a walking Christmas tree. Your clothing combo doesn't quite match your wedding ring, unless of course the setting is made of cubic zirconium. Come to think of it, I used to have some vintage clothing like that from the 1950's. Opals bring bad luck in case you didn't already know. I make a practice to never wear them. Trent said your name is Stormy. Very unusual name. I'm familiar with the last name Sabblonti, but not Castins. Did your mother die recently? One of my relatives works for Lambents, and it seems like he mentioned a Sabblonti funeral not that long ago."

"It's nice to meet you, Gwen. Yes, Mother passed away Christmas Eve. Lambents were in charge of the funeral service."

"If you'll excuse me, I need to talk with another one of the rodeo board members before he gives me the slip for the night."

Trent walked up behind Stormy. "Ready to meet a few more folks? All the big Kahuna rodeo people from far and wide are here tonight. I want to introduce you to the chairman of the Ignee County rodeo board, Carson Tayer." Stormy made her way through the crowd following Trent to the back corner of the building.

"Carson, I'd like you to meet Stormy Castins. You remember ol' Ace Sabblonti, don't you? Well, he was Stormy's dad."

The light above Carson's cowboy hat reflected Stormy's five carat wedding ring as he enthusiastically shook hands with her. "Why, Stormy, what a pleasure it is to meet you! We're so happy to have you join us for this grand celebration. It's not very often that we have an event as big and broad as this one. We ran completely out of barbequed beef. Can you imagine such a thing? With all the critters running around here, you'd think beef is the last thing we'd run short of."

"It's nice to meet you, Carson. I was running late so didn't get to taste the beef. I'm sure it was delicious."

Carson's head was spinning like a top as he was trying to connect the dots of the various Sabblonti family members. "Who's running the ranch now that both of your parents have passed on? That's an awfully big spread if memory serves me correctly."

"My husband, Chet Castins, was overseeing things until his bad auto accident about a month ago. I've hired a new professional ranch foreman until Chet can get back on his feet again."

"Sorry to hear about Chet's misfortune. Hopefully he heals quickly. Spring is fast approaching which requires lots of time in the saddle. Were you a rodeo queen in your day, too? I always wanted a daughter who could be crowned the Ignee County Rodeo Queen, but my wife and I have sons, so that never happened."

"No, I was never an official rodeo queen. I do have vast ranching and rodeo reserves, however. My husband is a real horse lover and used to work at a race track before we were married."

Trent interrupted Carson for a brief moment, "Could I have just two short minutes of your time?"

"Stay right here, Stormy. I'll be back before you can blink."

Carson joined Trent at another table. Trent leaned into him and spoke something to him in a muffled tone of voice. Carson nodded his head up and down.

In Stormy's mind, she'd never seen such a bunch of country hicks holed up all in one place at one time. As soon as Carson returned, she promptly thanked him, left the building, and drove back to the motel.

Checking the time, Stormy noted that it was not yet 10:00 in case she needed help unlocking the motel room door. She slid the key in the lock, turned it to the right, and it opened on the first try. Closing the door behind her, she peeled off both shoes and threw them against the wall. Three hours passed as she tossed and turned in the bed. It seemed as though she had just fallen asleep when she heard the clanging of cookware and loud country western music being played on the radio. Not having done a whole lot of cooking in her adult life, Stormy was uncertain as to what that particular smell was. Maybe it was burning grease. She felt like she was going to throw up if she didn't get out of the room as fast as she possibly could. Shoving her belongings into her suitcase and accessory bag, she bounded down the stairs and laid the key on the front counter. This was a night to forget!

CHAPTER TWENTY

Priscilla Fletcher and her mother, Francie, had worked all Saturday morning and afternoon in preparation for their supper guests. Nothing would do, but Francie insisted that the red tablecloth and matching red and white, heart-shaped napkins be ironed and folded just right. "I can remember when your father and I were courting and the first night he came to eat with our family. It seems like only yesterday. My heart longs for him more every day now that he's gone." Priscilla set the forks down on the table and gave her mother a hug. "Every child should be as loved and cared for as I was. Thank you."

Francie wiped a tear from her left eye with the edge of her red checkered apron. "I was just thinking that I wanted to nickname you *Prissy* the day we brought you home from the hospital, but your father wouldn't hear of it. Now that you're an adult, I'll have to admit that Priscilla sounds a whole lot better than Prissy! Did you check that shortcake in the oven? If we over bake it, we'll be serving bricks. No amount of whipping cream and plum berry jelly will sell it."

Glancing at the kitchen timer, Priscilla commented, "I thought it smelled close to being done. I'll get a toothpick and check the center of it."

"It's best if it's still a little moist in the middle. It will finish setting up after it's placed on the cooling rack. That arm roast I purchased from The Shadowy Merc cost me a small fortune. It was $2.65 a pound! It would be so nice to have a steady supply of meat from somewhere. Then we wouldn't have to schedule three meatless meals a week. Oh well, we haven't missed any servings yet. I can still fit into my wedding dress from all those years ago."

Priscilla had determined long ago that she was going to wear her own wedding dress someday. "It would sure be nice to have some fresh flowers for the center of our kitchen table. I guess we'll just have to use those plastic roses in the vase sitting on the coffee table in the den. Say, we could add some food coloring to a little water in the vase for the plastic flowers and colored water effect."

Francie poured a little wood polish onto the cloth in her left hand and crawled underneath the table to apply some to the individual legs. She instructed, "I think it's best to wipe the outside of the vase to make sure it's clean and set it on the kitchen table. Most men folk don't even notice things like that. They pay far more attention to what's inside the serving dishes."

With the meal preparation completed, Priscilla devoted extra time and attention to her personal appearance. She tried on several clothing combinations, but none of them seemed to strike her fancy. She took the footstool by the side of her bed and set it next to her closet. Standing on her tiptoes, she pulled a see-through plastic, zippered garment bag down to eye level. *Now, here's an idea. Let me see if I like the way I look in this get-up.*

Priscilla unzipped the bag and turned the sweater right side out. She pulled it over her head, but could not zip it up in the back as the zipper was quite short, so she enlisted her mother's help. Looking in the hallway mirror, she frowned as the sweater was a bit tighter fitting than she was used to wearing.

"I don't think I've ever seen you wear that before. It sort of looks like one of those pink and white coconut and marshmallow covered cakes with the creamy fillings. I'd not remembered those rabbit foot looking things tied together off to the side of the neck of the sweater. Whoever designed this certainly had an imagination and then some."

Pretending she was a ballerina dancing in the middle of the floor, Priscilla announced, "I'm in the mood to wear something different, so this will fit the bill. Shall I go with jeans or a skirt?"

"Heavens, Priscilla, with all of the work we've put into this project you're not going to ruin it by wearing jeans! A pink or red skirt would look lovely."

"I think I'll wear that red linen skirt with the French godet in the back that you made for me a few years back. You know, the one where you had to take the pattern to the home economics teacher at the high school to ask her how to cut out and sew the godet. I'd never heard of such a thing, but it sure looks snazzy when a girl walks into the room. If I wear my pink boots, it will really be over the top. Maybe I'll wear a pink ribbon in my hair, too."

Francie advised, "You'll look older if you leave the ribbon in your hair accessory box."

"You're right, Mother."

The doorbell rang at 7:00 on the dot. As soon as Priscilla opened the front door, Miggy jumped from Spence's arms and tried to jump into hers. "You're a wild little girl tonight, aren't you? All of the food smells are probably driving you crazy! Spence, please come in. We've been waiting for you and Miggy all day."

Spence removed his hat and smoothed his hair. "Good evening, Priscilla. It's so nice to see you. You're right. Supper smells so good. I have one more thing to get from my pickup. Back in a flash."

Standing on the porch, Spence rang the doorbell a second time. Priscilla carried Miggy in her arms like a baby as she walked toward the front door. "Spence, you're so silly. It isn't necessary to ring the doorbell again. Just come in. Can I hang your coat up and take your hat?"

"Sure. Please lay my hat with the top down. And these are for you."

Priscilla was concentrating on positioning Spence's cowboy hat correctly. With her back still turned to him, she asked, "What's for me?" When she faced him, she let out a loud squeal. "These are so beautiful! Where did you get such gorgeous, fresh, pink roses this time of year?"

"I have my connections. I hope you like them. They're

sort of an early Valentine's gift, too."

"This solves the predicament for our kitchen table. If you'll take a seat in the living room, I'll be in there in a couple of minutes to join you."

Priscilla hurried into the kitchen and replaced the plastic red roses with the fresh pink ones. "Those really light up my world."

Francie was covering the shortcake with extra whipping cream. "Priscilla," she whispered, "you turned the oven off, but forgot to remove the shortcake. I think it'll be okay. We'll just have to act like everything is hunky-dory."

"Sorry, Mother. Speaking of hunky, there's a real hunk with a low baritone voice sitting in our living room. Did you see these flowers Spence brought us?"

"Honey, he didn't bring them to us. He brought them to you."

Priscilla motioned for her mother to step forward. "Come and meet Spence. Then you can go back into the kitchen and finish what you were doing."

Francie wiped her hands on her apron as she entered the living room. "Spence, it's nice to meet you."

"It's super to meet you, too, Francie."

Spence stopped short of commenting on the fact that Priscilla looked absolutely nothing like her mother, a tall, thin brunette with light brown eyes. She must have taken after her father's side of the family. His eyes darted around the room in search of a family picture, but there wasn't one.

Miggy followed Francie back into the kitchen and stood below her as she put the finishing touches on the dessert. "I just know you're waiting for some sweet morsels to fall to the floor. You can have the bone from the roast. That will be your special treat for the night."

Francie removed her apron, folded it, and placed it inside the second drawer beneath the kitchen counter. She surveyed the table one more time to make sure she'd not forgotten anything. She paused for a short while to listen to the laughter coming from the living room. She couldn't remember the last time she'd seen her daughter brimming with such joy, and wanted to be happy for her, but Spence was nothing like what Francie had pictured for her one and only daughter.

"Supper's ready, so please come into the kitchen. Spence, if you'd like to wash before we eat, there's a clean hand towel on the bathroom counter just down the hall, second room on your left."

Spence headed to the bathroom, flipped on the light switch and looked down at his hands. They looked plenty clean to him, but he washed them anyway. He returned and stood at the corner of the kitchen table. "Where would you like me to sit?"

Francie gestured with her left hand, "You can sit across from me. Priscilla, you can sit on the end. We always leave the chair empty at the head of the table where my husband used to sit. No one will ever take his place."

Looking across the table at the spread of home cooked food, Spence let his shoulders relax. "I feel so honored to be here. Thank you for inviting me into your home. It's so quiet here compared to that noisy bunkhouse where I'm living."

Spence reached for the large serving fork lying across the top of the meat platter.

"Just a moment, Spence," said Francie. "We say grace before we eat meals."

"Oh, pardon me. I completely forgot."

"Would you like to ask the blessing over our food, Spence?" asked Priscilla.

"I think I'll pass on that for now. Thank you."

Francie said a short prayer and passed the meat platter so Spence could take a serving. He wiped his hands on his jeans before grabbing hold of the dish. "Spence, we're keenly interested in you and your family history. Could you please enlighten us?"

Priscilla felt like swimmers were practicing for the butterfly stroke inside her stomach. Her appetite flew right out the kitchen window when Spence began to speak. Her first instinct was to demand that her mother allow Spence to eat his meal while it was hot. Her legs were too short to nudge her mother's feet under the table. Francie could tell that her daughter was sorely displeased because Spence had not even taken his first bite, but she persisted nonetheless.

"Francie, could you please get my vest from your coat closet? I brought something that I'd like to show you. It might help explain a few things to help put your mind at ease."

"Yes, I'd be happy to do that. Excuse me for a moment, please."

Priscilla stared down at her plate and pushed her food around with her fork until her mother returned. Spence sat still as a statue.

"Here you go, Spence."

Reaching inside the interior pocket of his black, fur-lined vest, Spence pulled out a small black and white photograph and handed it to Francie.

i

"Some kids know from the time they're five years old

that they want to be a mechanic, truck driver, baseball coach or whatever. Well, I knew from the first moment I stepped inside one of the cattle pens of the Omaha Stockyards when I was just a little shaver that the western lifestyle was where I wanted to be when I grew up.

"My grandfather, Preston, and my father, Wayne, worked at the stockyards until they went out of business. They would sort cattle, feed them, water them, and get ready for every day which was different. The trucks would be lined up for miles delivering animals. It was like Vegas in its heyday, except the reason Omaha never slept was for an entirely different reason than Vegas never sleeps.

"Now don't get the wrong idea here. I've never been to Vegas, but I've heard some rather interesting travel stories. The record of the most cattle sold in a single day in the Omaha market was set in October of 1955 when 42,817 cattle passed through the yards. Of course, that was before my time, but it still made a big impression on me when I figured it out years later. Can you just imagine that huge cattle operation is now an industrial park? It's really a sad deal.

"I only got to visit the stock yard a handful of times when I was growing up since my parents divorced when I was eight years old. My dad never had time for us. When he wasn't at the stock yard, he was at the local bar drinking beer and playing cards. When I was an adult, Mom told me that my dad could gamble away his entire monthly paycheck in one night. Mom and I went to stay with her sister, Maviss Living, in West Virginia. Mom remarried a guy who worked in the coal mines. He was very physically and verbally abusive to me which made it hard to fully concentrate on my studies.

"After I graduated from high school, my mother tried to talk me into enlisting in the Navy, but I wanted nothing to do with that. I'm a land person in every way, shape, and form. She and my Aunt Maviss told me I just needed to do something constructive with my life and be a good citizen which they knew that I would be. I really appreciated that they allowed me to figure out my own future and be my own man.

"A high school buddy of mine got the wild idea in the middle of July 1988 that we should head to the Lone Star State where everything's big. His uncle Frank owned a medium-sized cattle spread down in the southern part of the state. The timing was great because the cattle market had just started to turn around and seven bullish years followed. Frank just about lost his shirt with the ranch when the cattle trade plunged into a bear market. That was around '95. You savvy the bulls and bears routine, right?"

"I know what a bull is and also a bear, if that's what you mean," replied Francie. She shot some curious glances toward Priscilla who leaned back in her chair and folded her arms. Spence covered his mouth with his napkin and cleared his throat. Francie continued, "Speak on, Spence. You're the storyteller here tonight."

"We stayed on and helped Frank transition his ranch into a place for hunting leases. My lifetime dream just about died there. I got out in the nick of time. In my head and heart, I knew it was time to *head west young man.* So here I am. I started working for the Toppens Ranch a while back, and it's been a great fit for me. Someday I want to own a cattle ranch and be able to look out my kitchen window and see the baby calves kicking up their heels in the pasture followed by some little whippersnappers wearing their little cowboy hats and blue bibbed overalls. I better get back to eating my supper."

Priscilla offered to reheat Spence's food in the microwave, but he politely declined. She barely touched her food. Her mother seemed to be in another world.

Silence ensued except for Miggy's crawling beneath their feet in search of crumbs and scraps. Spence slipped her a nice thick chunk of meat under the table. Francie spotted the act which she deemed to be horribly uncouth. Animals were to be fed in their own dishes. She pondered how many years Spence had packed that photograph around with him or where he might have obtained it in the first place.

"My hat's off to the cooks tonight. That was some mighty tasty food. I especially like mashed potatoes and gravy.

They are some of my faves."

Francie suggested, "Speaking of tasty food, shall we retire to the living room so we can have dessert? I will plate it and Priscilla can serve us. Spence, would you like a cup of coffee or tea?"

"No, thanks. Just some dessert, please. I do like my sweets, so I might ask for an extra-large serving if you don't mind. Batching in that bunkhouse does not lend itself to much cooking other than the main course."

Francie had originally intended to use her nicest dessert plates, but since she was already skeptical of Spence, she opted for paper plates. She tried cutting into the shortbread, but her knife did not seem to want to cooperate. She grabbed the serrated-edged knife from the wooden block and had little success with that. For some reason, the cake seemed quite rubbery. Eventually, she was able to break a large chunk off and put it on the paper plate. Francie had eaten quite a bit of the roast, vegetables, and mashed potatoes with gravy along with fresh dinner rolls, so she was stuffed. Priscilla declined dessert as well.

"I've added some extra whipping cream," said Francie. "Enjoy. Say, before I forget about asking you, what's the capital of Nebraska?"

"Why, it's Omaha, of course! Everybody knows that." Spence tried to stick the dessert fork into the shortcake, but couldn't get it to stay. He gingerly slid some of the whipping cream to the side so that he could concentrate on just the shortcake. After several attempts, he placed the fork on the plate and set it on the coffee table. "I apologize for not eating the dessert. My eyes were bigger than my stomach."

Ten o'clock came and went. Miggy was curled up asleep on Priscilla's lap after having tried repeatedly to bite the pink and white rabbit foot looking tassels attached to the neck of her sweater.

"Well, ladies, I've kept you up quite late this evening. How can I thank you and return the favor?"

"You're welcome, Spence. Priscilla and I wouldn't mind having you join us again sometime for supper because there are always things around our house that we need help with. In fact, the gate in our back yard is broken and part of the fence is falling down. I could always call a repairman, but we would welcome the help."

"Not a problem. I'd be happy to assist you. We'll figure out a time." Spence asked for his hat and coat as he reached to take Miggy from Priscilla's arm.

"Good grief, you two, you act like that pup is a baby. It's got four legs. It needs to exercise them. Oh, before I forget, here's Miggy's doggy bag with the bone from the roast. I didn't want her eating it on my floors that took me all day Friday to clean."

Priscilla returned with Spence's hat in hand along with his winter muffler.

"Wait just a doggone minute! Did you make me a brand new one? This doesn't look exactly like the other one."

Priscilla beamed. "I decided to make this one a little fancier. Do you like the triangle pattern? I thought it looked very masculine, and I made it a little bit longer than the first one."

"Yes, the design looks mighty fine. Your handiwork is superb!" When Spence set Miggy on the floor so he could tie the muffler around his neck, she jumped up and tried to bite the ends.

"Oh, no you don't, you little scamp. I'm not about to lose another gift. Not on your life!"

"Good night, Francie. Good night, Priscilla."

Spence and Miggy walked through the threshold of the front door and onto the front porch. Spence turned around and winked at Priscilla. She winked back at him, walked inside, and leaned against the closed door.

"What did you think of tonight, Mother?"

"What did I think of Spence or the night all together?"

"Both."

"I will have to think on it. I'm trying not to make a rush to judgment. I don't know of a way to double check that whole Omaha story to find out if there's any truth to it. There's no telling where Spence actually got that picture. He could have just memorized a few numbers and incidents to tell a tall tale. The majority of the time, desperation leads to disastrous consequences. Something isn't always better than nothing. I couldn't believe that Spence didn't know that Lincoln is the capital city of Nebraska. For decades we didn't have much trouble with drifters in this area, but we're definitely living in a different time these days."

Placing her hands on her hips, Priscilla glared at her mother. "Just because Spence could not remember the correct city does not mean he wasn't telling us the whole truth. We must extend grace to him based upon his challenging childhood. I think you're trying to paint with too narrow of a brush on this project. Just because someone doesn't seem to come in the right package doesn't mean they're not the right person. Worry is a thief that steals from tomorrow before it ever gets here. By the way, have you ever thought of what you'd do if some kind widower started paying attention to you? Would you cut off your nose to spite your face?"

Francie could feel her temples starting to throb. "Don't worry about me. I'm old enough to take care of myself. Spence strikes me as one of those types of men who's always looking around the river's bend for a new adventure and will never really belong anywhere."

"Well, he could belong here, couldn't he?"

"He's a complete stranger to us, Priscilla."

"Mother, sometimes it takes a complete stranger to remind us of who we are."

Francie shook her head back and forth in frustration. "Priscilla, please understand that I'm much more cautious since I've learned that Lane has been prowling the streets of Ridgemonte. Can't he be arrested or ordered out of town or something like that? Where's he staying?"

"How should I know? He's living his life inside a bottle right now."

CHAPTER TWENTY-ONE

Daisy's Floral Shop was humming like a swarm of bees bright and early Monday morning. She'd called Catherine Harrison along with two other part-time employees to help make the special arrangements and deliveries later in the day.

"Girls, I have a special running this Valentine's Day. If anyone buys a dozen roses of any color, I'm adding a box of chocolates to go with them. Maybe that's why I've nearly sold out already. Either that or there are more bachelors in the county than I ever imagined."

Having warmed the inside of her silver Subaru for approximately fifteen minutes while the engine idled, Catherine lifted the hatchback and quickly loaded the first group of flowers for delivery. To save time and gas, she'd sketched out the addresses and attached the list to her small clipboard on the dashboard. "I'm so glad it's not blowing and snowing out there. That would make for one long day to say the least. You must have ordered this sunshine, Daisy."

"Like I have any control over the weather!"

Catherine parked in front of Mintner Medical Center. *I'm going inside to see if I can borrow a cart from the information desk. Some of these employees made out like bandits today.* She loaded the floral arrangements with accompanying gift-wrapped boxes of chocolates onto the cart and wheeled it inside. She didn't even have to stop a second time and ask for permission to make the individual deliveries as the young man at the desk nodded and said, "Deliver away. I don't suppose there are any for me?"

"All of these are for women. I double checked before I left Daisy's. Since when do men get flowers and candy on Cupid's holiday?"

Nurse Dawn Rowann was overseeing nurse's station number three when Catherine arrived. Standing to her feet and peering over the counter, she queried, "Any surprises in your load? I'll bet one of them is for Charge Nurse Joyce Stone. Her husband has a bouquet of roses delivered every Valentine's Day. You can bet the ranch on it."

"Hi, Dawn. These soft, velvety, light orange ones are for Joyce. I'm sorry there are none for you. Maybe Joyce will share her candy with you and the other nurses. This one with the oversized card attached is for Macey Meadows. Aren't those yellow roses gorgeous?"

"Yellow roses are my number one flower. Too bad they're not for me. Macey must be holding out on us. I don't think she's expecting anything."

"That's the nice thing about unexpected surprises. They can come in all sorts of shapes and sizes. I'd best be on my way as I have lots more cheer to spread around."

Dawn could tell from twenty feet away that Macey must have gotten into yet another discussion with Dr. Linke and he'd prevailed. "No need to say anything. King Linke, correct?"

"Unfortunately, yes. You know me all too well. Too bad he doesn't find some woman and get married. Maybe she could soften him and remove that crusty exterior. There's no one I know that would have him, however."

"Now, Macey, that's a bit harsh on a Monday. Is that any way to start our week at Mintner? I've got something that will brighten your day."

"Like what? I'm starting to think that I made the biggest mistake of my life coming to this country hospital. I should have listened to my mother, but I don't want to admit that she was right. She told me to cast my line in a bigger fish pond and move to the capital city. I didn't think I could land a job there, but now I know I could have done it. I completed my clinicals in a small community and didn't expand my horizons much beyond there. So, where's the bright spot? I don't see any flashing neon lights."

Dawn set the box of candy on the counter. "Let's dive in, shall we? How about you open them?"

"I could use a nice chewy, chocolate-covered caramel. I can taste it already. That's the pick-me-up I need."

Macey unwrapped the box, but didn't bother to read the fine print. "Sterling's Sensations. That's kind of a different name for a candy company. Well, at least it doesn't say Sterling's Sinsations."

Lifting the dark brown, corrugated paper from the top of the chocolates, which had the diagrams and descriptions on the reverse side, Macey set it to the side, and selected the one in the middle. Closing her eyes and biting into the center, she swished the confection inside her mouth. Suddenly, her cheeks puffed out as she motioned for Dawn to hand her a paper towel. Macey spit the candy into it. "That's gaggy whatever it's supposed to be. Where'd you get these anyway?"

"They were delivered with the other illumination in your day. Sorry, I should have given you these first, but I was really needing something sweet to boost my blood sugar."

"My, these are lovely! Where are they from? Was there a card?"

"The card is taped on the back of the vase. It's a good thing you returned to the nurse's station as soon as you did. Curiosity was getting the best of me. I just might have opened the card, read it, and taped it shut again."

"You wouldn't have! These are from Daisy's Floral Shop. I've never gotten flowers from there before. I talked to my parents over the weekend, and my daddy could tell I was getting pretty discouraged. He probably told my mom to order some flowers for me."

"Don't just stand there all day. Read it to me."

"First I have to finish reading it myself. Then I'll decide if I'm going to read it to you. Are you sure you don't have some patients to check on? I think I hear one of them calling your name."

Macey opened the card and frowned. "This really is some kind of a joke. You know how much I dislike horses! Dawn, are you pulling another fast one on me like that one not too long ago where you filled my car with balloons so I couldn't get inside? Prankster does not run in my bloodline."

"I'm not taking the blame for this one. Now read."

Macey ~~

Isn't he regal? Both of us are just biding our time to get better acquainted with you. I've located a saddle that's just your size. There's no need to be afraid as *Beau Cheval* has been gelded. I like to call him *Beau.* We're both as gentle as a mild country breeze on a glorious spring day. I hope you enjoy the candy and flowers. Happy Valentine's Day!

Dr. Ben Shaw

"Who's Dr. Ben Shaw?"

"He's the guy that came to pick Chet Castins up from the hospital the day he was discharged. You know, the one that wears those daffy looking hats. I could still see that hat in my mind for a week after he was in here. I have no idea what he would look like all decked out in his country finest."

"Oh, now I remember! He's the guy with the intriguing smile." Macey studied the photograph some more. "How would he know what size of a saddle I would need? Aren't they all the same?"

"There's one way to find out."

"I'm not interested in finding out. Doctor this, doctor that, I think I'll look elsewhere, thank you very much."

Shaking her finger at Macey, Dawn cautioned, "Don't be too hasty on this one, Macey. He might be one of those kinds that have high expectations, and you just might fit the bill."

"I don't have the time or energy for a relationship right now. Every day I go home so exhausted all I want to do is sleep. Sometimes I'm too tired to eat."

"Maybe you should have Dr. Linke do a routine exam and order blood work."

"Forget about it. I'm not that sick or wrung out."

"Maybe Dr. Shaw could examine you."

"Stop trying to play doctor, doctor. You only have *RN* after your name, remember?"

Dawn looked down at her badge and laughed. "You should at least thank Dr. Shaw for your roses and chocolates. He could have just as easily sent them to someone else."

"I don't even know how to contact him."

"I'm sure he's listed in the phone book. Most veterinarians are."

"Do you want to pen him a thank you note and I'll just sign it?" Macey asked.

"You'd give me that kind of liberty?"

"On second thought, no. I'll figure out some way to let him know how much I enjoyed getting the flowers, but not the candy. He probably thinks he has good taste in all things."

Dr. Diller was standing at the counter inside his office when he noticed Catherine struggling to open the front door. "Just a minute, I can get that for you. It looks like you have your hands full and then some."

"Thank you, Dr. Diller. Yes, I still have some more in my car if you would be so kind as to help me with opening the door."

"Only four arrangements this year? I have five female employees. I thought for sure they'd all get one. No one likes to feel left out."

When Molly saw the flowers Catherine had, she let out a big gasp from behind the counter. "He did remember! Just when I was thinking of giving him the boot, he starts to show some manners." She hand delivered the Valentine bouquets to her fellow workers.

Dr. Diller's ears perked up when he heard Molly say, "Sarita, there doesn't appear to be anything for you. I'm sorry. I'm sure Wyn was just busy and completely forgot."

"It's not a big deal, Molly. Just because a guy doesn't send flowers on Valentine's Day doesn't make him a loser. Wyn is very careful with his money which I appreciate. We have a lot of big expenses coming up this summer. The flowers in my bridal bouquet will be the important ones."

Catherine returned to the flower shop around 3:30 in the afternoon. "All deliveries have been completed, Daisy. I'm so thankful the roads were clear today. What's that you're working on? I've never seen one quite like it before."

Daisy adjusted the black plastic apron she was wearing.

"Do you remember that phone call I made to you a few weeks back when you were working in your alpine studio designing your greeting card line? The same lady that came into the shop that day ordered a dozen of these black and white roses. Some flowers give the illusion they are black because their blooms are purple or dark red, such as the Schwarzwalder Calla Lily, but if you want a truly black masculine looking one, you have to create it yourself. There are three basic methods you can use. I like the dipping one the best. The trick is you have to choose a flower with a fully opened bloom so the dye will be able to more easily coat each petal. That's why I used some of the older roses to make this special-order bouquet.

"I have an old bucket that I pour the liquid dye into so it's easier to dip each rose into the solution for a couple of seconds. Then you have to carefully shake off the excess color so the dye falls back into the bucket, rinse each of the roses under the faucet, and shake it to remove excess water and dye. I'm on rose number twelve now and am cutting it very close because they need to dry some more before she picks them up."

"You do beautiful work, Daisy. I hope you're charging enough for these. Do they come with the box of candy as well?"

"They sure do. I ended up with four extra boxes of chocolates, so please select one for yourself."

"Thanks. That will make James happy when I get home tonight."

"How many years have you been his valentine?"

"Twenty-four and counting. I think we'll go to Hawaii for our 25th wedding anniversary."

"Be my guest. I have no desire to go to some islands that sit on top of a ring of fire."

Daisy sat on the stool behind the counter in her shop and turned the sign to read *Closed.* She wasn't about to close up shop until the last of the special orders had been picked up.

Salina Bevvins didn't arrive until 5:45 p.m. "I sincerely apologize for making you wait. I was unpacking freight in the back of the store today, and it took me a lot longer than I anticipated. That arrangement turned out far better than I imagined. How much is the total?"

"$60.00 and it comes with your choice of a gift-wrapped box of chocolates. That's by far the most labor-intensive arrangement I've made all day."

Salina reached into her wallet and pulled out three $20 bills and laid them on the counter.

"Sorry, I forgot to add the tax. It's $63.90 with tax."

"Here's a five-dollar bill. The black won't rub off onto anything will it?"

"It shouldn't. Be careful. I have an extra-large, white, empty, plastic bucket that I could place the flowers inside while you make your delivery. You could set the bucket on the floorboard, and it should be fine. Here's your change of $1.10. Thanks for your business. Happy Valentine's Day."

"Let's see, I think I'll take this box with the solid red wrapping. Hope the candy's dandy. Thanks."

Prior to driving to the lower Sabblonti ranch house, Salina double checked the amount of gas in the pickup tank to avoid a disastrous repeat of her last trip. She arrived at 7:35. It took Evan a few minutes to answer her knock on the front door.

"Good evening, Evan. I hope you and Chet haven't eaten supper just quite yet. Here, these are for Chet. Can you please deliver them to him?"

"I'll do that. Flowers are not usually on the menu, but there's always a first."

"The box of goodies is for dessert. Just a minute, I need to run to the pickup and get the food."

Evan closed the door to prevent a draft coming in.

Chet turned the TV volume down. "Evan, is that Stormy coming to see me? Have her come into the living room. I'm sure she's been helping do the chores at the main ranch house, so she couldn't get down here until after dark."

"Chet, I'm sorry to say it's not Stormy who knocked on the door."

"Rats! Is that who I think it is?"

"Yes, it's who you think it is."

"Don't open the door again until I get back down the hall and safely into my bedroom."

Evan turned the lock on the inside of the front door. Salina stood outside holding the cardboard box in both arms. She eventually laid it on the front steps and started to walk back to her vehicle.

"Salina, we were busy in here for a few minutes. It's nice of you to bring supper all the way out here. That's special delivery with a capital *S*."

"You're quite welcome. Sorry I didn't get it cooked up for you. I had to work in the back of the mercantile today, so was unable to use the stove in the employee break room. It's just one of those pre-frozen turkey pot pies. I hope Chet doesn't mind that it's not beef just this one time. How's he doing?"

"He's coming along slowly."

"Please give him by best, and tell him that I miss him oh, so much!"

Evan smiled faintly. "Drive safely."

Salina waved with her right hand as she walked toward her Aunt June Slader's pickup.

Taking the cardboard box inside and unpacking the groceries, Evan placed the pot pie inside the freezer. He walked down the hall to find Chet sitting on the edge of his bed. "I'll never understand women."

"Join the club. Neither will I."

CHAPTER TWENTY-TWO

Contemplating paying Chet a long overdue visit, Stormy finished washing and rinsing the remainder of the dishes in the kitchen sink. She watched the last of the soap bubbles swirl around the bottom of the drain. *Is my life going down the drain as well?*

The telephone rang just as she started to walk up the steep flight of stairs to her bedroom. *Do I answer it or just let it ring off the hook? I think I'd better. It's probably that dolt Chet trying to reach me. By now he's sure to have realized he forgot to have my Valentine bouquet delivered to the house along with my syrupy-sweet Valentine card.*

"What do you need now?"

"Hello, this is Trent Davies. I'm not sure I have the correct number. Is this the Sabblonti residence, and if so, does Stormy happen to be around?"

Stormy feigned a cough, cleared her throat, and answered in a high-pitched voice, "Just a moment while I get her for you." She laid the receiver on the end table while she went back into the kitchen to get her cup of hot, lemon-ginger tea. Returning to the living room, she sat in the recliner. "This is Stormy Sabblonti. How may I help you?"

"Hi Stormy, this is Trent Davies from the Ignee County Rodeo Board. Do you remember me? We met at Gwen Hybrenth's retirement dinner."

"Why, yes, of course I remember you, Trent. How are things with you?"

"They're just fine. Before I continue with official

business, I need to inquire as to your husband's welfare and see if there's anything the board can do to help out."

"Chet's just fine. Thanks for asking. That's such a generous offer, but we don't need a single thing. Remember, I told you that I'd hired a professional foreman, so things are ranching right along. I manage everything and everyone but the cattle and horses, so there are no worries, thankfully."

Trent kicked his boots off, placed his stocking feet on the desk, and fully launched, "That's great news! This might not work with your schedule since you're so busy, but the next meeting of the Ignee County Rodeo Board is scheduled for Friday, March 3rd, at 6:00 p.m. at the Grange Hall in Cinder Valley. I don't know if you'd already heard about our big blowout event scheduled for Saturday, July 29th, but it will be the 75th celebration of the Ignee Rodeo & Roundup. We want to make it the best ever. To that end, we're hand picking one representative from each of the counties from these parts, so that would be Blunte, Chrebine, Clarey, Ignee, Shadow Butte, and Tranquility Falls counties. You, of course, are our number one choice to represent Shadow Butte County.

"I realize this is a lot to lay on you all at once, so please feel free to take some time and think about it. I'm sure you're devoting a lot of time to your injured husband to help him get healed quickly. One of my fellow board members, Stanley Elson, just dreamed up this idea of the reps from each county a few days ago, so we've got to throw it into overdrive and get someone selected from each area. I think it's beyond brilliant. You know what they say, 'Teamwork makes it happen.' We're hiring a professional rodeo announcer along with *The Tall Blues,* the hottest country western singers in these parts and some other first-rate acts for the big day."

Stormy had been taking notes on the back of a catalog. "Trent, I'd be honored to represent Shadow Butte County, and it's only befitting that I should since the Sabblonti Ranch is the premier one in this area. Truth be told, it's probably the largest in the entire state. It's certainly a showpiece. I don't have anything else planned for July 29th. I can clear my busy schedule to attend all of your upcoming meetings. Is there anything in particular that you'd like me to bring to the March 3rd meeting?"

"Just your charming self. Oh, come to think of it, you might bring your calendar along, too. Sounds good, and I will count you in. On behalf of the Ignee County Rodeo Board, welcome aboard! Have a nice day, and take good care of that husband of yours. Good cattlemen are hard to come by or so they tell me."

"Thank you, Trent."

Stormy carefully set the phone receiver inside the cradle as she finished sipping her herbal tea. She walked into the kitchen, got the telephone book from the drawer, and placed the call.

"Silver Jack Motel, need a reservation?"

"I most certainly do, and there's no way you're going to fob that room above the kitchen off on me again. This is Stormy Sabblonti and I want your best room for the evening of March 3rd."

"The grand champion room has a king size bed and rents for the high dollah price of $175.00 per night. And that's just one night."

"I only need it for one night, and I don't care how much it costs. There's nothing Sabblonti money cannot buy."

S

Meg calculated this would be as good a time as any to make her request known to Stormy. Grabbing her green, columnar, accounting sheet pad in her left-hand listing all of her extravagant dollar amounts along with her mechanical pencil, she descended down the steep staircase. "Sorry to bother you on such a busy personal business morning, Stormy, but I need to run something past you. On your next trip to Ridgemonte, can you please stop at Cattlemen's Central and transfer a large amount of money into the operating account? I've listed the various expenditures in these columns on the green sheets here if you would like to take a look at them. It seems there have been a lot of expenses of late for repairs, feed, vet bills, supplies, and not to mention all of Chet's medical bills."

"I don't plan on driving to Ridgemonte anytime soon. The longer I live, I despise that town even more. I'll call the bank and have them transfer the money into the operating account. How much do you need?"

Meg held the pad about a foot in front of her and glanced down, "It looks like $260,000 should cover it for now. I just thought it would be much simpler for you to take care of it. I could drive in there and make the request. I also thought about calling, but since I'm so new on the job, it's a lot of money to be transferring all at once. I'm going to walk down and collect the mail from the mailbox now. Thanks for your help."

Sorely displeased at having to be bothered with busywork, Stormy contacted the bank.

"Cattlemen's Central, Chara Tankton speaking, how may I help you?"

"Hi Chara, this is Stormy Sabblonti. I'm super busy and don't have time to drive into town. Can I speak with either Lonnie Browne or Stewart Sanders to get some money transferred to one of my accounts?"

"Sure, Stormy, whatever you need. Mr. Sanders isn't here right now, but Lonnie can help you. Just a moment, please."

Lonnie cradled the phone between his shoulder and the left side of his face as he added figures on his calculator pertaining to the processing of a loan for a local company. "Hello, Stormy, this is Lonnie. I understand you would like me to transfer some money for you today?"

"Yes, I need $260,000 transferred into the operating account."

"Just a moment please while I get into your accounts so I can see what we're looking at for current balances and so forth. There's been quite a bit of check writing activity on the household account and miscellaneous account, so there's not that much in there. Since Jantzi passed away, there have been no deposits made directly into the CC Account, which is of course for your husband, Chet. Speaking of whom, how's he doing anyway?"

Stormy continued to draw hearts on her tablet and pen Chet's name in the middle of them. "Chet's doing just fine. I've been so busy finishing up other odds and ends after Mother's death that I meet myself coming and going."

"I can only imagine how hard it's been. Back to your bank accounts, there's some in the general account, the three savings accounts, and the five interest-bearing certificates of deposit. I can transfer a total of $260,000 from all of those accounts if you'd like and deposit it into the operating account. You must have had a lot of big expenses all at once."

Cutting the pink paper hearts with her fancy scissors, Stormy replied, "Yes, according to Meg we have. I think Chet bought some bulls late last fall before Mother died and the invoices are just now coming in along with the continual need for feed, supplies, repairs, his doctor bills, and the list goes on. I've had to hire extra help here at the ranch, too. Thankfully, I have a great foreman."

Lonnie continued to enter figures on his keypad. "I'm happy to hear that your new foreman is working out well for you. I'll send you a copy of the various withdrawals and deposits pertaining to all of the accounts, so you'll have those for your year-end records. Is there anything else that we can help you with today?"

"No, Lonnie, you've wasted enough of my valuable time."

"If Cattlemen's Central can be of further assistance, please let us know."

Stormy let the phone dangle over the side of her chair.

"I'll hang it up later."

S

Evan helped Chet get inside the passenger side of the van. "I made your appointment for 1:30 so we wouldn't be rushed this morning and would have ample time to drive into town. It will be good to get your current medical evaluation. It's only been seven weeks since your accident, and you're probably looking at about nineteen total for recovery."

Chet's chin dropped to his chest. "You could've talked all day and not laid that on me. That puts it about the middle of May. Pretty much wastes a half a year."

"Try not to get discouraged. That's why it's very important to follow the regimen the doctor prescribes for you. I think you're doing quite well actually."

"Thanks, Evan. I hope to be able to return the favor to you someday. I realize you're getting paid in dollars, but you're tailor made for what you've chosen to do with your life."

Parking on the south side of the Evergreene Medical Clinic to take advantage of the sun-soaked concrete, Evan walked around to the passenger side to open the door and hand Chet's crutches to him. "It doesn't feel like there's any ice on the sidewalk, and I don't see any, but just take it slow and easy."

Chet sat down in the oversized chair in the waiting room and rested his crutches between his legs. The past seven weeks seemed liked seven years. He didn't hear his name called by the nurse. Evan wondered if Chet had started to slip into a depression as he wasn't eating much.

Dr. Den Merenspinn entered the examining room. His hair was completely white, but his eyebrows were still black. It looked like he'd used a curling iron on the front locks of his hair. The remainder was combed straight back and cropped close to his head. His slender, oval face made him look taller than he was. The tip of his Roman nose was redder than normal this morning. Evan viewed him as quite intense and a bit on the serious side. He spent extra time with Chet during his examination. When he excused himself from the room, Evan followed him into the hallway. "I need a couple of minutes with you in your office, Doctor."

"Evan, what's your concern?"

"Chet's lost ten pounds. I'm living down at the lower ranch house with him until he can get around better. The infection that set in after he was discharged from the hospital didn't help much. He's compliant with his brief exercises, but doesn't communicate often. I thought I would just express my concerns which may not be justifiable at all."

"Does he have good emotional support at home, and are his meals nutritious?"

"Therein lies the major problem. I've yet to see his wife, Stormy, in all the time I've been there, and the ranching community doesn't seem overly supportive. Granted, it's the dead of winter when folks have a tendency to hole up more. I'm not much of a cook, so we've been eating canned foods, TV dinners, and an occasional meal that's been delivered. Some days he's steadier on his feet than others, and I've not felt he should be totally staying by himself, especially in that remote of an area."

"Stormy's not one of my patients, so I can't address that issue. Hopefully she'll come to her senses sooner than later."

Dr. Merenspinn and Evan returned to exam room No. 5. "Chet, I'm going to prescribe some increased range of motion, balance, muscle strengthening, and circulation exercises for you. Evan can help you with all of them as there needs to be a balance when working on the knee, ankle, and hip areas. Also, I want you taking extra iron and calcium. You can get those at the Ridgemonte Rx.

"Your right leg still seems weak. By the time of your next visit, you should be able to transition from crutches to a cane. When we get to that point, the cane will go in the hand opposite the injured leg since it moves in tandem with it. That's why it's so very important to balance the amount of stress that you are putting on that leg, too. Again, Evan will be able to assist you with all of that when the time is right. You're fortunate that he can be with you around the clock. Not everyone can afford that luxury.

"Continue with the massages to help reduce the scar adhesions and improve the mobility around that particular area. Just think of the stories you can spin to your kids about that scar and how you got it. So, I think that's about it for now. You've been awfully quiet today. I realize these major setbacks can take quite a toll on someone. Do you have any questions or concerns, and there are no steps to go up or down at home, correct?"

Chet peered intently into Dr. Merenspinn's serious, brown eyes. "There are just two steps to get onto the front porch from the front yard. If I take my time, I manage fine with those. I haven't been out of the house much since it's been so cold. The main question I have for you is when can I return to my normal busy ranch duties and get back in the saddle again?"

Furrowing his brow while tilting his head slightly downward, Dr. Merenspinn placed his right hand on Chet's left shoulder. "It's vital to get your leg fully healed before you even think of returning to your normal rigorous ranching routine. Think of it this way. That ranch is going to be around for centuries. It isn't going anywhere. If you even entertain the thought of trying to get on a horse or lift hay bales or anything of the sort before you're fully healed, you're going to be out of commission for probably another year or more. Stop by the grocery store and buy some healthy food to go with all of those T-bones and Rib-eyes you've got in your well-stocked freezer. Shop around the inside perimeter of the store where they sell the fresh produce. Avoid the center aisles with all the cans full of sodium and preservatives. See you in three weeks." Gently patting Chet's shoulder twice more, Dr. Merenspinn left the room.

After making Chet's next appointment, Evan helped him inside the front seat of the van. "I'll stop by the drug store really quick and get those supplements and leave the motor running, so it's nice and toasty in here for you. Do you have an account at The Shadowy Merc that I can get some groceries as suggested by Dr. Merenspinn? If not, I can write a check, and you can reimburse me. Help me think of some high calorie food. Enjoy it while you can. You're fortunate that you've got some height to you. Do you like cheeses, ice cream, and ranch dressing? I'll get some sour cream, butter, and bacon to go with spuds. I know how to bake those in the oven. They've got those Western Sidekick brand, frozen, cherry pies. We could try one of those, so we could have pie a la mode. I'll get a bunch of fresh veggies to go in salads. It can't be that hard to make a salad. I could even boil some eggs, cut them up, and put them in your salad. Are there any veggies or fruits you really don't like to eat?"

"Beets and bananas. That's about it. Keep that up and my appetite just might return pretty quick."

Evan reminded himself that he did need to start eating more salads with less dressing. He'd won the fraternity weight lifting contest during his collegiate years. When his roommate needed help loading an old refrigerator into the back of his pickup, Evan just muckled onto the bottom of it and hoisted it in. During his recent family reunion in Michigan, one of his uncles quipped, "Still have that Briarley build along with that 'toehead' look to you plus the big dimple in your chin, so I guess we can still claim you along with the rest of the clan."

The western magazine selection inside the Ridgemonte Rx was pretty marginal, but Evan selected two that he thought might interest Chet. He pulled into the parking lot of The Shadowy Merc, rolled down the windshield on Chet's side about two inches, and covered him with a blanket that he had in the back seat. "I'll be back before you know it. Time for this PT to fly low around that store."

When Evan returned with the cart mounded over with grocery sacks and small boxes, Chet's head was tilted to his left as he snored softly. Evan opened the side door and placed the supplies across the back seat and onto the floorboard.

"Chet, old boy, I deserve a leather medal for that one! I can still feel my heart thumping. I ran around that store like a race horse. I think you'll be really proud of my efforts. We'll eat like kings for the next three weeks."

"Were you able to shop by yourself or did the grocery clerk pull the cart in front of you and help you shop?"

Evan adjusted the brown and white stocking cap on his head. "What are you talking about? I've never gone shopping when a clerk pulled the cart in front of me. Chet, I think your medication is giving you funny thoughts."

"Shortly before my accident, I stopped in there one day and Salina helped me by pulling the cart in front of me and placing items in the bottom."

"She did? I didn't see hide nor hair of her today. There was a real friendly blonde checker named Cannaleah that rung up the groceries. I put the receipt inside one of the boxes back there. In fact, she asked me if I wanted bags or boxes."

"Maybe the clerks have to swear to be that way once they get hired there," said Chet.

"Every clerk in every store is supposed to be accommodating. Let's head to your ranch house. I can already taste that chef's salad, decorated baked potato, and T-bone cooked medium-rare."

Chet rubbed his stomach with his right hand. "I like mine just barely pan seared to where you can still hear the steer bellering. Make that two baked spuds for me with all the trimmings. Evan, did you get did get a bottle of steak sauce and some creamy horseradish?"

"Chet, believe it or not, I did. We must be on the same wave length, whatever that's supposed to mean."

"Happy to hear I'm on someone's wave length."

S

Stormy drove to the lower ranch house. Carrying the paper cut-out hearts and the Bundt cake mix she'd baked for Chet onto the front porch, she turned the handle of the door only to discover that it was locked. Blue barked loudly. She felt her jean pockets which were empty as were those of her coat. She had also forgotten to transfer the set of extra keys from Jantzi Belle's pickup into her new red one. Chet used to keep an extra key underneath a large piece of obsidian on the northeast side of the house. When Stormy checked there, the key was gone. She walked to the front door and knocked on it several times. There was no answer. She tried the back door and couldn't raise anyone either.

The living room curtains were fully opened, so Stormy pressed her face against the window and cupped her hands around her eyes. She surveyed the room as best she could looking for clues as to where Chet might be. It was mid-afternoon. *Perhaps Chet and Evan were both taking a nap.* Blue was inside curled up on a small mat. "Too bad you can't open the door for me. Chet seems to think of endless ways to continue to wade through my money. I don't want to know how much that caretaker is charging him. Can't be that much. Those are below minimum wage jobs. Any wash-out can be a caretaker or physical therapist."

A glint of white caught her right eye just as Stormy was ready to walk back to her pickup. She pressed into the glass harder to try to determine what it was. "Who sends black flowers in a milky white vase to anybody? Why didn't I get any roses? I'll bet I know who those are from, and it's not that lame stand-in, Evan. I'm such a fool! Why did I waste my time baking something and driving down here? There's no telling where that cheater is. This is proof positive that I need to devote my time, energy, and resources elsewhere. I rest my case."

Stormy drove back to the main ranch house, waited a couple of hours, and called the lower ranch house. Evan answered.

"Hi there, Evan. This is Mrs. Chet Castins. Can I please talk to my handsome husband?"

"Why sure, Stormy. He's sitting right here. I'll hand the phone to him."

Chet's face brightened as Evan left the room. "Well, hello darlin'! So glad you called. It's great to hear your voice. It's been so long since I've seen you. I could sure use a big hug."

"Explain the flowers, Chet."

"Flowers, what flowers?"

Stormy tightly gripped the receiver. "The ones in the vase on the coffee table in your living room that you're probably looking at right now while you're talking to me. Evan give those to you?"

Chet leaned to his left to relieve some of the pressure from his right leg. "Stormy, I can explain. Evan hasn't collected the trash yet."

All Chet heard was a dial tone.

Stormy walked into the kitchen and removed the garbage can from under the kitchen sink. After mashing the paper hearts into the cake and watching the frosting ooze through her fingers, she threw it away.

CHAPTER TWENTY-THREE

Sarita sat with her back against her two bed pillows which she'd placed on the living room couch in her apartment. She'd not gotten out of bed until after 10:00 since it was the weekend. Having recently purchased a used cookbook and cast-iron fry pan at the *Second Time Around* during her lunch hour the previous Tuesday, she practiced making a chorizo, potato, and egg frittata. It had turned out very well, so her day was off to a good start. She'd also purchased a partial boxed set of *Sagebrush Susan's* note cards. Selecting her favorite calligraphy pen, she began to write:

Dear Aunt Jonsey,

Let me begin by saying thank you for the lovely sympathy card and kind words of encouragement. Since Stormy was in charge of Mother's funeral arrangements, I assumed she'd contacted you. Please accept my deepest apologies for not letting you know. You mentioned that you'd not heard from Aunt Jillian or any of her family members for the past five years. My relationship with Mother became very strained prior to her death, especially after my fiancé, Wyn Moreland, and I became engaged at Christmas. She highly disapproved of him and was not shy about letting everyone else know her opinion. Someday you'll have to enlighten me as to how you managed to stay so sweet during your lifetime. Mother and Jillian seemed to grow like tall, bitter trees from deep, sour roots during their years. You must take after Grammy Mabel Siddonz, one of the kindest people to ever inhabit the planet. When I was a young girl, I thought she was just like pure maple syrup!

Wyn and I plan to be married on Saturday, July 29th, at Tom and Merna Toppens' Ranch. Merna has gone to great lengths to create a lovely high desert mountain backyard complete with wildflowers, rock cress, evergreens, decorative rocks, a pine gazebo, and the like.

I'd be honored if you could be my matron of honor. I have such fond memories of when I lived with you and Uncle Kent after graduating from high school. I learned so much from working in your store, Jonsey's Novelties. Those road trips to the county fairs and art shows were so much fun! It seems like only yesterday. Where have eighteen years gone?

My second request pertains to your precious great-grandchildren. Wyn and I would love to have Lilac be our flower girl and Logan be our ring bearer. You mentioned in your card that your granddaughter, Donna Mae Novis, had moved recently, so I don't have her current address. Also, I need mailing addresses for extended family members if you have them.

My third request would be if Uncle Kent could walk me down the aisle. Silly me, it will be an aisle of sorts in Toppens' back yard. What I'm really asking is if he would give me into the care of my lifelong, beloved husband?

Tom and Merna have basically adopted Wyn as their son since their only son, Toby, drowned when he was very young. Wyn was recently promoted to ranch foreman and is really in his element. I only wish Daddy were still alive so he could meet Wyn. He would love Wyn as a son, just like Tom does.

Last weekend Wyn and I were able to go to Tranquility Falls and pick out the floor plan and colors for our new manufactured home. As soon as the ground thaws, Wyn and Spence, Toppens' assistant ranch foreman, will level the area and make the necessary preparations for placement of the home. I'm beyond excited for this new chapter in my life!

My special day will be here before we know it. I have a lot of planning still left to do. Stormy isn't the least bit interested in helping me, but some of my co-workers in Dr. Diller's office have been very supportive. Dr. Diller's wife, Anne-Marie, will be giving me a bridal shower before my wedding.

Back to Anne-Marie for a moment, she mentioned an old time custom that I would like to use for my wedding. My "something new" will be my wedding dress that Merna has so graciously offered to make along with my veil. One of my co-workers, Bonnie, is letting me borrow her white pearl necklace. For the "something blue", I don't have to look too far as I still have one blue eye to go with my brown one. Do you have something from your wedding to Uncle Kent in 1944 that would work for the "something old?"

I had a funny thought the other day. Do twins run in the Siddonz family? Your set, Quentin and Quinn, were already out of high school by the time I was born. Wouldn't it be something if Wyn and I eventually ended up with some of our own? It saddens my heart that Stormy has suffered three miscarriages. I hope that she and Chet can have some children soon and very soon, so the young cousins can make fond memories together.

Oh, my goodness! Before I completely forget to tell you, Chet was involved in a very bad accident on January 2nd. He rolled his pickup and ended up in the bottom of a ravine. He broke his right leg and is having quite a difficult time. Stormy did not bother to notify us when it happened. We finally found out from Spence. You know how Stormy is about things. I'm sure she has everyone jumping to her verbal commands as she controls the reins of The Sabblonti Empire now.

That's about all the news from my little spot of the world. Please let me know your thoughts on my special requests and say hello to the rest of the family for me.

Love always,
Sarita Marie Sabblonti
soon to be Moreland

S

Since Dr. Ben Shaw had slept overnight in the bed in the back room of his vet clinic, he decided to heat a breakfast burrito in the microwave before driving to his ranchette to tend to his animals. When he walked through the building to make sure all lights were off and the front door was secure, he spotted a large stack of mail sitting on the front counter. *That's odd. Jacobe rarely leaves for the weekend without processing, sorting, and pitching all this paper. Oh, I completely forgot. He asked for Friday off work to help his elderly widower neighbor move to a new apartment.*

The cuff of Dr. Shaw's coat caught the corner of the mail stack as he turned to walk to the back of the clinic. Several pieces fell onto the floor. When he reached down to pick them up, he saw what appeared to be a picture of a ship with long, black billows flowing from the smoke stacks on top. Addressing his border collie, Jetter, Dr. Shaw said, "Well, lookee here. Interesting postage stamp with the Titanic. What a horrible night that would have been! A typewritten addressed envelope sent to me? It's probably someone hitting me up for a donation. It's too late for that as I already gave to the Shadow Butte Burn-Out Fund and three other organizations."

The envelope crinkled as Dr. Shaw pressed it between his thumb and fingers. His inquiring mind got the best of him. Slitting the top of the envelope with Jacobe's personal letter opener, he pulled the card out which contained a small piece of brown corrugated paper. Dr. Shaw walked around the side of Jacobe's desk and sat down. Leaning forward in the chair, he began to read to Jetter.

Dr. Shaw,

The lovely yellow roses for Valentine's Day were such a thoughtful gesture. Thank you very much. The box of candy left a lot to be desired, however. They contained cream centers such as apricot, cherry, raspberry, maple and so forth covered with milk chocolate. I suppose they would be fine for someone who liked that variety.

Beau Cheval is certainly a beautiful horse. I will freely admit that he looks way too wild in his picture. Does he like to have his photo taken? How long have you owned him? Did you train him yourself? Is he a show horse? Has he always had those strange spots all over him?

How do you know what size of saddle I would require? That sort of statement is a bit intrusive if you ask me.

With our current daytime temperatures, it's hard to even think about a gentle country breeze on a splendid spring day.

Sincerely,

MM

Dr. Shaw folded the note and tucked the small corrugated insert inside. He placed both of them back inside the envelope, creased it in half, and shoved it in his coat pocket. "Who types up a thank you note anyway? I wonder if Macey did this herself. She does not appear so cold, dull, and uninterested in person as she comes across in her writing. How was I supposed to know what kind of candy was in the box? I have far more important things to concern myself with than that. Are all women this finicky or high maintenance? Dealing with animals that can't talk is far easier at times. Speaking of animals, I'd best head home and get them fed. I know they appreciate me. Come on, Jetter."

CHAPTER TWENTY-FOUR

Carson Tayer, Chairman of the Ignee County Rodeo Board, had asked fellow board member, Trent Davies, to be at the Ignee Grange Hall an hour before the regularly scheduled meeting on Friday evening, March 3rd.

Having arrived first, Trent had shoved two rectangular banquet tables together and placed eight chairs around the edges. He wiped the top of one of them clean with his green and black wild rag and shoved it in his back pocket. He turned the heat register on the wall to read 72 degrees.

Carson could smell the aroma of freshly-brewed coffee as soon as he entered the building. "Trent, no wonder we're broke. You've got every light in the joint on. Do you own stock in Parson's Power Company or what's your deal?"

"Jack down, Car, ol' buddy. You said you wanted everything set up by six, so I've been running around like a cut duck tryin' to get 'er done. You did bring that freshly-baked peach pie like you promised, didn't you? Guess I better get out the glass plates and coffee mugs without chips around the rims for our meeting since we're having company."

"Company? Are you holding out on me again?"

"No, just following orders. I'm sure countin' on everybody being on time because we've got a lot of ground to cover."

"Thanks, Trent. Feels pretty warm in here. Did you

forget to wear your thermal undershirt? We don't need anybody falling asleep on us. I'm sure you don't require my help, so I'm going to review my agenda a couple more times before we get started." Carson had forgotten his zippered briefcase in his pickup, so he went outside to get it. When he walked inside, he heard a loud crash coming from the kitchen.

"Now what have you done, Trent? Is this your first meeting or what? I've never seen you so out of sorts before. Those fine, white, glass chards are all over this cement floor. There's a shop vac in the back closet."

Carson shook his head back and forth in disgust. Returning to the table, he made some notes on his large tablet. Trent was making so much racket in the kitchen, he couldn't make sense of his own handwriting. *This night's getting off to a disastrous start. It can only improve from here on.*

Fellow board members, Stanley Elson, Dean Kendall, Mitch Bentz, Neil Rolan, and Al Gibson were all in attendance by ten minutes before seven and staked their places around the table. All seven men including Carson and Trent were huddled in the kitchen, so they did not hear their guest arrive since Trent had left the door ajar. Al was in the middle of telling a story about a sheepherder living inside his wagon with his sheep dog when Carson looked at his watch and asked him to cut it short so they could get on with their business.

Stormy entered the building at 7:00 sharp and sat down at the far end of the tables. Her mouth felt very dry inside and she could hear her stomach growling. She regretted not having eaten a snack prior to driving to the grange hall, but she didn't have a minute to spare after getting her hair styled at The Mane Event, checking into The Silver Jack Motel, and dressing to the nines for her first attendance.

The board members dutifully walked behind Carson as they filed into the meeting room. Trent rushed over to where Stormy was sitting. "So happy you were able to join us this evening. Let me know if I need to increase the heat. Do you know these fine gents? If not, I'm confident Carson will follow his usual routine of going around the table and giving each one two minutes to introduce themselves. By the way, pretty hat for a pretty woman. Red looks good on you."

"No, I don't know any of the men here this evening. Where are the representatives from the other counties that you've selected for the upcoming event?"

"Glad you asked. That's still a work in progress. It's been a busy few weeks. There's a lot more to organizing a big shindig than meets the casual eye. Can I get you a cup of coffee? Do you take anything in it or just blacker than the Ace of spades? We're having dessert later."

"Yes, a cup of coffee would be very nice, and no, I take it straight black. I can get it myself. Is it in the kitchen?"

"You sit tight since you're our guest this evening. I'm more than happy to wait on you."

Stormy smiled inwardly. Trent seemed so kind and servant-like. When he returned with a mug of piping hot coffee, she glanced at his left hand, and noticed that he didn't appear to be wearing a wedding band. Most ranchers and cattlemen that she knew didn't wear much jewelry, so not a lot of stock could be put into a casual glance. It did appeal to her that he was so accommodating and attentive. She made a mental note to inquire if there happened to be a Mrs. Trent Davies at the same time she noticed the top of his wild rag hanging from his rear pant pocket. She was sure she could help refine him. He just needed a little Stormy touch every now and then.

The remainder of the board members selected their seats. Stormy was shocked that none of them greeted her with a handshake and made a big to-do over her appearance which included her red hat; semi-sheer, long-sleeved, black blouse with glittery accents; red and black, ankle-length tartan, 100% pure virgin wool skirt; and fancy, black, dress boots. Perhaps Trent was the only one with any class after all.

Carson called the meeting to order. He welcomed Stormy and per his usual custom, had each board member say a few words about themselves. "Introduce yourself gents, right on. Let Stormy know a little about you." Carson had to cut the long-winded ones off and gently remind the others that he didn't want to end up burning the midnight oil.

In his brief remarks, Trent mentioned nothing about a spouse, children, ranch, or anything of the sort. He was the most ambiguous of the entire lot. Just what did he do for a living anyway?

As the meeting continued, Carson asked each of the men for updates regarding the various tasks to which they had been assigned for the 75th Annual Ignee Rodeo & Roundup. When it came time for Dean's report, he lamented the fact that the country western singing group, *The Tall Blues*, the rodeo clown, Caper Sadler, and the rodeo announcer, Cord Calhoun, were going to cost far more than had been previously budgeted. "I don't know who these characters think they are. They act like they've got the golden voices, comedy acts, and the monopoly on the announcer's market. Granted, we aimed for the top horse in each category, but their normal fees would choke seven horses. I told them we were meeting tonight and would get back to them right away."

Carson sneezed, removed his dark red bandana from his hip pocket, blew his nose which sounded like a goose honking, and shoved the bandana in his front shirt pocket, so the end of it dangled about three inches. "Dean, just lay the figures on us. You don't have to apologize for those clowns."

Mitch piped up, "Carson, for the record, there's only one clown." Belly laughs could be heard all around the table. Stormy even enjoyed that line.

After reaching inside his rust-colored vest pocket and taking out a small notebook, Dean droned on, "Okay, you asked for it, so here we go. Now, keep in mind, this is for just one Saturday night. It's a good thing that's all we planned on. Plus, we have to pay their hotel bills, and each of them has traveling fees in addition to their specialty performances and acts.

"*The Tall Blues'* standard rate is $7,500, Caper's caper is

$10,000, and Cord's announcing gig is $15,500. So, if we add just those three plus their expenses it's around 40 Grand. Maybe we should scale down from the national scene and just look in the lower southeastern part of the state, so we can go with somebody not quite so high dollar. It's only March, so we still have a little bit of time to round up some statewide suspects."

Neil chimed in, "Maybe we better bag the idea of the celebrity line up. I had no idea it was going to cost that much. I mean we still have to buy more portable corrals, install two new chutes and repair some of the other ones, paint that entire fence all the way around the rodeo grounds, and the list goes on. It was quite a jolt when Al and I went down there last week and put the heavy scope on the rodeo grounds. We've got to really spiff it up. It's in quite a state of disrepair to say the least. I vote we put the money into the essentials and stay within budget. Speaking of which, just what is our working budget anyhow?"

Treasurer Stanley Elson replied, "Since we've gone in the hole the past three years for the annual rodeo, according to our last bank statement we had $4,327.82." Stormy glanced to her left and saw that the rodeo board banked with Cattlemen's Central as did most everyone in the region.

"Do you balance that bank statement every month, Stan?" asked Mitch. "I mean, have all of the outstanding checks cleared from last year?"

"Yes, the statements are balanced every month, and we have no outstanding or uncleared checks. So, what you see is what you get. Not much, huh?"

Mitch continued, "I finally heard from Shade Rodeo Stock Company and they gave me a bid of $22,790. It will be another 6 G's if we want the top bulls for the bull riding event. That's what really draws the crowds from far and wide, so I'm really hoping we can swing that."

"Any other bomb shells or expenses?" asked Carson.

"The city and county increased their fees about 200%, so we're looking at around $3,980 for those," Stanley added.

A pin drop could have been heard in the room. Mitch

leaned forward, placed his elbows on the table, and rested his cheeks inside his palms. Dean removed his cowboy hat and set it on the table in front of him. Stormy looked down at her lap and straightened the fabric of her black tunic. She shifted in her metal folding chair and rubbed her lips together. Her usual nervous mannerism of twisting her left earring resumed. "Excuse me, can you point me to the restroom, please?"

Trent jumped to his feet. "At the back of the room, turn left, go down the hallway, and it's the first door on your right."

After Stormy was out of earshot, wide-eyed Carson asked, "Trent, did you remember to clean the can?"

"Sure did, Boss. It was one of the umpteen piddly things on my list. What'd you think I was doing between six and seven, filing my fingernails?"

Neil narrowed his eyes as he looked at Trent, "Just what was the big idea of inviting that Sabblonti woman here tonight? We can't even have an honest to goodness discussion about anything. We don't know her from Adam's Off Ox. I don't feel like I can freely talk about anything. What could she possibly contribute to our association?" Dean and Stan agreed.

Mitch added, "Well, did any of you rodeo hands happen to look at that rock on her left hand? I don't know if it's real or not, but if it is, I vote we keep the chatter to a minimum and let her talk awhile. I'm sure she feels pretty strange being the only woman here tonight. I'm sure my honey would feel the same way. Stormy just might be a horse of a different color. Give her a chance. Don't be so narrow minded. Everyone brings something to the table, don't they?"

"Neil, in case you've so quickly forgotten, we voted during our last meeting to invite a representative from each of the counties around here," explained Trent. "You'd really be batty if all of them had showed up at once."

Trent walked into the kitchen and dished the pie onto the plates. Stormy emerged from the restroom just as he was finishing. She followed him into the kitchen. "Can I be of some assistance?"

"No, thanks. Got the pie taken care of. You can fill that coffee carafe, and take it out there for me. Oh, and we need some forks, too."

Dean polished off his piece of pie in three bites. "Delish peach pie, Carson. Please tell the Mrs. thanks."

Carson left his pie untouched. "Stormy, please excuse my poor manners this evening. It seems as though I've been overly consumed with all of the planning details and neglected to ask for your input. Being the outstanding business woman that you no doubt are, I'm confident you can add quite a bit of expertise or first-hand knowledge to our discussion."

Stormy had eaten only one bite of her serving of pie. She gently laid the fork down on her plate and wiped her mouth with the corner of the green paper napkin. She took a drink of her coffee, sat the mug down, and pushed her plate ten inches in front of her. Reaching down inside her purse, she located her hand-tooled leather checkbook showcasing the Sabblonti cattle brand and set it on the table in front of her.

Before she could make her next move, Stan reached into his vest pocket, drew out a ball point pen, clicked it, and handed it to Stormy. "Here, need something to write with?"

"Yes, thank you." Stormy instantly recalled an article she'd read within the past few days in one of Chet's ranching magazines that had been delivered in the mail to the Main Sabblonti Ranch house.

"Carson, you asked for my input. Class acts require class cash. It's as simple as that. Obviously, each of you has a heart to serve your community and keep the cattle country alive.

"We live in the finest one in the nation, so I would advise you not to scrimp on any detail, large or small. Many entities have to fold before their fifth year, much less their 75th. Long-standing traditions help to lend strength and stability to a region. I've been hearing reports of certain areas in our country where people have not stepped up to the chute, rolled up their country western shirt sleeves, and gone to work to preserve what the generations before them worked so tirelessly to establish. There are times in life when we cannot settle for second best or cut rate. I make it a policy to never operate in that manner.

"I have exceptional expertise and experience in a lot of areas. Granted, I've never worked directly with the owner of a company that provides rodeo stock for an event, but it certainly cannot be that complex. I'm ready to make my most important contribution this evening. To whom do I make my check payable?"

"Ignee County Rodeo Board would be just fine," said Stan.

All eyes were fixed on Stormy as she wrote the check. Her five-carat diamond ring on her left hand glistened like Orion in the night sky. Her hands began to shake when she tried to remove the check from the paper register. Stan offered to assist Stormy. When doing so, his hand brushed across the top of her left hand. "Your hands are like icebergs! Trent, did you forget to turn the heat on tonight?"

"Nope. It's humming at a flat 72. Should be warm enough for everyone. Feels pretty toasty to me, but Stormy's blouse is a bit sheer to say the least."

"Thank you for your assistance, Stan. My fingers don't seem very flexible this evening. That should be enough to take care of round one of the expenses."

"Well, thank you, Stormy," said Stan as he walked to the front of the table and presented the check to Carson.

"Yes, Stormy, on behalf of the Ignee County Rodeo Board, we are most appreciative. This will enable us to contact the performers and everyone else involved to tell them it's a go. Head 'em up, and move 'em out, boys."

"It's been my distinct pleasure meeting all of you fine gentlemen this evening. If you'll excuse me, I need to be on my way. My schedule keeps me very busy, and I must get plenty of rest to exercise my mental gymnastics."

All of the board members bid Stormy good evening and safe travels.

The meeting resumed. Trent mentioned that he'd forgotten to ask how Chet was doing.

Dean pressed, "Well, Carson, don't keep us in suspense for the rest of the night. How much did she pony up?"

"Looks like one fifty."

"A hundred and fifty dollars?"

"No, genius. A hundred and fifty large ones."

CHAPTER TWENTY-FIVE

Less Alotto decided to surprise his wife, Meg, early Thursday afternoon. He quietly opened the front door, slipped his cowboy boots off, and made his way up the steep flight of stairs in his stocking feet. His big toe protruded from the top of the left one. He could hear Meg's fingers vigorously working the adding machine inside Stormy's office on the third floor of the main ranch house. When Less stuck his foot into the office, Meg let out a shrill shriek. "Who's there?"

Jumping inside the office, Less bent forward as he laughed. "It's only me, catnip! Are you always so jittery?"

Meg pushed the adding machine back a few inches. "I sure wasn't expecting you today. What's going on? Why aren't you working? Have you been fired again?"

"Now don't get testy. Everything's under control, and no, I've not been dismissed from my job. This one is by far the cushiest setup I've ever had. Since you mentioned your boss is never around to keep an eye on you, I thought I'd surprise you and whisk you away for the rest of the day. You're going to love what I have to show you. I've even been working overtime."

"I hope it's some new baby calves. I've missed seeing them."

"It's still a little early for all that business to start. Maybe another month. All of the calving barns are ready to go though. You gotta remember we're in the high country now."

Standing behind Meg with both arms draped over her shoulders, Less's eyes widened. "What are you working on? That's one long drawn-out list of figures. I can see why you would need an adding machine. Are those the bills that Stormy owes this month? This is one high-dollar operation to say the least."

Meg picked up the small stool under the desk and put it in the closet. "You tend to the cow-calf operation and let me secure the dollars and cents. Sound like a plan?"

"Yes, sounds like a grand plan. I've come to the conclusion there are all sorts of treasures littered everywhere on this ranch."

"Have you had the chance to drive over the whole thing yet?"

Less sat on the floor trying to cover his big toe with his sock. "Not quite. I've been waiting for it to warm up a bit, and I've wanted to stay pretty close to home base since Chet has been laid up just in case he had any questions or needed my help with anything. Strange thing though. I've never met the character yet. Guess I could pop on down there and see him, but I've heard he's not doing too well, so I've not wanted to be a bother. Stormy seems pretty no nonsense, so I've been trying to tend to business. I'm aiming for that year-end bonus."

Meg opened the closet to get her coat and purse. "I should hope so! We need every dime we can get and then some."

"Now don't you worry your pretty little head over a little cash and a few T-bone steaks. You know you can always count on me. Have I ever let you down?"

"No, not exactly."

"Cut the lights and button 'er up, so we can get outta here while we still have plenty of daylight. I can't show you what I need to show you in the dark. Not effectively anyway."

"Less, you know how to get my attention in most anything. Give me about five minutes here, so I can make sure I've got everything it its place."

Less emerged from the third-floor bathroom wiping his hands on the front of his jeans. “I tried not to touch anything in the can so no one would know I visited. Ready to hightail it outta here?” They left the house hurriedly.

Meg opened the passenger door to Less’s pickup and got inside. She removed her shoes and placed her feet on the heating vents. “That was awfully sweet of you to leave your pickup running so the cab would be nice and cozy for me. Are we going for a short or long ride?”

“I guess you could say it’s longer than shorter. I thought about blindfolding you for this part of the drive to add extra suspense, but didn’t think you’d cotton to that.”

“I’m definitely not in the mood for those kinds of games today. I left my migraine medicine home this morning. I thought I had a few extra pills in my purse. Have you given any thought to renting a place of our own, so we can be out from under Blake Benson’s nose every night? A little bit of him goes a long way.”

“I told you when we had to leave South Dakota so suddenly that beggars couldn’t be choosers. I’m calling in a lot of favors from mutual friends who knew Blake long before I did in order to be able to stay with him until we can find something of our own. This part of the country shows real promise if we can just bide our time. Besides, Blake usually leaves real early most mornings and gets home right before we go to bed. I’ll bet he spends half of his monthly paycheck at the Sage Hen Café. He eats there at least twice a day most days. And, let’s not forget, Blake is allowing us to live in his house and enjoy his quiet ranchette rent-free for the first three months. I think that’s very generous. You could be a little bit kinder to him.”

After Less drove for a while, he turned onto the less traveled side road which needed to be graded and have some of the rocks removed.

“Is this even a road, Less, or are you trying to get us lost?”

“There’s no way to get lost on this big spread. You just keep driving, and you’re sure to get to some kind of a road sooner or later. Where's your spirit of adventure?"

S

Stormy returned home from her dental appointment in Cinder Valley at 2:15 in the afternoon. She walked onto the front porch carrying her groceries in both arms. The front door was open about a foot, so she entered the kitchen and set the bags on the table. Running up the stairs, she called for Meg, but there was no answer. Stormy searched throughout the house to no avail. She didn't have the home phone number for Blake Benson, so that wouldn't do her any good at the moment. *Meg's a big girl. I'm sure she can take care of herself. She must have had some kind of an emergency. She's worked from 9:00 to 5:00 every day since I hired her. She's as honest and faithful as they come. Now that Mother's gone, I would be sunk without her financial expertise.*

Putting away supplies was not one of Stormy's favorite activities. Meg was supposed to still be working so she could take care of the mundane chores. Stormy had far more important things to do these days. Maybe she needed to hire that personal assistant after all. She gathered her receipts from her various expenditures in town and made her way up the stairs to her office.

Stormy glanced at the numbers on the accounting sheet, but paid no attention to them. She contemplated putting the stack of papers inside the desk drawer, but thought better of it, and decided to leave them where they were. When she lifted her left thumb, the title *Bosner's* caught her eye. *Who or what is Bosner's? Never heard of that place. I'll have to make a mental note to ask Meg about that since it's for the* *sum of $9,207.14. Maybe it's for one of the bulls Chet purchased last fall. I don't remember him saying anything about it though, and there's no way I'm going to stoop so low as to bounce him about it now. I just know in my heart of hearts that he's faking most everything about the injuries he supposedly sustained in that accident. Serves him right if he was daydreaming about Salina. He was probably headed for a secret rendezvous with her. I'm so thankful I have a real purpose for my life now.*

The telephone rang in the upstairs office. *That's probably Meg calling now.* "Hello, Meg, is everything all right?"

"It sure is, but I'm not Meg! Are you kidding? I was calling Chet, but just realized I dialed the wrong number. I'm on my afternoon break from The Shadowy Merc, so wanted to touch base with either him or Evan to see how things were going and find out what the men would like for supper tonight. I'm in the mood to make something really special for Chet. Hopefully it will cheer him up. I'm still learning about what recipes he likes the best. I'd like to sit on the couch very close to him and spoon feed him every bite."

Stormy felt like pulling the phone from the wall, wires and all.

S

Less and Meg traveled for about another hour and a half.

"Are we there yet, Less? You have a very distorted sense of humor. There's no possible way some lavish surprise could be stuck this far out in the ding weeds."

Less patted Meg's left thigh. "Be patient. I know that's not one of your long suits, but maybe you need to start working on it." He crested the small hill and started the descent into the small meadow. "There it is! Isn't it a gem? I'll drive a little closer so we can both get out and take a good look."

"What am I supposed to be looking at? All I can see is a dry piece of land with a tree or two at the far end. What's that faded, reddish-brown thing over there?"

Less parked his pickup at the edge of the meadow. Looking down at Meg's feet he said, "I forgot you wore those little bunny foo-foo shoes today to match your working wardrobe. Can you hoof it across the meadow in those? You should plan to get you some new shoes as soon as you can. Your clothing is looking a bit tattered for a working woman."

"I plan on getting a lot of new things sooner than later, and yes, I can get across the meadow. You'll have to walk slower if you expect me to keep up with you. It's rather rude of you to haul me all the way out here and not walk by my side for the big reveal."

"I'll slow down. I'm just so excited I can hardly contain myself!"

Less ran for the last fifty yards and stretched the top half of his body across the old pickup. He patted the hood with both of his hands as he laid face down.

"Less, have you gone stark raving mad? Look at this thing! It's rusted out above the wheel wells, and there's a hole in the pickup bed. I doubt the stupid thing even starts. You have a perfectly good running pickup. How did you even find this hunk of junk in the first place? Are you sure you have been tending to ranching business seven days a week or is there something else you need to tell me?"

Placing his hands firmly on the hood, Less raised the top half of his body, stood up straight, and leaned against the side of the old pickup. "It's just you and me, kid, and this old junk heap!"

Meg bent over, shook her head back and forth, and leaned back as far as she could. Pulling her long hair into the air, she asked, "Can we go now? I'm getting cold and it will be dark soon. I don't want to be so far from the main road when night falls."

Taking her hand, Less asked, "Don't you want to get inside the cab and take a closer look? I think it would be good for you to sit in there and see how comfortable it is. They say, 'Don't judge a book by the cover.' Well, I say, don't judge an old rig by the number of days it's been in the sun. That just helps to add a little extra character to it."

"Who did this vehicle belong to originally? Where's the license plates? I don't see one on either the front or back bumper."

"South Dakota required both, but fortunately, in this state, you only need one. Same with some of the other states."

"In the short amount of time we've been here you've already researched that? The things you waste your time on sadden me." Meg zipped her coat and stuck her hands in the pockets as she started to walk across the meadow.

Less ran behind her and put his arm on her shoulder. "Don't try to carry the weight of our problems, honey. That's my job. I just need you to believe in me like you have since the day you became a C.P.A."

"I guess I can try."

CHAPTER TWENTY-SIX

Arriving twenty minutes early for Chet's appointment with Dr. Merenspinn, Evan parked in the sunniest spot he could find. The normal March winds had already arrived, much to his dismay. Unfortunately, Chet had fallen the prior Saturday evening when getting out of the bathtub. He had complained of increased pain in his right side as a result and gingerly made his way inside the waiting room. He sat down in the chair and shifted all of his weight to his left side. The doctor was running behind schedule for a Monday morning which did not help matters at all.

An hour after his regularly scheduled appointment, the nurse finally opened the door to the overcrowded waiting room and called Chet's name. She placed him in Exam Room No. 3 as she commented, "Chet, your blood pressure is very low today, but the good news is that you've put on five pounds since we saw you three weeks ago. Tell the chief cook and bottle washer to keep up the good work."

Dr. Merenspinn seemed quite harried when he entered the exam room. "Chet, the nurse's notes say you fell a couple of nights ago. Let's get you on the exam table, so you can tell me what happened."

"Well, Doc, I wasn't really paying attention as to how it happened exactly. The tub is sort of one of those high rise on the sides kind. When I started to get out, I didn't lift my right leg high enough. I lost my balance and fell over the side onto the floor. Evan was watching a TV show and didn't hear me fall, so it was a while before I made my way into the living room where he was sitting. After that, he had me try to walk and do some muscle strength tests and said he didn't think anything was broken. Since we had the appointment with you two days later, I just decided to tough it out at home. I've got quite a large bruise in that area."

Dr. Merenspinn laid Chet's medical folder on the counter. "You got out of the tub on your right side instead of your left? Have you been doing that since your accident? I thought you were taking showers instead of bathing in the tub. Remove your jeans so I can take a closer look at that leg."

Evan assisted Chet with Dr. Merenspinn's request.

"I guess you did a number on that leg!" The doctor continued with a thorough examination of Chet. "Just to be on the safe side, I'm going to order a new set of x-rays. When you're finished here, stop by Mintner Medical Center and get them done today. You may have to wait awhile at the hospital, but this will give me a better idea of what's going on. I don't think any bones are fractured or broken, but we'll just have to wait and see. I'll have my nurse call you if there are any concerns, otherwise continue the same PT regimen as you've been doing. I was in hopes of transitioning you from the crutches to a cane this time, but that nasty fall in your bathroom has set things back a bit."

Dr. Merenspinn looked at Chet's recorded weight. "The good news, however, is that you're starting to gain back some of your weight. Your blood pressure isn't terribly low, but we definitely need to keep an eye on it. We'll see what it's doing when I see you in a month. And no riding horses or driving during that time. You have the rest of your life to do those things. Do you have any questions or concerns?"

"Well, Doc, this sure isn't the report I was hoping for. I'm not sure the physical therapy routine is doing much good at all. It's pretty hard to stay upbeat to say the least."

Patting Chet on the back, Dr. Merenspinn said, "Keep a stiff upper lip, Chet. You're going to make it just fine.

Perseverance always pays off. Take it from me as I've had lots of first-hand experience in that category."

Evan helped Chet outside and into the van. "I have a suggestion. How about I take you to MMC and while you're getting the x-rays I'll head over to The Shadowy Merc and get us some more supplies? Is there anything that sounds good to you for a change of pace? How about some Italian food? Do you like Mexican dishes?"

"Real cowboys don't eat Italian food, Evan!"

"Sure they do, if they get hungry enough! You know, spaghetti and meatballs, garlic French bread lathered with fresh garlic chunks and slabs of real butter, salad with a half cup of Italian salad dressing so you can't tell you're eating anything green, and tiramisu."

"I think you've been watching too much TV. What's that tira thing again? It's probably something you just made up to take my mind off my life that continues to go south."

Evan explained, "Tiramisu is an Italian dessert consisting of layers of sponge cake soaked in coffee and brandy or liqueur with powdered chocolate and mascarpone cheese."

"Never heard of it, and I seriously doubt there's even such a thing. Who makes a cake out of sponges anyway? I've heard of coffee, brandy, and liqueur, but not that microphone cheese. Is it shaped like a microphone or something is why it's called that?"

Evan could not contain himself. He sat in the driver's seat and laughed out loud. "I think I'm going to take a stab at making us some new kinds of food. It might help to break up the boredom a bit. You don't like to play cards, watch TV, read, or do much of anything except sit there and stare out the window waiting for Stormy to show up.

"I'm not trying to be overly critical, but I'm just very concerned about you and your overall health. If you think of something to help pass the time of day, let me know. I can help you with the paperwork for your insurance company regarding your replacement pickup if you'd like. Just give it some thought. I'm only wanting you to know that I'm ready when you are. No rush. Be back in a few, and I'll try to avoid the Black Raven."

Chet reared back in the seat. "The black what? There's no birds in The Shadowy Merc. The minute they start letting those inside is when I no longer get my groceries from there. Just a minute, you must be referring to Salina."

"Just trying to keep things light, Chet. The end of the year will be here before we know it."

"What's that supposed to mean? What's so significant about the end of the year? I'm just trying to get to tomorrow."

S

Wyn Moreland drove away from the Lower Sabblonti Ranch house more confused than when he'd arrived. He'd assumed that as dusk settled over ranch land would be a good time to stop in and see Chet. No one answered his repeated knocks on the front door. The cattle and all but two of Chet's horses had been moved from the barns and loafing sheds. The place felt more deserted than ever. When he drove past the main ranch, there were no vehicles parked in the drive way. The scene during the afternoon of January 2nd and the reading of Jantzi Belle Sabblonti's Last Will and Testament flashed through his mind.

What bothered him even more was the insulated cooler he saw on the front porch of the lower ranch house. There was an envelope taped to the top of it which had red and black hearts drawn on the outside. Chet's name was penned inside the largest heart. Wyn presumed it was a woman's handwriting and that it was not Stormy's. If it was, she most certainly had a key since she lived there at one time and could have taken the cooler inside. When he bent down to take a closer look at the cooler, he could smell the aroma of what seemed like fish or fish tacos. "Who leaves a cooler full of food on a door step when the coyotes come down so low during the winter?"

Wyn had no paper inside the cab of his pickup or anything to write on so he could leave Chet a note to let him know that he'd stopped by to check on him.

Merna Toppens had just finished taking some food scraps to her chickens when Wyn arrived back at the ranch. She invited him for supper which afforded him the opportunity to tell her and Tom about his recent visit to the Sabblonti Ranch.

Wyn didn't expect much sympathy from Tom. "Wyn, I've told you before that I don't make light of people's misfortunes, and I believe in helping people who are trying to help themselves."

"Chet's in dire straits and can't really help himself much right now. He's got that physical therapist to help him out, but that's about it. I was just trying to be neighborly before the flood of spring work hits us hard."

As Tom unlaced his work boots, he looked straight at Wyn, "I admire your good-neighbor intentions, but you're right when you speak of spring work. Don't forget that you're in charge of the whole shootin' match around here now. Chet's real problems aren't the ranch or his health. Those are fixable. It's that wife of his that's a constant storm in his life."

"I can't argue with that. Thank God her sister isn't anything like her."

Merna removed the blackberry crisp from the oven as she finished whipping the fresh cream and adding a teaspoon of sugar to it. "I've always thought Sarita's personality favored that of her dad, Ace. I don't think anyone ever really knew what he was like because Jantzi Belle kept him on such a short leash. The thing I could never understand is that the money and ranch came down through his family line. Her family *didn't have a pot or a window* as the old saying goes. They weren't destitute, but on the other hand, they most certainly weren't in the same league as the Sabblonti's. Then again, most people in these parts aren't. So how was it that Janzti Belle ruled the roost and the rooster?"

"You talk to that rooster of yours in the barnyard every morning," quipped Tom. "Ask him the next time you see him."

Wyn loved Tom's sense of humor. He wondered if his real father, whom he'd never known, might have had one. "Tom, I need to ask you about getting that well drilled where Sarita and I are going to place our manufactured home. Also, is there someone you know that can dig the drain field for the septic tank? Spence and I have pretty much finished clearing the area, but we'd like you to come down, take a look, and give it the final approval. I don't' want to get everything moved in there and then the first night my bride and I sit down to eat, the kitchen chairs start rolling toward the wall if the floor isn't level."

"Ah, come on now, that would sure help to keep the honeymoon week alive now, wouldn't it?" asked Tom.

Merna's cheeks blushed quickly. "Soup's on you two. I've got a real nice surprise for you tonight."

Before Tom sat at the head of the table, he lifted the piece of aluminum foil from the top of the main dish. "Well, I'll be double dipped! Speaking of roosters, is this the one we butchered late last fall? Let's hope we didn't let him get too old and tough. Wyn, you ever had rubber chicken for supper before?"

Wyn realized he still needed to clean up before eating, so he excused himself. Returning, he replied, "No, Tom, can't say as I have. It doesn't sound real appetizing. I'd sure be willing to give this rooster a try though. What I'm really holding out for is the mashed spuds and chicken gravy. I could eat Momma Merna's country gravies by the boatloads. I just might need to send Sarita down here for some cooking lessons. Come to think of it, I really don't know how much cooking she's done in her life."

"As old as she is now, she sure should've had lots of practice," Tom added.

"Tom, I think you'd best mind your P's and Q's and let Wyn eat his supper in peace. We certainly have more important things to discuss than cooking lessons. Now is a good time to talk a little more about the upcoming wedding. It will be here before we know it. Sarita's coming out this next weekend so we can get started on our projects."

"Wyn, you've got the most important thing in a marriage which is a good wife. Everything else after that is gravy." Looking at Merna with a big smile on his face, Tom continued, "I've sure had a lot of gravy in my lifetime." He got up from his chair, walked over to where Merna was seated, and kissed her on her left cheek.

"Tom Toppens, what has come over you anyway? You're acting and talking like you did the first week we got married."

"Merna, our honeymoon has never ended."

CHAPTER TWENTY-SEVEN

Priscilla called throughout the house, "Mother, I didn't find a note on the kitchen table. It's been decades since we played hide and seek! Where, oh where, are you hiding? April Fool's Day was last Saturday." She thought she heard laughter in the back yard. Walking to the kitchen window, she could hardly believe her eyes.

Francie Fletcher held the small, brown sack in her right hand as she passed the wood screws to Spence who was using his electric screwdriver to drill them into the cedar boards. Looking at him lean into the fence with all his might made Priscilla's heart flutter. *Had he ever loved another woman? If so, who was she?* She supposed she could ask him, but what good would that do?

Maybe she should try the big city life with its bright lights and taxi cabs before she settled down with one person for the rest of her life. Surely there would be county recorder positions or other state jobs available anywhere in the good ol' US of A. Suddenly an idea came to her. Just then her mother spotted her standing in the kitchen and motioned for her to join them outside.

Donning her pink hooded sweatshirt, Priscilla walked onto the lawn and into the front feet of some of her welcoming committee. "Miggy, my Miggy, I wondered where you were! Have you been chasing the neighbor's cats? That would be a real no-no."

"Since when is she *your* Miggy?" asked Spence. "I thought you gave her to me. Remember? Christmas wasn't that long ago."

Priscilla leaned against the tree trunk. "I have perfect recollection of that day. It's been an incredibly long week at work. One of the deputy clerks was out all five days due to the flu."

"Don't come near me! We're busier than we've ever been at the ranch, so I don't have time to get the galloping crud. I'm sorry. That's no way to greet you. I just sorta got caught up in the verbal moment. It's great to see you and hopefully you can get some much-needed rest this weekend."

"Spence, why didn't you let me know you were going to be here this afternoon, so I could have taken a half day off work or something?"

Looking at Priscilla instead of the head of the wood screw he was driving into the board, Spence nicked his thumb, "Ouch! I didn't even know I was going to be right here right now. I had to purchase some more fencing supplies for the ranch at The Merc, so I swung by here to see if your mother was home. We put our two heads together and decided with what daylight we had left that we would take a stab at fixing your gate and fence. I'm glad we tackled the gate first. It took a lot longer than I thought it would, but I put the "x" pattern reinforcement boards on the inside, so that should help quite a bit."

Walking closer, Priscilla asked, "Can you stay for supper? I would really like to visit some more with you, and I'd love to hold Miggy on my lap even though she's getting a bit too big for that now."

"Thanks, but I can't tonight. I have some pressing needs to tend to at the ranch now that I'm assistant foreman. Until Tom gets some more help hired, Wyn and I are working really long hours. Neither of us are complainers, however. Tom won't put up with bellyachers at all."

Standing back about ten feet from the repaired gate and fence, Spence leaned back on his heels and folded his arms across his chest. "Looks mighty fine to me. Well, not as pretty as you Priscilla, but you know what I mean."

Chuckling, Priscilla's cheeks flushed hot pink to match her outerwear.

"Ladies, I must be on my way. Let me know if you need anything else repaired or if there's any other way I can help you. Miggy, time to get inside that pickup. By the way Priscilla, has Lane been any more of a nuisance lately?"

"Betty Lou said he stopped by late last week, but I had gone to Cattlemen's Central to make a deposit, so I didn't encounter him. She said he asked for *the lady in pink*. Maybe I should stop wearing that color."

"Please don't. I think it suits you quite well."

Francie started to walk toward the house.

When repairing the gate, Spence had installed a black piece of metal that needed to be lifted when opening and closing it.

"Priscilla, I've already given your mother the one easy lesson on how this works, so she knows. If you'd like to walk a little closer, I can show you. Just lift this piece with the knob on the end of it. That's all it takes. Got it?" Spence winked with his left eye.

"Got it." Priscilla winked back with her right eye.

Sarita was barely inside her apartment when she slid her right forefinger underneath the top of the envelope. Walking into the kitchen, she flipped the light switch on and leaned against the counter. Her eyes darted from one end of the lines to the other.

"My dear Sarita,

It warmed my heart to hear from you. Your Uncle Kent and I read your letter several times. We were very sorry to hear of your mother's passing. Please express our sympathies to your sister as well.

I'd be honored to be in your wedding or to help in whatever area you need. Uncle Kent said he'd also be willing to give you away, but it would cost you at least three pieces of wedding cake. Do you remember how much he loves homemade pastries? We just want you to make whatever choices will make you happy. You've had a hard row to hoe, but it looks like life is on a real upswing for you now.

When speaking with our granddaughter, Donna, she said she would be delighted to have Logan and Lilac be in your wedding. And I do have something from my wedding to your Uncle Kent in 1944 that I'm bringing for your special day. I hope you'll like it.

I've written out the addresses for the family members on a separate sheet. I hope you can read my chicken scratching. It's a little harder for me to hold the pen still when writing than it used to be.

Part of the family will probably stay in Blunte County for the wedding and then just drive over to Toppens for the big doings. Our daughter-in-law, Lisha, who is married to Quentin, wants to visit the cemetery so she can see where some of the Siddonz family members are buried. She's really into that ancestry bit.

Your Uncle Kent asked if we would be staying at the big Sabblonti Ranch house, and I told him to get a grip on reality. He wants *to do some camping and fishing after the wedding, so we might just pull our fifth wheel behind our pickup.*

See you this summer and sending our love,

Aunt Jonsey

Sarita threw her aunt's letter into the air. "Yes, my life is on an upswing right now! I can't make everybody happy all of the time, so Dr. Diller will just have to accept that my decision is a sound one. It bothers me that he seems to be less friendly at work. I think he's just worried about me. It's nice to have someone other than Wyn concerned about my welfare."

S

Priscilla informed her mother, "I'm feeling very well rested this morning, so I'm going to run some errands. Is there anything you would like for me to get for the house or you personally?"

"I should hope your sleep tank is full, Miss Priscilla! It's one in the afternoon. The only thing I can think of is the day old bread at The Shadowy Merc. If they have the two day old bread it might be a few cents cheaper. Four loaves should probably feed us for the next couple of weeks."

Priscilla removed the grocery list from the small magnetic tablet on the refrigerator and finished buttoning her jacket.

"No pink today?"

"Not this afternoon. I might be overdoing that a bit. I think I need to look for some sage greens, golds, reds or purples. Those colors might make me look more mature. There's not a lot of money to devote to clothing at the moment, however. I guess I could stop by the *Second Time Around* and see if they might have anything that strikes my fancy. See you later this afternoon."

It was a couple of hours later by the time Priscilla finished getting supplies in town and drove from Ridgemonte to the main highway leading out of town. She turned onto the ranch road and parked in the driveway a short while later. After waiting for a few minutes with no answer at the door, she walked back to her car. Just then she heard a voice coming from the front porch.

"Priscilla, come back! I didn't see or hear you. I was washing the walls in the bedroom hallway. Please come in so we can have tea together. What brings you all the way out here? It's wonderful to see you. I can take your jacket if you'd like."

"Thank you, Merna. I just couldn't think of anyone else to talk to or who would understand."

"Are you in trouble, child?"

"No, not that I know of. I guess that did not come out quite like I intended. Spence isn't anywhere around is he?"

Merna walked to the window and looked outside. "I don't think so, but then again, it's real hard for me to know some days exactly where they're working. This is a real busy time of year, and the cows are calving. Tom went out after dinner to see if he could be of any help. He's having quite a hard time trying to totally let go of those reins. Wyn and Spence are doing a great job according to Tom."

While sipping her tea, Priscilla thanked Merna. "It helps to soothe the nerves. After Shane stole Spence's hand-knitted scarf that I gave him as a belated Christmas gift and hung it on the rabbit brush, Spence brought it over when he and Miggy came to supper at our house. Mother insisted that he tell us some of his family history during which time he showed us a photograph of the Omaha stock yards where his father and grandfather worked. She also asked him if he knew the capital of Nebraska, and Spence answered incorrectly. I think it was just because he was so nervous. There are lots of other types of learning in this world besides book learning. Mother seems highly suspicious of him and very skeptical. I was hoping you could help me sort it out or give me some motherly advice."

Merna rocked gently in her chair. "Matters of the heart are highly personal and quite subjective which is most unfortunate. When it comes to relationships, however, it's a challenge to not be influenced by personal feelings or opinions. Do you think Spence is telling the truth about his family and the time he spent in Omaha?"

"Yes, I do, but I feel like I don't know Spence very well at all. Since I work in town all week long and he's the assistant foreman for your ranch, he has hardly any spare time at all, so how can I get to know him? Mother's very old fashioned and is of the frame of mind that a man is supposed to pursue the woman, not the other way around. I believe that as well, but at the rate Spence and I are going, that would take about five years!"

Covering her mouth with her hand, Merna laughed. "Oh, I know and sense your frustration. Things were a bit different for Tom and me. I lived in town, and he grew up on a small acreage just a few miles away. The year we courted before we got married, he was not the number two ranch boss with all of the responsilibites that go with it. We lived with his wonderful parents for the first year of our marriage. Also, Tom had a nice nest egg saved up to purchase our first little chunk of land.

"I have no idea what Spence's financial condition is and don't feel like it's my place to ask right now. Keep in mind that he didn't have a vehicle until Tom gifted him his older model. Most of our hired hands haven't had much money when they started out. That's why they usually go to work for someone else until they get some experience under their belts and can set aside a little extra money.

"Everyone is at a different place in their lives at a different time. The key is knowing where and when that is. The other thing to keep in mind is that you're an only child, and your mother is a widow. This makes her overly protective to say the least. What parent doesn't want what's best for his or her child? Something tells me you really aren't able to discuss this with her. Please don't misunderstand me as I'm not trying to come between you and her."

Priscilla set her empty tea cup on the saucer. "Until she gets past her initial suspicions, I don't think I can make much progress. I feel like I'm going behind her back even coming out here this afternoon, but I'm getting ultra frustrated and really don't want to lose Spence. The marriage prospects in the city limits of Ridgemonte are slim to none. Perhaps my standards are too high, but Spence and I just sort of instantly connected at the Merrill's New Year's Eve barbeque. It feels like there's a good chemistry between us. Maybe I should just apply for a job in another state and get out of here for good."

Merna motioned for Priscilla to stand up. She walked over to her and gave her a big hug. "As far as I'm concerned, a young woman's standards need to be that way. I never took chemistry in high school, but I think I know what you're talking about. I've seen more than one sorry case where a young lady with so much potential and promise marries a young man who isn't really in it for the long haul and ends up creating a path of destruction for all concerned."

Tapping her right temple, Merna suggested, "Maybe you could come out to the ranch several Sunday afternoons and help me fix supper. Then we could invite Spence and that might be a way for you to get to know him a little better. You could also take an active interest in his ranching activities and plan to participate in some work days when they brand, dehorn, vaccinate, and so forth. If this whole Omaha business is the truth and cattle ranching is in his blood, you'd better find out if that's how you want to spend the rest of your adult life. You could even invite your mother every once in awhile if she's interested. The more the merrier!"

Hugging Merna a second time, Priscilla exclaimed, "That's a marvelous idea! I hope that's not going to be too awful much for you. I didn't come out here with the idea of mooching off you or anything of the sort. You've really helped to put my mind and heart at ease. Can I give you a call and let you know what weekends might work out best for me? It's not that my life is very busy, but I do help Mother quite a bit, especially on Saturdays."

Merna held Priscilla's small hands inside her own. "Your mother surely realizes that you're going to get married someday, so she might as well start untying the apron strings sooner than later. Better yet, she needs to take the apron off, fold it up, and put it in the kitchen drawer for good. In fairness to her, we've had some drifters in these parts in the past few years, but Tom's instincts are usually spot on. He wouldn't have promoted Spence and given him a pickup if he did not feel he could trust him. He was skeptical of Shane all along and that proved to be accurate. Human nature is fascinating to say the least.

"And yes, you can call me anytime. One more thing before we dispense with this Spence matter. I've watched the way he takes care of Miggy. It's as if she's his child. You know what they say. A dog is a pretty good judge of human character, and that dog is Spence's constant companion."

Priscilla brushed her hand across the faded wooden tray of the old highchair standing in the kitchen corner. The back rest featured a hand-painted picture of two little yellow bunnies riding a tricycle, one behind the other, wearing little blue spring jackets. There was even a little wood extension where Toby could rest his tiny feet.

Glancing at the clock, Priscilla exclaimed, "Oh my, it's five-thirty! I need to get going. Mother will wonder where I am if she doesn't see our car parked in the driveway by dark."

"Here's your jacket. It also occurs to me that your

mother needs to find some other things to occupy her time besides worrying about you. The other part of our long-range plan could be to locate a widower. Most of them need a loving, caring woman to make a fuss over them."

"Now there's a brilliant idea! How can I thank you for gifting me your afternoon and your listening ear?"

"Be an honorable Mrs. Woodson."

"Mrs. Woodson?"

"Mrs. Spence Woodson."

CHAPTER TWENTY-EIGHT

Two cans of cherry pie filling, one chocolate cake mix, but it needs to be the kind with the pudding in the mix, and one 20 oz. bottle of cherry cola. It seems like there should be more ingredients. I will take his word for it. Sarita reviewed the recipe twice more. Walking toward the check-out counter, she was secretly hoping Cannaleah was working. Sarita made two more revolutions around the store without spotting her. She glanced down at her watch and decided that she might as well pay and head home. Turning the corner on aisle 4, she almost ran into Dr. Shaw who was carrying a gallon jug of milk and adjusting his hat with his left hand.

"Oh, hello, Sarita! Sorry about that. I guess I need to watch where I'm going."

"I'm probably a little bit preoccupied, so it's me that should have been paying closer attention."

"With a big wedding on the horizon, you're most likely very busy. I've not had the opportunity to congratulate you and Wyn. Best wishes for a very happy marriage."

"Thank you, Dr. Shaw. That's very kind of you. Wyn and I'll be blissfully joyous together, and it's wonderful to have the well wishes of family and friends heading into our big day."

Dr. Shaw walked behind Sarita as she carried her small basket to the front of The Shadowy Merc. "Looks like you've got a sweet night dialed up with the cake mix and carbonated beverage."

"It's actually for the work day scheduled tomorrow at The Toppens Ranch. I guess you could say that I'm part of the chuck wagon outfit."

"And the dessert menu," added Dr. Shaw.

Salina's ears perked up. "What did you say about the chuck wagon outfit? Is there something happenin' at the Sabblonti spread that I should know about?"

Neither Sarita nor Dr. Shaw spoke.

"We're all adults here now aren't we or are we still playing the simple, snooty junior high game where we act like nobody knows what's going on anywhere? Trust me when I say that I can tell you just about everything that goes on in this entire county and beyond especially after the sun goes down. I have my trusted connections. I like to refer to them as *The Back Roads Boys.* They're not all boys, mind you. Some of them are ladies, too. Maybe I should start calling them *The Back Roads Crew.*

"I've enlisted their help even more now that Chet's chillin' down at the Lower Sabblonti Ranch House and his visitors are few and far between. He's my main concern these days. I've been trying to fix high calorie meals to put some more meat onto his bones. He looked mighty fine right before his accident. I'll get him back to where he can get in his saddle again. He should have posed for one of the pictures in that annual cowboy calendar instead of some of those lightweights they rounded up. Some of their pictures look more like mug shots than rodeo champions. Sarita, your total is $9.28."

Laying a $10 bill on the counter, Sarita waited for Salina to count out the change.

"Most people extend their hand to take the coins. What's the matter with you? I suppose you think that since you're a high and mighty, born and bred Sabblonti your hand can't touch mine. Fine. I'll lay them on this germ-infested counter, and you can pick them up there. Speaking of hands, you and your sister will never have the upper hand on me."

"I'm not so sure about that," said Sarita as she zipped her wallet shut without placing the change inside.

Dr. Shaw paid for his merchandise with the exact amount of money and quickly exited the store.

S

Saturday morning, May 20th dawned way too early for Wyn and Spence who'd gotten a short six hours of sleep at best. The sun peeked over the tallest butte and down through the lone mahogany tree to greet the few lazy clouds on the eastern horizon.

Tom decided to add a little extra country spirit for the day when he hitched his matched pair of draft horses, Bolo and Browny, to his old chuck wagon and headed down the road to Crescent Creek Corral which was located on the edge of the winter range. The clanging sound reminded him that he needed to stop and rearrange his cookware in the back. He climbed onto the seat again, gently lifted the reins, and commanded, "Giddy up."

Fifty yards down the road Bolo stopped abruptly and raised his right front hoof. "What happened, ol' boy?" Tom tied the reins to the brake lever, climbed off the wagon, walked to the right side of Bolo, and traced his hand down to his hoof. "Ah, I see why you halted in short order. Sure thought I'd pounded that nail in there securely. Let's just hope I remembered to bring my farrier's box."

Tom retrieved his equipment from underneath the canvas of the wagon and walked in front of Bolo. Pain radiated from the center of his back throughout his arms, legs, and face as he lifted the horse's right front leg, leaned backwards, and placed it between his thighs. He dug the small rock out using his hoof pick and removed the bent nails with his nail puller. Using the rasp, Tom filed the rough edges as smoothly as he could. He reached into his shirt pocket and fished out the nails one at a time. "There you go, Bolo! Good as new. Glad I got an early start. At the rate we're going, we might be eating after dark. If that's the case, we won't need much of a campfire since it's almost a full moon."

It was as if Tom's equines knew they needed to get the lead out and get on down the road sooner than later. As they approached the turn off, he didn't even need to voice his usual, "Haw." By the time he arrived, the place was hopping with activity. Sporting a big grin, he exclaimed, "Looks like my two foremen are really on top of things today! Makes me feel good even if my back is giving me fits."

Wyn had decided to man the chores inside the corral while Spence was assigned to those outside. Members of the ranching neighbors' families, the Broomfields and Drebners, were assisting Spence as he prepared to separate the cull cows for sale and send the remaining cows and calves through the portable squeeze shoot on the northern end of the corral. Nelson and Marita Merrill and their ranch hands were helping Wyn with the branding, deworming, castrating, and dehorning.

Suddenly, Tom remembered something else in the back of his chuck wagon. He grabbed the burlap sack tied with red baling twine and walked to the front of the corral. Wyn spotted him after placing the Toppens cattle brand on one of the young calves.

"Well, Boss, do you approve so far?"

"You're doing just fine, son. You and Spence are real naturals for all this cattle business. It puts my heart and mind at ease. Here's some cattle ranching goodies for you two."

Wyn untied the sack and stuffed the twine in his rear pocket. "Seriously, Tom? Which ones go on which calves?"

"You're in charge. Work it out with your assistant. Your best bet is to split it straight down the middle. Not the calf itself, of course!"

Wyn walked to the far end of the corral and motioned for Spence to ride near him. Spence dismounted and they held a brief discussion.

"If there's an odd number, you'd obviously get that one since you're the top dog, I mean the top hand," said Spence.

"That's fair enough," agreed Wyn. "I'll take the blue tags and you can have the yellow ones."

Tom returned to the corral a few minutes later. "Spence, who's that stirring up all that dust at the end of the road? It must be some city slicker or boiled egg eating character out for a scenic drive. Normal folk know better than to drive like that on a day like today. A little breeze would sure be nice."

Dr. Shaw parked a few feet from Tom's wagon. "Sorry I'm late. It's been one of those mornings. I started to drive out of town and had to go back and get the most important thing for today."

"Howdy, Doc. Didn't realize you were even going to be here, but always happy to see you. Did Wyn want you out here today in case the cattle stampeded?"

"When I talked to him a few days ago, I told him about the new live respiratory vaccine that's been developed especially for cattle in this region. I highly recommended that you consider using it. That's when he told me about the upcoming work day on the ranch and asked me to come out and dispense it. Let me grab my portable cooler in the back of my rig."

"How expensive is it? Sounds like it might cost both arms and both legs."

"Come on now, Tom. A rancher has got to keep up with new developments every now and then. When you break the price down per animal, it's not that much considering what would happen if most of your herd got wiped out all at once. I just assumed that Wyn had mentioned this to you and that you'd signed off on the deal."

"Wyn makes all the decisions now. If he gave you the go ahead, that's fine by me. He's got good sound judgment in everything I've seen up until now. I sure would not have named him the foreman otherwise."

"Wyn's in charge of your outfit now? Since when?"

"Since right after the first of the year when he and Sarita got engaged. Now she's the real plum prize for any young man in these parts."

"Don't remind me."

"Pardon? Didn't hear you on that one. What did you say?"

Dr. Shaw located some extra pairs of gloves. "Nothing of importance, Tom. I best head toward the corral. Have they just gotten started?"

"Yes, Wyn just branded and tagged the first one with his blue tag."

Tom busied himself with folding out the canvas flaps of his chuck wagon and laying out his Dutch ovens. He counted out the number of briquettes he would need for each recipe. Taking the paper egg carton from inside the wagon, Tom tore each cup from the carton and placed it inside the ovens. The prior summer he'd deposited a small amount of wood shavings in each indentation and poured a little wax over each pile. Taking the box of matches, Tom struck them against the heel of his boot and started the coals burning in each container. "Time to get a move on and get this Toppens Top Stew fired up. No time to waste. What did I do with that recipe anyway? Okay, here it is, so I need:

1/3 cup flour
½ tsp. salt
½ tsp. celery salt
¼ tsp. pepper
¼ tsp. garlic powder
1 ½ lbs. beef stew meat cut into one-inch cubes
¼ cup oil
4 cups hot water
½ tsp. salt
½ tsp. Worcestershire Sauce
Cut up spuds, onions, and carrots

Then multiply this times five, and I think that should be enough to go along with all the other fixins."

"Tom, are you talking to yourself again?" asked Merna as she and Sarita joined him near the wagon. "Howdy! I could sure use some help. Sarita, did you bring the goodies for the dessert? We don't need to get that Dutch oven fired up quite yet."

Sarita handed the grocery bag to Tom. "Who's that standing next to Wyn in the corral? The sun is in my eyes which makes it hard to see."

"Why that's none other than Dr. Shaw."

"I didn't know he was going to be here today. I saw him at The Merc last night and he didn't say anything about it."

"Wyn asked him to come out and doctor the herd with the newest vaccine for cattle in these parts. Too much for me to keep up with these days. Glad I handed the reins to your soon-to-be-hubby."

Merna glanced at Sarita as she bent her head down. "Everything's going to be fine, Sarita. Dr. Shaw knows that you and Wyn are engaged. I'm sure he feels as awkward as you do being here. When he asked you to go on that sleigh ride New Year's Day, he had no idea Wyn had proposed to you. Things like that happen all of the time."

"No, they don't happen all of the time," commented Tom.

"What are you doing listening to our womanly conversation? You're supposed to be cooking."

Adjusting his old, gray felt hat with the rooster pheasant feather secured inside the hatband, Tom announced, "I am cooking. I can do more than one thing a time. That's why you married me, remember?"

Merna walked toward Tom and gave him a kiss on his cheek. "Forever my favorite rancher!"

A few of the cows and calves got separated from the herd when the Broomfields and their ranch hands were helping to drive them closer to the corral. It took part of the morning to locate them. Sim, their Australian cattle dog, saved the day when he flushed them out of a dry creek bed a few miles away.

Spence was so preoccupied with his work that he failed to notice the last vehicle to arrive mid-afternoon.

The sun was starting down the west side of the mountain when all work pertaining to the herd had been completed. Marita, Merna, Sarita, and Priscilla had set up a portable wash station of sorts with white basins full of warmed water, bars of homemade soap scented with sagebrush, and old towels for drying. Tom set out the camp stools and combined them with the lawn chairs brought by the other families.

It was quite a sight to behold as the working ranch crew filed through the chow line. Tom had prepared an assortment of delicious Dutch oven recipes, and Sarita's Cherry Dump Cake was the big hit of the entire day.

Nelson Merrill kept ribbing Rees Broomfield about which outfit worked the hardest during the day. Rees opted to let Nelson spin the yarn any old way he wanted to since his spread was next on the schedule for the ranching community work day. Nelson shoveled in the groceries as fast as he talked. At one point, Rees set his fork down on his tin plate, and just stared at Nelson. How could anyone shove that much food in his mouth at one time and still talk? Maybe this gave new meaning to *talking a mile a minute.*

Nelson looked across the group and yelled, "Priscilla, how'd we get you to join us today? You givin' up that easy city life, so you can become a hard workin' ranchin' girl?"

Marita chimed in before Priscilla could respond. "Now, Nelson, mind your manners. Priscilla was a big help at our New Year's Eve barbeque in the barn. If you would've been doing something besides battin' the breeze, you would have seen how hard she worked."

"Seems to me like that interest Priscilla sparked during our barbeque is still burning brightly."

"Nelson, leave the younger ones be. They can figure out things for themselves just like all of us did all those years ago. But, I've got to admit, it's fun to watch a romance blossom."

Sarita scooted her stool closer to Wyn as Dr. Shaw squirmed in his seat.

"Speaking of romances, Doc, you got any blossomin' or even startin' to bud?" asked Nelson.

"Working on it."

"Well, when will we get to meet her? Will she be showing up at any of these gatherings to learn how to work cattle or to fix chow?"

"Working on it."

"Does she even like cattle or horses? Can't imagine you signing on with some woman that doesn't. Course, stranger things than that have happened."

"Working on it."

"Look there at city girl, Priscilla. She figured out in no time at all how to get what she wants."

"Nelson Weston Merrill," scolded Marita. "That's enough. We're blessed and highly favored to have more young people joining in our ranching community and learning that wonderful way of life. I think you'd better have another helping of Tom's stew and diced green chilies cornbread and listen for a while instead of trying to do all of the talking."

Nelson rose from his seat and made another trip down the line of Dutch ovens.

To shift the focus from Dr. Shaw, Marita asked, "Priscilla, how's your mother doing these days?"

"Oh, she's fine, but she definitely needs some other

things to keep her busy."

"Other than what?"

"Other than monitoring my life day and night."

"It sounds to me like she needs *someone* rather than *something* to occupy her time. Well, come to think of it, the something usually happens when that certain someone comes along."

"My thoughts exactly," added Priscilla.

"Spence, did you bring your harmonica?" Wyn asked.

"Sure did. It's in my saddle bag. I'm just about finished here and then I'll get it."

Marita, Merna, Sarita, and Priscilla started to clean up after the meal. The extra-large, blue, campfire coffee pot was filled to the brim. Priscilla passed out cups to those wanting coffee, and Marita came along behind her and filled them.

Rees had built a nice campfire which drew everyone in just a bit closer. Miggy was dozing as she lay on Priscilla's lap. Spence played his harmonica as the group sang along to "The Happy Wanderer", "Come Away with Me", "America the Beautiful", "Camptown Races", and "Home on The Range." He started to cough, so he excused himself to get a drink of water from the bucket hanging on the edge of the chuck wagon.

Dr. Shaw looked up at the night sky.

"No use looking up there for your woman, Doc," kidded Nelson. "You best be looking in these parts somewhere I would think."

"I was just checking to see if I could spot Taurus. It hosts two of the nearest open clusters to our planet, the Pleiades and the Hyades, both of which are visible to the naked eye this time of year. Can anyone else see them?"

Nelson didn't let up, "Sounds to me like you'd better be lookin' for some pretty young thing that's got some book learnin' like you do who can talk your lingo."

"Working on it, Nelson."

CHAPTER TWENTY-NINE

Less Alotto had just about finished loading the odds and ends into the back of his pickup. Checking to make sure that his wife, Meg, had already gone to bed and fallen into a deep sleep, he made one more trip through the kitchen. He reached into the cupboard to grab a handful of salted peanuts.

"Looking for a midnight snack?" asked Blake.

Whirling around and dropping a few nuts onto the floor, Less jumped back a foot. "You scared the wits out of me! How long have you been standing there?"

Blake leaned against the counter and crossed his legs. "Long enough to wonder what all of those trips from my storage shed to your parked pickup are all about. I don't mind you and Meg staying with me until you can bootstrap yourselves from your last fiasco, but I've got a lot at stake here and can't afford any funny business. Everything has got to be on the up and up. It seems like more ranchers are starting to connect the dots and poke their big *Elliott beaks* into places they don't belong."

Less smirked as he chomped on his snack, and small pieces mixed with saliva dripped from the left side of his mouth. "So, what you're telling me is there are some rustling noises starting to come from some of your fellow rustlers when you guys carved off part of the Toppens herd a few years back? You can cool your horse heels on that one.

"Keep in mind that Chet Castins is going to be out of commission for probably at least a year or so, and you know he isn't going to talk. Jantzi Belle Sabblonti is pushing up daisies. You can thank your lucky stars on that one. If Chet didn't have that yard bird named Evan down there taking care of him along with that grocery store cashier with the long, sleek, black hair ferrying him meals back and forth, he'd really be in a bind. I can only imagine how much Chet's paying that character to adult sit him. No telling either what he and The Shadowy Merc cashier have cooked up. That Stormy is beyond high maintenance. She doesn't know up from down about ranching or cattle."

"Less, I don't know who told you what about any cattle rustling deals involving me in this part of the country." Blake reached inside the cupboard to get some peanuts, but the plastic bottle was empty. "The rumor mill runs day and night around here. If I would've been involved in any shady or illegal dealings, I most certainly wouldn't have been named Southwest District Brand Inspector."

"Say what you want. Don't forget that I have my connections with long memories, too."

Blake stepped closer to Less. "You did not answer my question. What's with all the junk in the back of your truck?"

"I need to go check on some of the cows and calves. I'm just hauling it to the dump at the same time. You know, kill the two birds with the one stone."

"After midnight? Does Meg even know you're striking out this early in the morning?"

Less wiped his mouth with the sleeve of his shirt as food particles fell to the floor. "Meg has no clue what all is involved in managing a spread as big as the Sabblonti's. Stormy should be paying me at least 100 Grand for what I'm doing as I'm completing the work of about four men as it is. I've sent the word down the wire that we need to hire a lot more help. There must have been some kind of major shake-up or a bunch of their ranch hands bolted after Jantzi Belle died."

"I've heard the same thing. It could be that Stormy ran some of them off. Jantzi Belle and Stormy seem to be cut from the same cloth. Kinda like a pair of twin rattlesnakes.

Come to think of it, if you look carefully at that Sabblonti cattle brand, it does sorta look like a walking snake."

S

"Speaking of branding," said Less, "we're way behind on all of the spring chores on the ranch. Don't suppose you'd like to lend us a hand the next couple of weekends so we could get caught up? Wouldn't you like to get your fingers on just a little bit of that Sabblonti bank roll? Meg could cut you the check for the hours you put in if you told her how many."

"No wonder you're chasing the clock and the calendar. Why would you haul junk from the Sabblonti Ranch, unload it here, and load it up again only to haul it to the dump? I've got district meetings in Chrebine and Tranquility Falls the next two Saturdays. I'm going to be talking to my fellow brand inspectors about ways to prevent cattle rustling. How rich is that?"

Less raised his right index finger and pressed it against his closed lips. "Sssshhhhh. Don't wait up for me." He tiptoed across the kitchen floor, opened the front door, and walked into the moonlight. Carefully opening the driver's door of his pickup, he got inside, and shifted it into neutral. He got out, leaned against the open door, and started rolling it down the small decline. At the bottom of the hill, he turned the ignition on and shifted it into gear. *Blake just needs to tend to his brandin' and leave Meg and me to our twosome.*

Midway to his dumping grounds, Less turned the engine off. He filled his two pickup tanks using the gas inside some of the cans located in the bed of his pickup. Arriving at his destination, he unloaded a set of spare tires, some small hand tools, four five-gallon gas cans filled to the brim, one hundred feet of heavy-duty rope, various lengths of chain, several old horse blankets, two shovels, a five-gallon bucket, a jack for changing tires, ten horse bridles and bits, three sets of solid silver spurs, a large black tarp, five gallons of paint, a roll of chicken wire, and a selection of old paint brushes. Brushing the palms of his hands together in satisfaction, he removed his gloves and got back inside the cab.

Less awakened to the aroma of fried bacon and maple syrup. He rolled over and looked at the clock with his left eye closed and his right eye open. *Time to milk this one for all it's worth.* Drawing a bathroom sink full of cold water, he splashed it onto his face and dunked his hair into it. He opened the medicine cabinet and took out his long, black, barber comb to slick his hair straight back. *Could use a haircut. No time for that stuff right now. Too much to do. Guess I could get that metal bowl, put it on top of my head, hand Meg some scissors, and tell her to go snip-snip.* He sauntered down the stairs and waited for Meg's first words. That would determine whether or not his *snow-job routine* was still working after all these years.

Meg was dressed in her housecoat and had her feet propped up on the glass-covered coffee table as she read from her paperback novel. "Good morning, or I should say, Good afternoon, Lovey. You must have had to pull a calf using your flashlight, the headlights of your pickup, or just the good ol' moonlight. It's been quite a while since you've had to do that. I just didn't have the heart to awaken you since it was around sixish when you finally crawled into bed. I have your bacon and waffles in a pie plate warming in the oven. How about some coffee and a tall glass of milk?"

"Sounds fabulous, Meg, my favorite C.P.A. What would I ever do without you? Yes, it was quite a night. Had to work really hard. Just never know where those cows are on this big spread. You know what they say, 'Sometimes you just have to wait 'til the cows come home.'"

"Are there times when the cows don't come home at all?"

"Might be, but that's never happened to me, because I

train them all the right way to start with. It's the same way with a good wife. If you train her the right way from the beginning, she always comes home when she's supposed to."

"You can train cows to come home when they're supposed to?"

"Sure," assured Less. "You can train animals to do anything you need or want them to do if you're talented like I am. Whatcha got planned for your leisurely afternoon anyway? Blake around or is he making himself scarce?"

"Blake was gone by the time I got up mid-morning. You were snoring like a freight train, so I had to use my ear plugs and black sleeping mask. I don't know if we're getting on his nerves lately or what as he doesn't seem to be home much. He eats at The Sage Hen Café most days. Maybe he's setting a snare for some pretty waitress.

"I'm trying to get some money saved so we can at least rent our own place soon. The Cresner Apartments might be a possibility, but that would mean driving to and from Ridgemonte every day to the Sabblonti Ranch. We would spend more in gas coming and going, so we wouldn't be money ahead in the long run. With it being $1.72 a gallon in this part of the country, it adds up quickly."

Meg placed her purpled baubled bookmark inside her paperback and set it on the coffee table. She walked into the kitchen, stood at the sink, and looked out the window. "Nice view of the ranchette today."

Less crept up behind her and placed his chin on the left side of her neck as he glanced down at her left hand. Meg squealed in delight. "Lesster Alotto! How many times have I told you not to do that?"

"Meg, good night, what's the matter with your hands and forearms? It looks like you've got the measles, but I thought you had those when you were a kid. Can you get them more than once? Guess I'll have to ask Blake. He knows all about those infectious diseases and all that related stuff or at least he says he does. Never know when he's actually telling the truth. Wonder if he could ever pass a lie detector test."

Turning her hands from side to side, Meg carefully

examined them. "The eczema has returned again. I've not had it for years. It itches to high heaven. All I want to do is to scratch it which doesn't help at all."

"I can't remember the last time you broke out like this! What causes it?"

"It's usually when I get stressed out about everything."

Taking Meg by the hand, Less led her into the living room. "Let's sit on the couch. Look, I told you that we can weather this slight storm and then things will settle down. There's real hope and promise here if we ride it out. At least we have a roof over our heads even if it's not our own roof. Blake can be a skunk and a half, but at least he's letting us stay here. Since Stormy flits hither and yon like a dragonfly at least you can eat most of your meals there every day and manage to slip a little extra food in your knapsack to bring home."

Meg placed three pillows behind her back so her feet could reach the carpeted floor. "I think one of the things that's adding to my stress is working in that ranch house."

"How tough can that be? I mean Stormy's never there, and you have free run of the place. You can hear someone coming from a long way off if you keep those windahs open upstairs. You said yourself that you've read umpteen books since you started."

Standing up and pacing inside the room, Meg continued, "There are strange noises inside that house, especially on the third floor. I can hear footsteps running up and down the hallway. If I close the windahs, somehow, they get opened again. If I open them, somehow they get closed."

Less eyed the blanket rolled up like a sleeping bag sitting in Blake's worn-out arm chair. He'd like to cover up and think for a spell. "What? I've never heard of such a thing. I mean I've heard of *hearing things* before, but nothing like this. Can you turn on the radio and listen to country western music?"

"I keep the radio off most of the time because there have been days when Stormy comes home early or returns from Cinder Valley or Ridgemonte sooner than expected. I don't want to lose my Cadillac gig there at all. There's no way I could find another job as beneficial as this one. If we moved to Texas or California, I might be able to, but not in this remote area."

"Is there some kind of cream or salve you can put on your skin to help? Do you think you should see a doctor?"

Meg's tears freely flowed. "I would rather spend my money on things other than a doctor at the moment. This too shall pass. I'm planning to wear rubber gloves to wash the dishes and mop the floors which will help."

"That's my girl! Tough as nails when she needs to be and soft as velvet the rest of the time. How lucky am I? Say, you plow through one of those extra thick romance novels about every four or five days. Where are you finding them? Does Stormy have them throughout the main ranch house? I feel badly you don't have a way to get to and from work except when you can catch a ride with me. That's going to be even more difficult now that the spring season has kicked into high gear. Blake's been good enough to get the groceries at The Merc before he leaves town."

Drying her face, Meg asked, "The paperbacks? That guest room next to our bedroom is full of them. Since there's no Mrs. Blake Benson, I have no clue where they came from or how long they've been in there. The last time I looked, there were literally a dozen brown grocery sacks filled with them. In fact, that one whole side of the closet is stacked knee deep. Maybe Blake reads them."

Less commented, "There are many chapters to him, or so it would seem. I just don't have much time to read."

CHAPTER THIRTY

Chet winced as he walked slowly out the back door of the Lower Sabblonti Ranch house. After Evan hung the bedding on the clothes line, he sat down in the green metal lawn chair across from him. "Is your cane helping? You're still walking with quite a limp which is odd since your last x-rays didn't show anything out of the ordinary."

"Despite what they show, my legs feel like rubber when I try to walk any distance at all. I really don't know what's going on. Doc Merenspinn says everything looks fine, but my body doesn't feel that way."

"Even though you've done your exercises as prescribed, your muscles have atrophied over the past few months which is what usually happens. It's going to take a while to get them back to where they were before your accident. I've got an idea. Do you feel up to going for a ride around some of the ranch? It's a beautiful spring day. I'll drive slowly."

Chet extended his right leg as he held it with both hands. "I've spiked quite a headache, but a short drive might not be too bad. It could help to lift my spirits a bit. When did I take my last pain pill?"

Evan checked his watch. "You took one-half of it two hours ago. It's another couple of hours before you can have any more, so now would be a good time to head out. Do you want to take Blue with us?"

"No, not Blue. Leave him here to guard the place. Let's take Beebee with us. Come on, boy, get in the van."

Beebee balked and did not want to load. Evan picked him up, set him across the back seat and slid the door closed. "I should add that to my monthly bill."

"Add what?"

"Doggie care along with my physical therapy charges along with holding down the fort, and you name it."

"Ah, I get it now. You're being paid, aren't you? Have you been driving to the main ranch house and collecting your check from Her Highness, Mrs. Stormy Sabblonti Castins?"

"Actually, strange as it may sound, I've been mailing my bills from town when we drive in for your doctor appointments. That's when I collect my mail at the post office as well. I figured that might be the best method until Stormy thaws out. She must have hired a bookkeeper, though. My checks have been signed by *Megan Francine Alotto, C.P.A.* That seems pretty formal to me, but to each his own. Or I guess you could say, 'to each her own' in this case."

"Well, at least Stormy's keeping all the bills paid current. No surprise really that she's hired a CPA. Jantzi had hers in Blunte County do all of her tax stuff, so maybe Stormy's following suit. I just can't imagine what Stormy's doing with all of her free time. You'd think she could spend some of it with me."

Evan had no suggestions for how to remedy Chet's longing for his wife. Not being married yet, he had zero advice. There might be a prospect, however, who just may appear at Wyn and Sarita's upcoming wedding. "Is there some place in particular that you'd like to see this afternoon? It's been quite a spell since you've been able to do much of anything at all."

"Just head up the road, and I'll give you directions as we go along."

"Sounds good to me."

Chet started to doze off while riding in the front seat of the van, so Evan kept on driving. He had no clue where he was going.

Chet lifted his head and rubbed both eyes. "Turn left

here and drive down yonder. What? Who's running this outfit anyway? Those bulls are not supposed to be in the pasture yet! I only see twelve and there are supposed to be seventeen of them."

Evan started counting out loud. "I came up with thirteen. One is lying down on the other side of those tall bushes. Can you see his head sticking out?"

"Where?"

"At 2:00 on the clock face. You can't miss him."

Chet leaned his head forward and narrowed his eyes. "I don't see anything over in that direction. When I look into the far distance, things look slightly fuzzy. It just might be my headache."

"Next time we see the doc, we'll have him check your vision. I have no idea where the other bulls would be. Maybe they're over that little hill, so they're out of sight temporarily."

"Yes, Sabblonti Ranch had seventeen breeding bulls. Maybe Stormy sold some of them. Who knows what she's done? My back and leg are very uncomfortable, so let's head home. On the way, we can stop by and ask Stormy about those bulls."

Evan drove into the driveway and parked right in front of the main ranch house. "Chet, do you want to try to get out of the van or shall I see if I can get Stormy to come outside so you can talk to her? I can do the disappearing act, so you can have some privacy."

"That'd be great, Evan."

No one answered Evan's repeated knocks on the front door. He thought he heard something around the far side of the house, so he walked around to check it out. He could have sworn he saw the window closing just as he rounded the corner. Meg slid her hand down the inside wall of Stormy's upstairs office and waited patiently. She dared not move a muscle.

Evan called out, "Stormy, if you're here Chet would like to see you." After waiting several minutes, he walked back to the van. "I have no idea, Chet. I couldn't raise anybody.

Strange thing happened. I thought I saw a window closing upstairs, but maybe my eyes were just playing tricks on me."

Returning to the lower ranch house, Chet explained, "Evan, before you fix my supper, give me some more pain pills, and feed my horses, I need to call Stormy to find out about my bulls."

Stormy was just getting home from yet another shopping spree in Ignee County. Meg held the door open for her as she walked through with her arms heavily laden with colorful sacks. "Thanks, Meg. Looks like Less is waiting for you in the driveway. Get gone, I mean see you later."

The phone rang as Stormy set her purse on the kitchen counter. Thinking it was Trent Davies of the Ignee County rodeo board, she answered quickly, "Hi, Trent! I thought you might be calling this evening, so I hurried home from my busy day. I was able to really score some fabulous finds in Cinder Valley. I'm finally getting those clerks whipped into shape. How's your day gone, and what's the latest report ahead of our next meeting? Silly me, I'm doing all of the talking. I guess I should let you try to get a word in edge wise."

"Trent? Who's Trent?"

Stormy almost hung the phone up. "Oh, it's you again. What do you want this time?"

"Stormy, where are all of my bulls?"

"Bulls? What are you talking about? I have no idea where they are. It's not my day to watch them. Besides that, don't you recall that the ranch and all its holdings belong to me now that Mother has passed? If you want to talk on the phone, perhaps you should call that low-life grocery store clerk in Ridgemonte. I'm sure she'd love to hear your scratchy, sad voice."

Chet started to say Stormy's name again, but heard the dial tone. "Evan, it's no use."

"What's no use?"

"Trying to talk to Stormy or reason with her."

"What did she say about your bulls?"

"She reminded me, once again, that the Sabblonti Ranch

and all that goes with it now belong to her."

Evan set a frying pan on the stove. "This is a community property state, Chet."

"Try telling that to Stormy."

"I think I'll work on supper. What sounds good?"

"Nothing."

"Sorry, that's not on the menu. I'm not getting paid to fix you nothing for supper. Chef Evan will whip up some kind of cowboy magic. Chill and watch. And I'm not even a cowboy!"

Chet hobbled to the kitchen counter and removed the phone book from the drawer. He dialed the number for the Shaw Vet Clinic which automatically went to voice mail. Then he remembered that he had Dr. Shaw's home phone number penciled inside the front cover. "Come on, Doc, answer your blasted phone, will you?"

Dr. Shaw was right in the middle of enjoying a home-cooked beef stroganoff dinner to which he'd added diced cook bacon and sour cream. He contemplated not answering the call, but mercy got the better of him.

"Ben Shaw here."

"Howdy, Doc, sorry to bother you at home."

Realizing few people had his private number, Dr. Shaw continued, "Who's calling, please?"

"Chet. You know, Chet Castins."

"Oh, it's you, Chet. Is something wrong with your voice? You don't sound like your normal self. Sorry I did not recognize you. You sounded a little bit like a cartoon character on TV. What's going on?"

"I need to talk to you about my bulls at the ranch. Do you have a few minutes to answer some questions?"

"Yes, what's wrong with them?" Dr. Shaw held the phone from his ear a few inches as he savored every bite and listened to Chet.

"Did you get a call from anyone at the ranch to check the bulls with electrostimulation or have you been out to treat any of them? I was especially concerned about those six young ones we have. Also, I have no idea if anybody started giving those older ones extra feed a couple of months ago, so they would be in primo condition for the upcoming breeding season. Worst of all, Evan and I went for a ride this afternoon and discovered that the bulls have already been put in their pasture."

Dr. Shaw gently set his plate inside the sink. "Already? I didn't think you put them out quite this soon."

"Normally we don't. Slinky, my oldest Aberdeen Angus bull, was starting to develop that rigid straightness in his left rear leg, so I wanted to keep a sharp eye on him. That *post-legged* issue could end up costing me a few calves next spring. You know how hard I've worked to maintain a top-notch herd, especially after Ace Sabblonti died."

"Yes, I can attest to that. Do you want me to drive to the ranch and see what I can find out? I don't own a bulletproof vest, but I guess I could round one up somewhere. Pardon me, that didn't sound quite right. For a moment, I completely forgot that there was a gun involved in your mother-in-law's death in a roundabout sort of way. I didn't mean any disrespect by that comment. What I was driving at was Stormy's possible reaction if I ask her about any ranching operations."

Chet motioned for Evan to bring him a chair so he could sit down. "Stormy's scared to death of guns, so you have no worries in that department. She's hired a ranch foreman, but I've not met him. I can only hope he knows what he's doing. I miss my cattle and horses more than you can imagine."

"There's one encouraging thing, Chet."

"One? What's that?"

"I've not heard you speak with such passion about anything for months now. It's a good sign that you want to get back in the corral again."

"I never wanted to leave it in the first place. Thanks for checking on my ranch for me. I really appreciate it."

Evan decided to inject a little humor into the evening. He'd removed the yellow and white checkered kitchen drapes and fashioned an apron of sorts for himself along with a matching serving towel which he spread across his left arm.

He tied a white dishcloth on top of his head to resemble a chef's hat. He hummed some soft dinner music and danced a few waltz steps by himself when serving Shepherd's Pie.

Chet tilted his head to the right, raised his left eyebrow, and said, "Evan, have you been dipping into my Dr. Feel Good bottles by any chance?"

"Not a chance, Monsieur."

"Not a chance, who?"

"Just waxing a little Francais this evening."

"You can eat your wax and mayo stuff while I scarf down some of this Sabblonti beef. Where'd you learn how to build this pie?"

"It's a long story that will have to wait for a shorter time."

S

Dr. Shaw set his alarm for 4:30 the next morning. During the night, he dreamed he was riding his gelding, Beau, in the hills when he shied after suddenly encountering a coiled diamondback rattler. Dr. Shaw sat bolt upright in the bed. *I know that was a dream, but it was all too real.* He tossed and turned until it was time to get up and get going with his day.

He addressed his border collie, Jetter, "You can come with me today. Let's play detective." They drove from the Shaw Ranchette toward the bull pasture on the Sabblonti Ranch and parked until the sun came up. Dr. Shaw retrieved his hand-held counter from one of the sections in his seat cover and put it in his pocket.

"Sorry, Jetter, you have to stay inside the cab. I will never get these bulls counted if you're out there herding the herd. No barking, understand?" Jetter lay on the seat, lowered his head, and laid it across his front paws. "You're master of the guilt trips. Have I told you that lately?"

Dr. Shaw spent the next hour and a half walking the area looking for Chet's bulls in the pasture. He could only account for fourteen of them. A portion of the fence was starting to sag in a couple of areas, so he made a note to mention that to Chet.

Using his mobile phone in his pickup, he called his office and left a message for his assistant, Jacobe Davone, to let him know that he was driving into Ridgemonte and would be there as soon as he could. As he headed toward the main highway, all he could see in his mind's eye was that rattlesnake which appeared in the dream. Suddenly, he spotted an approaching pickup. Since the road wasn't quite wide enough for two trucks, Dr. Shaw drove off the right-hand side about four feet, into the sagebrush, and came to a halt. He got out of his pickup and stood next to it. Jetter started barking.

The driver in the pickup accelerated as he drove past Dr. Shaw who was waving his left arm back and forth signaling for him to stop. Walking through the clouds of dust to the driver's side, Dr. Shaw spotted the license plate with the Mount Rushmore faces. He motioned for the driver to roll the window down, and asked, "What are you doing way out here this early in the morning?"

"What's it to you?"

"Just wondering since your license plate is not from our state."

"Don't you have more important things to worry about than my plate?"

"Yes, as a matter of fact I do. I was just checking on the bulls."

"That's not your job. It's my job. Get off this ranch or I'll have you arrested."

"The last time I checked, there weren't any *No Trespassing* signs posted. Since when is it your job to monitor those bulls?"

"Since I was hired by Stormy Sabblonti. That's when."

"Do you mean Stormy Castins?"

"What's in a name? I think she's shed the Castins part of it. You look like some Wannabe-Rancher with a black and white dog. It takes a whole lot more than a designer pickup and fancy hat to get the job done."

"How long have you worked for Stormy?"

"Long enough to know that I'm whistlin' in the wind talking to you."

"Well, you just might make use of some of that valuable time and get all of those bulls accounted for and that fence repaired before you get canned. You're three short with possibly a whole lot more if that fence gives way."

Dr. Shaw turned to walk toward his pickup when he heard, "Who's counting?"

"I am," he yelled back.

Less Alotto revved his engine and drove into the bright sunlight.

Dr. Shaw got inside his pickup. He looked at Jetter and stated, "I think I have an interpretation to that dream I had a few hours ago. I've just met the rattlesnake in person." As he drove west, he placed a call to the Lower Sabblonti Ranch house on his mobile phone. Much to his surprise, Chet answered right away.

"Good morning, Stormy, it's so nice of you to call me bright and early. Are you having trouble sleeping because you're missing me lying in the bed next to you?"

Dr. Shaw certainly wasn't prepared for that greeting. "Sorry to disappoint you, Chet. I didn't know if you'd be up and at'em already."

"Sure am, Doc. I never really went to bed. Some nights have been like that. What'd you find out, if anything?"

"I went to the pasture and located fourteen of the bulls, but couldn't find the other three. I spent all the time I could this morning. I'll try to go out later, but my day was already overflowing with appointments before the sun came up. When I was leaving, some character drove up in an older pickup with out-of-state plates. He's a real prize to say the least. He's very contrary and threatened to have me arrested if I did not get off the ranch. He never did give me his name, and I didn't ask. Stormy hired him or so he says."

Chet stroked his mustache. "It's probably that ranch foreman she brought on board."

"I told him that three of the bulls were missing. Also, the fence needs repaired in some places. I brought that to his attention as well."

"Thanks for checking this out for me. There's no guarantee what shape the ranch will be in by the time I'm well enough to start taking care of it again."

"Chet, there are never any guarantees in life. I found that out a long time ago."

CHAPTER THIRTY-ONE

"Come in Sarita dear. I apologize as I did not see you standing on the porch."

"Thank you, Merna. I hope I'm not arriving too early this morning. You said you had something else planned for this afternoon, so I got up early and drove to your ranch. I thought I could carry everything in one trip, but it looks like I'll have to make a second one. I feel so badly as I spotted this young woman on the side of the road who looked like she was having some trouble. It was in that narrow bend in the road, and there were two pickups following closely behind me, one of which was pulling a trailer, so I didn't dare stop. I thought about turning around and going back to see if I could help her, but time was getting away from me. I hope someone stopped to help her. If that was me, I would certainly want a good neighbor to come to my rescue. I'm not very physically strong, so I don't know if I could've been of much assistance anyway."

"Most men folk in these parts are pretty good about stopping and helping someone, especially a woman in distress."

Merna led Sarita into one of the back bedrooms in her house. She let out a squeal of delight, "Oh, my goodness, look at this! You've transformed this room into a bridal suite. It looks like a picture in a magazine. Is this the basic pattern for my gown?"

"Yes, it is. Tom was kind enough to get on a ladder and install that big hook in the ceiling for me, so when I start to fully assemble all the layers of your dress, the ceiling will bear the weight of it. It also helps a lot with my shoulders and neck as I can just stand flat footed on the floor and make the adjustments when necessary. For the preliminary fitting, I made the basic pattern from a set of old, solid, pastel bed sheets. I'll go finish folding the laundry while you try it on, okay?"

Sarita stepped into the dress and smiled with sheer satisfaction. *Just needs a couple of tucks.*

Merna tapped on the bedroom door. "Are you dressed, honey?"

"I am, and it's going to be perfect."

Merna walked to the dresser and picked up a wristband with a magnetic top which had pins stuck to it. She proceeded to gather small tucks here and there as she made notations on a small, lined tablet. "Your long torso is going to accentuate the Basque waist very nicely. The Queen Anne neckline bodice will be lovely with the white lace overlay. What do you think of having a variation of the Juliet sleeve to make it short without a puff at the top? When I shopped at the fabric store, I picked up a couple of swatches of white satin and white lace overlay. One is more of a stark white than the other one. Here, I've drawn a picture of your gown. Take a few minutes to study it and let me know what you think. I need to check the beef and barley soup on top of the stove."

Merna returned to the bedroom drying her hands on a dishtowel. "Have you thought about a necklace or something along that line?"

"Yes, I'm borrowing one."

"That will look exquisite with that particular neckline. Which of the satins do you prefer?"

Sarita held the fabric swatches up to the light. "I'm almost thinking the softer white. The stark one would suit Stormy and the color of her hair better than mine, but this is not about Stormy for once. It's about me and my special day."

"That's for sure. You'd said you didn't want a train or a bustle. I'm with you on that one. You and Wyn will want to mingle with your guests and dance your special song. Not having a train or bustle will make that a whole lot easier. Have you thought about shoes for the day?"

Lifting her right foot, Sarita said, "Great question! No, I hadn't gotten that far. I want to wear something super comfortable, almost like a pair of ballet slippers. I can't wear heels because I don't want to stand taller than Wyn. Come to think of it, I saw a pair of slippers that had sort of a white beaded-pearl design on them. I think they were in a magazine that I was reading during my lunch hour last week in Dr. Diller's office. I will double check when I go back to work on Monday. I can call and have them shipped in time for the wedding."

Merna measured Sarita's waist one more time. "Speaking of Dr. Diller, have you told him you won't be working for him after you get married?"

"Yes, I told him right after the first of the year. He has really been a huge disappointment to me. Like I could really take another one of those in my life. I fully expected him to be ecstatic about me getting married. He acts like Wyn is some second-class citizen. I doubt he'll even show up on the 29th. He'll probably schedule some sort of a vacation."

"What does he have against Wyn for heaven's sake? He doesn't even know him. Tom would come to Wyn's defense in a heartbeat. Tom has been crowing like a rooster telling all the ranchers in these parts how well Wyn and Spence are taking care of our ranch. I just might have to give Dr. Diller a piece of my mind when I go in for my next dental appointment."

"Now, Merna, I appreciate you defending Wyn to the hilt, but it's best to let sleeping dogs lie. There are times when the best way to prove someone wrong is through good, honest actions and hard work."

Merna grinned as she nodded her head up and down. "Wisdom has spoken from the younger woman. Upward and onward. Assuming you're able to order those slippers, let's measure your gown to determine how far from the floor you'll want it. The skirt is free flowing and this satin has a very nice drape to it. The clerk at *It's Sew Time* in Ridgemonte said she would give me the cardboard bolt carriers for the satin and the lace. I really like the ladies who work in there. They're so helpful and kind. A couple of more things, and I think that will do it for today. How about the design for your veil? Have you had time to give that some thought? Also, do you want a matching, satin, beaded pillow for your ring bearer?"

Sarita looked in the mirror and pulled her hair away from her face. "The easiest answer first. Wyn's already selected the perfect thing for Logan. Believe it or not, I spent some time drawing my veil. Could I have the kind that has a blusher with it? I'm really into this blusher thing as I think it will be something very meaningful for Wyn to unveil his bride, so to speak. Could you make this Juliet cap and attach the veil and blusher to it? Also, I would like some pearls on the cap if you have enough.

"Before we get too far down the trail, Merna, I should've asked you what all of this is going to cost me. I've had to set aside money each month in order to purchase Wyn's ring. The jeweler was kind enough not to charge me for the engraving. Here's what I'm going to have put on his band:

WM & SS ~~ 07-29-2000

Do you think he'll like that? I was going to ask him his middle name, but I didn't want to give away my surprise. I think he will be pleased with just WM, don't you?"

Merna handed the small piece of paper back to Sarita. "Yes, honey, I do. I can make everything just the way you want it, and don't worry for one minute about the cost of the fabric and accessories. That's one of my gifts to you. Okay, I think that does it for now. Let's plan to have you come out to the ranch in a couple of weeks. By that time, I'll have purchased everything I need, and we'll be ready for your first official bridal fitting."

"Thank you, Merna. You're precious. If anyone ever deserved to have a dozen kids, it's you!"

S

Earlier in the week Dr. Shaw had looked at his schedule in disbelief. Either his assistant, Jacobe, had zoned out and not recorded appointments or all of the critters were giving him a much-needed day off. He discovered one of the tires on his horse trailer was flat, so he changed it the night before. He'd also purchased a new one at *Gib's Gas* since his spare was also deflated. It might have been solely his imagination, but he could've sworn that his gelding, Beau, and his border collie, Jetter, were smiling right along with him as they headed down the highway for their mountain adventure. He looked at Jetter before gazing out the passenger window. "Yes, ol' Jetter, ol' buddy, ol' pal, I have this feeling that everything's coming up roses today!"

Approaching the narrow curve in the main road, Dr. Shaw felt Beau's weight shift in the horse trailer. He was thankful for the electric brakes he had installed in his pickup three years ago. Trying to concentrate on a pickup pulling a camper trailer coming toward him, he thought he saw something on the side of the road. He glanced in his rear-view mirror. The something was actually a someone. "Jetter, we might want to double back and check that out. I hope someone isn't injured. We know how to help in those kinds of situations, don't we buddy? Before long, you just might have your doggy license to practice medicine. Of course, the person we just saw would have to be on one of the most difficult and challenging sections of the road. It's another four miles or so until the next turn out."

Somewhat aggravated at trying to get his pickup and horse trailer turned around in a confined space, Dr. Shaw had calmed down a bit by the time he resumed driving. As he approached the curve from the opposite direction from where he first saw something along the side of the road, he slowed down to 5 mph. Rolling down the driver's window, he called out, "You need some help? What happened?"

The person was bent over and looking at some mangled metal on the ground. She stood up and nodded her head up and down. She did not turn around. Who was this mysterious woman?

"I'll have to drive down the road and park my pickup. Be there to help you as soon as I can. Doesn't look like you're going anywhere anyway."

Dr. Shaw drove to the next turn out, flipped on the hazard lights, and parked his vehicle. "Jetter, we'll be back before you know it. Take good care of Beau for me, okay?"

Jetter barked loudly as if to say, "Yes, Boss."

Arriving at the narrow spot in the road, Dr. Shaw bent down to render assistance. "Did you take a header over your handle bars? Here's my wild rag if you'd like to clean your hands and face. Oh, my goodness, your hand is bleeding! Here, let me take a look at it. I can't believe no one stopped to help you."

"I haven't been here that long. My hand's okay. Really it is. I know how to take care of it."

"It's a good thing you were wearing a helmet. That might have saved you from suffering a concussion or something worse. What happened?"

"I wanted to spend my Saturday morning in the glorious outdoors, but had never bicycled on this part of the highway, and didn't realize it was so narrow. I was going to turn around up the road a short distance as soon as I navigated that turn. Some hotshot drove up beside me in a big truck, revved the engine, and honked his horn. I felt like he was trying to force me off the road. I'd heard that some ranchers don't like people riding their motorcycles, bicycles, or even horses for that matter on these roads. In my opinion, it's a free country, so people can ride where they want to ride."

Dr. Shaw squinted to shield the sun from his eyes. He thought he recognized those teeth as she spoke. "Macey, is that you by chance?"

Stepping back, removing her helmet, and shaking her head so that her hair fell loose onto her shoulders, she replied, "Yes, my name's Macey, but who are you?"

"I'm Dr. Shaw, the local vet. Remember when I came to pick Chet Castins up when he was discharged from the hospital?"

Macey brushed the dirt from her cycling pants. "Yes, I do, but you don't look anything today like you did that day."

"What's that supposed to mean?"

"Nothing. Sorry. I'm a bit out of sorts to say the least. I would really appreciate some help. Maybe I'll take you up on your offer to use your wild rag." Macey got a bottle of water from her zippered pouch strapped to the seat of her bicycle. Drenching the rag, she cleansed her hand and wiped her face with the bottom half.

Dr. Shaw tried to contain himself, but couldn't. He looked at her and started to laugh. "You look like a raccoon."

Tossing Dr. Shaw's wild rag to him, Macey exclaimed, "Well, thanks a lot! I thought you were here to help, not stand there and laugh at me. You might be a professional man, but you sure could use some lessons on social skills. Are you related to Dr. Linke by any chance?"

Dr. Shaw did a complete turn so he could change his countenance. "You totally misunderstood me. I wasn't laughing at you, and no, I'm not in any way related to Dr. Linke. Why do you ask?"

"If you weren't laughing directly at me, then why did you laugh in the first place? As it pertains to Dr. Linke, well, we'll just table that discussion for now, shall we?"

"Okay, I owe you an apology. Please forgive me. When

you took off your helmet and wiped your face, there was still some dirt on your forehead, cheeks and chin. But I can still see the whites of your intense, emerald green eyes. Also, I didn't want you to think that I chuckled just because you wouldn't explain your earlier comment as to why I don't look anything today like I looked when I picked Chet up following his hospital stay."

"You're like a hunting dog on point, but I do forgive you. And that was a full-on laugh, so don't try to explain it away as a chuckle."

"We can continue our bantering later, but we'd better get your bike moved before there's more travel on this road. I'll carry it down to my pickup if you can collect your personal items next to the embankment."

As they approached Dr. Shaw's vehicle, Jetter spotted them and started moving back and forth across the front seat. He cocked his head to the right and barked as Macey walked to the passenger side.

"It would appear as though you were headed to the mountains yourself, Dr. Shaw."

"True story. I rather believe that my assistant, Jacobe, cleared my schedule for the day and moved everyone to next week. I didn't dare take a sneak peak at that. And please call me Ben."

"Fair enough, Ben it is then."

Macey stood by the side of the pickup until Dr. Shaw opened the door for her. "Jetter, this is Macey Meadows. Macey, it's my distinct pleasure to introduce you to Mr. Jetter Shaw."

"You assign your last name to your animals?"

"Sure do. Why not? It's a good thing your cycling pants were full length."

"No kidding. I managed to tear a big hole in the right leg of these. They were a little pick-me-up gift from my daddy. His package arrived last Wednesday."

"Pick-me-up gift?"

"Let's just call it a gift, shall we?"

"Yes, let's. I have the most splendid idea! How would

you like to accompany Beau, Jetter, and me to the mountains? We would definitely enjoy your company."

"Dressed like this and covered with dirt and grime?"

"Absolutely. You look just fine to me, uh, I mean that won't be any problem given our final destination."

"I really should go home. Could you please drive me there?"

"I could, but Beau and Jetter really want you to come with us."

Macey looked at Jetter who barked, licked his mouth, and scooted closer to her in the seat. Laughter overcame her. "Oh, I suppose I should."

"Well, don't sound so enthusiastic."

"It's not that. I don't even know you. Didn't your mother ever tell you not to talk to strangers much less get into their vehicles and ride with them?"

Dr. Shaw's shoulders tensed. "Macey, if you can't trust me, you can't trust anyone. My mother told me a lot of things. Wait until I let you know what advice she gave me about women. I need to practically drive back to my place before I can turn around, so let's get started."

Macey remained quiet and collected her thoughts for the next few miles. Pushing the lever for the right turn signal, Dr. Shaw drove through his circular driveway.

"Is this where you live?"

"Yes, this is the official Shaw Ranchette in all of its glory. If it's okay with you, I'm going to unload your bike here. We can pick it up on the way home."

"Nice place. Carefully manicured. When do you have time to do all that or do you hire it done?"

"No, I do it all myself. I'm a pretty high-energy person. Actually, the *manicuring*, as you call it, is a great stress reliever."

"I sure need to find one. That's why I thought I would start riding my bike more often."

"You could replace the bike riding with horseback riding."

"I've never been on a horse."

"Oh, that's right. Now I remember."

"You remember what?"

"Never mind. Let our big adventure begin."

Dr. Shaw could see Macey settling into her seat on the passenger side as he drove. Just as the sun rays of providence were starting to shine upon him, he didn't want to head for the shade. He opted for a period of nonverbal activity. When he entered the portion of the road that was as straight as an arrow, he glanced over to see that Jetter had rested his chin on Macey's left thigh. Both of them were napping quietly. A rush of adrenaline laced with protection came over him.

Macey's head jerked to the left after which she sat up straight.

"Are you okay?" asked Dr. Shaw. "Do you need me to stop?"

"Yes, I'm fine. Thanks. I nodded off briefly. When I closed my eyes, I could see myself going end over teakettle on those handlebars when my bike slammed into the embankment."

"The turn off is just ahead up here, and then it's about another ten miles as we start to climb into the high country. Are you up for that?"

"Sure. Are there switchbacks on the road or is it pretty straight?"

"There are only a couple of moderate turns. Other than that, the road is pretty good. I wouldn't have trailed Beau up here if it was not a suitable route. His stomach does not need that kind of turmoil."

Dr. Shaw parked under a group of quaking aspen trees. "Macey, I'm going to unload Beau and tie him in the shade. There's a nice stream just over that bluff if you'd like to wash your face. I keep some old towels in one of the side panels of my pickup. Just a second, and I'll unlock it for you. I might have stuck some other odds and ends in that same compartment. I believe I have a small bottle of castile soap in there. You're welcome to whatever you can use. We'll give you some privacy before I water Beau and Jetter up the stream."

Macey found two towels and walked toward the bluff. She joined Dr. Shaw after rinsing her hands and face in the cool stream. "Well, would you look at this? Is there anything you don't know how to do?"

Patting the old camping quilt, he said, "Come, have a sit. I hope you like egg salad sandwiches, garlic dill pickles, and potato salad. I might have used a titch too much mayo in the salad, but I think you'll like the dill flavoring. I'll confess up front that the double-dark chocolate fudge, supreme brownies with nuts were a box mix. I didn't have time to melt the chocolate in my double broiler to make them from scratch."

Macey almost dumped her plate onto the quilt. "Seriously? You cook in addition to everything else you do?"

"I've had to learn how to prepare my own food. I'm not real keen on fast food or frozen foods that contain a lot of preservatives. How about you?"

"I can cook, but it's not my favorite thing to do. My mother makes scrumptious food. I would rather spend my time baking and making fancy desserts."

"You don't look like you eat a lot of desserts or does your bike riding deplete the calories for you?"

In between taking bites of her sandwich, Macey replied, "Working with Dr. Linke does that for me."

"You've mentioned him a couple of times already. Would you like to talk about it?"

"Negative. I want to enjoy the rest of my day. These sandwiches are really tasty. Is there a secret ingredient?"

"Of sorts. I add some hot sauce, but not just any old hot sauce. I have my favorite brand that enhances my specialty dishes. I've got a super-duper suggestion. Would you like to try to ride Beau today?"

"My day has been stressful enough. I think I'll pass on that. Maybe Jetter and I can stay here in the shade."

"There's no way he'll stand for that. The minute I get in that saddle he starts walking in lockstep with Beau." Before flashing that intriguing smile, he added, "I'll be back after while, pretty soon, maybe."

Waving her left hand back and forth, Macey motioned for Dr. Shaw to take off. She curled up on the blanket, fell into a deep sleep, and started to dream. She awakened to Jetter licking her face. "Silly dog. Are you helping me clean my pan?"

"How was your siesta? Beau is broken in for you now. Come stand by him and stick your arm out. Let him smell you, and we'll see how he reacts."

"He'll probably be just fine since I smell like the earth, the flora, and the fauna," Macey said as she stood up. Beau wrinkled his nose as he brushed it across Macey's forearm and down onto her hand. Holding the reins, Dr. Shaw instructed her to put her foot in the left stirrup and swing her body weight across the saddle. Despite trying repeatedly, she could not accomplish that. He considered assisting her by helping to hoist part of her body weight, but reconsidered. "Go sit on that big rock over there. I'll lead Beau next to it, and you can get on that way."

The suggestion worked brilliantly. After Macey got in the saddle, Dr. Shaw led Beau for a few minutes around the side of the hill. "Here, take the reins. I'll walk right beside you. I know you can do this."

Macey looked down at Dr. Shaw. "Uh, I don't think I'm quite ready yet. The saddle is way too big for me. I feel like I'm going to fall or get bucked off."

"Give it a try. It's important that a horse not be able to sense that you're afraid of him. If you can handle working in the ER, you most certainly can handle one of the gentlest equines on the planet. I mentioned to you before that I knew just the right size saddle for you."

Macey sensed Dr. Shaw throwing down his gauntlet, so she announced, "I can do this and I will do this. Just watch me." Securing her feet in the stirrups, she took hold of the reins as Beau started walking northwest. Jetter assumed his normal position beside Beau.

"Mission One accomplished," said Dr. Shaw as he stretched out on the blanket, covered his face with his cowboy hat, and fell fast asleep. He had no idea how much time had elapsed. He awakened to Beau's whiskers nuzzling his knuckles as he lifted his hat. Standing to his feet, he asked, "Do you think you can get off by yourself or do you need some help?"

"I've already gotten off and back on twice by myself."

"You have? What time is it anyway?"

"Two hairs past a freckle. How should I know? My watch broke during my morning escapade. Judging from the western sky, I would say 4:30ish or later. Where would you like me to tie Beau?"

"I can do that. You don't need to worry about it."

"No, I want to do it. I watched you tie him, and I want to make sure I've learned the proper way."

"So happy you're a quick study. Please tie him under the shadiest spot of the aspen grove."

"Look over there!" exclaimed Macey. "What is that dirt flying in the air?"

"That's just a friendly badger sending dirt signals. He's probably digging deeper to make room for his soon-to-be bride badger. When you're done there, please join me on the ledge overlooking the valley."

Macey and Jetter walked to where Dr. Shaw was sitting on the large rock and joined him. He spoke from the stillness, "Look at that reflection pool below that lower crossing. I think it's neat how the water gathers in those eroded pockets of basalt worn smooth by the rushing waters. This time of the year there's a purplish-bluish hue to the rocks accentuated by the green moss that grows in the background. The small rock outcroppings form their own little pools in the stream. The sun's rays reflecting off that water makes it look like liquid gold. The buckwheat is in full bloom. I love the desert."

Macey took a deep breath and exhaled slowly. "I had no idea it was so beautiful and peaceful up here. Just think, if I would not have crashed on my bike, I might never have discovered this area." Macey's feet dangled over the ledge. When Dr. Shaw looked a second time, her left pinky finger was less than an inch from his right one. He resisted the urge to touch it or open his palm to see if she would place her hand inside his.

"When we left our ranchette this morning, I had a feeling everything was coming up roses today, and it sure has!"

"Speaking of roses, I absolutely loved my Valentine bouquet, but you do need some serious help choosing chocolates."

"I received your typed thank you note telling me as much. I did not hand select those candies. Daisy's Floral Shop delivered those with the flowers. I never saw either of them."

Macey gasped, "You didn't? You just totally took a chance on both?"

"Yes, just like I totally took a chance on inviting you up here today. The majority of the time, you just have to go with the stirrings of your spirit providing you know who's doing the stirring."

Moving her right hand in a circular motion, Macey said, "Speaking of stirring, I make unbelievable chocolates, the hand-dipped variety. It's quite a time-consuming project, but so worth it. I could polish off a platter in no time all by myself. Would you like to join me some time to learn how?"

"You bet I would. Aren't chocolates more of a holiday item?"

"Not necessarily. Chocoholics never take a holiday, so I make them the year round. The mint and coconut-flavored ones are my favorites. I have the candy making supplies at my little house. You would need to come over there. Before I left this morning, I looked at my work schedule to see when I might be able to carve out some time to go bike riding. The best time for you to visit would be next Saturday evening. You could bring Jetter with you so he could be our chaperone. Given your age, we'll probably need one."

Dr. Shaw felt Macey's left hand brush ever so slightly against his right one. She sensed it simultaneously and scooted to her right. "Sorry, I didn't realize I was in your space."

Looking closely at Macey, Dr. Shaw commented, “I’m not the one who moved.”

“I know.” She smiled, lifted her legs, and stood on top of the rock. “My ribs are telling me they’re not happy. I hope I’ve not cracked one of them.” Raising her cycling pants about four inches, she exclaimed, “That’s one wicked bruise!”

“Since we’re both medical professionals, do I need to suggest that you should be examined by doctor just as a preventative measure?”

Macey answered as she walked toward the shade trees, “I’ll keep an eye on the bruise and monitor the rib pain level.”

Dr. Shaw joined Macey under the trees. “Speaking of invitations, next Saturday evening sounds great, and would you do me the honor of being my guest at an upcoming wedding?”

Macey looked down to re-examine her leg and massaged both sides of it. Dr. Shaw wondered if she would ultimately deny his request. “When and where is it? I’m scheduled to work most weekends for the next two months. We’re having a staff meeting on Monday to finish calendaring everyone’s summer schedule. Days like today remind me that I’ve spent way too much time inside the walls of Mintner Medical Center since I moved here.”

“It’s Saturday, July 29th, at the Toppens Ranch which is in Shadow Butte County. It would be best if you could take that whole day off work. You might want to take Sunday off, too, if you can swing it. Some of those country wedding dances last until after the midnight hour or so I’m told. Maybe one of the other nurses could sub for you.”

The sun filtered through the trees into Macey’s eyes, so she stepped a few feet to her right. “Who’s getting married? Friends of yours?”

Dr. Shaw moved his shoulders up and down and pulled his hat brim lower to cover his forehead. “More acquaintances than friends I guess you could say. In these parts, most everyone is invited to special gatherings whether they receive a paper invite or not. It’s one of the things I especially like about this area."

"You still didn't answer the question, did you?"

"Oh, the who's getting married question. Toppens Ranch Foreman, Wyn, and his fiancé, Sarita."

"I don't believe I've met either one of them before. As the county vet, you probably know everybody, his brother, and his dog, right?"

"Pretty much. Speaking of pretty, you sure, uh, well, we'd best get Beau loaded into that trailer and head on down the mountain. Thanks for spending this day with me and taking a chance."

"You're welcome. Thank you for a splendid day. I'm glad I took that chance."

CHAPTER THIRTY-TWO

Miggy was surely dreaming she was chasing the newly born calves, her legs twitching as she dozed on the well-worn green and brown plaid couch in the Toppens bunkhouse. No one noticed that she'd used the lower right-hand side as a teething tool.

Wyn had just finished eating his second helping of biscuits and gravy when Spence sat down for a late breakfast. Gravy spilled over the side, through the crack in the breakfast table, and onto the floor.

Wyn set a tall mug in front of Spence's faded, green, chipped platter. "I made the coffee extra strong this morning since you haven't been to bed yet. Was there enough dew between 2:00 and 5:30 to keep the leaves on the hay?"

"As near as I could determine there was. The grass is so thin since we've not had any rain this spring. I got off the tractor a couple of times to check the rollers. It looks like one of the belts is wearing really thin. We need to keep an eye on that. Also, I hadn't realized that there was such a sharp slope on the other side of that meadow. I don't think any of bales fell down the other side. Looks like it's going to be one long day. Do you have time to attach that grapple fork to the other tractor's bucket loader?" asked Spence between sips of coffee.

Drying the last of the dishes, Wyn said, "I wish I did. I'm meeting myself coming and going these days. I probably miscalculated when agreeing to a wedding date of July 29th. At the time it seemed like it would be no problem. That wagon train is already too far down the trail to stop it now. Sarita would be super chapped if I even suggested such a thing. We'll have to wait 'til winter time to take our honeymoon. I just remembered one more thing on that hay." Wyn removed a paper towel from the roll and a pen from his shirt pocket. He proceeded to draw on the towel as he instructed Spence. "When you stack it, make sure to lay those bales on their sides for the bottom row. Then stack every other row with the bales lying flat."

Spence looked at Wyn's diagram a little more closely. "With not getting much sleep, I appreciate the reminder on stacking those bales," said Spence. "You make these biscuits and gravy yourself?"

"Absolutely. When I sent our grocery list with Merna a couple of weeks ago, I included four boxes of biscuit mix and eight packets of country sausage gravy mix. If you add enough butter and pepper to stuff, it makes it taste like something other than cardboard. I like a little biscuit with my gravy, so I use a two to one ratio."

"You might want to hold off on adding so much water," added Spence. "Pretty runny gravy. Oh well, Miggy's snack is on the floor. Does Sarita like to cook?"

With his hands in the sink rinsing out the coffee pot, Wyn turned around slowly. "That I could not tell you. Let's hope she does. We've not spent a whole lot of time together actually."

"Sounds like Priscilla and me. Even though she lives and works in Ridgemonte, she might as well live in Rhode Island or some such place."

"I'm not worried about not knowing Sarita all that well. When I was in the boy's home, I read all kinds of stories about sailors and marines knowing some gal three weeks, getting married, and shipping out. Their marriages lasted for over fifty years."

Spence countered, "Yeah, but that was a totally different time in our country. The war didn't afford long courtships.

Seems to me like a guy can feel it in his gut whether or not he should marry the young filly or get on down the trail."

"Agreed. Do you feel that way about Priscilla?"

"Felt that way the first time I laid eyes on her at the New Year's Eve Barbeque in Merrill's barn. Shane totally fouled that one up for me. He was such a glutton and started power drinkin' the cider. Before I knew it, he was rolled up on the ground like a bloated steer, and I had to take him home. After what he did to all of us here at the ranch, I should've just let him fend for himself."

Wyn squirted all of the kitchen counters with the antiseptic mixture he'd placed inside the plastic bottle. "Where would you say your relationship with Priscilla stands today? If you offered her a ring would she take it?"

"She's not the problem. It's her mother," stated Spence.

"Well, now, that's one problem I don't have. My would-be-mother-in-law expired before the end of last year. That's when I knew beyond a shadow of a doubt that our marriage would stand a fighting chance."

Spence opened the creases of the cardboard milk carton and stuck his nose inside. "Speaking of expiring, this milk smells funny. The container says it was supposed to have been consumed three weeks ago."

"You can't pay any attention to that stuff. Those companies just put those dates on there to force customers to buy them by such and such a time. Cattle ranchers don't fall for scams like that. Smarten up, Spence. Here's some maple syrup. Just pour a little of that in there and down the hatch with it. I gotta get a move on.

"One last thing, Merna came down yesterday and wanted me to remind you to stop by the house so she could get your measurements for your vest for the wedding. I need my best man looking his best on my big day!"

Spence closed the milk carton and placed it inside the fridge. "I completely forgot about that. All of this wedding business is giving me some sorely needed experience in that area."

Wyn continued, "Merna's been sewin' up a storm in that

house. I can't wait to see Sarita in her dress. Speaking of the wedding, you did invite her, didn't you?"

"Who?"

"Priscilla. Who'd you think I meant? The Tooth Fairy or Cinderella?"

"I sorely need sleep."

"That makes two of us."

S

Salina strained her eyes as she peered into the display window of the *Second Time Around.* She glanced down at her watch as she walked through the door. "Hi Verntoola, it's me again! Have you rounded up anything since my last visit?"

"There are a couple of ensembles that I've set aside in my office in the back. You still haven't told me exactly what you need them for, so it's been hard for me to know what to sell and what to hold back. I'm operating on a pretty slim margin, so I need to have everything on the sales floor at once."

"As I told you before, just a very feminine occasion. You know, general stuff along those lines. Let's see if you and I are on the same page."

As soon as she entered Verntoola's small office, Salina was drawn like a magnet to the floral print, powder blue, summer dress. It was sleeveless with a very low neckline, tapered waist and mid-ankle length. She rubbed the bottom of the dress between her fingers, lifted the skirt, and brushed it across her right cheek. "This stuff is heavenly. I just know the target of my desires will want to reach out and grab each of these lovely white flowers on this dress. Thankfully, there are a lot of them. What's this dress made from?"

Verntoola put her glasses on and held the dress closer to her eyes. "It's silk chiffon fabric. Mandrake silk or so the tag sewn inside the hem of the skirt reads."

"I thought chiffon was a kind of pie. One time I splurged and bought a piece of lemon chiffon pie at The Sage Hen Café. Of course, that was back when I was not devoting my spare change to my present project."

"Yes, there are chiffon pies," agreed Verntoola, "but the name *chiffon* comes from the French word for *rag* or *cloth*. What's your present project?"

"This dress is certainly no rag!" huffed Salina. "I should've said my future project."

"Quit being coy. Here I've done nice things for you. The least you could do is let me know what you're planning."

"It's an unveiling of sorts. A big shocker."

Touching some of the flowers in the dress fabric, Verntoola asked, "And this dress will be your big surprise?"

"Let's just say I'll incorporate it."

"You should try it on in the dressing room over there. It looks like it might be a titch too small."

Salina pushed the floor-length, fabric curtain of the dressing room to the far side. She was so excited to try on the dress that she forgot to pull the curtain back until Verntoola cleared her throat loudly which caught Salina's attention. Emerging from the dressing room, Salina picked up a mannequin and started dancing with it. "Give me your honest opinion, Verntoola. It instantly peels ten years off me, doesn't it?"

Verntoola didn't open her mouth.

Salina continued to demand an opinion.

"Okay, you asked for it," said Verntoola. "The dress looks like it's at least two sizes too small for you. The V-neckline opens almost to your navel. That's probably the reason it ended up here in the first place. The original owner might not have known how to alter her clothes, so she donated it instead. I see that every now and then with these new designs. I much prefer the older ones myself. You know, in the days when women were ladies and men were gentlemen."

"You're such a prude, Verntoola. No wonder you're still looking to get married. You should've lived during the Victorian era."

"Last time I looked, you didn't have a ring on your left hand either."

"That's just because I'm not willing to settle."

Salina's words weren't very settling. "Settle?" asked Verntoola.

"Yes, you know. Just take the first cowpoke that comes along. That's a recipe for disaster to be sure. I'm biding my time for the real prize. I decided that it's just as easy to marry a rich man as a poor one. In fact, I'm slowly reading a book which addresses that very subject."

"The only rich men I know in these parts are the big cattle ranchers. It seems like their sons and daughters continue to marry into the big ranching families, so it's hard to worm your way into one of those."

A bit out of breath, Salina set the mannequin back in its original place. "Ah, Verntoola, you just gotta know how to do it. I forgot to look at the price tag on this dress. What color of tags are discounted this week? This one has a black tag."

"This must be your lucky day, Salina, as the black ones are 40% off. Are you sure you still want this dress as snuggly as it fits?"

"Why wouldn't I?" snapped Salina.

Gesturing to her jewelry display case, Verntoola offered, "There's some nice jewelry in there. That necklace with the dogwood flower in the center of it would complement your outfit. It could serve as the centerpiece."

"The last thing I need is something else to try to be the focal point. You're looking at the centerpiece, Verntoola."

"Somewhere you lost me, but that's okay. I feel like I've been lost most of my life. The only reason I leased this shop was because I received a small inheritance from my great aunt. Most days I wish I would have invested elsewhere. Your total is $18.48 with tax."

Salina laid a well-worn Jackson on the counter and waited for Verntoola to make change.

"Salina, can I ask you a very personal question?"

"As long as it doesn't pertain to me, yes. Shoot."

"Do you like my first name?"

Salina slowly dropped the coins, one by one, in the bottom of her purse, hesitated, then said, "It would not be one of my favorites, but I don't want to hurt your feelings. Don't you like it?"

"I think it makes me sound eighty years old or beyond. I want a young, vibrant name like Kayla or Kyley. That's a first name I think all cowboys would really like."

"That's easy enough to remedy. Just go to the Shadow Butte County Courthouse. You ask for permission from the court and obtain an order from the judge. I've heard that Judge Jerry Jofton is a decent sort of fellow. After he signs the order it allows you to change your birth certificate and other documents. Reinvent yourself. People do it all of the time. I'll let you in on a little secret, if you promise not to tell a single, solitary soul. I'm in the process of doing it myself. It's not as hard as you think it might be. Use your imagination. Set your sights on what you want. Go after it with gusto. It's a free world out there, honey. Better grab hold or it will pass you by."

"Gee, thanks, Salina. I feel like you've just given me a solid gold coin instead of a measly $20 bill. Where do you get all of your ideas anyway?"

"I check out a lot of books from the public library, and if you recall, I've purchased a lot of used western romance novels from your shelf over there. The real finds are inside those old *True Confessions* stacked just below the paperbacks."

Verntoola walked to the shelf and picked up the entire stack of magazines. "I completely forgot about those. Maybe I should start reading some of them at night. Shall I hang your dress on a hanger or would you prefer I fold it and put it inside the recycled grocery bag?"

"Folded, of course. I don't want anyone in town to see

me carrying it down the street. That would foil my plot."

"Plot? Are you a writer?" asked Verntoola.

"Not so much a writer as a planner."

"I've not heard of any big upcoming doins' in Ridgemonte. What am I missing?"

"Nothing that I know of in Ridgemonte."

Tom scraped his plate with the heel of homemade bread and scooted his chair from the table. "Merna, you might want to gather your clothes off the line before I start with that brush mower this afternoon. It looks like the breeze has shifted, and it's blowing right toward the house. We need to make sure our bedroom windows are closed."

Merna ran to the back of the house arriving just ahead of the hot desert wind. The guest bedroom which she had transformed into wedding headquarters was her number one concern. She was having trouble turning the metal bracket around the circular knob to secure the windows. "Tom, I need some help, please. Come quickly!"

"No wonder I haven't seen much of you lately. When did you whip all of this out?"

"Sorry, Tom. It's been a busy few weeks. Are you sure you want to clear that area today? Can't it wait a few days?"

Tom double checked the latches on the windows. "Maybe, but I won't know how many cars and pickups can park there 'til I get rid of that tall brush. I'll wear those protective glasses and tie my wild rag to protect the lower half of my face. Let's hope the stampede strings keep my hat on my head. I'll be fine."

Locating a clean wild rag for her husband, Merna asked, "Do you think you should ask either Wyn or Spence to do it for you?"

"Nah, those young pups are running to keep up as it is. Looking ahead to that wedding, what time of day is it anyway?"

"It's 7:30 at night," said Merna.

Tom wiped the beads of sweat from his forehead. "Sure hope it cools off some before then. I heard on the radio this morning that it's been fifty-six days since we've had a drop of rain. The storms have been splitting and going around us. They're calling them the *splitters*. So, I think 7:30 will be a good time as the temps will start dropping on toward midnight."

"Midnight?"

"Yes, said Tom, "And you'd best take a nap that afternoon because the last time I checked, your name completely filled my dance card."

Merna took a break from her sewing so she could rest her back and shoulders. Looking out the bedroom window, she had a hard time seeing Tom through the clouds of dirt. She could tell there was a moving object and that was about it.

All of a sudden, she sunk down in her sewing chair. Several loud knocks on the front door brought her back to reality. Marita Merrill arrived with clipboard and paper in hand. "Merna, you look frightened. Can I help?"

"It just occurred to me that I've been so busy sewing for everyone else that I don't know what I'll wear. I want something very special. It's like my own children are getting married. I'm running very short on time."

"I'd offer to help you, Merna, but have my hands full with the reception. I wouldn't know how to cut out a pattern much less how to piece it together. I wanted to get here a little earlier, but had to help Nelson round up a couple of stray calves. Before we get started can I see the wedding dress?"

Marita followed Merna down the hallway into the guest bedroom and saw the dress hanging from the big hook in the ceiling. "This is absolutely gorgeous! I had no idea you could do this. Are you keeping it hidden from Wyn?"

"Yes, I've been careful to do that. He's been so busy I've not even had time to measure him for his vest."

Merna handed the pattern envelope to Marita who pointed to the drawing in the middle and asked, "Is that what Wyn's wearing?"

"That was what he decided. He wanted me to make one for him and Spence. Wyn's will be this silk, ivory, brocade, western wedding vest that he'll wear over his long-sleeved, white shirt with ivory snaps. Spence's will be this silver colored, silk, brocade vest. Don't they look sharp? This pattern is called *The Sunset Wedding Vest.* They sure never had anything this fancy when Tom and I were married in 1947."

"Nor when I married Nelson. It warms my heart to see some of this next generation getting hitched. Pretty soon we'll have a crop of youngins' running all over the place. I know it's your house, but how about I fix us a cup of tea, so we can put our feet up and plan away?"

"Sold me on the idea," said Merna. "You know where my tea makings are in the kitchen. There's a fresh rhubarb pie in the tin with the lid on it. Please cut us a piece of that to go with our tea. I'm sure those will move our wedding menu along more smoothly."

CHAPTER THIRTY-THREE

Evan and Chet left the ophthalmologist's office in Cinder Valley.

"Chet, any place else in town you'd like to stop before we head home?"

"None that I can think of. It's like a whole other world over here. Too many people for me. Sorta gives me hives." Just the mention of the word picture caused Chet to start scratching his thighs.

"Well, Chet, you don't need hives in addition to everything else you have going on. It's a huge relief to know that your vision is okay, and you don't need glasses right now. Do things still look blurry to you?"

Chet looked at a brick office building in the distance. "Not as much as they used to, but I still see the waves in both eyes every now and then. It usually happens when I'm walking. If I sit down, the waves calm down and disappear eventually."

Evan kept his foot on the van's brakes at the end of the street. A flash of red caught his eye. "Say, isn't that your cattle brand?"

Glancing to both sides, Chet asked, "Isn't what my cattle brand? I don't see any brands anywhere. Now I think it's you that needs to have your eyes checked."

Evan insisted, "I could've sworn I saw that upright S with

the dot on its tail on that red pickup truck back there."

"Couldn't have been. There's nobody that owns anything red that has the Sabblonti brand on it. I'd bet the whole spread on that one."

"Okay, Chet. Have it your way. I thought we could play detective for a few minutes before we left the big town. Where's your sense of adventure these days? It would drive me nuts to live here with all of these high-rise streets. It reminds me a lot of driving in downtown San Francisco. You'd wear your brakes out in short order."

Any place that didn't raise cattle was of little interest to Chet. "I lost my sense of adventure the night of my wreck, except new adventures with my wife. I hope she returns to her senses sooner than later. As for Frisco, I've no clue. Never been there. Don't want to go either."

Evan noticed Chet's frayed shirt collar. "Hold on a second. I knew there was something else we needed to do before we left town. Is there a western store in this town so we can get you a new shirt for the shindig?"

"What shindig?"

"Your sis-in-law's wedding. Remember?"

"When is that anyway?"

"It's coming right up."

"I don't plan on going, so let's not waste our time or money."

"Chet, I would highly encourage you to attend the gathering for several reasons. Before Wyn got super busy with ranch work this spring, he stopped by several times to see you. By your own admission, you've said Sarita is a very nice person. It's important to rejoice with people when it's time to rejoice. Besides, that will be the perfect opportunity to spend some real quality time with Stormy. You can sit by her, hold her hand, tell her that you love her, and relive your own wedding day. Don't miss your big chance to reunite with your wife. I'll make myself invisible, so no one will even know I'm there if that's what's bothering you."

Breaking into one of his few smiles of late, Chet admitted, "You're right. Thanks for the pep talk, Evan. I really don't feel like getting in and out of the van again. Can you just drive to the store, go in, and select a shirt for me? All I need is a size 17 neck and 36 ½ inch sleeve. I like the kind that has the pearl snaps on the cuffs if they have them. Hopefully you can score a parking spot in the shade and roll the window down. Better get me a new pair of jeans, too: 38 x 34, boot cut, solid black."

Being unfamiliar with Cinder Valley, Evan drove around for a while trying to find the store.

After feeling like they were driving around in circles, Chet suggested, "You could stop at that stop n' rob convenience store and ask someone if there's a western clothing store in town. I'd think there would be."

"Real men don't stop and ask directions, Chet. They just go on the hunt until they find what or who they're looking for. That's my philosophy which has served me well for decades."

Chet thought he saw a sign that read County Wear. "Evan, turn right at the next corner and then take another right. I think they've got what we're looking for down that way."

Evan parked near Country Cate's Western Wear. "Now there's a name and half for you." As he entered the store, all he saw were women's western clothes.

The clerk emerged from the back of the store. "Hi, what brings you in today?"

"I need some men's clothing, but don't see any."

Store clerk Shasta replied, "All of our men's wear is in the back. You can tell who buys most stuff in this store. If you'd like to follow me, I can show you what we have. Anything in particular that you're looking for?"

"White, western, dress shirt with fancy, pearl snaps and new jeans."

"We've got plenty of those on hand. They've been selling like hotcakes ahead of our big event."

"What's that?" asked Evan.

"The 75th annual Ignee County Rodeo and Roundup. People are coming from far and wide for it."

"Must be nice."

Shasta started looking through the stacks of jeans. "What size on the shirt and jeans?"

"I need a 17-neck size with 36 ½ inch sleeve and 38 x 34, boot-cut jeans in black."

"I know I have those jeans in that color and size. If you'd have said the regular blue denim, you would've been sorry out of luck. As for the shirt, the closest thing I would have is an XLT."

"I'll take your word for it."

"Anything else?" asked Shasta.

Evan surveyed the racks of shirts one more time. "I was looking for a bright purple men's shirt with matching lavender snaps, but it doesn't like you have anything like that in here, so that'll do it for now."

Looking toward the back wall of the store and back to the front counter, Shasta surmised, "Actually, purple is not a color we sell to menfolk that often. Sorry about that. Also, I would wash and iron that white shirt before I wore it if I were you. The original fabric straight from the factory can be sort of itchy and scratchy."

Before glancing at her name tag, Evan wondered if she'd been a western model or if she was an exercise instructor since she was in such fine shape. He guessed he could learn to like bleached blonde hair. "Is Shasta your real name?"

"It sure is! Isn't it lovely? Reminds me of the soda brand or Mount Shasta in sunny Cali."

The phone rang inside the store. "Would you mind if I took a minute and answered that? My boss instructed me to take every call and not miss a sale."

"Not in the least."

Evan walked up and down the aisles throughout the front and back of the store to stretch his legs while Shasta took the special order. He checked the price tags on some of the clothes hanging on the mannequins and raised his eyebrows. As he approached the counter, he noticed an extra-large grouping of women's clothing covered in see through plastic garment bags. Notes taped to each bag read,

"Will pick up by 5:30 today." He gestured with his left hand, "It looks like someone went on a super shopping spree. Nice women's clothing you have in here."

Shasta straightened each of the garment bags. "Thank you. Yes, we pride ourselves on carrying the top of the line in women's western wear. As for these inside the bags, they're all for one person if you can imagine that. I wish I got a commission on the amount I've sold her just since the first of the year. I might be able to take a vacation with the extra funds. The woman who ordered all of that stuff is sort of the new darling of the rodeo board now that Gwen Hybrenth retired. She, the new darling as I like to call her, always pays cash. Amazing."

Making a mental calculation in his head as to what might be an approximate tab for the clothing, Evan agreed, "Yes, that's amazing. But, then again, some of these cattle barons are really worth a lot of money in these parts."

"True story. Here's your merchandise. Enjoy."

"Oh, they're not for me."

"Looking at you, I didn't think you'd wear a 38 x 34."

Evan smiled and left the store.

When he returned to the van, Chet was napping. "You were gone long enough to make an offer on the store. Or was it the help that waylaid you?"

Evan opened his mouth, pressed his bottom teeth against his upper lip, and said. "The clerk shows some promise. Things take time sometimes, Chet."

"Evan, just when I thought I could go to the wedding, now I don't think I can."

"Why's that?"

"I don't have a gift to give Wyn & Sarita. I can't go empty-handed."

Checking his pocket to make sure he had his wallet and not finding it, Evan braked suddenly. "Chet, is my wallet inside that clothing sack?"

"Sure enough is. You're all shook up, aren't you, Evan?"

"Back to this wedding gift dilemma, Stormy will be taking care of that stuff. Those are the sorts of things that wives do."

"You're right. For a minute there, I completely forgot I was married. Another Friday night and weekend alone. I wonder how much longer I can continue with this baloney. About all I have left is a band of gold that I never wear anymore."

S

Dr. Shaw parked his pickup in front of 812 Flame Street. For once, he was on time. Fastening the leash to Jetter's collar, he stood on the street, adjusted his white beaver Stetson, and walked onto the front porch. "No barking." Jetter nipped at the leash as he looked into the flickering eyes of his master. No one answered the door. Dr. Shaw rang the doorbell again.

"I'm on the patio. Come around back." Macey opened the gate for her guests. "It's been so hot today that I thought we'd have some fruited tea to start with. Jetter, we don't have a leash law in Ridgemonte."

"Would you mind if I secured this gate? Jetter likes to herd, so we better keep him corralled."

"Yes, please do. You can leave him in the back yard if you'd like. I could use a hand carrying the bevs and snacks from the kitchen to the patio."

Dr. Shaw removed his hat after closing the patio screen behind him.

"Nice hat," commented Macey. "I'd be happy to take that for you if you'd like. It accentuates your square jaw and chiseled chin." Macey laid it top down on the corner of her solid oak bookcase. As he stroked his chin, Dr. Shaw made a mental note of how she treated his hat and that she knew the proper way to lay it.

"Thankfully my kitchen is well shaded. I decided to make cold snacks and not heat the kitchen until we make our confections."

Dr. Shaw drank in the colors of Macey's kitchen as he sipped his iced tea. "Interesting combination of turquoise with the greens, blues, and coppers. I would've never thought of using this color in a dining area. It looks more bathroomish or some other room in a house."

"I especially enjoy it as it's soothing when I need it to be and energetic when necessary. Sort of the best of both worlds. I have the greatest landlady. When I moved in, she told me I could paint any of the rooms whatever color I wanted. It's been a lot of fun to experiment. When I'd finished decorating, I invited her over to see it. She offered to sell it to me. My parents were willing to help me with the down payment. I simply need to decide if I want to stay in Ridgemonte or move to greener pastures."

Just then a flurry of white scampered from behind the island in the kitchen and ran to hide underneath Macey's couch in the living room.

"I think I just spotted your guard cat."

Macey got on the floor on her hands and knees. Reaching as far back as she could, she gently pulled her cat forward and scooped her into her arms. "Emmy, meet your new veterinarian."

Dr. Shaw looked back and forth at Macey's eyes and then Emmy's. "How'd you get her eyes to match the color of yours? Was that your criteria for selecting her?"

"Not at all. She belonged to my college roommate. When she got married, her husband was severely allergic to cats, so I adopted her and brought her to Ridgemonte with me. I renamed her *Emmy* to match her eyes. I think they're gorgeous. Plus, both of us were born in May, so our birthstones would be emeralds. I've always wanted an emerald ring, but they are terribly expensive. I inquired of a private gemstone dealer one time. He quoted me somewhere between $3,500 and $4,000 for a dark emerald which he maintained were the best and purest kind."

Macey ran her fingers through Emmy's hair. "There's one thing that I should probably ask you about as far as Emmy's concerned. Can you see those clumps of matted fur on her back? I've tried brushing her and even asked the groomer to clip the globs, but they keep growing back."

Dr. Shaw studied Macey's hands. He wondered how many patients she'd lovingly cared for already. "Has Emmy been gaining weight rapidly?"

"Come to think of it, yes she has. I've cut her food portions in half lately. I just attributed it to the hot dry weather we've been having. I've not really felt like eating much myself and have put on two and a half pounds."

Dr. Shaw stroked Emmy's head softly. "Matted fur can be a sign of diabetes or hypothyroidism. You can bring her into my clinic, and I'll run some lab tests on her."

"That's a great idea! I just need to carve out the time to do it. I've been giving her daily massages, rubbing her chest, patting her forehead, and giving her all of the love I know how."

Lifting Emmy up and down as if weighing her in mid-air before she jumped from his hands, Dr. Shaw commented, "You nurses and your mercy gifting."

"What do you mean by that?"

Dr. Shaw explained, "A lot of people go into the health profession because they have a lot of mercy to help mankind."

"Never really thought of that before. Agreed, some of us do. I've no idea why others have chosen it. Having a pet can help keep our hearts healthier, too."

Raising his turquoise glass to hers, Dr. Shaw said, "Cheers! Here's to two healthy hearts."

Macey clinked her glass against his.

Drinking all of his tea, Dr. Shaw asked, "What's in here anyway?"

"For the basic mix, I used black, lemon, and raspberry tea bags. I let it sit in the sun for about four to six hours. Then I've added fresh strawberry, peach, and lemon slices.

Do you like it?"

"Very much. The peach is an especially nice touch."

"Excuse me a minute, please. I want to make sure I didn't stick that sack of cat food in front of Emmy's kitty door so she can't get outside when she needs to."

Dr. Shaw stood with his back against the kitchen island. He spotted a greeting card in the window sill which read, "Happy Birthday to ONE OF THE LOVES of my life." He stepped closer to the window and breathed a sigh of relief when he saw who'd signed it. Sitting next to it was a photo of an adorable little girl about five years old. She was sitting on a white settee with light grey cushions wearing a pink and white plaid, taffeta dress and white pumps. Her hands were folded on her lap. Her smile was rather subdued as she sported a white hat with a pink ribbon tied off to one side. The hat looked more like an inverted flower pot than a bonnet. Her dark chocolate brown ringlets were tied to the left with a matching pink ribbon. A solid sea of pink and white peonies formed the background. Macey reentered the kitchen.

"Cute little girl. Is she your niece?"

Macey giggled as she placed her right hand over her mouth. "Niece? I have no nieces. That's me before I started kindergarten. It's my daddy's favorite picture of me. As you can tell, I was not overly fond of the photographer on that particular day. I spend a lot of time in my kitchen, so it helps me when I have to go many months without seeing my family. I'll open the door if you can carry this tray and set it on the patio table for me."

They emerged just in time to see Jetter drinking water from the brass style, spill fountain. Macey was unfazed. Dr. Shaw deemed this a good sign. "Jetter, I'm glad you like my fountain. It's one of my stress relievers, too."

Dr. Shaw stood next to the small garden shed. "Shade is perfect out here. Did you design this backyard as well?"

"Sort of. Some of the plants and furnishings were here when I moved in. I've added more evergreens, succulents, grasses, and herbs. I cook with a lot of rosemary and lemon thyme. I like to alternate the Black-Eyed Susans and the Wild White Daisies."

"You must like yellow, Macey. That Cat Claw Vine looks very happy along with the Red Ice Spike."

Macey picked up her watering can to moisten the pot where the spearmint was growing. "Yellow is becoming one of my select colors. I painted the guest bedroom in a soft buttercup yellow and accented it with red blended with blue undertones. It's a real eye catcher using colors which are opposites on the spectrum. I think we can eat before the bug invasion. Then we can move inside. I can light the tiki torches if need be."

"The miniature, all white, Christmas tree lights add a lot to the ambience out here. Do you keep them up year-round?"

"Yes, I decided to. Every day is Christmas if you're still alive and breathing."

Dr. Shaw made five trips in and out of the house carrying platters and containers from the kitchen counter to the patio table. On the last one, he spotted a humming bird near the bee balm bush. "Look Macey, we've got company!"

Macey joined Dr. Shaw. "Where's our guest?"

"Look at that pretty little messenger."

Macey looked around the yard. "I don't see anyone except us and Jetter racked out over there."

Dr. Shaw pointed to the bee balm. "It's the hummingbird. They're symbolic of messengers."

"Then I'll wait for my message," Macey said.

"You really pulled out all the stops for presentation tonight. Nicely done, Macey. Awesome hummus. Did you make this yourself? Very tasty with the fresh cuke slices."

A small bit of cucumber skin stuck to the corner of Dr. Shaw's mouth. Macey almost stepped closer to remove it with her finger. She motioned for him to brush his mouth off which he promptly did.

"I have a secret hummus recipe that I make in my food processor."

Looking around the perimeter of the patio, Dr. Shaw did

not spot any cucumbers. "Well, it does not appear that you grew these?"

"Correct. Too short of a growing season."

After consuming two of the sliders, Dr. Shaw asked, "What's that spice I can taste?"

"Probably sage. Have you ever cooked a pork shoulder roast?"

"Can't say as I have."

"Dried sage is the secret ingredient. I used my slow cooker this morning so as not to add extra heat to the kitchen. Worked better than I thought it would. I let the meat rest and then shredded it. I took a chance that you would like coleslaw on top of the shredded pork with the final condiment being a sliced garlic dill pickle."

Flashing that intriguing smile, Dr. Shaw said, "And here I thought you were not one to take many chances at all."

"Normally I don't. Shall we venture inside for your one easy lesson?"

"I completely forgot. I was going to bring my double broiler for tonight. Sorry about that."

Checking around to find Jetter, Dr. Shaw saw him napping underneath a wooden wheelbarrow planter filled with orange marigolds with red centers.

"I've got you covered," Macey said. "What I'll need help with is cutting small chunks off this ten-pound brick of sweet dark chocolate."

Dr. Shaw lifted the brick and pretended he was doing curls with it. "Where'd you get this? I doubt The Shadowy Merc carries this top-shelf brand."

Macey had filled cereal bowls with various kinds of nuts and shredded coconut. "From my constant secret admirer. It came in my monthly care package."

Dr. Shaw filled the bottom portion of the pan with water and turned the burner to the number one position.

"You're putting the cart before the horse there, good doctor. Heat the water in the tea kettle and then pour it into the bottom. Fill the top with the chunks, turn the burner on low, and stir away. If the water is allowed to boil, steam is produced and released around the dark chocolate which will tighten it. Then we can't use it for dipping."

Dr. Shaw stepped away from the stove. "You mean I almost ruined everything before we got started?"

"I wouldn't say ruined, but I'm giving the lesson tonight, remember?"

Macey set an overly large, metal, lasagna pan on the counter. To the right of that, she lined a jelly-roll pan with waxed paper. She reached into the cupboard and got her box of latex gloves, slipping one over her right hand.

"Since when do you use your nursing gloves to make chocolates?"

"Just watch." Placing four handfuls of chocolate into the metal pan, Macey selected her filling. Cupping her hand slightly as she made gentle *S* motions through the chocolate, she made certain each one was completely covered before sliding the completed product onto the waxed paper. "Now here is where the artist enters the picture. Tap the surface of the chocolate with your middle finger and pull up a string about an inch or so long. Move your finger over the top to create the design you like. I make mine with an M. Now it's your turn to try your hand at this."

Dr. Shaw traced a "B" in the air with his finger. "Here goes nothing. One thing's for sure. That dish of processed coconut is all yours. Those mixed nuts are talking to me."

As Macey glanced at Dr. Shaw's shaking hand, she realized she was probably making him very nervous, so she excused herself to go outside and check on Jetter. When she came back, much to her surprise, Dr. Shaw had dipped three chocolates and placed his initial on top of each one.

"Are you sure you've never done this before? You're just pulling my leg!"

"As God is my witness, I've never even attempted making hand-dipped chocolates before this evening."

Macey peered across Dr. Shaw's forearm. "What's the *B* stand for again?"

"Ben. Benjamin, actually."

"A superb idea is coming to me. Do you mind if I call you Benny?"

Dr. Shaw pursed his lips together as he hunched forward. Standing straight, he asked, "Benny, as in B E N N Y?"

"Yes, as in B E N N Y! You no like?"

"It would take some getting used to."

"Never mind. It was just a playful idea. You scholarly types need to lighten up sometimes. No wonder so many of you die so young. I had so looked forward to today. Please don't ruin it on a note of rejection. I had this little jingle going through my head, "Benny, Macey, Jetty, and Emmy."

"That little ditty came together quite quickly." Dr. Shaw removed his latex glove and laid it on the counter. He took a small spatula from the white, ceramic, circular, cooking-utensil container and placed one of his chocolates and one of Macey's on a saucer. He walked over to her and extended his offering. "Let's sample these, shall we?" He thought he saw her left eye glisten with extra moisture.

"You first."

"No, it's always ladies first."

Macey bit into the center of her hand dipped confection, but not before a full tear dropped onto the top of it.

Dr. Shaw froze. He didn't know what to do now. If he could have physically kicked himself in the rear, he would have done so right then and there. He picked up his chocolate, and barely took a bite from the corner of it. "Flavor is beyond delicious." Without thinking, he offered his chocolate to Macey to take a bite from it. She turned to her right and started to walk away. Reconsidering, she turned back, turned his already eaten side of his chocolate toward him, and took a bite from the other side as he was still holding it. "The coconut is better than the nut filling."

Macey quickly regained her composure. Smiling from ear to ear, she offered the remainder to Dr. Shaw who gladly consumed all of it without somehow touching her fingers. She stood motionless and so did he. She did not blink and neither did he. Finally, he did. Macey laughed. "You blinked first."

"Yes, I did. I'd be honored if you would call me Benny."

"On that note, shall we retire to the living room for a cup of coffee?" asked Macey.

"I think I've had enough caffeine, but thanks anyway. I'd take a tall water though." Dr. Shaw sat down on Macey's overstuffed white brocade couch. Emmy still had not resurfaced. "Sitting on this couch makes me nervous."

"How so?"

"A white couch. All I have to do is look at it, and I'll probably leave a stain somehow."

Macey smoothed a portion of the brocade covering. "That's what they make stain remover for. A white couch works well with a long haired, snow white cat, especially when I only vacuum once a week."

Peering into his glass, Dr. Shaw inquired, "How'd you know I liked lime wedges in my glass of water?"

"Just took a calculated risk."

Dr. Shaw reached down and picked up a book titled *Corrals & Gates* from the center of the octagonal shaped coffee table draped with a hand embroidered, flower garden design cloth. The book cover featured a middle-aged woman dressed in dark blue, mottled fabric that made her look like the ocean floor. Her long, red locks and matching shade of lipstick clashed with the reddish-brown coat of the horse whose bridle she was holding in her left hand. "That equine looks like it has mange. What's the book about, anyway?"

Macey explained, "It's about how to set healthy boundaries which is one of the keys to having a successful, happy life and family."

The corners of Dr. Shaw's mouth turned downward which accentuated the two small lines in his cheeks. He flipped through a few of the pages. "Have you read it, and do you agree with what the author espouses?"

"I checked it out from the library recently, so I've not had a chance to finish reading it. I can usually tell from the first few pages whether or not it's worth my valuable free time to spend on it."

Closing the book and carefully laying it on the coffee table, Dr. Shaw asked, “Do you mind if I ask you something?”

“Not at all.”

“The day we went riding in the mountains you mentioned Dr. Linke. Is he difficult to work with?”

Macey sat across from Dr. Shaw in the matching white brocade chair. “He’s beyond impossible. I’m thinking of switching to the night shift, so I don’t have to see him as often. There’s a psychiatric nurse in Tranquility Falls that specializes in hard cases like him. I just need to find a way to suggest that he should make an appointment with her. He would go ballistic if I said anything along those lines. At one point during school, I’d considered specializing in psychiatric nursing after I got my Bachelor of Science, but am glad I changed my mind. Hospice isn’t for me either. Let’s move to another subject. My turn to ask the question this time. Also, the day of our mountain adventure, you said to ask you what advice your mother gave you about women.”

Dr. Shaw flashed that intriguing smile which seemed to last for a full five minutes. “My mother told me to marry a woman just like her.”

Macey said, “Please tell me about her.”

Sliding down on the couch to make himself more comfortable, Dr. Shaw explained, “From the day I arrived on planet earth, she has been my devoted madre, biggest fan, supporter, cheerleader, encourager, and you name it. She called me her *Crown Prince*. Mom would discipline me if I needed it, but I knew she always had my best interest at heart. On my birthday and special holidays, she would make at least one recipe that was my favorite. Her Montmorency cherry pies were to die for. She didn’t spoil me. I knew when the chips were down, I could always count on her. She’s still there for me. I don’t know how *Benny* would go over with her, but if something’s okay with me, it’ll be okay with her. Now it’s my turn again. You said your dad gave you marital advice, too.”

Macey put her hands over her eyes, then uncovered one. “I hesitate telling you this because you’re probably going to think it's silly, but here goes. When I was a little girl, about the same age as I was in that picture you saw of me earlier this evening, I would ask my daddy if I could marry him when I grew up. He would just laugh. He told me to look for a man just like him, and I would be MHEA."

"MHEA?" asked Dr. Shaw.

"Yes, surely you know," Macey said. "Married Happily Ever After."

"Please describe your father to me, Macey."

"He's basically a lot like your mother, only rarely cooks. He just picks up the check at the restaurant. Do you want to know the real reason I wanted to call you Benny?"

Dr. Shaw placed his hands on the couch cushions and sat straight up. "I guess."

"Well, don't sound so enthusiastic."

"I think it makes me sound like a young boy," commented Dr. Shaw.

Macey squealed with delight. "That's the whole object! I wish I would have met you when we were both about seven years old. You know, before you had given parts of your heart to others, one chunk at a time."

Placing his right hand over his heart, Dr. Shaw stated, "I still have my whole heart. Pieces of it have not been given away to anyone. What are you talking about?"

Holding up her right forefinger, Macey asked, "Not one piece given to anyone at all ever in the past?"

"No, not one. Would it make a difference if I would have given it all away not once, but several times?"

"Maybe. I would have to think about it. That's a very deep question with several layers to it."

"I'm just now getting to the point where I can even concentrate on matters of the heart. Undergrad, vet school, and setting up my practice have been an extremely long haul. And, while we're on the delicate subject of hearts, how about putting yours under the microscope as well? Turnabout is fair play."

Macey explained, "I was very shy and introverted in high school. My nose was in a book most of the time. My steady dates in college were my textbooks, classes, and clinicals. I moved to Ridgemonte straight out of college. Don't ask me why. I couldn't even tell you myself."

Dr. Shaw challenged, "So you're telling me that with those looks of yours you never had a steady boyfriend in either high school or college before receiving your BSN degree?"

"We need to insert a completely different slide with a challenging specimen under the microscope," announced Macey. "When I was a sophomore in high school, my best friend met her early demise. Nikkie worked at one of the local restaurants, The Red Jar. It catered to families, especially those with lots of children. Their Friday night special was all of the meatless spaghetti you could eat for $1.99 per person. It was the first week of June, and I'd talked with Nikkie on the phone right before she left to go to work. She was so excited as she got to help close that night. It would've been early morning actually because the place stayed open until midnight on Friday and Saturday nights.

"Nikkie's body was found in a pool of blood the next morning when the owner unlocked the door at 8:30. She died of multiple stab wounds. The largest meat cleaver normally used by the kitchen staff was missing. A thorough investigation was conducted, but the killer was never found or at least that's what the authorities reported. It left our city in turmoil for years. That's what unsolved murders do. I cried until I had no tears left. To say that episode made me set even stricter boundaries is a mild understatement. Back to your comment regarding the looks department, beauty lies in the eye of the beholder. I don't look in the mirror very much. I got way off in the ditch telling you my high school story. Back to the subject at hand. How old are you now anyway?"

Quite taken aback, Dr. Shaw answered, "Old enough, and I want you to know that you are stunningly beautiful. You should look in the mirror every now and then and find out for yourself."

Dr. Shaw and Macey continued to talk for another two

and a half hours. He passed her facial tissues to dry her tears and blow her nose every time she needed to do so. The wastebasket overflowed with discarded ones.

Macey entered the kitchen and turned the light off above the sink. After splashing cold water on her face and patting it dry, she glanced out the window and saw Jetter sound asleep on her chaise lounge. Dr. Shaw walked up behind her. She turned to face him. He was standing three inches from her. She deemed the next move was in his court. His shoulders relaxed as he formed a gentle smile.

"Such restraint, Dr. Shaw. I like it that you shave so closely."

"It's Benny from now on."

"Thank you, Benny, for this evening. Most of all, thanks for helping me to unburden. I'd not cried a single tear from the evening Nikkie died until tonight. Then the dam broke."

"I'm the one who should be thanking you, Macey. Everything was beyond wonderful. No worries about the breakage. I know how to manage the flow of water."

"Well, that's good to know. I think I received something I didn't realize I needed."

"Such as?" asked Dr. Shaw.

"The start of an inner healing," said Macey.

"I scored as well."

"You did? How so?"

"One wall tumbled."

Macey secretly wished Dr. Shaw would have lingered a little longer as she watched him adjust his Stetson, clip Jetter's leash to his collar, and walk into the front yard. When she washed the last of the dishes in her sink and hung the dishcloth on the magnetized clip on her refrigerator, she narrowed her eyes in the dim light to read the handwriting on a small piece of paper affixed thereto,

"Macey, I miss you already, Benny."

CHAPTER THIRTY-FOUR

At long last the big day had arrived. The Silver Jack Motel was coining the jack, Cinder Valley's voluminous sun bleached, blue, water tower was all but dry, and the horse flies had just hatched which fried the nerves of most equines and folks in attendance.

Saturday, July 29th, dawned with the Cinder Cone Club serving their annual Buckwheat Pancake Buckaroo Breakfast complete with Bacon Bow Ties, Fruit Compote, pure maple syrup, crocks of homemade butter, and gallons of black sheepherder coffee. Blue and white plaid tablecloths checkered the city park as far as the eye could see. Waves of dark denim were spotted as the young whistle britches crawled over the old army tanks which formed the southern perimeter. The forecast called for 110 degrees in the shade if there was any to be found.

Carson Tayer, Chairman of the Ignee County Rodeo Board, had tried to dissuade the Cimmarron Sorority Sisters from conducting their annual parade down Flintlock Street, but was completely unsuccessful despite his repeated requests.

Luetta Lonnders, Parade Committee Chairwoman, was in full command mode as she barked orders, blew the black and white striped whistle hanging around her neck, and heaped praise upon each of the parade entrants. When

Carson couldn't stand it a minute longer, he marched up to Luetta, "Get rid of your whistle already. These horses are not used to that shrill sound, especially those in the Silver Dollar Riding Club."

"What's the matter, Carson? Afraid someone is going to outshine you today? Whistles don't bother horses in the least. If anybody should know that, it's you. I've waited forty-six years for this occasion. I'm not about to cave into you or anyone else!"

"Forty-six years? What does that have to do with anything? We're all supposed to be working together to make this Cinder Valley's finest day ever."

"You do have a very short memory, Carson. Does Saturday night, April 24, 1954 ring a bell in the concrete between your ears?"

Carson pulled the brim of his oversized, black, cowboy hat lower onto his forehead to avoid the 11:00 rays. "I have far more important things to concern myself with today besides some random dates you've thrown out in a feeble attempt to snare me."

Luetta moved the clipboard in her right hand close to Carson's face. "The only feeble attempt I recall is your last-minute cancellation of our date to our Senior Prom at eight in the evening. You asked me what color of dress I was wearing, and if I preferred a wrist or pin-on corsage. You promised to dance with me to 'Honky Tonk Girl.' Not only did I never receive a petal of any kind of flower from you, but was left standing in my living room that evening staring at myself in the beveled mirror. And, for the record, I never fulfilled the lyrics to that song. Not even one word of it. To this day, you've never uttered an apology to me. Over the years, you've grown way too big for your britches. There's coming a day when someone is going to whittle you down to size. One last thing, you might consider getting rid of those *roll-your-own* cigarettes. You fancy yourself as a real rodeo man, so you should probably switch to something a little milder that might not leave as much yellow stain on your sorry teeth, lips, and chin."

Removing his pouch of tobacco, Carson dangled it by the brown string in front of Luetta's face. "The size of my britches, as you call them, and anything else pertaining to my appearance is my business, not yours. Speaking of jeans, another layer of skin, and you couldn't fit into the ones you're wearing. Did one of your sorority sisters paint those on you earlier this morning?" With that, Carson patted his left rear pocket to make sure he'd not lost his leather gloves and turned to walk toward the park. He felt something very hard under his cowboy boots at the same time he ran smack dab into solid burgundy.

"Gee, I'm sorry, I couldn't get out of your way fast enough," said Stormy.

"If you were standing that close, your intention was probably eavesdropping."

"I apologize if it appeared that way, but it's so noisy over here I was waiting for you to finish conversing as I need to talk to you right away. You're like trying to find a needle in a haystack this morning."

Removing his hat and running his hand through his overgrown hair, Carson suggested they locate a table in the park. As Stormy followed behind him, Luetta's words replayed in her mind. Even though she was not directing them at Stormy, they felt like swords being thrust into every ounce of her being. It reminded her of how her mother, Jantzi Belle, had spoken to her father, Ace, before he died. Oh, the power of the spoken word!

"Did you get any breakfast yet, Carson?" Stormy asked. "I would be happy to fix a plate for you if you tell me exactly how much butter and syrup to put on each pancake."

"I think they've shut the chow line down by now."

Stormy looked in the area where the Cinder Cone Club had set up shop for the morning. "The cooks are still turning their pancake turners, so they're not done yet."

"Yes, I guess I better eat now. The only things I've had this morning are five cups of coffee to go with my half a can of tobacco. You don't mind if I light up, do you, Stormy?"

"Personally speaking, I mind it very much, but who am I

to say anything to you? I wouldn't dare even suggest a word of correction to the most important person in all of Ignee County today."

Carson continued, "I've tried to quit smoking for years, but nothing ever works. I think I'd better try licking it sooner than later. Four of those big buckwheats and a plate of bow ties ought to do it. Oodles of butter and ladles of syrup on top. I'm coffeed out for now. A couple bottles of water, too. Thanks, Stormy. Sure am glad you know how to really treat a man like he's supposed to be treated. If you'd have been in my senior class in high school, well, never mind. I'll cool my heels over here. You'll save me an extra slow one at the Rodeo Dance later tonight, won't you? Yes, indeedie, I've got it made in the shade with a masquerade."

In all of the hustle and bustle of the past few months leading up to the main event, Stormy had completely forgotten about the dance. She dared not concern herself with that right now. She needed to get through the remainder of the day first. Sticking a bottle of water inside each pocket of her split riding skirt, she walked slowly toward Carson balancing the lopsided paper plate of pancakes in her left hand and the bow ties in her right. "I hope I didn't drown your breakfast in too much syrup, Carson."

"'Bout time you showed up. I could've cooked and served my own meal in the time it took you to do it. Pick it up a pace or two. Now what was so all-fire important that you're taking up so much of my valuable time?"

Stormy couldn't quite believe what she was hearing. Watching Carson inhale both plates of his food reminded her of the demonstrations by the traveling vacuum cleaner salesmen when they would visit the ranch during her childhood years. A combination of syrup and butter ran down the deep crease from the corner of Carson's lower left lip off his chin and onto his bright red, western, monogrammed shirt. He paid no never mind. He wiped his mouth and jaw with his right shirt sleeve. "It'll dry in the sun. No biggie. You're wilting like a petunia. I've got about two more minutes and that's it."

"I just heard about the Draysn Family," said Stormy.

"What about them? They're hardly my number one priority at this particular moment."

Stormy explained, "Their house burned to the ground this morning. It's a total loss. Fortunately, the fire department was able to get everyone out alive. Even their household pets are dead. They have no insurance, so a community drive is being conducted since there are so many people here for the rodeo. Hopefully, a generous amount can be collected and gifted to them. I thought it would a kind gesture for the Rodeo Board to donate something."

Carson lifted his left hand and extended it straight up. He started sliding his left index finger across his overgrown left thumbnail. He continued doing this for two minutes. Finally, Stormy threw her hands up in the air and asked, "What are you doing? What's that supposed to mean?"

"This is the world's smallest violin playing 'My Heart Bleeds for Them.' Nolan Draysn hasn't worked a day in over fifteen years. If he'd get a job, the family could have insurance and everything else they need."

"Nolan Draysn isn't able to work!"

"You don't know that. You're not even from this county, Stormy. Since when have you become an expert on every citizen?"

Stormy stood her ground. "Since I watched him try to stand and walk. He has multiple sclerosis which has gotten progressively worse every year. His wife works as a motel maid and all of his young children look for whatever work they can find to put beans in the pot. Have you no heart?"

"I have a heart, and the last time I checked, it was beating just fine. Not too fast, not too slow, just right. If you're so concerned about them, put your money where your mouth is, Mrs. Money Bags."

"My personal donation has already been made, Mr. Tayer. I was petitioning you on behalf of the Ignee County Rodeo Board. You do want to look good, don't you? I would think positive PR would be something you wouldn't let slide.

You don't have to put a lot into the hat when it's passed around."

Taking his small black comb from his shirt pocket, Carson removed his hat and combed his hair. "I look good all the time no matter what. Just being on the board is positive PR as you like to call it. Last time I checked you were not an official member."

"What have I been doing non-stop then for the past four and a half months if not working toward becoming one?" asked Stormy.

"If you need me to help you figure that out, then you'd better quit while you're ahead. Watch your step if you want to be introduced in the middle of the arena tonight."

"I'm watching very closely. And, it's Stormy Sabblonti. Don't bother to mention the Castins."

Sneering, Carson asked, "Are the Castins now the Castouts? Or are they the Castoffs?"

"Sure, just like you're Carson Chameleon Tayer."

"That's not my middle name!"

"Are you sure about that? Could've fooled me."

S

Never before in the history of the Toppens Ranch had there been so much concentrated activity in just a few short hours. Spence had recruited some help from nearby ranch hands to take care of the cattle and horses for the weekend. He asked himself why he was so nervous. All he had to do was corral Miggy, don his duds for the big event, and not lose Sarita's real wedding band. The fake one was already tied to the bridle around Logan's little plastic horse that he would be carrying down the yellow-carpeted aisle.

Wyn had moved to his manufactured home two weeks

ago upon completion of placing it on the foundation, leveling it, hooking up the water, and the umpteen other related tasks. Spence had offered to host a bachelor party of sorts, but truth be known, there wasn't time for such a thing. Wyn had commented that the last ranching community workday at the Drebners equated to the same thing for him when the men folk went around the circle late in the evening and gave him some tried and true marital advice. Spence had paid Wyn one more visit late last evening just to make sure all systems were go. Wyn had mentioned to Spence that he in no way expected any funny business tonight following the wedding ceremony. He said if there was any, he would hold Spence responsible no matter what or who and that payback was sure to be painful.

Sarita arrived at the ranch shortly after lunch. It was her second trip of the day, having forgotten Wyn's wedding band and her throw-away bouquet on the first one. Tonette, one of her co-workers from Dr. Dillers' office who had also hosted Sarita's bridal shower, had driven her to the ranch. The two women had spent the last two Saturdays working on ideas for Sarita's hair, makeup, and last-minute wedding day plans. Never having been married, but desperately desiring to be, Tonette had assured Sarita that she'd read enough bridal magazines and historical romance stories to qualify her as an expert wedding coordinator.

At 2:00 the phone rang. Wyn was in the middle of shaving. He sauntered into the living room.

"Hello, if this is Sarita, I can't talk to you. It's bad luck to see you or talk to you before tonight."

"No, Wyn, this is not Sarita. It's your best man. Remember to bring your marriage license with you so I can sign it following the ceremony."

"License? I would imagine Sarita has taken care of that."

"Better make sure," said Spence.

"Can you do me a huge favor and ask? Might be better to walk up there than call. I want my bride to have as stress free a day as humanly possible. Lemme know."

Spence dutifully inquired only to discover that Sarita

knew nothing of the sort. That was the groom's job.

Tom was sitting in the shadiest seat in the back yard sipping a quart jar filled with iced tea flavored with a sprig of fresh mint. It was the oldest generation who had wisdom in these tight places, so Spence sought him out. Tom laughed so hard he nearly popped the middle button of his shirt. "Whoever heard of such a thing anyway? Wyn hasn't been that busy, has he? You're supposed to be helping him out, too. Looks like you fellers are still a little green around both ears. This calls for a quick trip to town. Just when I thought I could rest up before the big dance tonight, I've got to high tail it into town. Sometimes it's not what you know, but who you know. Call Wyn and tell him there's nothing to worry about. Keep all your cards close to your vest, Spence."

Tom was careful not to upset the bridal headquarters humming like a grist of bees. He called Merna into the kitchen and informed her that he was driving into Ridgemonte to get a little something special for the bride and groom to which she queried, "At this late hour? Did you just think of it?"

"Sorta last minute stuff. Being the only male around here this afternoon might make all you women folk at little nervous, so I'll do all of you a big favor and skeedaddle. Should be back around 5:00."

Merna frowned. "It's going to take that long?"

"I'm not sure exactly how much time it's going to take to find exactly what I'm looking for so best to allow for a little extra if I need it."

"Tom, after being married to you for fifty-three years you'd think I'd have you figured out, but then you go and throw me for a loop."

"Actually, I threw my loop around you a long time ago." As Tom hugged Merna he lifted her feet completely off the ground and swung her around.

"You act like you're reliving our wedding day all over again."

"Funny you should say that. For some reason, I feel like I am. I don't know when I've ever been happier."

"Me either," agreed Merna.

Tom left his ranch and drove to the pickup dealership on the outskirts of Ridgemonte. He parked right next to the showroom and walked in. "Delbert around here somewhere?"

One of the salesmen informed Tom that Delbert had left the dealership shortly after lunch, so Tom drove to the Dawson residence. He thought he heard conversation in their back yard. Tom hollered over the fence, "Delbert, let's go for a ride."

Delbert's son, Brent, greeted Tom. "What brings you to our digs today? Don't stand there like a stranger. Come on in and take a load off."

"Where's your dad?"

"Believe it or not, he and mom are downstairs painting her craft room."

"On a day like today? You've got to be kidding me. Painting a craft room? I think I've just about heard it all," Tom said.

"Have a seat and I'll round him up for you. There's a cooler full of cold bevs if you need one."

Delbert emerged from the basement of the Dawson residence wearing his official painting t-shirt, cutoff jeans, and old tennis shoes. Tom couldn't help but chuckle.

"Knock it off! I wouldn't have climbed those stairs for just anybody." Within the next minute, both grown men were belly laughing.

"Delbert, I need to call in all of my favors on this one. We need to go for a ride right now."

"Can't it wait until I change my clothes?"

"We won't be gone that long," assured Tom. "Besides, you'd just have to change back into them once you got home again unless you're all finished painting for the day."

"No such luck. We've got the ceiling done and two walls, but still have the other two walls and the trim to go."

"Couldn't you hire it done, Delbert?"

"We could have, but the wife says she likes to spend time with me in close quarters doing mutual things."

Tom didn't want to touch that one with a ten-foot-pole as he informed Brent, "Please tell your mother that we'll be back shortly."

Not thinking he would need to get out of Tom's pickup once he got inside of it until he got back home again, Delbert deemed Tom's request extremely urgent and fastened his seat belt on the passenger side.

"How do you like this F-350, Tom?"

"It's mighty fine. Sure am glad I went with the larger size this time. Thanks for holding it for me. Seems like I've owned it a lot longer than a few months."

"Where are we headed in such a blasted hurry?"

"I have no idea," replied Tom.

"What do you mean you have no idea? You told me we were going for a ride."

"We are. I just don't know where he lives."

"Cut the baloney. Name and address please."

"I can give you the name. You need to supply the address for the Jofton residence."

"They moved last year," said Delbert. "I think I know where they live now. Their youngest son bought a rig from us recently. Turn right here, Tom, and then it's the fifth house down on the left-hand side of the street. I'll wait inside the cab of the pickup for you."

Tom descended upon the Jofton's doorstep. The window washing service was just wrapping up their semi-annual visit. After ringing the doorbell several times, he waited for a few minutes, but couldn't locate any family members.

Since the pickup was not parked in the shade, Delbert felt like he was in a bake oven. Tom had taken his keys with him, so Delbert couldn't turn on the AC. He deemed he'd better get out of the pickup as his clothing was already starting to stick to him.

Jerry Jofton was securing the window screens behind the workers on the back side of the house. He entered the front yard. "You two fine gents need your windows done, too? Delbert, stay put! I need to get my camera."

"Oh, no you don't dare, Jerry. I'll run and hide. The

theme of this day is sacrificing self for the benefit of all, otherwise I never would've left the house. All I had to do was provide the location." Delbert ducked behind some shrubs on the side of the house.

Tom returned to his pickup a few minutes later where Delbert was waiting for him inside the cab. "Everything's set, Delbert. We'll just follow Jerry."

"Can't you take me home first, Tom?"

"Don't reckon as I can right yet. I have no idea where Betty Lou Bradford lives. You're already this far into it, so you might as well enjoy the ride. Which do you like better, T-bones or Rib-eyes?"

"T-bones any day of the week, why?"

"I'm sensing I better sweeten the pot with some of that Toppens' beef before the day is over, custom cut order, any way you and the family like it."

Tom followed Jerry to Betty Lou's house. He and Delbert sat inside their pickup waiting for Jerry to talk to Betty Lou and ask her to get her keys and drive downtown.

When they arrived at the Shadow Butte County Courthouse, Delbert opted to stay inside the pickup once again. Twenty minutes later, Tom, Jerry, and Betty Lou walked out the front door sporting grins as big as all outdoors as Tom carried the over-sized, all important white envelope in his left hand.

En route to the Dawson residence, Delbert was so preoccupied with his appearance that he sounded like a magpie squawking about the new arrivals for his dealership and the promotions offered by various manufacturers. He never did bother to ask what was obtained from inside the courthouse on a late Saturday afternoon.

Tom stopped in front of Delbert's house and turned the engine off. "Will we see you tonight?"

"Tonight?" asked Delbert.

"Yes. You know, the big doins' at the ranch?"

"That's tonight? I thought it was in a couple of weeks. I wonder if the wife remembers. I better milk this paint job for all it's worth, so I can sweet talk her into going with me."

"First you might need some paint thinner."

"What?"

"Take a look in the mirror, Delbert."

Running his hands through the top of his hair, Delbert felt a large clump that was stuck together.

"Are you using water based or oil-based paint?" asked Tom.

"I don't know. I didn't check the label. The wife rounded up all the materials."

"Let's hope it's water. See you in three hours."

CHAPTER THIRTY-FIVE

Stormy had gone back to her room at The Silver Jack Motel for a brief rest late Saturday afternoon after such a hectic morning at the park. Perhaps she should have eaten one of those buckwheat pancakes, minus the butter and syrup, of course. In her haste to pack for the big day, she had forgotten her house slippers along with her every day shoes at the main ranch house. Country Cate's Western Wear closed a half hour ago as did the regular department store in Cinder Valley. There wasn't time to drive to the ranch and be back before the start of the main event. She had neglected to include adhesive bandages in her toiletry bag to cover the red-hot blisters on both heels. No amount of liquid makeup foundation would cover her sunburned nose and cheeks.

Several months ago, Stormy had made the decision that she would travel back in time and purchase women's western wear circa the 1800's. Surely this would help her to be noticed in the large evening crowd. Her dark blue, split, riding skirt was cut with a slight flair, side pockets, and front flat opening. It allowed for ample movement when walking. Twelve Victorian-style, metal buttons highlighted the front of the skirt. The 100% antique, white silk, walking jacket was deemed to be the perfect match paired with the skirt. The tightly fitted lines and turn-of-the-century details made Stormy feel like a Victorian queen. Small piping, tiny covered buttons, and back ruffled peplum were details no roving eye could miss. A high-collared, high-dollar brooch featuring an Imperial Topaz in the center surrounded by accompanying smaller topazes in the dark pinkish-red and orange-red colors was a real eye catcher. She didn't bother with any in the blue hues since she had no way of knowing if any of them had been artificially irradiated to enhance the color. One must have the real McCoy when it comes to precious gems and stones.

Stormy grimaced as she slipped her tired feet into her fancy, lace, genuine leather boots that were supposed to fit like a dream. She struggled to lace up the nine-inch area and teetered on the two-and-a-half-inch frontier heel that was intended to be balanced by the pointed toe. Fluffing her hair one more time and slipping her left hand through the loop of her white, Battenburg lace parasol, she locked her motel room door and headed for the rodeo grounds.

Parking was a premium. Stormy had completely neglected to factor in this all-important aspect and ended up having to walk a quarter of a mile. As she limped near the arena, but still with 100 yards to go, she heard her name over the PA system. "Stormy Sablonteeeee." A pause followed and then Ignee County Rodeo Board Chairman, Carson Tayer, continued to introduce the work force who'd made this evening possible. She arrived at the bottom of the main section of bleachers just as the committee members and other associates walked single file past her. None of them even looked her way.

Rodeo Announcer, Cord Calhoun, with his silver baritone voice and innumerable one-liners, had the overflowing crowd on their feet immediately when the Grand Entry began. Rodeo Clown, Caper Sadler, was waiting in the wings with his first act. Stormy wondered if clowns ever had a sad day. The lead singer for *The Tall Blues*, sporting his blue velvet cowboy hat, led everyone in the national anthem and "America the Beautiful." When doing so, he turned lots of women's heads.

Not only was parking non-existent, so was seating.

Stormy had assumed that there would be designated places for the rodeo board and committee members. She unfolded her parasol, pushed in the piece of metal on the shaft to secure it, and shaded the left side of her face as her eyes searched all sections of the bleachers for a place to sit down. Just then Ignee County Rodeo Board Member, Trent Davies, walked past Stormy. There was no way he didn't recognize her. She had spoken with him earlier in the afternoon when he was by himself. He had mentioned the rodeo dance later that evening and hinted that he would be asking her for at least one slow dance with him just as Carson had also done earlier in the day. Suddenly, Trent reached his arm around the waist of a young woman with reddish-brown hair and drew her very close to the right side of his chest. She did not resist as she patted his right hand, looked up, and grinned at him.

The steer wrestlers opened the night's competition as six cowboys posted qualified rides. Stormy looked down at the program. The two events she really wanted to see, bull riding and women's barrel racing, were way down the list. Her feet were really talking to her despite having taken four over-the-counter pain relievers prior to leaving her motel room. She thought she saw an opening in a row of seats in the section to her right. Making her way through the thick crowd, she leaned against the side of the bleachers before climbing up the stairs. Since her parasol was shading part of her face, she didn't pay close attention to who was standing in front of her, but she did overhear their conversation. The three of them were in a tightly-knit huddle.

The woman's voice crackled when she spoke. "Real star-studded line up you got here tonight. Well done if I say so myself. Perhaps I should have retired much sooner."

One cowboy's speech was a little slurred when he answered. "Nah, Gwen, truth be known, we still need you on that board to keep us on the straight and narrow," said Stanley Elson, Ignee County Rodeo Board Treasurer.

Fellow board member, Dean Kendall, threw in his two cents worth, "Felt so bloomin' good to spend that flush

Sabblonti cash. I could do that from now 'til the cows come home. Boy, howdy, did we ever take that young, dumb thing on the snipe hunt of all snipe hunts! If Ace knew she'd parted with that much of his hard-earned money, he'd rear straight up outta his grave and give her a piece of his mind."

Gwen, Stanley, and Dean laughed uproariously.

Aunt Jonsey helped Sarita into her wedding gown and fastened the clasp of her borrowed, pearl necklace at the nape of her neck.

"Sit down here sweetie for just a minute so I can position your veil evenly on the top of your head. I can't even imagine how many hours it took Merna to make this pearled, beaded Juliet cap and attach the two layers of tulle. I want to make sure I don't smudge your lip gloss."

"Aunt Jonsey, I just thought of something. Can you please get me a moist washcloth? I think I'd better remove the gloss. It's so sticky. It might leave Wyn with soft, pink, shimmery lips, and he would have a hard time living that down!"

"Good catch. I'm sure he'll appreciate that in advance. Before the ceremony starts, I want you to open this. It's from me to you."

Sarita untied the powder blue, satin ribbon bow securing the small box and laid it on the dresser. Carefully lifting the lid, she gasped, "These are lovely! It doesn't look like they've been worn very much."

"Believe it or not, your grandfather Siddonz made these for my wedding to your uncle Kent in 1944. They are 100% silver. Even though my married name is Kiddle, my father wanted me to always have a reminder of my maiden name, so that's why he fashioned them in the shape of an "S". Little did I know that your mother would name you Sarita. I can think of no one else that I'd rather gift these to besides you. After my wedding, I put them back in my cedar chest and completely forgot about them until I got your letter."

Tall, thin, silver-haired, and elegant as ever adorned in her blue lace, summer dress, Aunt Jonsey helped Sarita adjust the earrings and gave her a big hug as she brushed a tear from Sarita's left cheek.

Merna tapped on the bedroom door before opening it. "Everyone is seated, so we're ready for the ceremony to begin. Sarita, you look radiant!"

Aunt Jonsey admired the bridal bouquet of Yellow Missionbells, Black-eyed Susans, and Blue Sugarbowls. "Merna, you never cease to amaze me. You must not have slept much for the past two months."

"It's been such a pleasure that I've not thought of it as work at all. I'll tell Kent that the bride is ready and corral Lilac and Logan."

As Coye's Stringers consisting of a banjo, fiddle, and violin commenced the processional, Judge Jerry Jofton, Wyn, and Spence entered the back yard and took their places to the right of the gazebo. The matron of honor, Aunt Jonsey, walked down the yellow-carpeted aisle followed by her great-grandson, Logan. He carried a plastic, bay horse with a ring from a box of caramel popcorn tied to its bridal. Lilac was taking her own sweet time as she reached inside the white wicker flower basket. Instead of walking slowly and dispersing the blue flower petals, she took them out one by one, bent over, and laid each one carefully on the yellow aisle.

Sarita couldn't figure out what was taking so long as the laughter of the crowd could be heard above the music which suddenly changed to the wedding march. Uncle Kent extended his right arm to Sarita as they walked through the door and entered the yard. She had no idea all eyes were on her as she was looking only at Wyn. Sarita had chosen to walk on the right side so that no one was between her and the love of her life when she arrived in front of the gazebo.

Merna stayed at the very back of the crowd with tears streaming down her face when she realized there were no biological parents present to celebrate one of the most important milestones in the lives of their children.

Judge Jerry Jofton welcomed everyone and asked them to be seated on the bales of hay adorned with quilts, sleeping bags, horse blankets, and miscellaneous western coverings. A pair of bluebirds landed on the branch of a pine tree behind his left shoulder. He did not ask who gave Sarita to be married to Wyn as was the usual custom.

Wyn and Sarita had written their own vows culminating in the salt covenant which was something new to those in attendance. Several ranching women craned their necks as they witnessed Wyn pouring the salt from his container into the larger receptacle and Sarita doing likewise. Faithfulness, loyalty, trust, friendship, and love were the hallmarks of the vows. When Judge Jofton announced, "You may now kiss your beautiful bride," Wyn lifted Sarita's blusher veil and wholeheartedly embraced her. The crowd really whooped and hollered.

After the judge introduced the couple as Mr. & Mrs. Wyn Moreland, they walked down the aisle as Coye's Stringers played "Keeper of the Stars" and formed their receiving line. Well-wishers quickly responded. When Dr. Diller's wife, Anne-Marie, came through the line without him, Sarita inquired as to his whereabouts to which she replied, "The good doctor is less than."

Somewhat puzzled, Sarita asked, "Less than? Less than what?"

Anne-Marie hesitated. "You fill in the blank, honey."

Somehow Dr. Shaw and Macey never did make it through the line which could have been by design. Macey drank in every detail of the wedding and reception.

Judge Jerry Jofton assembled the wedding party along with Tom, Delbert Dawson, and Betty Lou Bradford, so the witnesses could sign the marriage license. The judge commented, "Now this is Shadow Butte County teamwork at its finest, if I say so myself." Tom shook the judge's hand applying several extra shakes of gratitude.

Spence said, "The real credit goes to Tom. He jumped into action and made sure that marriage license got issued in short order, even if it was just in the nick of time!"

Tom shrugged his shoulders, "It wasn't that big of a deal. I was happy to do it for Wyn and Sarita. Say, Delbert, why don't you remove your cowboy hat, so we can see if the paint thinner worked?"

Delbert started to respond, but thought better of it. He shrugged his shoulders just as Tom had done, smiled, and walked toward his wife who was sitting in the shade.

The bride and groom worked their way to the horseshoe-shaped buffet area. Neighboring rancher, Nelson Merrill, had barbequed a steer on a spit during the day, and Marita Merrill had her culinary troops busy for days with the rest of the fixins.

Spence and Priscilla were in charge of collecting the wedding gifts and securing them in Wyn's former bedroom inside the bunkhouse for the weekend. Miggy was none too happy at having to be corralled inside the bunkhouse while the crowd partied into the night.

Tom had fashioned a portable dance floor of sorts which was placed near the gazebo following the ceremony. Wyn had never danced with anyone before in his whole life, so he was relying upon the few movies that he'd watched. He had requested "Can I Have This Dance for The Rest of My Life?" It felt as if he and Sarita did not move more than a two-foot radius during the entire song. The younger cowboys and cowgirls soon joined them on the dance floor. Truth be known, the lawn soon became the enlarged floor. Merna could have cared less. More grass seed could be purchased at The Shadowy Merc if need be. There was never going to be another night like this one.

Francie Fletcher offered to serve the pieces of wedding cake that had been placed on the paper plates. She loaded as many as possible onto the tray and made her way in between the rows of hay bales. When she held it in front of Dr. Den Merenspinn, he looked at Francie and smiled softly. "Any chance I could get a cup of coffee to go with this?" She just laughed. "I've not seen any hot coffee this hot summer evening, but that doesn't mean that the kitchen's closed."

Locating Merna, Francie informed her of Dr. Merenspinn's request.

"I had a hunch I should've brewed some," said Merna. "No problem at all. I'll get the coffee pot plugged in. It should be ready in about fifteen minutes. He probably won't mind waiting."

It was time for Sarita to toss her throw away bouquet to the single girls in the audience. About twenty young ladies gathered a few feet behind her. When the bouquet was flying mid-air, Tonette dove in front of Priscilla to catch it, but tripped and fell at her feet. Priscilla reached out to grab it. She wasn't sure how soon she should tell Spence that she'd been the recipient, so she laid it behind the hay bale where she'd been sitting and enjoying her dinner.

Francie had been in the kitchen pouring coffee and missed the bouquet transfer. She located Dr. Merenspinn on the opposite side of the yard from where he was sitting a few minutes ago. It was a good thing she'd included a few extra cups on her serving tray as they seemed to disappear into the night air. All she saw were well-callused, tanned, masculine hands grabbing them.

"Francie, you missed all the excitement," said Dr. Merenspinn.

"I did? How's that?"

"Your daughter caught the bouquet. If that tradition means the same thing today that it did when I got married, it looks like you might have a busy season ahead."

"Priscilla is nowhere near ready to get married. Besides that, there's no serious prospect on her horizon."

Dr. Merenspinn's full, thick, black eyebrows were in full view as he fully raised them. "It's more than obvious to even the casual observer here this evening that Spence has quite a case on Priscilla. She's not exactly telling him to get lost. I might be getting up in years, but my radar detector still works just fine. It looks to me like you'd better take that apron off or at least cut the strings and let it fall off." Dr. Merenspinn turned around to join the ranchers in their horse tales.

Priscilla had given those in attendance small bags of tulle containing the rice from the box that Wyn had gifted Sarita last Christmas when he proposed to her. Before getting into their horse-drawn carriage to take them to their new abode, they were showered from head to toe.

Following the ceremony, Chet and Evan were sitting on a bench at the edge of the yard where it was easier to hear above the music. Some of the neighboring ranchers sought Chet out to inquire as to his well-being and that of the Sabblonti Ranch. Chet was not overly talkative. When the men would glance at Evan, he just shrugged his shoulders.

Spence had requested the song "When A Man Loves a Woman." He and Priscilla made their way onto the dance floor.

Dr. Shaw remembered hearing this song years ago. Rees Broomfield cornered him and wanted to ask a myriad of cattle related questions. Dr. Shaw tired hard to end the conversation, short of being rude. He was standing across the yard from Macey at the time when he saw several young cowboys approach her to ask her to dance with them. Finally, Dr. Shaw just walked away and left Rees talking to himself. He just might have answered himself, too. By the time he made his way through the crowd, the song had ended.

There were so many people milling around and visiting that no one seemed to notice the late arrivals. Chet agreed to Evan's offer to refill his lemonade cup. Sitting alone on the bench and staring at the shadows of the leaves of the quaking aspen trees dancing in the light, Chet thought he felt a large bug crawling across the back of his neck. He rubbed the yoke area of his white shirt and shook his head a couple of times. The sensation returned. Finally, Chet stood up, shook his arms, and brushed his pant legs. It felt like something was crawling over him. Then he saw a shadow emerge from behind the boxwood bush.

"What are you doing here?" demanded Chet.

"Waiting to keep you company," said Salina. "You look awfully lonely tonight, but handsome as ever. This band is awesome. I would love to dance with you, especially to this song, and unwrap your smile in the process."

Chet sat down. "Didn't anyone ever tell you that wedding crashing is outlawed in these parts?"

"I've been studying the statutes and ordinances, and I could find no such thing. You're going to have to try a little harder than that to run me off."

Salina bent down very closely in front of Chet and started moving her fingertips across his fingers like she was playing a piano as she hummed the lyrics to the song being sung by Coye.

Evan arrived with two cups filled to the brim with lemonade. He cleared his throat loudly. "Excuse me, please. Chet, here's something to quench your thirst. Salina, you need to make yourself scarce."

"Speak for yourself, Evan. This is a free country. I didn't see any *No Trespassing* signs posted anywhere. Speaking of making yourself scarce, why don't you follow your own advice and leave Chet and me alone for a while?"

Evan replied, "Stuff a sock in it, Salina!"

"I'm not wearing any socks in case you hadn't noticed. Chet, we have something very important to discuss, don't we? Something beyond what kind of dinners you would like for me to continue to bring to you in the evenings. How do you like my new dress? Did I get close enough so you could examine my extra-large centerpieces and smell my perfume?"

Aunt Jonsey walked toward Chet. "Stormy, is that you? I was hoping you'd be here. I've not seen you in so many years. What are you doing holding that bouquet? You've been married several years by now."

Salina turned around ever so slowly. "I've never been married. Don't you worry about my bouquet for Chet. And you would be who, pray tell?"

Extending her right hand, Aunt Jonsey replied, "I'm Sarita's and Stormy's Aunt Jonsey. And who would you be, pray tell?"

Shaking hands with Aunt Jonsey, Salina said, "A very good and close friend of Chet's. Someone who definitely has his best interest at heart."

Evan quickly interrupted, "Aunt Jonsey, not everything is at is appears."

Folding her arms, Aunt Jonsey stated, "Well, I most certainly hope not! Young lady, I'm sure there are other eligible cowboys in attendance this evening."

"None I'm interested in. That's for sure. There's one thing about me that all of you should probably know. Once I set my sights on someone or something, I hit the mark. I don't miss. And, I don't give up 'til I get it."

Evan stepped in front of Salina and almost fell into Chet's chest in the process. "Down this stuff, Chet, and let's hit the road. I've had about all the excitement I can stand for one evening."

Chet acted like he would just as soon toss the contents of his cup onto Salina as drink it. As he extended his right hand, some of the lemonade sloshed onto the ground.

Salina raised her voice, "Oh, I was so hoping you were going to throw that on my dress, so then you'd have to wipe it off. How exciting!"

Evan grabbed hold of Chet's arm and helped him to his feet. Chet announced, "We're outta here this minute!"

Chet leaned on his cane until he felt like his body was balanced enough to walk across the loose gravel to Evan's van. Looking to his side, he thought he saw a silhouette of someone standing on the edge of the lawn where he'd been sitting. He narrowed his eyes to try to determine who it might be. Then again, maybe he was seeing things. It wouldn't be the first time. His eyes still weren't 100%.

Evan drove down the long lane toward the main highway. In his rear-view mirror, he saw the new red pickup with the Sabblonti cattle brand on the side door. "Say, Chet, there's that red pickup again. You know, the one with your brand on the side. I've got three pickup trucks behind me or else I would stop and take a closer look."

"Evan, I've told you before that there's no such thing as a new red pickup with my cattle brand on it anywhere in these parts. We stayed way too long at that wedding reception."

"Yes, Chet, we probably did. When you said that, it made me wonder if Wyn had the same opinion of spending more time than he'd wanted to before leaving with his beautiful bride."

A short distance from their new home, Wyn brought the team of horses to a stop. Searching the moonless night sky and locating the constellation, *Bootes the Herdsmen,* he showed Sarita where it was.

"Wyn, we'll have a herd of our own someday. Surely, we must name one of them Bootes."

"We shall. Let our adventure begin. What's that in the back of the carriage? I thought I asked Spence to take all of our wedding gifts and place them inside the bunk house."

"It's a very special gift that I wrapped for our first night together in our new home. Grammy Mabel made it for me when I was seven years old. She must have seen a long way into the future as she stitched every stitch of our double wedding ring quilt with double love."

Wyn stretched his hand across his chest to join Sarita's left hand as both of them touched each other's wedding rings.

Wyn broke the brief silence, "A circle symbolizes eternity where there's no end."

"My very own cowboy, our love will endure for eternity."

CHAPTER THIRTY-SIX

Silence shrouded Stormy as she lay on the living room couch covered with the multi-colored baby afghan. It was 1:30 Sunday morning following one of the warmest days on record in Shadow Butte County. Despite a hot wind of reality having blown completely throughout her body, her teeth were still chattering. She couldn't sleep despite having consumed a cup of chamomile, slippery elm, sleepy tea after taking a hot, relaxing bath. Perhaps she should build a fire in the fireplace. Never having done that before, she scrapped the idea as she didn't know where to begin. She did know that one would need to light a match, however. The conversation she overheard about members of the rodeo board leading her on a snipe hunt and the scene involving Chet and Salina during the wedding reception ran through her mind like a race horse. At that very instant, Stormy remembered something she'd heard while listening to the radio during one of her many road trips to and from Cinder Valley since March. What a waste of time the past four months had been! Well, it could have been worse. At least she hadn't squandered four years.

Radio Station KCVW featured an hour-long program titled *Medical Lowdown.* One of the presenters had been a psychotherapist who'd spoken on the subject of rejection. His sage advice had been that no matter how unpleasant your experience had been and/or how much shame and rejection one had felt, if you refused to focus upon it, you could take away its power. But what would that look like in a practical sense?

Stormy pulled the afghan to her chin and drifted off to sleep. The eight-day clock on the mantle awakened her at 8:00 a.m. She dressed quickly, made a to-go cup of coffee, and drove to the burial grounds. Walking to her parents' gravesite, she sat down cross-legged in front of the headstone.

"Mother, I really need you. There's no one else I can turn to at a time like this. Did you ever suffer an intruder in your marriage to Daddy? How did you get my father to love you so much and do most everything and anything for you? You left me all that money along with the ranch, but you didn't bequeath me what I really needed. I just know you'll find a way to get the message to me as to what I should do. I miss you so!"

Not feeling inclined to drive back to the ranch house, Stormy turned onto the main highway and headed toward Cinder Valley. She had the road virtually to herself. There was no shortage of foals kicking up their heels in Samuel Stixson's broodmare pasture which birthed a splendid idea. She'd taken so many chances since the first day of the year that another one wouldn't make an ounce of difference at this point.

Slim Shade was in the process of loading his rodeo stock into one of his semi-trailer trucks when Stormy arrived at the Ignee County rodeo grounds. Armed with a new-found confidence, she approached him to help with her hunt.

Slim, ever his pleasant self, removed his cowboy hat and wiped his forehead with his left shirt cuff. "Howdy, Miss, who or what are you looking for?"

"Slim, you remember me, don't you?"

"Can't rightly say as I recognize you for sure. There were throngs of folks meandering around here the past day or so. They sorta swam in front of my face. I was introduced to some of them. I'm not one much for names. Remembering faces is much easier for me."

"I understand. I'm Stormy Castins and helped the other

members of the Ignee County Rodeo Board conduct their big event."

"Stormy? Yep, I remember that name now. Real unusual is the reason it stuck in my mind, but you sure don't look anything like you did when I first met you. Seems you were all dolled up in high-dollah fancy, western, wear. Stock buyers keep an eye on the money and what it can buy if you know what I mean."

"That's exactly the kind of help I need right now."

"Buying stock?" Slim asked.

Stormy stepped a few feet away from the semi-trailer avoiding the strong smell. She probably had not yet figured out that to some people that was the smell of money. "In a manner of speaking, Slim. I know that you probably work primarily with rodeo bulls and the like, but do you know anything about race horses?"

Slim explained, "There are horses that race if that's what you mean. Quarter horses, Thoroughbreds, Arabians, Paints, and Appaloosas can be found on tracks in most places. What'd you have in mind?"

"I'm looking to purchase a prized race horse for someone very special."

Leaning against the cab of his semi, Slim asked, "Will this someone special be racing the horse himself or will someone else most likely be the jockey? The most popular race horse is usually a Thoroughbred. The prices vary a whole bunch depending on pedigree, age, overall body confirmation, and some other market factors. So, the easiest way to figure this out might be for you to tell me how much you're looking to spend, and I'll try to help you from there. Deal?"

"Yes, that's fair," agreed Stormy. "The figure that's coming to me is around $70,000 or so. I could go a little higher if necessary. $100,000 would probably be my maximum amount."

"I charge a commission. Some people call it gypo type work. You would need to add that to whatever figure you float out there."

"Is your commission a flat rate or percentage?" Stormy asked.

"Flat rate. Sorta like a finder's fee in this case which I could probably do for $10,000."

"$10,000 just to locate a race horse?" gasped Stormy. "You made it sound like they're running everywhere."

Tucking his large thumbs underneath the straps of his bib overalls to help him stand straighter, Slim stated, "You said earlier that you wanted it for someone very special. That takes time, effort, energy, and money. Keep in mind I've got rodeos booked through the end of October which keeps me on a dead run. If you want just any old plug, I can round one up for a finder's fee of a grand or so."

Stormy paused as she made her mental calculations. "I see. $100,000 for the race horse and your fee of $10,000. Do we have a deal?"

"We do after you fork over my finder's fee," Slim said with a slight edge to his voice. "I've been burned way too many times in the past, so I require my money up front."

"What happens if you don't find me a horse? Do I get the $10,000 back?"

Slim snorted like a sow, "Hardly. It's like a criminal defense attorney who requires his money up front from his client before he ever turns a wheel or scrawls one word on one of those important-looking, yellow, legal pads of his. He looks for a way to keep his client out of the clink, but can't always guarantee it. I'm looking just like he's looking. Only difference is he's looking for weasels, you know, a way to weasel outta certain things, and I'm looking for horses."

Stormy looked at Slim from the soles of his boots to the top of his white ten-gallon hat. "How do you know so much about what a criminal defense attorney does? Have you been in trouble with the law or served time in jail or prison?"

"Never. And don't plan on it in the future." Slim moved his right arm in an arc motion in front of him and gestured toward his semi and trailer. "I'm Slim, and this is my shade. I operate in the wide-open spaces, not behind bars. I knew a character one time that got rung up for cattle rustling.

Served him right for tryin' to outrun the law. There's just something about money that tests everybody's character, isn't there? Any other concerns?"

"Not that I can think of right now," Stormy said. "I can cut you a check for the amount. I don't have that much cash on me this morning."

"Non-rubber checks spend just like cash, so it's sixes to me."

Stormy returned from her pickup waving her check in the air as she sang, "Let it fly, let it fly, let it fly!"

Slim had no comeback for that repetitive line. "You best give me your telephone number. It's going to be much easier for me to contact you than you trying to run me down. I'm headed to Colorado next and New Mexico after that. But don't you worry all your curly hair any 'cause I can guarantee you a real genuine race horse."

"That's perfect, because at this stage of the game, that's exactly what I need."

"Don't call me. I'll call you."

S

Tom Toppens turned on the radio in his kitchen at 6:00 a.m. as was his usual custom. The voice on the other end didn't proclaim any good news again. "Top of the morning to all you early risers out there. You might want to get your chores done as soon as you can. The temperatures are headed into the triple digits again today. On my drive home from the station yesterday, bleached beige blanketed the landscape. Maybe some of you better get out there and do a rain dance or two."

After pouring his second cup of coffee, Tom removed the calendar from the wall and flipped five pages back. March 3rd was the last square where a large red *X* had been made. One hundred and twenty-nine days had come and gone since there'd been a drop of rain fall from the sky. Prior to that, there had been about three months of combined moisture, rain and snow mix, which produced an ample supply of spring grazing grasses.

Merna, still recuperating from having overextended herself with all of the wedding preparations, walked from their bedroom into the kitchen as she buttoned her housecoat. Glancing at her beloved she said, "I'm familiar with that look after fifty-three years. "Worry gives small things big shadows. What are your plans for today?"

"Equipment maintenance under the big cottonwood tree. That will help take my mind off a few things. Busy hands help to calm a busy mind. How about you whip up my favorite coffee cake with extra crumb topping? I'll head in around ten o'clock for a refueling."

"I most certainly can do that for you, but not before I get a big squeeze." They hugged until Merna could feel Tom's torso relax. "Looks like we have an early morning visitor. I'd better get dressed." The small sedan went past the main ranch house toward the bunkhouse.

Spence had cooked breakfast for Fennel Bridgemore, better known as "Fenn", himself, and Miggy. Fenn was the newest addition to the bunkhouse following Wyn and Sarita's marriage. He had few cooking skills, but his Oklahoma ranching experience more than made up for Spence having to pull double KP duty. He gently reminded Fenn this morning that this was his last week of doing so. Next week, Fenn had better start reading the lone western cookbook located above the kitchen stove before bedtime each night. After all, most any adult should at least be able to fry a hamburger, a pound of bacon, or fix boxed Mac & Cheese. Fenn's remedy seemed to be that applying enough catsup, salsa, hot sauce, salt and paper could repair most any cooking failure. Spence reminded him that not everyone came equipped with a cast iron gut.

Miggy's barking announced the arrival of today's guest. Fenn welcomed Priscilla. "Whoa, I think I need my sunglasses for all that pink this early in the morning. You won't have to worry about Spence losing you on the range."

Priscilla waved her hand in front of Fenn as she walked by and pulled up a chair. "Spence, did you save me a piece of salt pork fried with extra black pepper? I've been wanting to taste it. Or did you use white pepper this morning?"

Spence moved closer and tapped Priscilla's right shoulder. "White pepper, and where'd you get that shirt? Pretty snazzy, if I say so myself!"

"I was hoping it was not too over the top."

"Over the top? I think it's picture pink perfect, just like you. I'm glad you remembered a hat, too. Your mother would be none too happy if you looked like a baked lobster when you got home tonight."

Fenn commented, "Nice detail. Pink with white print, snap flap pockets, white-marbled snaps, western, single-point front and back yokes with a spread collar. It's probably a size small."

Priscilla eyed Fenn, "Have you worked in a western clothing store previously or do you make a habit of memorizing catalogs?"

"Neither one. I just have an eye for detail, double eyes for detail, actually. Looks like the dots in that fabric aren't exactly lined up straight."

"Fenn, you best feast your eyes elsewhere, pal." Spence lined Fenn out concerning the chores to be completed for the day. He also reminded him that he'd better hold up his half of the kitchen bargain and have it cleaned up by the time he and Priscilla returned from riding the range and repairing the broken stretch of fence.

Priscilla filled the water canteens in the kitchen sink and joined Spence down at the hitching post next to the horse barn.

"Did you remember our lunches?" asked Spence. "And you know how much I like treats, so I hope you remembered to bring one of those, too."

"Inside every man there's still a little bit of boy. Yes, I made us some goodies."

"I'm saddling the oldest gelding on the ranch so you can ride him. He was part of a pack train before Tom bought him. Nothing spooks him. You just plod along, don't you Gimmer? Don't ask me where people come up with the names they tag on their animals. I need to round up a hammer, wire stretcher, and other odds and ends."

"I take it we aren't able to drive to the area where the fence needs to be mended?"

"Correct," said Spence. "Like I explained during our phone convo, it's in that real rocky place. Wyn spotted a couple of predators last week, so we want to make sure the cattle stay where they're supposed to be."

Fenn watched from the barn yard as Spence and Priscilla rode away with Miggy in tow. For a brief moment, the scene could have been taken from a country western movie, minus the perpetual pink, of course. *That lucky duck. What I wouldn't give to be repairing fences today rather than clearing that area to stack the second cutting. Hope they hire somebody else soon, so I'm not the low man on the totem pole around here.*

As they rode along the fence line, Spence began to process verbally, "I've been plum pleased that you've come so well-equipped."

Priscilla slid the stampede strings on her hat a little closer to her chin. "It has helped to walk to and from work every day, mow the lawn on Wednesday nights, and complete my bench- stepping exercises before supper at least four evenings each week. I've also weaned myself, so that I eat desserts only on Sundays. It used to be all week long."

"You misread the equipped part of it. What I should have said was that you know how to ride a horse, prepare meals, record county records, and treat a man like he deserves to be treated."

Sensing she could sure use a blast of air conditioning at this point in the ride, Priscilla commented, "That looks like a splendid place to tie up the horses over there."

"Good eye. Let's water them first and head for the shade."

Laying down her pink and white checkered tablecloth she'd packed inside the lunch, Priscilla offered Spence a beef sandwich.

"I could polish off about three of these. How'd you make the filling?"

"It's leftover beef arm roast. My mom has a meat grinder that she mounts onto the counter. You just insert the desired blade inside and crank the handle. I added mayo, dill pickle relish, creamy horseradish, and lots of salt and pepper because I thought that's what you'd like. I've been making fruit leather in our back yard. I took those old screens from the windows, cleaned them, and made some drying racks."

Spence envisioned window screens in his mind's eye. "Humpf, there's just no end to what you're capable of doing, is there?"

"As far as everyday things go, maybe not, but the thing I really want to do, I don't seem to be capable of."

"Get your mother on board?" asked Spence.

"Exactly. We're at an impasse. She's at the point now where she refuses to even talk about my relationship with you. Somehow, she's gotten it in her head that you cannot be trusted because you supplied the incorrect answer for the capital of Nebraska. She says that if you can't be honest about that, there's no telling what else you're withholding from us."

Spence tossed the remainder of his sandwich into the nearby pine tree so Miggy couldn't get it. The horseradish would have lit her up in a hurry. "I don't know what else to tell you. What you see is what you get. Just don't plan on stringing me along, because I don't play games with strings or anything else for that matter. I don't want that to sound harsh, but at some point, you've got to decide who and what you want in life. It's not like you're fifteen years old and trying to make one of the most important decisions of your life.

Wyn and I had several man-to-man discussions regarding this very subject before he married Sarita. I'm so proud of both of them for sticking to their guns and not allowing outside influences to hijack their marriage. I assumed your mother was warming up to the idea of our relationship since she attended the wedding and helped serve cake."

"She did that just so she could keep a very close eye on both of us."

"I don't need anyone keeping a close eye on me," huffed Spence. "I'm a principled grown man who's walking the line."

"The line?"

"Yes, that straight and narrow one. Ever heard of it?"

Spence jumped off the rock and tossed his fruit leather as far as he could. He busied himself removing the horses' saddles and brushing their coats. He was trying to prevent a saddle sore from forming on Gimmer's left side.

Priscilla placed the remainder of her sandwich inside the small bag. She tucked the unopened fruit leather next to it. Sliding off the rock and approaching Spence, she stuck out her right hand. He whirled around to face her, "Whose side are you on, anyway? Hers or mine? Or I should say ours?"

"Ours, but I want to continue to honor my mother. If my dad was still alive, it would be a completely different story. She would not be acting like this. I think she's growing strangely paranoid."

Spence unleashed, "I agree with you that you should honor your mother, but that does not give her a license to control every aspect of your adult life. And it's not like you're some derelict daughter that neglects her and does not pull your own weight. As it is, you're pulling the whole wagon load as near as I can determine. What more does she want? Some milquetoast character that can't even tie his own boot laces? If you don't stand up to her now, she'll ride roughshod over every single day of your marriage. Are you confusing honor with control?"

Priscilla clenched her teeth together inflicting

momentary pain so she would not shed a tear. She gathered her tablecloth and remainder of the lunch from the rock outcropping. Spence did not offer to help her get into her saddle to ride Gimmer. She had no idea what time it was. From the afternoon sun on the horizon, she assumed it was approaching four o'clock or later. They continued to repair the remaining portion of the five-strand barbed wire fence. The cat had Spence's tongue tied tightly. Priscilla followed him back down the trail and secured Gimmer to the hitching post after which she emptied her saddle bags.

Standing next to her opened car door, Spence said, "Thank you for all of your help today. You can listen to your mind, but you've got to follow your heart. The only way to know what's real is to dig deeply into your spirit. I apologize for getting so amped up on the fence line, but at some point, we've got to get this thing ironed out. I'd rather do it where only the critters can hear us. Ants, birds, butterflies, cows, cougars, coyotes, dogs, and horses don't gossip."

"Will I see you again?" Priscilla asked.

"The next move is yours. Or should I say, your mother's? Let me know what you decide. You know where to find me."

S

The sun had long since slipped down the western side of the mountains as the eighteen-wheeler rolled down the highway. The driver had planned on stopping in Cinder Valley for the night, but his passenger persuaded him to take him further up the highway. "I think this is where I need to get off. It's harder to tell than I thought it would be. It's one of these side roads along this stretch of highway somewhere. There's no traffic coming either way. If you can grind 'er to a halt, I'll get out here. Much obliged."

"You got kin folk in these parts that can give you a hand out?" asked the driver.

"Know folk but no kin. I'll be just fine."

With that the driver shifted into gear and continued to drive his truck and trailer down the highway.

The passenger slid his backpack under the fence and crawled on his stomach until he was clear of the barbed wire. The moon was full five days ago, so there was still ample light to crawl through the brush and grass without being seen or heard. When he was about a half mile from the main road, he started walking upright and continued for what seemed like miles. As he crested the side of the hill and looked into the meadow, he could see cattle bedded down for the night. He was unsure if he was in the exact place he desired to be, but surely this would be close enough. Even though he was not that tall, his shadow loomed large when he stood up after eating the four cold biscuits he'd stolen from a plate of leftover food at a truck stop earlier in the day.

S

Francie Fletcher had stayed up late watching an old black and white World War II movie. She had the volume turned up so loud it was hard for Priscilla to fall asleep. She entered the living room just as the film ended.

"Another war movie?"

"Yes. You know me. I could watch them over and over again until they're completely worn out. I thought after your rigorous day, you'd be spent and counting sheep by now."

"What's the movie about?" asked Priscilla.

"V-E Day. May 8, 1945 when Germany unconditionally

surrendered its armed forces. The terrible war machine was finally defeated. Thank God for that!"

Priscilla hesitated for a moment knowing there would be no turning back once she started the next part of their conversation. She drew in a deep breath, sat up straight, and looked directly at her mother. "Speaking of war machines, this is the perfect time to address ours."

Francie let out a cackle and waved her hand at her daughter. "War machines? The U. S. isn't involved in any conflicts right now."

Rolling her eyes, Priscilla explained, "Mother, that's just a figure of speech. It's time to talk about the elephant that's been sitting in this room since Saturday, February 5th."

Leaning forward in her chair, Franice smirked and pointed her finger at her daughter. "You truly are sleep deprived. There's no animal, much less an elephant weighing more than a ton, in our midst. I need more clues than that."

"Forget clues. Straight talk is what's needed. I've decided to marry Spence Woodson."

The smirk was replaced with a look of shock and quickly escalated to a wind of flailing arms. "You what? When did he ask you? Is that why you went out there today under the guise of pretending that you were going to ride the range with him? What did you tell him?"

Francie jumped to her feet and started pacing. Priscilla jumped up also, taking her turn with waving her arms as she spoke. "You've never trusted Spence, and based upon your last remark, you don't trust me either! I did in fact ride the range with Spence and helped him repair broken barbed wire fence all day long."

Priscilla rubbed her temples. "What has gotten into you anyway?" Her softened tone made Francie take a step back, bracing herself for another unexpected attack. Priscilla continued, "Since Dad died, you're becoming stranger and more difficult by the day. Isn't it enough that I pay rent, help with all of the bills, and do more than my share around here? I've done it for years. What more do you want from me? Am

I not allowed to grow up?" She sounded as if the wind had been knocked out of her. She knew she would let her emotions take over if she didn't move.

Stomping into the kitchen, Priscilla removed a pair of scissors from the junk drawer. Opening the second drawer on the right-hand side of the stove, she removed one of Francie's well-used aprons. She walked into the living room and tied it behind her back. Handing the scissors to her mother, she directed, "Now cut the strings."

Taking another step back, Francie's left hand flew to cover her mouth as she stifled a sob. Two huge tears spilled from her eyes as she shook her head. "I'm not about to!"

Knowing she had to follow through, Priscilla grabbed hold of the strips of faded, orange plaid cloth strings. "Not a problem. I'll cut them for you." Light as two feathers, they made no sound when they fell onto the hardwood floor, but in Francie's heart, it was deafening. Surprised by the lump that was forming in her own throat, Priscilla kept her eyes on the fallen strings. Quietly, she said, "I overheard Dr. Merenspinn talking to you at the wedding about aprons."

"Priscilla, you weren't supposed to be listening to our conversation."

"I just happened to be walking by at the time. Also, a little birdie told me about it afterwards. Did you happen to notice the way Dr. Merenspinn was looking at you during Wyn and Sarita's wedding?"

Sitting down again, Francie asked, "Just what's that supposed to mean? You're exaggerating because you're trying to change the subject."

Priscilla realized she'd incorrectly buttoned her pajama top when she'd gone to bed. She pulled the bottom edges together. "The younger generation not only pays attention to what their peers are doing, but they keep a close eye on the older one as well, especially if it happens to pertain to their parents."

"Dr. Merenspinn was not looking at me any differently at the wedding than any other woman!"

"How do you know? Have you received your diploma in

Mind Reading? If you weren't so grouchy, you just might have danced the night away. Ever thought about that?"

Francie looked away for a few minutes. "Enough of this goofy Dr. Merenspinn business. It's starting to make my head spin. He's been a widower for years. The last I heard, he has all sorts of women making appointments with him under the guise of needing medical help. They are serious gold diggers with stars in their eyes. He continues to ignore them, so I guess there's nothing wrong with his eyes."

"Maybe you need to have your vision checked," suggested Priscilla.

Francie pressed, "Back to this Spence business, so we can dispense of it once and for all. Are you making this decision in haste because you're already in a family way?"

Priscilla flushed hot pink. "You don't respect me either, do you? Just like an apron is put on a toddler to keep her clean, I've kept myself chaste to this very day and plan on it until the day I say *I do*. Spence Woodson is such a country gentleman; he hasn't even kissed me yet.

You don't give me an ounce of credit for trying to do things correctly, taking my time to make sure I choose a lifelong mate, and honoring you the entire time. I need to learn the difference between honor and control. Find someone or something else to control because I'm no longer playing that game. If it wasn't so late tonight, I'd literally drive to the Toppens Ranch, climb on top of the bunkhouse, and shout from the rooftop, 'I'm free, and I'm marrying Spence Woodson after as he proposes to me!'"

CHAPTER THIRTY-SEVEN

Opening his backpack and lighting the edge of the brown and burgundy yarn, the intruder ran swiftly across the edge of the meadow, dragging the broken tree limb with the handiwork tied on the end of it behind him. With the wheel lines having been turned off for a while, the sudden wind gusts rapidly spread the sparks to the dry hillside. Gaining momentum quickly, the fire roared through the boxed canyon where the herd had bedded down for the night. Running in the opposite direction, he could smell burned hides as he listened to the final bellowing of some of the bovines as they drew their last breaths and collapsed on the sagebrush and indigenous grasses. It was impossible for them to outrun the leaping flames. The arsonist's energy drink would propel him across his imaginary finish line before he plunged into the creek. No one heard him yell, "Take that, Spence, and all you Toppens' Top Hands!"

Varying shades of orange quickly blanketed the night's horizon. Yellow flames whipped across the landscape as billows of smoke, propelled by increased wind flurries, rose toward the heavens. Deer, elk, mountain lions, rodents, and other wildlife made a futile attempt to outrun it. The destructive conflagration finally met its demise when it ran into the sheer, solid, igneous rock wall.

Blake Benson awakened when he heard a piece of metal crash into the side of one of his outbuildings. Peering through his opened bedroom window, he determined one of the panels from the car port had flown through the air into the wall of his shop. Walking up the stairs, he knocked on the door of his guest bedroom. There was no immediate answer.

Blake slipped into his jeans and walked barefoot into the night air. He strained to listen for the sounds, if any, from his animals inside the corral. Sensing nothing was amiss, he went back to bed.

Less Alotto feigned sleep for three more hours until he heard Blake's pickup leave the driveway. The wind died down as he eased out of bed, got dressed, and headed outside to sort through his pile of odds and ends and load them onto the large utility trailer.

Since Blake's house had few shade trees around the perimeter along with insufficient air conditioning, Meg had not slept well during most nights for the last month which inflamed the eczema on her forearms and hands even more. The racket coming from Less's activity did nothing to soothe her nerves. She looked inside the refrigerator for something for breakfast, but the pickins' were pretty slim. Stormy's pantry would just have to provide for today and maybe the rest of the week. Normally Meg applied her makeup prior to heading to her bookkeeping job at the Sabblonti Ranch, but since her supplies were running low, she opted not to. Locking the front door behind her, she embarked upon her work-a-day world.

"Less, what are you doing with that boat? You don't even like to fish! We need to leave right now. I don't want to be late for work. I have this sneaky feeling that Stormy writes down what time I arrive at the ranch house every day that she happens to be there. It wouldn't surprise me in the least."

Less decided to wear one of his mesh, lightweight, baseball caps for the day since it'd been so hot. "Boat? I don't own any boat."

"What's that thing on the trailer that looks like it has light blue life jackets draped over both sides?"

"It's an old pickup camper shell. Far cry from a boat, Meg!"

"You're supposed to be managing a cattle ranch, not horsing around with camping stuff."

"Just might need to sleep underneath one some night. Never know for sure. Doesn't that sound romantic? You and me all cozy inside a camper shell. Sorta like honey-mooners. The life vests could be our pillows."

"Less, our honeymoon was a very long time ago."

"Did you get some breakfast and coffee before we left the house?"

"There were no eggs or sausage in the fridge. Those instant coffee granules mixed with hot water smell like leftover engine oil."

Less knew it was time to zip his lip and drive.

S

Just finishing his breakfast, Slim Shade spotted the pay phone in the far corner of the restaurant. He asked the waitress for enough quarters to place a long-distance call.

The greasy spoon background noise from several states away blared in her ear as Stormy, sipping her green tea inside her turquoise-colored peacock mug, answered her phone.

"Stormy, Slim Shade checking in. I've scored you a real winner of a race horse! He's almost a three-year-old chestnut with a snip on his nose and half stocking on his right hind leg. I looked over prit near every square inch of him and he's as sound and strong as an obsidian wall. They've named him 'Rascal Racer.' His sire is Fire Racer and his dam is Savannah Sable. If you ask anybody worth their quirt in the racing world, he can tell you that there's no finer breeding stock than Fire Racer. The only catch is I can't take possession of him until the middle of November."

Stormy turned the calendar pages hanging on the kitchen wall. "That's a ways off, but as long as you can guarantee delivery before the holidays, I'm fine with that. Did the seller require a down payment?"

Slim leaned against the restaurant wall as he watched one of the customers pull several $100 bills from his billfold and lay them across the table from another rancher. "No, and that's where hiring me really paid off. I've put in my time with these characters, so we're all one big happy circuit. You know, you plug one of us in, and it lights up the whole herd! I told my contact that you were good for the money. He'd actually heard of the Sabblonti outfit before from somewhere."

Picking at her rough cuticles, Stormy decided she just might treat herself to a mani and a pedi real soon. "That does not surprise me in the least. Anyone worth their cattle knows that the Sabblonti influence reaches far and wide. Just a minute. I've got to write that name down before I forget it. Is it spelled just like it sounds - R A S C A L R A C E R?"

"Don't ask me. I'd put a *K* in there where you said *C*. I flunked most spelling tests in school. What I paid attention to was math. Never sorry about that one. It's more important to know how to count your money than spell your name or anyone else's for that matter."

"Okay, I'll just go with that spelling and hope it's correct. You'll provide the registration papers when you deliver Rascal, won't you?"

"Guaranteed. Rascal is a papered horse, for sure. Cuttin' no corners there. When you shell out a hundred grand, you get the full racing deal. I'll contact you when I'm ready to load him up and head for your ranch."

"Thanks, Slim. I can't wait. I'm so excited!"

"Women." Slim hung up the receiver of the pay phone. Two quarters fell from the slot into the bottom receptacle and made their way into the coin pocket of his bib overalls.

S

Less let the pickup engine idle in the driveway by the Main Sabblonti Ranch house. Meg didn't even feel like telling him goodbye or have a nice day. Stormy had been watching from her kitchen window.

Inserting the key into the lock, Meg realized the door was already open.

"Rough morning?" asked Stormy.

"You could say that. Sorry I'm late."

"Don't make a habit of it. Bookkeepers looking for jobs around here are standing behind every sagebrush, so best not to push your luck."

"Again, I'm sorry. It won't happen again. You look lovely today, Stormy."

"Thanks. I've got a very important business day ahead, so I need to get a move on. No time to waste."

No sooner was Stormy gone from the main ranch house than Meg ran upstairs and opened the closet. She retrieved the three large boxes containing many small boxes from Bosner's and threw them down the staircase. When she arrived at the bottom, she carried them outside to the burn barrels. Making sure no one else was around, she turned on the black hose which produced a steady stream of water. Meg struck the side of the barrel with the match and monitored every box, large or small, until it was completely consumed inside the barrel. Then she doused it with water.

Ascending the stairs, Meg entered her daily sanctuary. She grabbed the heavy striped wool blanket on the closet shelf and laid it out carefully on the floor. The black notebook with plastic inserts was growing to be a daily delight. She rolled the office chair back to just the right spot, crossed her legs, placed them on top of the desk and started to flip the pages. Meg marveled at the artistic design given to some people since that was not her talent. She wanted to finger each coin inside the plastic inserts, but knew that the value was decreased dramatically if touched by the human hand with all of its natural oils. Meg closed the notebook, wrapped the blanket around it, and set it back on the closet shelf. Purloined coffee and breakfast would follow as soon as her boss was further down the highway.

S

Stormy hadn't been this elated in years. Her daydreams propelled her into downtown Cinder Valley. She parked in front of Earl's Saddle Shop. The sound of the bell mounted inside the front door announced her arrival.

"Good morning. How can I help you?"

"I need you to make a horse bridle, but just not any old run of the track one. It's got to be top notch made from your most expensive leather."

"I can probably do that for you," agreed Earl. "Here are my samples along with some of my specialty designs. I also have a book over here on the counter that you can look through. I've been in business so many years it's easier to take pictures and file them away than try to display the actual work. I end up selling most of them as soon as I get them made anyhow. What color's the horse?"

"It's a chestnut."

"Let's see here. I would suggest using this color, but feel free to take your time."

Stormy started to open the notebook when she noticed one strap of a bridle lying across the opposite counter. She walked over, picked it up, and ran her right index finger down the left side of it. "Earl, is all of this done by hand? It must take you forever!"

"Yes, it's done by hand and requires a set of very specialized tools for cutting, piercing, forming, stitching and decorating. This particular one happens to be a top adjusting bridle. Some of my customers prefer those."

"Instead of this scrolling design on the sides can I have you put the horse's name which is Rascal Racer? I would like Rascal down the left side and Racer down the right side. Then I want our cattle brand on each side, too."

"I can do that for you. What does your brand look like?"

"If you have a piece of paper and a pen, I can draw it for you."

Earl walked to the cash register and handed Stormy paper and pencil. "Write down the exact spelling of the horse's name for me too, please."

Stormy proceeded to draw the Sabblonti cattle brand for Earl.

RASCAL RACER.

"Here, Earl, that should do it."

"How soon do you need it? I'm a little behind in my custom orders at the moment."

Stormy looked at the calendar on the counter. "As long as I have it by the first of December that should be okay."

Earl explained, "This is my most expensive leather, so all total it will be around seven fifty."

"Only $7.50 for this?" asked Stormy. "Wow, that's a steal."

Smiling faintly, Earl said, "You have the decimal point in the wrong place. It's $750.00."

"There's nothing Sabblonti money cannot buy."

Tucking that statement into his memory bank, Earl asked, "Is this for you or someone else?"

"One half for me and one half for someone else."

"So which half is yours, the Rascal or the Racer?"

"Definitely not the Rascal, but since I'm racing toward the winner's line, more than likely the Racer."

Keenly interested, Earl continued, "Where are you racing? Which track?"

"I don't know if there's an official name for it."

"Well, every track that I've ever heard of has a name. Just asking."

"Do you want me to pay you in advance?" asked Stormy.

"Yes, for a custom order with specific lettering, I require 50% down and the balance on delivery."

Stormy noticed a stack of undeposited checks secured with a black clip next to Earl's cash register. "I'll just pay you in full right now."

"Your total including tax will be $804.38."

"Thanks, Earl. I'm sure glad there are people like you who know how to do this kind of stuff."

"Well, everybody knows how to do something. Finding that something is the key."

S

It took Less longer than expected to pull the trailer to his secret stockpile. After unloading it, he decided to unhitch it and leave it next to the old pickup for the time being. His stomach reminded him that his early morning haste produced hunger. Since he was already in the remote region of the Sabblonti Ranch, Less decided to check the cows and calves that were on the upper summer range. As he crested the hill and started his descent into the area, he slammed on his pickup brakes and bailed out. It had been a full three weeks or longer since he'd been here. He looked toward the boxed canyon. What'd happened here?

Less kicked the ashes as he walked around gazing upon the carcasses. In some places, all he saw were outlines of what looked like an animal that had been completely fried while standing still. Throwing his baseball cap in the air, falling onto his knees into the ashes, and pulling the skin on both of his cheeks downward, he screamed at the top of his lungs, "Whoever did this will pay big time!" He got in his pickup and drove like there was no tomorrow. He stopped in the middle of the street in front of The Sage Hen Café in Ridgemonte. Blake looked up from his lunch plate just as Less entered the restaurant with his hair standing straight on end and leftover ash streaks on his cheeks. He looked like something straight from a horror movie.

Blake directed his co-worker who was having lunch with him, "Pay my bill, call Ted to come pick you up, and cover for me the rest of the day. Later."

Spinning Less around to face the front door, Blake grabbed his right arm, ushered him outside, and around the back of the building.

"Shake yourself, Less. Where have you been? It looks like you've gone stark raving mad! You don't come into a public place looking like this. Where's your hat?"

"That's all you can say at a time like this?"

"Time like what? You didn't torch anything on my place did you? You better not have or you'll pay dearly. I'll boot your boots off my place so fast it'll make your head swim."

"They've gone up in smoke!"

"Who's gone up in smoke?" demanded Blake.

"The Sabblonti cows and calves."

"All of them?"

"I don't know how many. I didn't count them."

"Give me your keys and don't go anywhere. Stay put."

Blake went inside the restaurant and sat across from his co-worker in the booth. "Here's the keys to Less's pickup, so you don't need to call Ted to come get you. It's the rig with the South Dakota plates parked outside. Drive it to my ranchette. Now!"

Driving the state brand inspector's vehicle to the back alley, Blake ordered Less to get inside. "You better start explaining."

Less recounted his discovery of the range fire and dead animals. "Just when I thought Meg and I were going to start getting ahead, this goes and happens."

"How did the blaze start in the first place?"

"Search me," said Less.

"When was the last time you checked on that part of the herd over there?"

Less rested his head on the back of the passenger seat and closed his eyes. "I can't remember how long ago it was."

"Seems to me you've been spending way too much time collecting stuff that should be hauled to the dump. Since you're the foreman, you should be farming that kind of stuff out to your hired hands. Those are the kinds of things you take care of during the dead of winter."

"Well, I haven't wanted to hire very many extra hands," explained Less. "I thought if I could show Stormy that I could operate this spread without it costing an arm and a leg, she'd give me a bonus."

Blake accelerated until he was driving twenty miles over the speed limit. "I'm taking you straight to my place. Your pickup will be waiting for you there. Since it's just lost, missing, strayed or stolen livestock that fall under my jurisdiction and control, you don't need me to clean up behind you. You're totally on your own. Tread carefully henceforth."

CHAPTER THIRTY-EIGHT

Less stood under the cold-water shower until he could tolerate it no longer. He rehearsed several tall tales in front of the bathroom mirror. If he'd been in the acting business, his upcoming performance would have to be his all-time best. He rummaged around in Blake's office until he found a small lined memo pad and scrawled some titles and tally marks on the pages. Arriving at the Main Sabblonti Ranch house at straight up quitting time for Meg, his usual custom was to sit inside the cab of his pickup and wait for her to emerge, but today was slightly different. He opened the front door just as his bride descended to the bottom step of the stairs. "Your boss around by any chance?"

"She just got home about ten minutes ago, so she's putting her personal purchases away."

"Can you fetch her for me? Got some information to pass along."

Less kept a tight grip on the doorknob to help steady himself.

"Yes, Less, you need to speak to me?"

"Stormy, seems as though there was a bit of misfortune during last night's storm."

Looking outside, Stormy asked, "Last night's storm? Whatever are you talking about? There was no such thing."

"Sure there was," pressed Less. "Didn't you hear the wind or thunder and see the dry lightning?"

"There was no wind or lightning down here. I didn't

hear or see anything. I'm a very light sleeper. If there'd been anything of the sort, I most certainly would've noticed it, especially thunder."

Less stepped inside, closed the front door, and leaned against it. "Well, the storm might've split and gone around you. Seems like there's been a lot of those this summer. Anywho, I make it a regular practice to keep a careful eye on all the herds on the various spreads. Been watchin' the cattle prit near round the clock. Even write it down in a little notebook I keep in my front shirt pocket. When I checked one of upper areas earlier this morning, I found some dead carcasses in one of the canyons. Looked like they couldn't outrun the grass fire. Both cows and calves."

Placing her left forefinger on the left side of her nose as she gripped her chin with her remaining fingers, Stormy asked, "How many are you talking about?"

"Didn't tromp all over the hillside and down into the gully to try to count 'em. Pretty ashy and all."

Carefully surveying Less and raising her left eyebrow, Stormy commented, "I don't see a speck of any kind of ash on you or your boots."

"I've got real sensitive lungs and have had bouts of walking pneumonia in the past. I had to rush to Blake's and get in the shower to get all that residue washed off me, so I wouldn't start hacking for days on end."

"If you keep as meticulous records as you claim you do then all you'll have to do is count the remaining ones and you'll know how many you've lost. When I inquire as to the average cost of a cow and a calf, I'll calculate that and deduct it from your wages. You just might have to work several months into the new year and not collect a paycheck."

Less slammed his right fist into his cupped left palm. "That's grossly unfair! Do I have control over the weather? How am I supposed to know when the lighting is going to strike or the wind is going to blow?"

Cool as a summer cucumber, Stormy calmly said, "As Sabblonti Range foreman, you're absolutely in charge of those things. Also, you should've had man-made barriers in place so that if a range fire starts it burns out very quickly and no cattle are lost in the process. I have far more important things to concern myself with than the loss of a couple of cow and calf pairs. Now if you'll be on your way, I have things to do. Meg, I'll see you at eight sharp in the morning."

Less and Meg got inside their pickup. As Less hunched over the steering wheel and drove down the lane onto the main highway, he looked straight ahead and asked, "No questions, Mrs. Alotto?"

"Questions? About what?"

"The range fire. The cattle. You know, my job."

"I have no questions, Less. You've assured me everything's fine."

"You're correct, Meg darling. Everything's just fine. What do we possibly have to be worried about?"

Tossing and turning in the double bed during the night, Less moaned and groaned as he flailed his arms. Meg shook him until he was wide awake. "Are you having a bad dream?"

"Nightmare. I was trying to save 'em."

"Save who?" Meg asked.

"The cows and their calves."

"Forget about those stupid cattle so we can get some sleep."

Blake seemed to be arriving home later in the evenings and leaving earlier in the mornings. Meg tried to engage him in small talk, but Blake wasn't talking.

After Less delivered Meg at work the next morning, he decided to drive to the lower range to check on the cattle. He noticed one of the calves swaying back and forth as it tried to stand and was having difficulty breathing. Less looked as far as the eye could see, but couldn't spot Yatey or Ruston who he'd assigned to ride herd on this part of the herd. Granted, there were miles to cover on any given day as the cattle were spread out all over the place. He determined there was only one smart thing to do now, so Less drove to Ridgemonte and parked in front of the Shaw Vet Clinic.

Jacobe Davone was helping his boss load supplies into the various compartments of his truck.

Looking at the license plates on the pickup and at Less a second time, Dr. Shaw remembered his dream and the previous encounter on the road.

Less walked a little closer. "Got a calf or two on the lower summer range that seems to be having lotsa trouble breathing. Can I get you to come out and take a look? I have no idea what it could be. In all my ranching experience, I've never seen anything like that before. I can do some doctoring of the herd, but this is probably way above my pay grade."

As Dr. Shaw counted the syringes he had in the container, he asked, "Did you vaccinate your herd with the modified live respiratory vaccine during your branding? We administered two rounds for the Toppens herd."

"I was so busy I didn't get around to it. Ridin' herd on the Sabblonti herd is beyond a full-time job."

"I can follow you to the ranch and take a look. Jacobe, please call Rees Broomfield's ranch house and leave a message that I'll be there as soon as I can."

Dr. Shaw followed Less in his truck to the lower range. He parked under a small outcropping of trees and walked toward the wobbly calf.

Continuing with his initial examination, Dr. Shaw commented, "There's no sign of nasal or lacrimal discharge and no coughing. Let me check for pyrexia. It's 105.8 which is in the normal range. Whatever the calf is consuming is going right through him based upon the scour deposits on the ground. Where's your closest water source? We'd better have a look at that while we're at it."

"Over the next hill is a small reservoir. I assume it drank from there."

As soon as Dr. Shaw walked over the hill and next to the bank of the reservoir, he opined, "Holy smokes, look at that blooming algae! Your water level here is dangerously low. If you combine that with increased heat and light along with limited water circulation, it's a recipe ripe for toxins to be released into the water."

Less bent down and scooped a handful of the water letting it filter slowly through his fingers. He sniffed his palm. "Why would the cows and calves drink it if there were toxins in it?"

"Do you have another water source close to this reservoir?"

"I have no idea how far away the next water source is located," Less replied.

"You have no idea? Aren't you Sabblonti Ranch Foreman?"

"Yes, I am," said Less as he squished a big stink bug with the heel of his boot. "Yatey and Ruston are ridin' out here somewhere. We've been very short handed since I signed on here. Course this is one gigantic ranch."

Dr. Shaw surveyed some of the rest of the herd. "I would imagine that the Sabblonti enterprise certainly has enough funds to hire some range riders. Back to your original question regarding animals drinking from this reservoir, some water is better than no water. The cattle aren't always going to be able to discern toxins in water. Have you apprized Chet Castins of what's going on here or his wife, Stormy?"

Patting the memo pad in his shirt pocket, Less said, "Haven't had a chance to tell her about the algae yet. I knew the best thing to do was to round you up first to get out here to lemme know what's the problem. As far as Chet goes, haven't seen him since I got hired on here. Last I heard he was still hobbling around and can't even ride a horse yet. It may be years down the road before he can get back in the saddle again. What's the cure for treating the part of the herd that's consumed the water with the toxic stuff in it?"

Dr. Shaw started to walk back to his pickup. "The immediate one is to move the herd to a different part of the Sabblonti Ranch. As late as it's getting in the fall, that should've been done already. Another thing to keep in mind is there are three to four common toxins in the algae that can ultimately affect the liver. This is nothing to horse around with. Get some additional hands hired so you can gather the entire herd and make an assessment.

One more suggestion, Less. You're letting these cattle overgraze in some areas, so they won't be up to par with their weight and marketing time is fast approaching when you'll want the top price for prime beef. With the drought we've had this summer, the grass on the range is not nearly as plentiful."

"Thanks, Doc. Appreciate you driving all the way out here. Send the bill to Stormy. I'll give some thought to the round up."

S

Spence stopped by the Toppens Ranch house right before dinner to talk with Tom. Merna was just returning from the bunkhouse.

"There you are, Spence. I delivered your mail. Were you needing something?"

"Has Tom gotten back from Ridgemonte yet?"

"No, his appointment with Dr. Diller wasn't until 11:00 and then he was going to stop by to visit with Delbert Dawson. The running lights on Tom's new pickup aren't working correctly. There's no telling exactly what time he'll be home, but know for certain that it'll be before suppertime."

"Sounds good. It's nothing urgent. Wyn and I need to ask his opinion on seeding some more ground. I'll catch him later. I'm going to grab some dinner at the bunkhouse and head out again. Thanks."

Miggy jumped from the pickup bed onto the ground after Spence turned the ignition off. "Fried lunch meat for dinner. How many slices do you want, Miggy? Oops, forgot that Merna said there was some mail she left in the wooden box. Back in a second."

When tearing the end of the envelope open, Spence nearly tore the letter in half as the scrap of faded, orange plaid cloth fell to the floor.

Hello, Spence!

I can only imagine how busy you've been with the fall roundup. Our time apart has given me a lot of time to ponder and prioritize. Your parting words to me were, "You know where to find me." I opted to write to you instead of paying you a visit.

You have no idea how much I enjoyed riding the range with you. Even though city life is the only thing I've ever really known except for visiting my grandparents' Big Sky Country ranch every summer, it's not where I want to spend the rest of my life.

I'm at a real crossroads now. I've spent several years formulating the criteria for my future husband. I would like to be married and live happily ever after. You know, HEA. How about you? If the man of my dreams doesn't act soon, I've decided to either move to another city in our state and get a job or move to another state altogether. One thing's for sure, I'm moving from my mother's house.

The night I returned home from helping you at the Toppens Ranch, I spoke with my mother about the difference between honor and control. I suggested she cut the apron strings and let me live my adult life. She refused, so I cut them for her. I've enclosed a sample for your consideration.

How's Miggy? I miss her so much! She's beyond adorable. Please give her a BIG hug for me. Make sure to tell her it's from me. I just know she can understand some human words. After all, love truly is a universal language.

As busy as you are, I would imagine this is all the free time you have to read, so I'll make this short and sweet.

Thanks for the memories,

Priscilla

P.S. You fit the criteria perfectly.

Spence jumped up and opened the kitchen drawer. Turning the yellow pages to ***D***, he traced his finger down the page to locate the number. He placed his order straightaway.

After collecting and preparing the order, Catherine Harrison stepped onto the elevator at 4:52 p.m. and into the Shadow Butte County recorder's office at 4:55. Assigned the closing for the day, Priscilla emerged from the Employee Break Room carrying her personal belongings.

"Since you're decked out in pink today, I'm guessing you're Priscilla?"

"I certainly am!"

"Lucky you. Enjoy. I had the sender repeat the message he wanted printed on the card. It made no sense to me, but maybe you can figure it out. Of course, I get the whole short hand, intimate, personal message routine once people have been together for a long time. Are you married or about to be?"

"Planning on it. These pink roses are gorgeous!"

Catherine admired the bouquet accented with baby's breath. "I've spent years studying the symbolism of flowers, some of which are simpler than others. Pink roses represent happiness. Obviously, your fiancé is happy with your relationship."

"Obviously. Thanks for the personal delivery and words of encouragement."

"You're welcome. I'm merely a messenger."

Priscilla settled into her office chair as she gingerly removed the petite card from the envelope.

"Roger the criteria. Sample looks great.

S & M."

"Catherine may have been confused, but I'm certainly not."

Removing one of the dozen roses, Priscilla proceeded to remove each of the velvety soft petals as she recited, "He loves me, he loves me not, he loves me, he loves me not . . . ending with *HE LOVES ME*! I just know he does! This last pink rose petal confirms it."

S

Between Dr. Shaw's clinic appointments and Macey Meadows' hospital shifts, they'd not been able to spend much time together since Wyn and Sarita's wedding. Somewhat nervous, Dr. Shaw placed a call to the nurse's station at Mintner Medical Center. Macey's shift ended an hour ago. His next call was bound to test the mettle of their friendship thus far.

As soon as Macey picked the phone receiver up and before she could answer, Dr. Shaw launched, "Macey, I'm so sorry. I'm going to have to cancel getting together tonight. I discovered something possibly threatening some cattle on the Sabblonti range and need to talk to Chet right away."

"Benny, it's totally fine. I've been on my feet for nine and a half hours today. I only sat down for two fifteen-minute breaks. What I wouldn't give for a foot massage right now and someone to serve me a bowl of hot soup!"

Dr. Shaw wouldn't mind having a foot massage himself. "Do you have one of those small units where you pour water into the bottom of it and your feet get massaged when you activate the power button?"

"No, unfortunately. I'm going to take a hot mineral salts

bath and crawl into bed. We need at least two more nurses at the hospital. For some reason, we've not had any applicants lately. I'm sure it has something to do with remote high mountain regions and not a lot of women wanting to live in those sorts of places."

"I'm sorry. Thanks for understanding about the cattle emergency. I'd be happy to give you a foot massage sometime in the future."

As she lay on the couch, Macey spread her toes apart so she could view them better. "I'll think about it. I don't let just anyone off the street touch my feet."

Laughing, Dr. Shaw suggested, "I had this snazzy idea before this whole toxic algae debacle."

Lowering her voice quite a bit, Macey answered slowly, "That sounds serious."

"It is. That's why I appreciate your maturity along with your medical experience and background. Back to my idea for a minute. Do you work this weekend?"

"No, thank God! Friday is my last day this week. I need to remember to be grateful that I can work afternoons and have some weekends off."

Without thinking, Dr. Shaw continued, "Just imagine. If we were Shaw & Shaw, we could double our efforts and get my work done in half the time or less, and your feet would be a lot less tired."

Macey rolled off her couch onto the floor. "Shaw & Shaw? That sounds like some investment or law firm."

"Never mind the double Shaw. I still owe you a dance from the wedding, remember? A very slow dance."

"Actually, I do, now that you mention it."

"My assistant, Jacobe, is going to come to my house and help me rearrange my living room furniture. Some of those pieces are solid mahogany and quite heavy."

Macey continued her leg exercises on the floor. "You don't have to rearrange your furniture just for me!"

"Oh, yes I do. Did you plan on dancing on top of my glass-topped coffee table or my sectional?"

Macey laughed and laughed. "Benny, you're the best!"

"What kind of soup do you like?"

"Soup? Can you make me a shrimp cocktail instead using seven shrimps and whip up some homemade cocktail sauce with horseradish?"

Sitting at his desk, Dr. Shaw quickly drew a picture of a shrimp on a piece of scrap paper. "It can't be that tough to make. Finding the shrimp in the mountains will be the biggest challenge."

"That's what they make grocery stores for, Benny. I realize it'll be thawed frozen shrimp, but it's better than no shrimp. When we take our trip to the coast, we can have some fabulous fresh fish."

"What trip to the coast?" asked Dr. Shaw.

"Oops! I guess the coastal trip belongs in the same category as the Shaw & Shaw. Nothing personal, but I'm headed to take a bath and then to bed."

"Sweet dreams."

"Thanks, Vet Det."

"Vet Det?"

"Yes, you know, Veterinarian Detective."

Dr. Shaw drove to the Lower Sabblonti Ranch house in search of Chet Castins. Upon arrival, it alarmed him somewhat that Chet had already gone to bed for the evening even though it was only three minutes past 6:00. Evan was able to roust him out of bed when he announced the name of his visitor.

Observing Chet's current physical condition, including his leather belt cinched ever so tightly around his waist, Dr. Shaw opted not to fully inform him right then of his recent visit to the Sabblonti Ranch at the request of ranch foreman, Less Alotto.

"It's good to see you, Chet. I hadn't been by to talk to you since the wedding, so just thought I'd stop in and see how you were doing. If I drove down here early tomorrow morning, would you like to take a ride to look at the range before the weather starts to change?"

"Sounds great! I could sure use a change of scenery."

"If I'm here around 8:30 would that give you enough time to do your morning exercises and so forth?"

"I'll be ready and waiting."

CHAPTER THIRTY-NINE

After picking Chet up and exchanging early morning pleasantries, Dr. Shaw eased into the important part of the conversation in order to prepare his passenger for his eventual jolt of reality. "Stormy's ranch foreman, Less, paid me a visit yesterday morning. He was in quite a panic. When I drove to the lower summer range, I observed one of the calves laboring to breathe and stand on all fours. When I inquired about the water source, Less led me over the hill to show me the reservoir. That's when I discovered the blooming algae."

Chet commented instantly, "Any rancher in his right mind knows that spells trouble, and you get your cattle as far away from there as fast as you can."

"Apparently Less wasn't in his right mind. I suggested he get the herd moved right away. We'll see when we get there."

Perking right up when they neared the range, Chet said, "Yep, sure fire, looks like we've got some that fell prey to the algae. I wonder if Yatey knows about this."

Dr. Shaw opined, "It looks like Less heeded my advice. I don't know how he could've moved the cattle that quickly though. He's living with Blake Benson who probably rounded up some of his buddies, and they may have herded them down even lower."

Strumming the dashboard with his right fingers, Dr.

Shaw searched for more words. He'd never seen a sadder face than Chet's. "Would you like to get out and stretch your legs a little?"

"There's nothing I can do out here now. What's done is done. When will the river of adversity stop running right through me, Doc?"

Again, normal verbose Dr. Shaw could find no words.

Chet said, "I know you're taking valuable time away from your schedule, so let's head back to the ranch, shall we?"

"Yes, I should probably get back to my appointments for the day. Speaking of my schedule, I could sure use some help."

"Have you thought about contacting any of your vet school buddies to see if they would want to go into partnership with you?"

So thankful that he'd been able to shift conversational gears quickly, Dr. Shaw said, "That's not a half bad idea. I'd been able to pretty much keep the fires put out until a few months ago."

"What happened a few months ago? As you can tell, I'm almost a full year behind. Never in a thousand years did I dream I would lose that much time. I'm way too young for all these setbacks."

"If you can even possibly look at it this way, Chet, the day you needed me to take you home from the hospital was a game changer for me."

Chet craned his neck far to his left, "How so?"

"I met a certain nurse whose smile has kept me smiling ever since."

"Let me guess," said Chet. "Macey with the milky white teeth and emerald eyes?"

"Oh, so you noticed as well."

"A guy would have to be half blind to miss all that came with that package." Chet drank some more coffee from the travel mug Dr. Shaw had Jacobe prepare for him earlier in the morning.

"Package? Don't make it sound so impersonal."

"Have you forgotten that I'm a married man, Doc?"

"Not in the least. A very long suffering one, I might add. We should probably find something else to talk about besides mutual marriage or engagement advice or we could resume it next time we take a drive."

"Thanks for giving up your morning for me, Doc. Just add that to my ongoing tab."

"I'm not keeping one, but happy to help any way I can, Chet."

Despite using his cane, Chet walked into the Lower Sabblonti Ranch house with an increased bounce in his step. Evan couldn't help but notice.

"That trip must have been just what the doctor ordered. Did you finally find that rumored silver on the Sabblonti Ranch?"

"All we found were some dead cows and calves."

"What gives?" Evan asked.

"Bloomin' algae in the bloomin' pond," replied Chet who drank a full glass of cold milk along with eating three chocolate chip coconut cookies. "Let's head to the main ranch house. Time to have a talk with the Mrs."

"Shall I don my full body armor or is this a peaceful visit?" Evan asked.

"You can give me front porch curb service and park down the driveway a ways if you'd like as you croon along with your country tunes."

"Sounds like a perfect plan, Chet. I don't like confrontation in any way, shape, or form. Count me out."

"I'm not expecting confrontation. Just explanation."

The early arrival of the crisp fall weather caused Chet to zip his coat up as soon as he got out of Evan's van. Since it was the weekend, he didn't bother to knock. "Hello, anybody home?"

Stormy glided down the stairs in her red bedroom slippers, stopping on the second to the bottom step.

Looking directing at Stormy, Chet stated, "Salina, I need to have a word with you about those cows and calves. Come into the kitchen so we can talk. Right now."

Resisting the urge to correct Chet, Stormy replied,

"Would you like a nice cup of hot coffee? How about some orange cinnamon rolls to go with it? I just took them out of the oven."

"You must have eaten at least a dozen of them already because you've not been that sweet in almost a year."

"Please come in and sit down. Can I take your coat and cane?"

"No. I won't be staying that long. Dr. Shaw and I just returned from the range. Lost some cows and calves there. Have you spoken with your hotshot range foreman about that or has he even let you know?"

Stormy gingerly touched Chet's right leg as she pulled up a chair and sat near him. "When I spoke to Less, he assured me that he kept careful watch on all of the herds in the various places on the ranch. He carried a small tablet in his shirt pocket where he kept daily records. I instructed him to count the herd once he'd completed his survey and subtract the ones that had perished. I plan to deduct that amount from his wages. I don't deem it a serious problem at all. There've probably been only a couple of cow-calf pairs that are gone. It can't be that much. There's nothing that Sabblonti money cannot buy."

Chet glared at Stormy. "So, you knew about this and didn't tell me?"

"I just found out myself. Besides, I wanted to wait until you were further along with your healing until I told you. I was just trying to be considerate."

Having not initially noticed Stormy's hand resting on his leg, Chet looked down. Stormy didn't remove her hand, but applied a few loving strokes as though she thought that would usher in some healing. Everything's going to be fine, Chet. Really it is. How are you getting along down there at the lower ranch house?"

"Evan's a good physical therapist."

"I'm thankful to hear that. I hope I never need one."

As Chet stood and positioned his cane in front of him to help his balance, Stormy placed her hand on top of his. She spoke very softly, "Heal quickly. Take care. By the way, the last time I checked, my name was Stormy, not Salina."

Chet reminded himself not to take the bait. Stormy closed the front door behind him as Evan opened the passenger door of the van.

"Now where?"

"To the Moreland residence, please. We should arrive there just about the right time if you can step on the gas a little."

Evan marveled at the sudden change in Chet, but didn't want to drill down on it. Hopefully it was permanent with a full healing ahead, both emotionally and physically. Evan felt he could author a two volume physical therapy series on just the last few months alone.

Sarita walked into the front yard carrying a full egg basket. Wyn had worked long into the evenings securing the hen house to keep the foxes out. Chet and Evan settled right into the comfy chairs in the living room as Sarita served them hot tea. The aroma of cornbread and navy bean soup wafted through every room of the house.

"Thank you for stopping by to see us," Sarita said. "Wyn should be home any minute for supper. We'd love to have you join us. Do you have time?"

Before Evan could agree, Chet answered for both of them, "We most certainly do."

Sarita busied herself in the kitchen setting the extra soup bowls at the table. Wyn emerged through the back of the house after having washed in the laundry room. He was as genuinely glad to see his visitors as was his new bride.

"What brings you by our way today, Chet? Are you getting around better? I couldn't really tell how upwardly mobile you were at the wedding. I was a bit distracted."

Sarita blushed and nearly burned her right hand dishing up the hot soup.

"Wyn, we lost some cattle on the lower range due to bloomin' algae in that one reservoir. Just wanted to stop by and see if your outfit was having any problems with your herd."

"Gee, so sorry to hear that, Chet. No, we're not having

any problems with the Toppens herd that I know of. When did you find out?"

Chet continued, "It's a long story, but the short version is that Stormy's ranch foreman took Dr. Shaw out there after he discovered some calves with severe scours and laboring to breathe. Doc figured out right away what was goin' on. Toxic algae in the water source."

Wyn replied, "The water on Tom's spread seems fine, course we don't have as many reservoirs as you guys do. Also, Dr. Shaw vaccinated the whole herd twice to prevent the upper respiratory infection."

Chet finally started eating his supper by the time Wyn had consumed his third piece of hot cornbread and butter. "We've been so busy with the Toppens herd that I couldn't even venture a guess as to what's been going on at the Sabblonti Ranch. Since Tom handed the reins over to me right after the first of the year, Spence and I've been on a dead run trying to keep up. Tom hired a couple of part timers, and then just recently we brought Fenn Bridgemore on board full time to replace Shane. He's living at the bunkhouse with Spence and Miggy. We needed to seed another meadow, and we just barely finished with that."

"Spence has a son now?" asked Chet. "When did he get married?"

Sarita swallowed too large amount of soup and started to cough. She excused herself and headed for the master bathroom.

"No, Miggy is Spence's new Bernese Mountain Dog. She's a real beauty and has taken to ranch work like a pro."

Chet consumed half of his bowl of soup which afforded Evan the opportunity to talk. "That's a real nice chicken house you've built, Wyn."

"Thanks. I've been burning the midnight oil trying to get that done. Those pesky foxes spoil the vines."

"I didn't see any vines growing anywhere," commented Evan. "Are you planning on planting some grapes way up here?"

"That's just a saying, but it can be applied to a lot of

areas of life. I plan on keeping those varmints out of every area of my life, especially my marriage."

"Foxes can't get inside your marriage!" Chet exclaimed.

"It's a type and shadow, so to speak. I'm blissfully happy and don't plan on allowing any intruders inside."

Sitting back down, Sarita chimed in, "Now, Wyn, here you are dispensing advice, and we've not been married that long."

"I've been married long enough to know that I want you all to my lonesome."

Sarita served hot fudge sundae cake straight out of the oven with heavy cream for dessert.

Chet hugged her as they prepared to depart. "Maybe I should plan to stop by a little more often for dinner. That dessert was a real treat."

"You're welcome any time, Chet. You too, Evan."

"Has your sister paid you a visit in your lovely new home? It's so peaceful and warm here. You've done a really nice job setting it up."

"Thank you, Chet. I've not seen my sister in a very long time, but she does know where I live. I have no hard feelings toward her. Maybe she can't bear to visit me since we live in a manufactured home. It's not four walls that make a home. I've stopped at the Main Sabblonti Ranch house several times to see Stormy, but the only person there is her bookkeeper, Meg. I can't imagine what Stormy has been doing that keeps her away from home so much. I'm using everything I have to concentrate on my new marriage. It takes way too much energy to play those hateful games, so I choose not to play. Mother played the games. Daddy didn't."

"How well I remember," said Chet. "Things become much clearer with the passage of time."

"Sarita and I had to wage a strong battle for our relationship, wedding, and marriage," stated Wyn. "The important things in life are worth fighting for."

Sarita continued, "It's still a ways off, but do either of you have Thanksgiving plans? If not, you're welcome to come over and spend the day with us. I'm insisting that Wyn take that day off work. Tom, Merna, and Fenn will be joining us, so we'll have a full house. There'll be lots of good food and great company."

"Count me in, Sarita," said Chet.

"Me too," agreed Evan.

CHAPTER FORTY

Yatey and Ruston were up early thirty as they planned to look for the last of the strays. "Better take extra sandwiches in your saddle bag today, Ruston. No tellin' how long we'll be gone. You fill the canteens, too?"

"Sure did, Boss. Glad to see my mount isn't limping this morning." Ruston had rubbed his horse's legs with some liniment the night before, applying a little extra to the right hind one.

Tying his bed roll on the back of his saddle, Yatey cinched it down as tightly as he could. Patting the hind quarter of his gelding and whistling for his dog, he mounted up, and they headed up the trail.

After riding for a couple of hours, Yatey glassed the area with his binoculars. Ruston followed suit. "Looks like we got 'em all on the last trip," he surmised. "Sure would be nice to head home before dark since the days are getting a little shorter."

Tucking his set of binoculars inside his dusty black duster, Yatey suggested, "You know, Ruston, I didn't sleep very well last night. I have this strange feeling that we should ride to the upper summer range and look for strays there. I'm just sure that's what Chet would want us to do. He's always so thorough and looks after each one of those bulls, cows, and calves like they're his kids."

"He doesn't have any kids, does he Yatey?"

"Nope. He and the Mrs. have lost three. Feel really sorry for them. If I didn't have my four beautiful daughters and that flock of grandkiddos, I don't know what I'd do, especially after the wife died. If Chet can't return to ranchin' next year, I'm gonna hang up my old silver spurs and retire this cowboy hat, so I can get on down the trail and spend more time with those little cowboys of mine. Funny how my girls have had nothing but boys. Sure makes me plum proud."

Not happy with what he'd just heard about the extended ride for the day, Ruston retied the dusty, light green, wild rag around his neck. He was not very talkative for several hours which didn't bother Yatey in the least. He loved the solitude. Suddenly, he spotted some birds circling quite high in the sky.

"Ruston, somethin's up over yonder. Let's head over there."

Not seeing anything obvious, Ruston asked, "What's over yonder? I think you're seein' things, Yatey."

"You gotta look somewhere other than straight ahead or straight down all the time. Have you been relyin' on your horse to just follow mine for a while as you've napped in your saddle?"

Yatey gently pulled back on the reins. "Whoa, Nickers!" Dismounting from his horse, Yatey led him by his bridle and stopped a few feet from one of the carcasses. "What happened here, Ruston?"

"You expect me to know, Boss? I can barely keep up as it is."

"Let's see if we can figure out where this fire started," suggested Yatey as he tied Nickers to a big juniper tree.

Ruston pulled his hat brim down, so he could survey the overall area much better. "Well, near as I can tell, it looks like it started at the edge of the meadow and spread into the canyon. Boxed those cattle clear inside there, so they didn't stand a fightin' chance. Odd thing is though, if there was a lightin' strike or somesuch, why did it burn only in that area? Rock wall woulda put 'er out when it got that far."

Yatey stood stark still and didn't move a muscle. Ruston wondered if he was going to keel over. Yatey said, "It's been bone dry here for months and wheel lines don't water the canyons. If there'd been a lightin' storm, I sure would've seen it, wouldn't you?"

"Yes, Boss." As Ruston moved the toe of his worn out, pointed cowboy boot across the dirt, he thought he spotted something. Bending down, he picked up what looked like about a four-inch scrap piece from a knitted blanket. "Look here, Yatey. What do you suppose this came from?"

Walking closer to Ruston and holding the brown and burgundy scrap in his left hand, Yatey said, "I've just about seen it all. Was Less sleeping up here? Did he cover himself with an afghan or something? Hard tellin' since there's not much of it." Placing it securely inside his saddle bag, Yatey looked straight at Ruston and said, "Time to head for the real Boss's house."

Yatey and Ruston rode to the line shack where they'd been staying. After taking care of the horses, they got in Yatey's old two-tone, light brown Mercury pickup with the gear shift on the column which couldn't be driven when there was snow on the ground or right after a sudden thunderstorm.

Evan and Chet had just sat down for a late supper to eat a bowl of beef stew when they heard several loud raps coming from the horseshoe knocker. Evan said, "I'll bet I know who that is. Shall I just ignore it?"

"Better check, Evan, just to make sure."

Pulling the curtain back a few inches, Evan didn't know exactly who it was standing there, but since it wasn't Salina, he opened the door.

"Howdy, Chet around by any chance?"

Chet had known that voice for many years. He was frustrated he couldn't jump up and run to the door. "Yatey, you come right on in here right now. So good to see you. I've missed you all year long! Oh, Ruston, great to see you, too. Pull up a chair, boys. Evan's got plenty of good ol' Sabblonti beef stew all fired up. Evan even made biscuits from a can for supper."

Yatey stood still as did Ruston. Chet continued, "Well, get those dusters off and wash that dust off. Whatcha waitin' for?"

With not much of an appetite, both cowhands washed up for the meal. Ruston was too nervous to eat much of anything. Evan sensed something was amiss, but Chet was so happy to see his hired hands, that he shoveled in his food as fast as he could. Evan hadn't seen him eat like this before."

Yatey took two bites and set his dripping spoon on the table. "Uh, Chet, this isn't entirely a social call, so to speak. It isn't that Ruston and I haven't wanted to stop by and check on how you were doin', but we've been runnin' to keep up all year long. You know how it is. There are practically no holidays or days off."

Reaching into his pocket and pulling out the singed, hand knitted, piece of whatever it was, Yatey laid it on the table. Chet picked it up with his left hand and dangled it in the air. "You came all the way over here to show me this?"

Ruston started to talk first, but Yatey interrupted him, and then explained to Chet and Evan what they'd discovered a short while ago.

Chet laid his face on the kitchen table. No one or nothing moved or spoke.

Raising his head and looking at the kitchen ceiling, Chet yelled, "I feel like the entire Sabblonti Ranch just caved in on me!"

Evan spoke first. "Chet, since you don't know for sure how many cattle perished in the fire, it's not like you've lost the entire ranch."

Yatey and Ruston quickly added positive remarks to help encourage Chet. Evan didn't have trouble selling every last drop of the beef stew he'd made or the biscuits he'd cooked from the can.

After Yatey and Ruston departed, Evan patted Chet on his back, and said, "I didn't want to mention this in front of your hired hands, but remember, there's still all that cash in all of those bank accounts at Cattlemen's Central you told me about. That can buy all kinds of cow and calf pairs."

"Whew, Even, you're right. You always know just what to say and when to say it."

S

The month of November seemed to slip right through Stormy's fingers as she tried to prepare herself to face another round of major holidays without her beloved mother, Jantzi Belle. She had made several trips to her gravesite over the past few weeks, but this had done nothing to cheer her up because Jantzi didn't answer back when Stormy had posed the questions to her. In addition, Stormy had declined Sarita and Wyn's invitation to join them for Thanksgiving dinner in their new home. Stormy had convinced herself beyond the shadow of a doubt that there was no way one could keep completely warm inside a drafty manufactured home during the cold winter months in the high desert mountains. Sarita had chosen her own path just like everyone else in life.

Friday, December 1st, Stormy drove into Cinder Valley to pick up the custom-made bridle for Rascal Racer. Earl had done an outstanding job of making it.

When she returned home later that evening, Stormy looked through some catalogs and magazines as she anxiously awaited the call from Slim Shade regarding the delivery of the race horse. The waxing crescent moon lulled her to sleep around midnight.

In the middle of a dream where Stormy was shoving Salina Bevvins and pulling her long, black hair, she awakened suddenly to the sound of footsteps walking down the long hallway toward the bedroom. Jumping out of bed and opening the door, she saw the window open and close in as much time as it would take for the grains of sand to flow through an hourglass. "Who are you, and what do you want?" she screamed. Trying to get any sleep the remainder of the early morning was an exercise in futility. She'd contemplated driving over to the lower ranch house to ask Chet and Evan to check out the Main Sabblonti Ranch house, but thought better of it. She'd heard of haunted houses. There was no way on God's green earth the main ranch house was one. Or was it?

A few minutes after ten Saturday morning the phone rang in the kitchen as Stormy was making herself a cup of strong coffee. "Hello, this is Stormy Castins."

"Stormy, Slim Shade here. Got that Rascal Racer dialed up for you. Need to get the money. Lemme see. Today is Saturday. I'm supposed to meet the seller on the 6th to take possession, so I'll need you to wire the money by that date. I can deliver Rascal on Friday the 8th. Will that work for you?"

Looking at her calendar, Stormy declared, "No, the 8th will not work. I need it to be on a Saturday. How about a week from today on the 9th? There won't be any men folk here that day, so can you help me put him in a barn or someplace?"

"An extra day would actually help me out a lot. There's no telling what the roads will be like over the next week, so if I hit a slippery stretch or two, I want to be able to take my time since I'm carrying expensive cargo. If you've got a paper and pencil, I can give you the number of where to send the money transfer."

Stormy wrote the information down. "I had something so snazzy made for Rascal. I can't wait to show it to you."

"That's real nice, Stormy. It makes me very happy when I know that a horse is going to a ranch where he'll be taken care of and appreciated. That's a whole lotta cash to be shelling out, especially around Christmas time and all."

"Slim, don't concern yourself so much with money.

There's nothing Sabblonti money cannot buy. With our firm plans, I'll meet you here at the ranch on Saturday the 9th. Do you need directions, Slim?"

"You told me how to get there once before, and I wrote it down. My sense of direction is pretty good. I doubt I'll get lost. Never have before."

"The 9th it is. Thanks, Slim."

"Don't mention it."

Stormy didn't enjoy a full night's sleep for the next four nights. When Meg arrived for work at 8:00 Wednesday morning, Stormy's nerves were worn quite thin.

"Meg, don't make so much noise when you come in the front door. Where are your manners, anyway?"

"I wasn't aware that my arrival was that loud." Meg noticed the large dark circles under Stormy's eyes.

"I need to go into the bank today, so I can send a wire transfer. If I can't get a morning nap, I'll need you to drive me."

"I'm happy to do that. Maybe that can be one of my Christmas gifts to you since I'm not able to buy much else on $500 per month." Meg was not really happy that Stormy had been spending a lot more time at home the last month or so. She was used to her being gone a lot, so she had free run of the place. Meg had long ago perfected the act of supposedly having so much office work to do that she could barely get it done in an eight-hour shift.

Stormy was unable to get any extra rest, so she donned her business attire, applied her makeup, and grabbed her briefcase. Stopping by the office down the hallway before descending down the staircase, she said, "I'll be back after a while. Make sure to listen for the phone to ring in case there are any messages for me."

"I can drive you into Ridgemonte if you'd like, Stormy."

"Thanks for the offer, Meg. I can drive."

"Isn't it something you can take care of over the phone like you usually do?"

"I probably could, but if the assistant manager, Lonnie Browne, is the only one working and something goes south, I cannot afford for that to happen."

"You must have a big project afoot."

"You could say that."

Meg carefully watched out the upstairs window for Stormy to leave the driveway. She located the cherry wood music box under Jantzi Belle's bed and removed the remaining cash inside. Dialing the number to Blake Benson's house, she fervently hoped Less had stopped in there to warm up a can of beans for dinner. She tried calling three different times. During each call, there was no answer. Finally, on the fourth attempt, Less answered. He sounded out of breath.

"Less, is that you? What's the matter with you? You sound winded."

"I've been loading some stuff in my little trailer and each time I got inside the house, the phone quit ringing, so I almost didn't come inside and answer it this time. You never call me in the middle of the day. What's up, catnip?"

"Stormy's being really witchy. I think she's getting ready to hire a new bookkeeper. Collect all our stuff as quickly as you can. I've put everything I own into those two black duffel bags inside the bedroom closet upstairs. Don't dally around in case Blake comes home unexpectedly. Even though it's cold outside, I'm going to try to walk to the end of the lane. I'll meet you there."

S

Stormy entered the lobby of Cattlemen's Central. Due to sheer fatigue, she felt like crying, but knew she must keep herself together for the next few minutes.

Chara's friendly greeting and smile never went out of

style. "Hello, Stormy. It's nice to see you this afternoon. What can we do for you today?"

"I need to send a wire transfer. I've written the information on this piece of paper. Hopefully I have everything you need."

Glancing at the phone number and the dollar amount, Chara said, "This should take care of it. Are you getting all ready for the holidays?"

"This will fully launch my Christmas season. I'm very excited to tell you the truth. I've been working on this gift for quite some time now."

"Excellent," said Chara who seemed to be taking longer than usual as she strained and squinted looking at the various Sabblonti bank accounts on her computer screen. "If you could have a seat in the lobby for just a couple of minutes that would be helpful. There's fresh coffee in the carafe if you would like a cup. I need to ask Lonnie Browne something."

Stormy was running on empty, so the mention of sitting down was a welcome sound. A jolt of caffeine would help for the drive home.

Chara huddled with Lonnie in his office as they studied the Sabblonti bank accounts. "Please ask Stormy to come into my office. Also, is Stewart inside the building?"

"I believe he is. Do you want him to come into your office right now?"

"No, not at this exact moment. Please ask him to stay inside the bank for at least the next hour in case there's an explosion."

"Explosion?" asked Chara.

"Outburst would be more correctly stated."

Chara walked toward Stormy and asked her to step into Lonnie's office for a few minutes after which she closed the door behind her.

"Stormy, you requested a wire transfer be sent to a Slim Shade in the sum of $100,000. I'm sorry to have to tell you that there's not that much combined in all of the Sabblonti accounts as of today."

Adrenaline rushed through Stormy as she jumped to her feet and screamed at the top of her lungs, "What do you mean there's not a hundred thousand dollars in the Sabblonti accounts? There's nothing Sabblonti money cannot buy! I never did think you knew one earthly thing about banking the first time I laid eyes on you. When my beloved mother died almost a year ago, there was over half of a million dollars inside Cattlemen's Central that belonged to her and her alone. What have you done with it? I'm calling the Ridgemonte Police Department or the Shadow Butte County Sheriff's office. There's no way you're getting away with this. Thieves! Thieves! And more thieves!"

Stewart Sanders, Cattlemen's Central Bank Manager, calmly entered Lonnie's office. "Lady and gentleman, is there a problem here?"

Lonnie explained that he'd looked through all of the various Sabblonti bank accounts, and there was not a total of $100,000 to wire to another bank.

"Stormy," said Stewart, "Lonnie and I would be happy to go through your banking records with you. Please come into my office. Lonnie will print off the various statements and bring them in so we can have a more detailed discussion. Three copies please, Lonnie. Thank you."

Chara delivered three cups of piping hot coffee on a tray. Lonnie handed a stapled set of bank statements to Stewart and Stormy. On days like today, Stewart, slower than slow, was in his prime, even if one had to drive stakes to see if he was moving.

Stewart directed, "Stormy, please refer to the statement for the Operating Account."

Never having balanced her own bank statement in forty years, Stormy flashed the *deer in the headlights* look. Steward sighed inwardly.

"Lonnie, could you please locate the correct page for Stormy and help her as we go down through these debits and credits? It might be easier if I refer to them as deposits and withdrawals."

"Sure, I'd be happy to do that." Lonnie had placed the

statement for the Operating Account on top of the set of stapled sheets of paper.

Stewart began, "Stormy, if you can please follow along with me as I read down through the first few pages of this statement that would be most helpful. It would appear as though a few months ago, $260,000 was transferred from some of your other accounts into your Operating Account. You telephoned the bank that day and asked Lonnie to do that for you. He followed that up by sending paper copies to your ranch address. There are an awful lot of checks made out to a company or business known as *Double A Enterprises*. Are you familiar with them by chance?"

Stormy cleared her throat. "No, I can't say as I am, Stewart."

Continuing with his explanation, Stewart said, "The memo in the lower left-hand corner of those checks states it's for supplies. That's a lot of supplies to buy from one vendor, but I do know that some cattlemen prefer to deal with just one or two outfits if they can find a good one. *Bosner's* is the other company where a lot of these checks are made payable. I've never heard of either one of these companies, have you Lonnie?"

"Not off the top of my head. When I reviewed the images, the checks made out to *Double A Enterprises* were deposited at the Bank of Blunte."

Stewart still wasn't finished with his observation, "Looking at some of these other printouts, there've been many checks issued to pay for Jantzi Belle's funeral expenses, Chet's medical bills, household expenses, a large check to Ignee County Rodeo Board, and so forth."

Stormy's eyes were swimming in an ocean of figures. There'd never been a worse time for sleep shortage.

"Stormy, perhaps the best place to start would be to talk with the bookkeeper you hired," suggested Stewart. "She might be able to shed some light on all of this. Cattlemen's Central keeps impeccable records. A banking institution does not stay in business this long and service as many cattle ranches as we do if they're not totally above board."

Lonnie added, "I recall the day you came into Cattlemen's with your new bookkeeper and authorized her to sign on all accounts. I thought she said she was a CPA as well."

"If she's an accountant and a CPA, she should be able to sift right through this and give a rapid explanation," said Stewart. "But as for right now, there's no way we can send a wire transfer for that much money."

Stormy wondered what her mother would do this very instant. "Mr. Sanders, can't you just wire the money on the good Sabblonti name?" asked Stormy. "There's nothing Sabblonti money cannot buy."

"Given the fact that your mother has passed away and Chet has been laid up for almost a full year, I deem we need to wait until we can get all of this sorted out first."

"How do you know Chet has been laid up for almost a year?" demanded Stormy.

Stewart calmly commented, "Stormy, Shadow Butte County is extremely large, but it's not so large that it cannot carry the smallest whisper or the loudest shout."

Folding the set of papers and placing them underneath her left arm, Stormy slowly stood to her feet and exited Cattlemen's Central.

Less turned off the main highway onto the road leading into the Sabblonti Ranch. Meg was waiting for him with a large backpack laying on the ground by her feet. Quickly getting inside the cab, she asked, "Did you get everything?"

"I hope so. We didn't have that much to start with, so if I forgot something it shouldn't matter. Did Stormy suddenly wig out? It's way past time to blow this popsicle stand anyway."

Meg looked to her left. "Glad you think so too. This last month has really been unbearable. It wasn't so bad when Stormy spent 99% of her time in Cinder Valley. When she decided to fly back to the coop, those made for very long days."

Less's hands trembled as he held onto the steering wheel. "Got a plan, Meg?"

"Sure do. Drive me straight to that place way out in the ding weeds that you took me to a few months ago."

Slapping the dashboard, Less yelled, "You mean my treasure island?"

"Yes, whatever you call it."

As Less drove, Meg drew in deep breaths and exhaled slowly. She repeated this twenty-two times.

"I'm not even going to ask what you're trying to accomplish."

"Good, Less. Just drive, and get out of here as fast as you possibly can."

Almost two hours passed on the road less traveled. Less crested the small hill and started the descent into the meadow.

"Where's that old, faded, reddish-brown, rusted-out rig that was here before?" asked Meg.

"Come away with me, my favorite C.P.A., and I'll show you where it is. Actually, we need to drive slowly across this meadow and over that next hill to where we're completely outta sight."

Less turned the pickup ignition off. The sun slipped over the western mountainside. Meg climbed out of the cab and let out a shriek. "Why, Less, my Less, it's beautiful! How did you manage to get this done way out here?"

"I busted my belly a bunch putting the finishing touches on this!" Opening the camper shell door, Less patted the mattress laying on top of the pickup bed. "Think we'll be cozy enough in here? Guess we can dine on love for one night, right?"

Meg gave Less the biggest hug she'd ever given him during their entire married life.

The right rear tire of Stormy's pickup blew out on her drive home from the bank. By the time she hailed down a trucker to change it for her and made another trip into town to get the spare inflated, it was after dark by the time she arrived home. Dialing Slim Shade's number on the kitchen phone, she leaned against the counter.

"Howdy, Slim's still in the shade today. What can I do for ya?"

"This is Stormy. I've just had a revolting development."

"Such as?"

"When I went to my bank to wire the funds to you, I miscalculated and didn't have quite that much in there. Is there any way that you could get the seller to reduce the price?"

"Not a chance on earth. I had to talk like a Dutch uncle to get him to agree to that price. You gotta realize what breeding stock we're talking about here. This just ain't any old plug. Sure sorry to hear about your bad luck. I do have a backup buyer. Always keep one of those in my back pocket. I've spent at least that 10 Grand finder's fee and then some. Course we already talked about that. It was mine for the keeping no matter what. Takes a lotta time to run around and dicker with these characters. If you can get the cash together in the future, lemme know, and I'll try to round up another one for you. Sorry, Stormy."

"I'm sorry too, Slim. Thanks for all of your help. You're

a real stand-up guy."

"Merry Christmas to you and your husband."

"Same to you and your family."

Never having been more disillusioned in her entire life, Stormy lay on the living room floor and stared at the ceiling. Surely when the sun dawned in the morning, she would know what to do.

CHAPTER FORTY-ONE

Stormy made sure she was awake, showered, and dressed by the time the mantle clock struck eight straight up. Two hours came and went. There was no sign of Meg. Stormy placed a call to Blake Benson's house which produced nothing, so she decided to drive there. Blake was just getting inside his pickup when Stormy entered the driveway. She blocked his pickup with hers, so he could not drive around her and head to the main road.

"Why, Stormy, what a pleasant surprise! I didn't even think you knew where I lived. Are you delivering early Christmas presents or what brings you my way today?"

"Where's Meg?"

Blake took his own sweet time sorting a stack of brand inspection papers on the seat of his pickup. "Meg? Isn't she at your place working?"

"Not so as one would notice. When's the last time you saw her?"

"I haven't seen her since last Friday. I've been in Tranquility Falls County since last weekend with brand inspector meetings and just got home. I'm doing a very quick turnaround and heading into The Sage Hen Café for some dinner. Want to join me? You could pay my tab with all of that Sabblonti cash you have."

"Don't be ridiculous!"

"You seem slightly agitated, Stormy. Is something wrong? Less and Meg have been with you for almost a year now. How's Chet getting along? Back in the saddle yet?"

"Chet's fine. It's Meg that I'm after at the moment."

Blake got inside the state vehicle and started the engine. Rolling down the window, he said, "They might have headed into town. We've had a slight mishap at the house this morning. I'd invite you inside, but the bathroom toilet overflowed down the hallway and into the kitchen."

Stormy tried to peer into the cab of Blake's rig to look for any of Meg's personal belongings or any other clues, but there was so much junk on the dashboard, floorboard, and passenger seat that nothing was readily discernible. "I'll drive into Ridgemonte and see if I can locate Alottos. Meg Alotto just might be in a lotta trouble."

"Stormy, you always did have an exaggerated imagination."

Blake waited until Stormy was completely out of sight, turned the engine off, and walked inside his house. He wasn't a bit surprised when he'd arrived an hour ago from meetings in Tranquility Falls to find there wasn't a trace of Alotto's belongings to be found. As for the overflowing bathroom story, well, some people will believe just about anything you tell them on any given day.

S

Before the morning sun poked its first rays over the mountain tops, Less and Meg had stripped the four tires from Less's pickup that he'd been driving for the past year and loaded them in the back of the trailer. Less also removed everything else of value from the rig that could be sold at a later date. He hooked the trailer to the refurbished pickup that he'd painted charcoal gray and parked it 100 yards away. After dumping a little more gas into the tank of the pickup he'd stolen from South Dakota, he dropped a lighted match inside and ran for his life, singing, "Match in the gas tank, no rig!"

Less jumped into the cab of the refurbished pickup, flashed a huge grin, and proclaimed, "It's just you and me, kid, and this old junk heap now! Off to our next adventure quite a bit more flush this time than last time. Let's see, there are Flushes, Straight Flushes, but there's nothing quite like a Sabblonti Flush!"

As Less drove to the Bank of Blunte, Meg removed the mirror from her purse and applied the makeup she'd stolen from Jantzi Belle's bathroom. She'd discovered there were several drawers full. Meg had no idea how old it was. All she needed it for was less than half of a day. "How do I look, Less?"

"Gorgeous as ever! Uh, where'd you get that wig or whatever it is you're wearing and that fake fur coat?"

"I found them in one of the upstairs bedrooms in the Main Sabblonti Ranch house. You wouldn't believe what else I found up there. There's no time to tell you about it now."

"You best be careful. The way you look now will not match your driver's license picture. We can't afford any delays."

"Which driver's license? Don't you remember that I carry several with me?"

Less parked at the edge of the feed store parking lot in Blademere. "Meg, can you hoof it to the bank from here?"

"I planned on it all along. I also found this extra-large black leather bag in one of the Sabblonti Ranch house upstairs bedrooms. Try to relax a bit until I return."

Meg entered the lobby of the Bank of Blunte and removed her sun glasses as she flicked her long hair behind her right shoulder. She waited for the teller to signal that it was her turn to approach the counter.

"Good morning, what I can do for you today?"

Glancing at her name tag, Meg replied, "Hi, Lindi. I'm getting ready to leave town for the holidays to visit my ailing mother, so I need to make a withdrawal. She's in hospice care now. I have to pay a bunch of her medical bills to boot. This is not the best thing to have to do around the holidays. There's never a good time for that sort of thing really, but as her one and only devoted daughter, I most certainly must take care of my dear mother." She dabbed her eyes with one of Jantzi Belle's old handkerchiefs.

"I'm very sorry to hear that. Where does she live?"

Meg pretended that she did not hear the question as she dug around in the bottom of her bag. "I need to write a check for *CASH*. Is that okay?"

"Yes, that's fine," assured Lindi. "Do you have your account number with you?"

Meg handed a blank check to Lindi who used the number to check her account. "This account is in the name of *Double A Enterprises*. Let's see, are you Meg Alotto? I will need to see your driver's license please."

"Of course. Just a moment while I remove it from my wallet." Meg handed her license to Lindi. At exactly the same time, a bank teller trainee approached Lindi to ask a question requiring a detailed explanation.

"I'm sorry to keep you waiting. This is my first month at the bank and my co-worker's first day on the job. Lindi was so flustered she didn't carefully compare Meg's picture on the driver's license she produced to her actual face. "Go ahead and write your check," directed Lindi.

Meg reached underneath her sweater and pinched herself sufficiently to produce tears. Continuing to dry her eyes, she explained, "You know, now that I think about it, there's no telling how much longer my mother will live, so I should probably just cash it out," Meg explained. "What's the balance in my business account as of today?"

"Just a minute while I double check that figure. It looks like it's $258,436.71. Gee, I wish I had that much in my checking account!"

Continuing with her remorseful tone, Meg replied, "Fine. I'll write a check for that amount since I don't know how soon I can get back to town. I might as well take care of it now just in case mother goes much quicker than I expect." Meg really produced the tears at this point. "Do I make the check out to the Bank of Blunte or just write *CASH* on the *Pay To The Order Of line*? I've not written that many checks before, so I'm unsure of exactly how I should handle this."

"Either one is fine," said Lindi. "I can cash it for you either way. Do you prefer large bills?"

"Mostly large and some small. It will be easiest to pay all of the medical bills with large ones."

Lindi disappeared into the vault for about ten minutes and resurfaced carrying a wooden tray with the bills stacked inside. "Could I please get you to step over here to the end of the counter, so I can count the cash out for you? It's in large strap bundles all except for the coins, but I can still count it out."

"I'll take your word for it," Meg said. "I'm so very worried about my mother and need to get to her bedside as soon as I can. I just don't know if I could live with myself if she died before I could get to her. I would feel guilty the rest of my life for that one. Do you have a piece of paper that I need to sign to close the account for good?"

A picture of Lindi's mother flashed through her mind, and she almost started crying as well. "Yes, Meg. Please sign down at the bottom of this piece of paper." Lindi helped secure the bundles of cash inside Meg's large black leather bag and her elongated purse which she'd emptied onto the pickup seat before walking to the bank. "Happy Holidays, and I hope you get to see your mother very soon."

"Me, too. Thank you, Lindi."

Just as Meg exited the building, she noticed the bank manager hanging up the telephone and walking into the lobby to greet customers. She walked two blocks west and spotted Less sitting in the cab of the newly painted pickup sporting the lone rear Arizona license plate. There'd been one nailed onto the back of the trailer as well. As soon as she got inside the cab, she removed the wig and started scratching her scalp. "Feels like there are bugs crawling in my hair."

"Sorry, darlin', no time to stop now. Just keep scratchin.' "

"Where we headed?"

"How does upstate New York sound to you, catnip?"

"Fabulous! Let's hit the road. It's just you and me, kid, and this old junk heap now!"

S

Stormy had spent the morning frantically driving around Ridgemonte looking for the Alottos to no avail. No one had seen them or a description matching their pickup with a South Dakota license plate. She contemplated stopping inside The Sage Hen Café for a bite to eat, but reconsidered knowing full well that Blake Benson would be inside. She drove to Blademere and entered the Bank of Blunte.

Lindi had just returned from her late lunch break. "Good afternoon, how can I help you today?"

Stormy started to explain her predicament and then asked to see the bank manager, Ed Tilmore. After closing the door behind her, Ed asked, "What brings you to our bank today, Stormy?"

"My family owns a large cattle ranch in Shadow Butte County, and we've banked with Cattlemen's Central for decades. When attempting to send a wire transfer yesterday, I discovered that there were insufficient funds to do so. A large number of checks had been written on my operating account and deposited into an account in your bank, so I drove over here to check it out. Has my bank manager, Stewart Sanders, called you to discuss this yet?"

"No, I've not talked with Stewart in a couple of weeks. I've been unusually busy most of the day with telephone calls and my regular customers. The extra dry spring and summer months have made ranching pretty rough heading into the end of the year. As a matter of fact, I've not even had time to eat dinner yet. Oh well, my lovely wife will have supper waiting for me."

"Oh, before I forget, here are the printouts of my various accounts from Cattlemen's Central. That might make it easier for you to check what's going on here at the Bank of Blunte. I sure hope you can get to the bottom of it quickly. It doesn't make a lick of sense to me."

Ed lifted his glasses toward the top of his head with his left hand as he scanned the information on the various pages. He set the papers down on his desk and lifted the phone receiver to ask for assistance in his office. When Lindi appeared, he requested print outs of the *Double A Enterprises* account. She returned shortly with them in hand. Since surveying these did not take long, Ed looked at Lindi and asked, "You closed this account earlier today?"

"Yes, Mr. Tilmore. The customer was in a real hurry."

"So, you just counted out the cold hard cash and handed it over to her without any supervision at all?"

"Why, yes, Mr. Tilmore. What else was I supposed to do? You were on the phone, our assistant manager and one other teller are sick today, and it's our newest teller's first day on the job. Meg said her mother was near death, and she was trying to get to her so she could say good-bye."

Ed sunk back in his chair. "Lindi, you've got to be kidding me!" He stopped just short of throwing the stack of papers straight in the air.

Stormy interrupted, "Did I hear you say the name *Meg*?"

"Yes, her name was Meg. She was the nicest lady all dressed up in a fancy fur coat, lots of makeup, long red hair. She looked sort of like a movie star. I hope she didn't notice me staring at her so much."

"Meg doesn't even own a fur coat and most certainly does not have long red hair. It's brown! The last time I visited with her about her family she didn't mention a thing about her mother being gravely ill. In fact, she said her parents were taking a trip to Italy. That was just three weeks ago."

Fire shot from Stormy's eyes directly into Ed Tilmore's eyes. Jumping to her feet, she screamed, "I've been fleeced out of hundreds of thousands of dollars and so have you! Is there not a person in this entire high desert mountain region with an IQ above three? I fully expect you to launch a full investigation and retrieve every single, solitary, last penny of my money. Do you hear me? Do I make myself plain?"

Stormy fainted and fell to the floor. Ed called emergency services which arrived within the next few minutes and revived her. Ed assured Stormy that he'd do everything within his power to try to locate the missing funds and offered to drive her back to the Sabblonti Ranch. Stormy stormed out of the Bank of Blunte.

The editor of the Blunte County newspaper loitered outside the bank building holding his camera in his right hand. Restraining himself from marching outside, grabbing the camera and wrapping it around the editor's neck, Ed motioned for him to come inside his office. "There will be no write up of this hullabaloo today, understood? We dare not cast Blunte in a bad light."

"Understood, Mr. Ed. I'll drop in next week to arrange for my 2001 small business loan. I've got my eye on a new printing press that's hot off the press."

"I'll make sure I'm around, and the coffee will be freshly brewed, just to your liking. Plenty of cream to boot."

CHAPTER FORTY-TWO

It was as if the doors to the storehouse in heaven which release the snow opened wide commencing the minute after midnight on Monday, December 25th blanketing the landscape with three feet of beautiful, white powder. Thankfully, most folks in the area were nestled inside their beds, some with stocking caps on their heads.

Tom and Merna slept in until 9 o'clock which was unheard of for them. Merna had baked her pies the day before along with the rolls for Christmas Dinner. Tom was feeling much better as evidenced by Merna not having to remind him to wear his new red and green plaid shirt which she'd sewn for him last week. A pair of bright red suspenders would complement his shirt nicely. He stood in front of the mirror in the hallway, pulled his suspenders forward, and watched them snap back onto his shirt. After several minutes of this, Merna suggested he find something else to do. Tom stepped into the kitchen, "Mrs. Toppens, did you place that large envelope inside your purse?"

"I certainly did."

"Good. Let's not forget that, so the Morelands will have more land."

Toppens' newly hired ranch hand, Fenn Bridgemore, would be riding with Tom and Merna to the dinner at the Moreland residence.

Spence and Fenn split the morning chores at the Toppens Bunkhouse along with the feeding of the cattle and horses. Priscilla wrapped the photograph of Miggy that she was gifting to Spence which highlighted Miggy's twenty-two small black specks on her nose, brown hair above her eyes and below her ears, and the perfect white stripe between her eyes which flowed onto her nose and under her chin onto her chest. When taking her picture, Priscilla was able to capture Miggy's tongue hanging out as if to say, "I'm so happy!" She placed the gift under the miniature decorated tree on top of the entryway table to prevent Miggy from attacking it. She'd called the bunkhouse earlier all in a dither as she wondered if Spence would be able to make it into Ridgemonte to dine with her and her mother, Francie, at Priscilla's newly rented, decorated duplex. Spence reminded her that since he now had a 4-wheel drive rig, there would be no problem at all. He was sincerely hoping, despite the fresh snowfall accompanied by frigid temperatures, that Francie would be thawed out enough to rejoice with him and her daughter following their Christmas gift exchange. Stay tuned for updates on that one.

Wyn found it hard to sleep in any day of the week including Christmas. Sarita had not been feeling very well the past few days. She had gotten sick to her stomach a few times first thing in the mornings. Wyn assumed it was just a touch of winter flu. Sarita was waiting a few more days to try to determine if it was something else. She was still dressed in her flannel nightgown when Wyn came inside after completing his morning chores. He encouraged her to go back to bed for a while and he would take care of setting the table and getting everything ready for their guests. Christmas Dinner was scheduled for four in the afternoon followed by a gift exchange. Evan had offered to cook a Christmas goose with orange sauce and bring all the trimmings. Chet said his contribution could be keeping a close eye on Chef Evan so he didn't foul up the meal. When they were several miles down the road, Chet reached inside his pocket and realized he'd forgotten the piece of mystery knitting that he'd wanted to show Wyn after dinner. *Oh, well, no use ruining a holiday with more bad news. That could wait until after the first of the year. Besides, Stormy still had all that hard-earned money safely secured inside the steel vault at Cattlemen's Central. Whew, what a relief!*

Dr. Shaw overslept resulting in a sudden panic as to whether or not his prized turkey dinner would be ready by one o'clock. He chided himself for guaranteeing that he could pull this off. Macey had traded holidays with

Nurse Dawn Rowann, so she could make sure to have Christmas Day to spend with the good doctor even if he was a veterinarian. To top it off, Dr. Shaw just remembered that he'd offered to drive into town to pick Macey up. When they returned to his ranchette, maybe they would just sit by the fire in his living room and play some more hands of cribbage while the turkey continued to cook. Dr. Shaw was totally frosted that he'd not yet beaten Macey at that game. She was a real competitor at most things which wasn't the only thing that Dr. Shaw loved about her. He had certainly met his match after meeting her! Before checking the turkey inside the large white roaster at high noon to see if it was browning sufficiently, Dr. Shaw spotted the custom-made saddle he'd ordered from Earl's Saddle Shop, complete with Macey's name hand tooled across the back cantle. Did he have holiday wrapping paper wide enough in his guest bedroom to cover it? He shrugged his shoulders, "Horse blankets come in so handy, just when you need them the most."

Free-lance artist and designer, Catherine Harrison, along with her husband, James, had invited Daisy Freemille and her family to their Alpine Mountain home for the day. James preferred a nicely baked holiday ham to turkey any old day of the week. Catherine planned to make their famous potatoes using shredded hash browns, sour cream, real butter, cheese, and a crushed potato chip topping. Freshly baked pecan pie slathered with whipping cream would be the final offering of the evening followed by short accounts of the holiday happenings inside Daisy's Floral Shop.

Salina had taken a full day off work from The Shadowy Merc on Sunday in order to prepare her Christmas Eve dinner for Chet. Since she wanted to make sure that there would be leftovers for Chet and Evan for a few days later in the week, Salina had cooked a 14-rib pork loin. Prior to placing it inside the baking pan, she slit the membrane between the rib bones to allow the pork to curl around and stand up. She fashioned little red and gold curly-q decorations to place on top of each of the rib bones after it was cooked. Pear and chestnut stuffing along with bread pudding would round out the meal perfectly. Since Chet was still a married man the last time Salina had inquired around the countryside, she deemed that her over-the-top meal and a sentimental greeting card would be her gifts this year.

Salina was beyond confident that next Christmas would be far different as she would have made great inroads by that time, and Evan would be completely out of the picture as would Stormy. It was after 9 o'clock in the evening by the time Salina arrived at the Lower Sabblonti Ranch house. She knocked on the door several times, but there was no answer. She could hear Chet and Evan talking inside as she turned the door knob in her feeble attempts to open it. It took a few minutes to unload the lavish dinner that had been placed inside coolers during transit. Salina left these on Chet's porch and stomped back to her pickup. Fifteen minutes later, Evan slowly pulled the living room window drapes to the left side, peered down at the porch and informed Chet of his gift who informed him to "leave it be for the coyotes."

1

Stormy, reminding herself that one is the loneliest number, especially on the major holiday of the year, spent the day in her upstairs bedroom since she had no gifts to open. She'd turned the electric blanket on, fixed a pot of pomegranate and juniper berry tea, and started reading a new book featuring letters written by women homesteaders which spawned several fresh ideas. After reading the one titled *Crying No More*, she sat straight up in bed, turned the blanket dial off, threw the covers to her left and glided down the steep staircase. Tomorrow would be a new day!

CHAPTER FORTY-THREE

Due to the overnight freezing temperatures coupled with the snow accumulation, it was a bit of a challenge for Stormy to get her red pickup started. She resembled a snow bunny hopping around as she swept the snow from the roof and scraped the windshields. The defrost dial was turned to *maximum*. She retrieved the owner's manual from the jockey box and went inside to peruse the same. Turning to the index, she located the section for instructions on shifting the vehicle into and out of 4-wheel drive.

Stormy was confident Chet would be proud of her at this point in time. Her hands trembled as she attempted to apply her makeup and lipstick. Donning her bright red hat, coat, and gloves, she turned out every light in the house. Leaving her various checkbooks upstairs in her office since there were virtually no funds for writing checks these days, Stormy embarked upon her trip to Cinder Valley. With only three days remaining in the year, she desperately hoped that the local businesses had not taken extended vacations between Christmas and New Year's.

The bell rang several times as Stormy carried the large, green garbage sacks into Country Cate's Western Wear store and piled them in front of the counter. Store clerk, Shasta, emerged from the back half of the store where she'd been working on year-end inventory. When Shasta saw that it was Stormy standing at the counter, she walked forward, but was not the first to speak.

"Hello, Shasta. It's nice to see you today. I hope you had a very special Christmas."

"Thank you, Stormy. Yes, I had a super day spending it with loving family and friends. I received a lot of gifts, too. What can I do for you?"

Stormy gestured with her right hand and asked, "I was wondering if it would be possible to return the items in these sacks?"

"That would depend upon when they were purchased. If it's more than 90 days, our store policy is to not take them back. You purchased most of them for the Ignee County Rodeo & Roundup, didn't you?"

"Yes, that's correct."

"So that would have made it sometime in July of this year?"

"Most probably."

Shasta walked around the counter and opened an orange notebook turning to the page starting with ***S***. "Yes, most of your orders were custom orders before the month of July. I don't show anything ordered or purchased after the date of July 29th. I'm sorry about that. It looks like you purchased several thousand dollars' worth of clothing. You live in Ridgemonte, don't you?"

"Our ranch is sort of between Ridgemonte and Cinder Valley."

"Do you shop in Ridgemonte very often?"

"Not too often. Why?"

"Well, there's a consignment clothing store in town called *Second Time Around*. You might try your luck there. I think the lady who owns it has a name that starts with a *V*, but I'm not sure."

Shasta opened one garbage bag and looked inside.

Stormy asked, "Is there a consignment store here in town?"

"No. There used to be, but not anymore. It closed. The thrift shop three streets over used to carry some clothing, but they've started selling more books, video games, housewares, TV's, appliances, and those sorts of things. Didn't you like the styles? Most women would give their eye teeth to be able to wear clothing like this."

"Oh, I loved the styles, and there's nothing wrong with the clothing."

"Then why are you trying to return all of these bags filled to the very top?"

"It's a long story," said Stormy.

"Most stories usually are."

"Shasta, I want to thank you for being so helpful to me during the months when I was making all of my clothing selections. I wasn't nearly as kind to you as you were to me. I appreciate you."

"Thank you, Stormy. I can work three months on such flattering words. I would offer to help carry the garbage bags back outside for you, but Cate has a store policy that someone must be inside and watch the cash at all times."

"I wish I would have kept a closer eye on my cash."

"Cash?" asked Shasta.

"Never mind. That's an even longer story."

Stormy parked in front of the next storefront, dug around in the bottom of her purse to locate what she was looking for and walked inside. The clerk was bent down behind the counter removing some cases from the very bottom shelf. Looking up, she greeted Stormy, "Good morning, how may I help you?"

"There used to be a young gentleman who worked in the store. I've forgotten his first name. Do you know if he still works here?"

"He hasn't worked here since Labor Day weekend."

Stormy laid the red velvet case on the counter top. Opening it carefully she said, "I wanted to return this ring to the store to see what I could get for it."

"I apologize but the owner, Mr. Jodell, doesn't deal in used jewelry."

"I purchased this ring here not that long ago, so I was hoping since it had only been a few months, I could return it and get my money back."

"Our store policy is that all sales are final."

The red velvet jewelry box started to slide off the counter, so the clerk reached down to catch it. Stormy noticed the jagged, *J*-shaped scar on her hand and looked at her name tag. "You're Aprilily! I remember your name from earlier this spring. Are you the lady that was in the street with your young children?"

"Yes, that was me. I was really down and out before fortune and providence smiled down upon me."

"What happened if you don't mind me asking?"

"Not at all. I will never forget that day when you offered me your old wedding ring inside this very same red velvet jewelry box. I declined it because I wanted a ring of my own. Shortly after that, I met some ladies in the community. They are known as the *Western Women of Destiny*. They took my children and me under their wing and helped to restore us. One of them had a son who'd lost his wife in an automobile accident. One of his children was badly injured as well. In the process of the women befriending me, I befriended the young widower, and we were married the Saturday after Thanksgiving. I have so much for which to be thankful. Sometimes, we don't appreciate what we have until it's gone or almost gone."

"Well said, Aprilily. I'm so very happy for you that you've found a wonderful husband."

"Thank you. I nearly lost my children due to neglect. I'm way too old to be learning lessons the hard way."

"Do you have any suggestions of how I could recoup my money from this ring?" asked Stormy.

"It's lovely. How many carats is it?"

"Five."

Well aware of what a five-carat, princess-cut, white gold wedding ring sold for, Aprilily suggested, "You could try the pawn shop in town and see what the owner would give you for it. I'm sorry, Stormy. I would really like to be able to help you."

"You already have, Aprilily. I admire your strength and courage under adversity. I was very mean to you and your daughters. I realize that now, and I'm very sorry."

Walking around the other side of the counter, Aprilily gave Stormy a big hug. “I understand, Stormy. I took no offense. I’ve closed that dark chapter on my life. I’m writing a new book now.”

Thankfully, Stormy had a few miles of driving time to reflect upon her conversations with Shasta and Aprilily before her next stop.

Clark, sales manager for Carl’s Car Corral, had just returned from test driving a new pickup. Stormy thought she recognized him, so she increased her steps to catch up with him in the parking lot. “Almost Happy New Year, Stormy! Your new rig looks as snappy as ever. How are you enjoying it?”

“Hello, Clark. It’s nice to see you. I’m enjoying it very much. Do you have a few minutes that I could talk with you in your office please?”

“Sure do. I’ve got nothing but time for you.”

Stormy didn’t beat around the bush when she pulled the beige envelope from her purse. “Clark, I need to sell my pickup.” She laid the paperwork in front of him. Just as he was about to ask his next rapid-fire question, he thought he saw a lone teardrop fall from Stormy’s right eye onto her cheek. He pretended that he was looking for something in his desk drawer until she could regain her composure.

“I’d be happy to take care of that for you. I see that you brought the title which is good. Can I see your key for a minute, please? Be right back.”

Clark returned a few minutes later. “Okay, Stormy, here’s the best I can do for you. The standard rule of thumb is that the vehicle depreciates a fast 10-12 G’s the minute it’s driven off the lot. Sorry about that, but it’s just the way the cookie crumbles. Believe it or not, most ranchers buy new in this area, so we don’t carry a lot of used pickups. I could probably offer you around $16,000 or $18,000 for it, but that’s about it. I’d also have to factor in removing those brands from the side doors, the body work to take the dings from the back panel, the high mileage, and so forth. It hasn’t been wrecked or anything since you bought it, has it?”

"No, it hasn't been wrecked, and you're right, I did put quite a few miles on it the past few months with all of my trips back and forth from the ranch to Cinder Valley."

"Were you working in Cinder Valley?" asked Clark.

"Sort of, but I definitely picked the wrong part-time volunteer work or something to keep me occupied."

"Yes, that happens every once in a while. I knew someone who did the same thing once upon a time. She eventually saw the light before the lights were turned out. I'll get your paperwork drawn up along with a check. Did you bring both sets of keys with you?"

"Yes, here's the other one."

Stormy sat inside Clark's warm office for a few minutes. Her mind was oblivious to everything and everyone around her. Clark returned and asked her to sign on the dotted line and handed her a red envelope containing the check. He extended his right hand to shake hers. "Stormy, thanks again for your business. We appreciate it. Stop in anytime you're in the market for a new rig. We'd be happy to help out."

"Speaking of help, I need some right now."

"Sure. What's that?"

"Can you please drive me back to the Sabblonti Ranch?"

"Now?" Clark asked.

"Whenever it's convenient. I'm in no hurry."

"I have a new rancher coming into the dealership in about a half hour. After I show him our new models, I would be happy to give you a lift."

The prospective rancher arrived two hours late, so three hours later Stormy rode in the cab of Clark's brand-new pickup en route to the Sabblonti Ranch. Clark, usually never at a loss for words which was one of a salesman's most valuable gifts, didn't say more than ten words during the entire trip. He didn't have an answer for overwhelming sadness as he lived his life on the bright and sunny side even in the chill of winter.

Arriving in the driveway of the main ranch house, Clark left the engine running and opened the passenger door for

Stormy. "It's pretty dark. Can you see your way?"

"Yes, I can. Thanks, Clark. I really appreciate your kindness to me."

"Stormy, just remember, it's always darkest before the dawn."

CHAPTER FORTY-FOUR

Tuesday Evening, January 2, 2001
6:00 p.m.
Main Sabblonti Ranch House

Stormy had spent the morning meticulously selecting her finest country western woman's ensemble, applying her makeup and one of Chet's favorite eau de parfums, a scent labeled *My Western Whisper* with rose hips, gardenia, and vanilla accents. Donning a bright, cheery apron, she went to great lengths to plan one of Chet's favorite winter meals which would include Sabblonti prime rib, sautéed mushrooms, baked potatoes, canned corn with half & half added to it, and several slices of buttered toast sprinkled with garlic powder.

Prior to making the dessert, Stormy had gone to her upstairs office to retrieve the recipe she'd found in a holiday magazine sitting on top of a pile of unopened mail. When sliding the mail a few inches to the left on top of the desk, she felt something heavy underneath the stack of envelopes, so she lifted it to the top.

Turning the picture frame over, she read the printing on the white sticker taped to the bottom:

"To Meg, My C.P.A., ~~
My Cute Petite Alotto
Always, Less, August 23, 1968"

Sitting in her office chair, Stormy studied the wedding photo. Less and Meg looked so different now than when they'd gotten married. Stormy coached herself, "Well, sitting here staring at this picture isn't going to change what's happened. Meg's definition of a CPA is certainly different from that of the rest of the world. When I accompanied Mother to her 1998 year-end tax appointment, her CPA was a real-life Certified Public Accountant, not a Cute Petite Alotto. Who could have imagined that three capital letters, **CPA**, could make such a financial difference? Meg's no more a CPA than I am!"

There was barely enough Sabblonti money remaining to

buy much of anything.

Stormy walked down the third-floor hallway and opened the door on her left to her dad's special room, *Ace's Place.* Hanging on the east wall was a framed display of different types of barbed wire. The aged wooden hammer Ace used to repair miles upon miles of fence over seven decades was displayed next to it.

Taking the wedding photograph and hammer downstairs, Stormy bundled up to brave the outside elements. Making her way through the deep snow to the tack shed, she went inside, flipped the lights on, and pounded the framed picture until the hearts were no longer recognizable, much less the photo of the Alottos. Taking the little wooden-handled light green broom, she swept the remains into the miniature, matching dust pan and dumped them in the small trash barrel. Chet would be pleased to find his tack room tidy when he was able to return there.

Experiencing a profound release, and determined to learn from her foolishness as opposed to continuing to remain foolish, Stormy returned to the house, replaced her daddy's hammer right where it belonged and decided to wear her new apron featuring the Sabblonti cattle brand on the front of it.

The dessert was the most time-consuming endeavor of the day consisting of three layers of a basic chocolate cake made from scratch, raspberry filling, and a triple chocolate glaze. All of this had kept the butterflies in Stormy's stomach at bay for the entire day. She could not remember being this nervous the day she married Chet ten years ago.

Evan parked right next to the front porch and kept the engine idling until Chet made his way safely inside the Main Sabblonti Ranch house. Oh, how he would love to have been invited to supper, but knew his place, and reflected upon the last several months as he drove back to the Lower Sabblonti Ranch house.

Chet leaned on his cane as he stood in the front entryway. Stormy helped remove his coat and hat.

"Supper sure smells good, Stormy. I really appreciate

the invite."

"I hope you enjoy it. Would you like to sit in the living room for a few minutes first?"

"Sure. That would be fine with me."

It hurt Stormy's heart to watch Chet continue to lean on his cane. "Is it painful to walk, Chet?"

"Sometimes. It just depends upon the surface. My leg has been bothering me a lot more now that the cold weather has set in."

Having spent the afternoon cooking and baking in the kitchen, Stormy hadn't noticed the chill in the living room. Chet rubbed both of his arms with his hands as he spotted the beautifully wrapped Christmas gift placed on the right side of the fireplace mantle.

"Would you like me to build a fire, Stormy?"

"If you feel up to it. If not, you can direct me, and I would be happy to try to get one going."

Chet walked slowly toward the fireplace and pulled the mesh screen back. Thankfully, there were several pieces of wood stacked inside the metal frame on casters that he'd fashioned for Jantzi Belle all those years ago. A few pieces of kindling were stacked on top. Chet started to walk toward the entryway.

"Is there something I can get for you so you don't have to walk so much?"

"Doc Merenspinn says walking is good for me which I know to be true. It'll take just a quick minute. Chet unzipped the inside pocket of his vest and returned to the fireplace. "I would like you to open your Christmas gift right now. Sorry, I couldn't find any holiday wrapping paper at the lower ranch house. Would you settle for just a brown envelope instead?"

Stormy gestured to the love seat. "Can we sit over there, Chet? And yes, a brown envelope is more than enough. It's the thought that counts." Stormy manifested a puzzled look on her face as she felt the irregular bumps protruding from the envelope. "What on earth is this, Chet?"

Chet had almost forgotten how good it felt to have his

wife by his side. "No hints, Stormy. Do you want to try to guess before you open it?"

"Not really. I was never very good at guessing games, so can I just open it?"

"Not even one, teensy weensy, little guess?"

Stormy leaned into Chet's right shoulder. "You really want me to guess, don't you?"

"Yes, I really do."

"Okay, then, I will venture a small guess, but promise me you won't laugh at me if I get it wrong."

"I promise," Chet said.

Tracing her fingers across the top of the envelope like she was playing the keys on a piano, Stormy said, "Um, let me see, it feels like it might be some flower bulbs to plant in the spring or something like that maybe."

Chet burst out laughing. Stormy realized just how handsome her husband looked all dressed up in his western best.

"They're not exactly flower bulbs," explained Chet, "but I think they're something that will give you great joy."

"Is there more than one object in this package?"

"Yes, there are several. Twelve to be exact."

Stormy started jumping up and down like a little kid waiting to open her presents from Santa. "I can't stand it any longer plus I'm getting cold. Can I open them now?"

"Yes, but you have to do it one at a time," instructed Chet.

"One at a time it is. Can I get your coat and drape it over me?"

Chet started to suggest she get a coat of her own, but caught himself just in the nick of time. "By all means."

Stormy removed the packaging tape from the back of the brown flap, looked inside, and recoiled. Her eyes met Chet's. Neither of them moved.

"It's okay, honest it is. Trust me with this."

Stormy read the name on the outside of the envelope as she scrutinized the feminine handwriting, *Chet*. "Is this what I think it is and from whom I think it is?"

"It's what you think it is, and it was written by whom you think it was, but stay with me. I told you that you could trust me, remember? Don't bother reading anything that's inside any of the envelopes because I didn't bother to read any of it. Please hand me the one that has *January* on the back of it."

With her right-hand trembling, Stormy passed the light blue envelope to Chet who struck a fireplace match and touched the corner. He dropped it on top of the kindling. There was just enough pitch for a couple of sparks. Quickly getting the idea of what she was supposed to do, Stormy handed Chet the envelopes for the months of *February – December*. By this time, both of them were laughing loudly and watching the flames flicker inside the fireplace. "Stormy, there's one for every month when you weren't near me and when I needed and wanted you more than anything else in this big wide world."

Suddenly, Stormy realized what she must do. Standing ever so close to Chet, she said, "Please take a seat, don't move, and I'll be right back." Bounding up the stairs, she ran into her mother's bedroom, opened the dresser drawer, grabbed what she needed, and glided down the railing. She approached Chet and asked him to open both hands. After Stormy placed the stack of Jokers inside, he walked near the fireplace, pulled the mesh screen back, and threw them on the fire. He'd never seen plastic burn so fast.

Stormy patted the cushions on the love seat. "Can you sit here again to open your gift?" There was no argument from Chet. "Before you open this, I have some very important things to say to you."

Looking deeply into both of his robin egg blue eyes, she commenced, "I don't completely understand why I've treated you the way I have since Mother died and why I've not been able to trust you. It wasn't you that should have been mistrusted. I'm beginning to figure that out now. I'm beyond thankful that you're such a forgiving man after how I've treated you and would even come here tonight for supper. It was as if a strange spirit entered me after Mother died. I must make every effort to boot it out and keep it out."

Chet handed Stormy his large white handkerchief to dry her genuine tears and blow her nose.

"You don't know how much it means to me to hear you say those words, Stormy. Right before my accident, I wondered if I'd been living a lie all these years and that maybe you didn't love me. Tonight, I do believe I have a solid future ahead, or I should say, we do." Both of them sat in silence as they watched the oversized juniper log burn in the fireplace. Stormy took one, long, last look at the ashes from Salina's love notes.

Stormy patted the top of Chet's gift. He shook it.

"Okay, turnabout's fair play, Chet. You have to make one guess as to what it is."

"It's pretty lightweight. Let's see, another vest, maybe? There's some kind of strange sound when I shake it though, so I don't rightly know what it could be. Maybe it's the metal buttons on the vest hitting the side of the cardboard box or something."

"Go ahead and open it then," suggested Stormy.

"The wrapping looks like a professional did it. Did you wrap it?"

"Yes, I did, and thank you."

Chet slid his right forefinger under the scotch tape and gingerly removed the wrapping paper. Stormy had taped the box shut as well. "Were you vying for Tape Queen of the Day, Stormy?" Again, they both laughed.

Chet opened the top flaps of the box and let out a gasp, "Stormy Suzanne Sabblonti Castins, this is beautiful, just like you!"

Lifting it to the light, Chet ran his fingers down both sides as he read, "*Rascal Racer*." What's Rascal Racer? Where did you get this?"

"I had it custom made for you. There's a very, very long story that goes with all that leather."

"I can wait to hear all about it. In the meantime, . . . " Chet slid the bridle gently over Stormy's head, pulled her very close to him, and kissed her passionately.

As the flames died down, Chet started to get up to put

another log on the fire. Just then, Stormy jumped up, "Wait, there's something else I need to do."

Running up three flights of stairs, Stormy fell on her knees in front of her mother's closet. Sitting cross-legged on the floor, she pulled Jantzi's red cowboy boots onto her feet. She danced around the room until her head was spinning like a top. Winding down, she glided back down the staircase and sat cross legged in front of the fire. Slipping the boots off, she laid them across the burning logs, and yelled,

"SABBLONTI RANCH, YOU'RE ALL OURS NOW!"

Leaning her head back, Stormy released a victorious laugh that echoed throughout every room in the three-story Main Sabblonti Ranch house.

"Mommie's red boots will no longer guide one single step of mine."

"And once the storm is over, you won't remember how you made it through, how you managed to survive. You won't even be sure, whether the storm is really over. But one thing is certain. When you come out of the storm, you won't be the same person who walked in. That's what the storm is all about." (Haruki Murakami)

ABOUT THE AUTHOR

Sheila Eismann, author and publisher of twelve books, is third in her lineage of five female writers and poets. She endeavors to enhance the lives of others through education and encouragement via penning her inspirational and fictional books. Eismann, co-founder of Idaho Creative Authors' Network (ICAN), speaks at Womens' and Writers' Conferences.

Please peruse Sheila's website www.sheilaeismann.com and sign up to receive her blog posts and newsletters. Send her an email at sheila@sheilaeismann.com to let her know which character was your most favorite in this novel along with the best part of the story. Happy Reading!

Where to find Sheila Eismann online:

Email: sheila@sheilaeismann.com

Website: www.sheilaeismann.com

Facebook: www.facebook.com/sheila.eismann

Blog: www.sheilaeismann.com

LinkedIn: Sheila Eismann

Etsy Store: www.etsy.com/shop/BooksbySheilaEismann

OTHER BOOKS AVAILABLE FROM AUTHOR SHEILA EISMANN & DESERT SAGE PRESS which can be purchased from: www.sheilaeismann.com or www.amazon.com.

Western Fiction Book One of The Sabblonti Series, ***Jantzi's Jokers***, features Jantzi Belle, matriarch of the Sabblonti family, who has worked for decades to keep her cattle empire intact. Life takes a drastic turn when she receives a late-night visitor. The brief disappearance of her Last Will and Testament could complicate matters between her daughters, Stormy and Sarita. Stormy and her husband, Chet Castins, are struggling to work through the loss of their three children. Against all odds, drifter Wyn Moreland makes a bold move when he decides that Sarita is his beauty to rescue. The county veterinarian, Dr. Ben Shaw, is also vying for her affections. Will Wyn emerge as the winner? Just prior to the dawn of the New Year, revelations come forth regarding forgery, cattle rustling, and land exploitation. Will the Sabblonti Empire survive, and more importantly, who will control its reins?

The Sabblonti Saga accelerates in Book Two of the Series, ***A Stormy Year***. Riding her high horse after inheriting the family fortune, Stormy Castins is determined to reinvent herself following her husband's accident. Blinded by jealousy, ambition, and naivety, she hires Less and Meg Alotto to oversee her vast high desert mountain domain. While Stormy is away, the cattle herd ends up in disarray.

Amidst the hot dry season, romance is blooming on several fronts despite a major showdown during a mid-summer celebration. The pesky Black Raven continues to wreak havoc at the most inopportune times.

Unable to overcome the vengeance which strikes by way of a mysterious range fire combined with the dire deeds of a cagey couple, the Sabblonti Ranch is in shambles just as Stormy starts to regain her senses. Humility is the prescription needed to open her eyes in order to realize what's truly important in life. The sparks from a belated holiday rendevous set Chet and Stormy on their path to recovery.

Desperation explodes when heiress Stormy Sabblonti Castins calculates her dwindling fortune in Book 3 of the Sabblonti Series, ***Love the Tie that Binds.*** Is she capable of learning the painful lessons of having to rely upon someone and something other than inherited wealth? As her husband, Chet, continues to heal from his near fatal accident, tormenting shadows of The Black Raven lurk in the background.

These high desert hills are alive with blessed babies, enchanting engagements, skillful scavengers, sophisticated scoundrels, rich revelations, timeless treasures, and western weddings.

The Main Sabblonti Ranch house abounds with an unexpected marriage, childrens' voices, and Sir Shelton sporting his silver bell.

In a captivating story of courage, trust, and faithfulness, will Stormy still be tied in knots or find lasting love by year's end?

Share the joys and sorrows of a mountain community in this swirling saga.

In this collection of true stories titled ***Stirrings of The Spirit***, author Sheila F. Eismann invites you to walk with her family through several valleys en route to some mountain tops as they learned to rely on God in the most harrowing of circumstances.

Have you ever wondered why you were the last one to hear of THE big social event of the year? Well, wonder no longer after reading this e-book titled ***Recognize Your Circles***! When volunteering for an organization years ago, author Sheila F. Eismann was introduced to the concept of "the circles of your life." Since the idea was so beneficial to her, she decided to share it with all of you.

Straight from the Horse's Trough is a humorous read to render assistance to the suburbanite or urbanite who desires to live a healthier lifestyle by growing his or her own food, but is faced with the challenge of a small space in which to do so. This e-book is chock full of how-to steps and includes pictures to remove guesswork from the project.

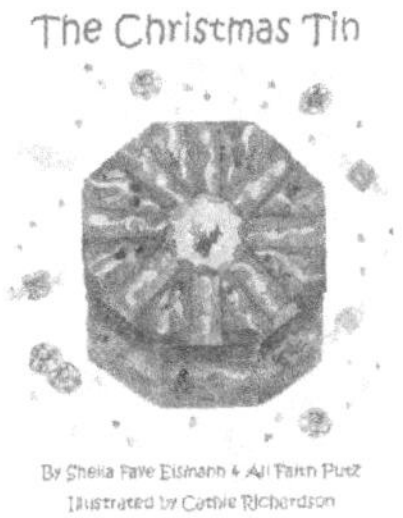

The Christmas Tin
By Sheila Faye Eismann & Ali Fann Putz
Illustrated by Cathie Richardson

The Christmas Tin is a most delightful read for the young at heart anytime during the year. This endearing book is based upon a true story featuring the older of the two authors when she was a young girl and conveys the timeless message that "love truly is the best gift of all." Children will especially enjoy all of the colorful illustrations contained within this treasure.

Everyone can use a little encouragement ~~ a dose of what is beneficial, ethical, and honorable. ***Heart to Heart From God's Word*** provides this for you. Penned with humor and wisdom, the daily tidbits are paired with Bible verses that convey life-changing principles which are designed for readers of all ages transcending cultures and continents. This devotional will challenge you to grow and fulfill your God-given destiny. It can also double as a prayer journal.

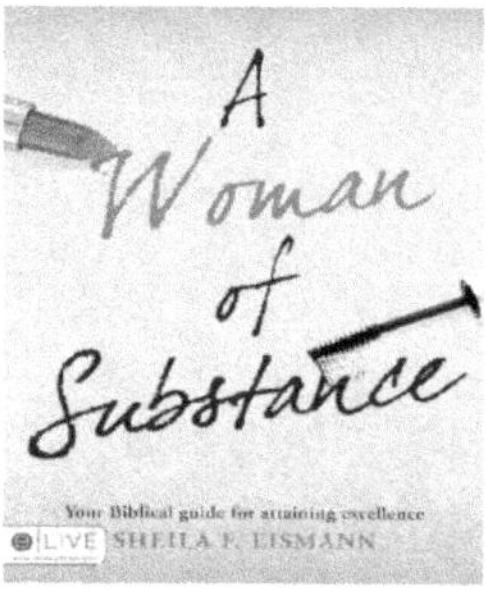

A Woman of Substance is a practical, interactive, and entertaining 12 week Bible study penned to help equip you to fulfill your God-given destiny and impact the culture for Jesus Christ at the same time. It can be used as a stand-alone study or devotional and works well in a group setting, too. It is designed for women ages junior high through adult.

Freedom is Your Destiny! Vietnam Veteran, Dan Eismann, using combat experiences to illustrate spiritual truths, invites you to take a journey with him as he presents a rock-solid strategy for not only fighting your spiritual battles, but winning the all-important war. In the midst thereof, the most vital aspect is that you realize you can experience freedom and become all that God has destined you to be!

Settle into your special reading spot; grab a cup of tea or your favorite meal. Be stirred as you read and ponder **Poetry Time, Volume One**; allow Sheila's words to encourage and heal.

CAST OF CHARACTERS

A

Ace Sabblonti, Stormy's and Sarita's deceased father
Al Gibson, member, Ignee County Rodeo Board, in charge of rodeo grounds and maintenance
Anne-Marie – Dr. Diller's wife
Aprilily – young homeless mother with two children; clerk, Jodell's Jeweler's, Cinder Valley
Aunt Jonsey Kiddle – Stormy and Sarita Sabblonti's maternal aunt

B

Beau Cheval, Dr. Ben Shaw's Appaloosa gelding
Betty Lou Bradford, elected Clerk and Recorder, Shadow Butte County
Bolo & Browny – Tom Toppens' matched pair of draft horses
Brent Dawson, employee, Dawson's Dealership, Ridgemonte; Delbert Dawson's son
Blake Benson, Southwest District Brand Inspector

C

Caper Sadler – rodeo clown
Carl's Car Corral – auto dealership, Cinder Valley
Caroline Crutchens – Mintner Medical Center Nurse
Carson Tayer – Chairman, Ignee County Rodeo Board
Catherine Harrison – free-lance artist, greeting card designer, flower shop supplier, and Daisy's childhood friend
Chara Tankton, bank teller, Cattlemen's Central
Chet Castins, Stormy Sabblonti's husband
Cinder Valley Scoop – Cinder Valley newspaper
Clark, salesman, Carl's Car Corral, Cinder Valley
Cord Calhoun – Rodeo Announcer
Coye's Stringers – Country Western Band

D

Daisy Freemille – owner, Daisy's Floral Shop, Ridgemonte
Dawn Rowann – Mintner Medical Center Nurse
Dean Kendall – member, Ignee County Rodeo Board, in charge of rodeo announcer, clown, and musical group
Delbert Dawson, owner, Dawson's Dealership, Ridgemonte
Dr. Ben Shaw – Veterinarian, Ridgemonte
Dr. Den Merenspinn, medical doctor, owner of Evergreene Medical Clinic, Ridgemonte
Dr. Diller – Dentist, Ridgemonte
Dr. Linke – Mintner Medical Center Physician

E

Earl's Saddle Shop – Cinder Valley
Ed Tilmore – manager, Bank of Blunte
Evan Briarley, Chet Castins' Physical Therapist
Evergreene Medical Clinic, Ridgemonte

F

Fenn Bridgemore – ranch hand, Toppens' Ranch
Francie Fletcher, Priscilla Fletcher's mother

G

Gib's Gas – gas station in Ridgemonte
Gwen Hybrenth – retiree, Ignee County Rodeo Board

I
Ignee Grange Hall, Cinder Valley
It's Sew Time – fabric store, Ridgemonte

J
Jacobe Davone – employee, Shaw Veterinarian Clinic, Ridgemonte
James Harrison, Catherine Harrison's husband
Jantzi Belle Siddonz Sabblonti, Stormy's and Sarita's deceased mother
Jed Brennon – owner, Jed's Appliance Center, Ridgemonte
Jodell's Jewelers – jewelry store, Cinder Valley
Joyce Stone – Mintner Medical Center Charge Nurse

L
Lane – cowboy drifter, Ridgemonte
Leo Jeelon – Shadow Butte Deputy County Sheriff
Less Alotto – Sabblonti Ranch Foreman
Lilac Novis – Aunt Jonsey Kiddle's great-granddaughter
Lindi – bank teller, Bank of Blunte, Blademere
Logan Novis – Aunt Jonsey Kiddle's great-grandson
Lonnie Browne, Assistant Manager, Cattlemen's Central, Ridgemonte
Lorena, head clerk, DMV, Shadow Butte County Courthouse
Luger – ranch hand, Toppens Ranch
Luetta Londers – Parade Chairwoman, 75th Annual Ignee County Rodeo & Roundup, Cinder Valley

M

Macey Meadows – Mintner Medical Center Nurse
Marita Merrill – Nelson Merrill's wife, Shadow Butte County
Meg Alotto, bookkeeper, Sabblonti Ranch
Merna Toppens – Tom Toppens' wife, Toppens' Ranch
Mintner Medical Center – Ridgemonte hospital
Mitch Bentz – member, Ignee County Rodeo Board, in charge of rodeo stock

N

Neil Rolan, member, Ignee County Rodeo Board, in charge of rodeo grounds and maintenance
Nelson Weston Merrill – rancher, Shadow Butte County

P

Priscilla Fletcher – employee, Shadow Butte County Recorder's Office

R

Res Broomfield – cattle rancher, Shadow Butte County
Ridgemonte Rider – Ridgemonte newspaper
Rory, motel clerk, Silver Jack Motel, Cinder Valley
Ruston – younger cowhand who works for Sabblonti Ranch

S

Sagebrush Sorority Sisters – in charge of annual parade for Ignee County Rodeo & Roundup, Cinder Valley
Sage Hen Café – restaurant, Ridgemonte
Salina Bevvins – store clerk, The Shadowy Merc, Ridgemonte
Samuel Stixon – owner, broodmare farm, Ridgemonte
Sarita Sabblonti – Stormy Castins' sister; Wyn Mooreland's wife
Shade Stock Company – rodeo stock supplier
Shane – cowboy, ranch hand employed by Toppens' Ranch
Shasta – sales clerk, County Cate's Western Wear, Cinder Valley
Sheriff Jeff Jensen – Shadow Butte County Sheriff
Silver Jack Motel – Cinder Valley
Slim Shade – owner, Shade Stock Company
Spence Woodson – Assistant Ranch Foreman, Toppens' Ranch
Stanley Elson, Treasurer, Ignee County Rodeo Board
Stewart Sanders, manager, Cattlemen's Central, Ridgemonte
Stormy Sabblonti Castins, heiress to the Sabblonti cattle ranch and family fortune; Sarita Sabblonti Moreland's sister

T

The Mane Place, hair styling salon, Cinder Valley
The Second Time Around – thrift shop, Ridgemonte
The Shadowy Merc – grocery store and mercantile, Ridgemonte
The Tall Blues – country western singing group
Tom Toppens – owner, Toppens' Ranch
Tonette – Sarita Sabblonti's co-worker, Dr. Diller's office, Ridgemonte
Travis Fisen – employee, Lambent's Funeral Home
Trent Davies – Assistant Chairman, Ignee County Rodeo Board

U
Uncle Kent Kiddle – Stormy and Sarita Sabblonti's maternal uncle

V
Verntoola – thrift shop owner, The Second Time Around, Ridgemonte
Vonnetta, hairstylist, The Mane Place, Cinder Valley

W
Wilbur Drebner – cattle rancher, Shadow Butte County
Wyn Moreland -Toppens Ranch Foreman, Sarita Sabblonti's husband

Y
Yatey – older cowhand that works for Sabblonti Ranch

Z
Zib's Towing – Ridgemonte Tow Truck Business

---

i

http://upload.wikimedia.org/wikipedia/commons/7/71/Livestock_chicago_1947. N.p.n.d. Mon. 19 Sept. 2016.

www.ingramcontent.com/pod-product-compliance
Lightning Source LLC
Chambersburg PA
CBHW050022030726
47506CB00001B/67
* 9 7 8 0 9 8 9 7 1 3 3 3 7 *